AND AWAY WE GO . . .

Changing neither his scowl nor his focus, Soult snorted angrily and said, "I've seen you do some boneheaded things over the years, but this is just that one step beyond stupid all the way to insanity."

"Oh, come on; I've done dumber stuff than this," Carrera said.

"Name o

"Flew to e⋯⋯⋯⋯⋯⋯⋯⋯ a girl?"

"That wa⋯⋯⋯⋯⋯⋯⋯⋯ This is just effing ri⋯⋯⋯⋯

Carrera fi⋯⋯⋯⋯⋯⋯⋯⋯ silently for a long minute. Finally, he wiped one hand across his face, sighed and said, "This is defensible, too, Jamey. Maybe more importantly, it's for the good of my soul."

Soult shook his head resignedly. "Still stupid,"

Carrera demanded, "Now tell me again what your orders are."

Velasquez, being senior, replied. "If they kill you, we butcher them to a man. If you're not back in an hour, same thing. But if they give up, you want us to stand and cheer, salute and give them an honor guard to the POW camp."

"Very good." Carrera twisted to take his pistol from its usual holster, then tossed that underhanded to Soult. "And away we go."

DAYS OF BURNING, DAYS OF WRATH

TOM KRATMAN

Days of Burning, Days of Wrath

Copyright © 2020 by Tom Kratman

A Baen Books Original

Baen Publishing Enterprises
P.O. Box 1403
Riverdale, NY 10471
www.baen.com

ISBN: 978-1-9821-2552-3

Cover art by Kurt Miller
Map by Randy Asplund

First printing, August 2020
First mass market printing, August 2021

Distributed by Simon & Schuster
1230 Avenue of the Americas
New York, NY 10020

Library of Congress Control Number: 2020019699

Printed in the United States of America

10 9 8 7 6 5 4 3 2 1

For:

Leo F. Casey, English Teacher Par Excellence,
Boston Latin School
(My errors are mine, not his.)

CONTENTS

Terra

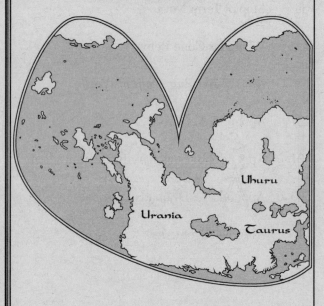

Urania

Uhuru

Taurus

Nova

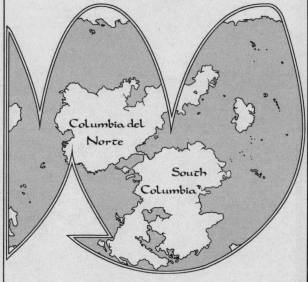

Columbia del Norte

South Columbia

WHAT HAS GONE BEFORE

Long ago, long before the appearance of man, there came to Earth the aliens known to us only as the "Noahs." About them, as a species, nothing is known, least of all what they called themselves. Their existence is surmised by the project they left behind. Somewhat like the biblical Noah, these aliens transported from Earth to another planet samples of virtually every species existing in the time period approximately five hundred thousand to five million years ago. They also appear to have modified the surface of the planet to create a weather pattern and general ecology suitable to the life-forms they brought there.

Having transported these species, and having left behind various other, genengineered species, apparently to inhibit the development of intelligent life on the new world, the Noahs disappeared, leaving no other trace beyond a few incomprehensible and inert artifacts, and possibly the rift through which they moved from the Earth to the new world. No other such rift has ever been found, suggesting, though not proving, that the Noahs can create and eliminate them at need.

It was through that rift that, in the year 2037 AD, a

robotic interstellar probe, the *Cristobal Colon*, disappeared en route to Alpha Centauri. Three years later it returned, under automated guidance, through the same rift. The *Colon* brought with it wonderful news of another Earthlike planet, orbiting another star. (Note, here, that not only is the other star *not* Alpha Centauri, it's not so far been proved that it is even in the same galaxy, or universe for that matter, as ours.) Here, finally, was a relatively cheap means to colonize another planet.

The first colonization effort failed to ethnic and religious strife. Thereafter, rather than risk further bloodshed by mixing colonies, the colonization effort would be run by regional supranationals such as NAFTA, the European Union, the Organization of African Unity, MERCOSUR, the Russian Empire and the Chinese Hegemony. Each of these groups were given colonization rights to specific areas on the new world, which was named—with a stunning lack of originality—"Terra Nova" or something in another tongue that meant the same thing. Most groups elected to establish national colonies within their respective mandates, some of them under United Nations' "guidance."

With the removal from Earth of substantial numbers of the most difficult and unprogressive people, the power and influence of supranational organizations such as the UN and EU increased dramatically. With the increase of supranational power, often enough expressed in corruption, even more of Earth's more ethnocentric and traditionalist population volunteered to leave. Still others were deported forcibly. Within not much more than a century and a quarter, and much less in many cases, nations had ceased to have much meaning or importance on Earth. On the other hand, and over about the same time scale, nations had become preeminent on Terra Nova. Moreover, because of the way the surface of the new world had been created by the Noahs and divided by the supranationals, these nations tended to reflect—if only generally—the nations of Old Earth.

Warfare was endemic, beginning with the wars of liberation by many of the weaker colonies to throw off the yoke of Earth's United Nations.

In this environment Patrick Hennessey was born, grew to manhood, and was a soldier for many years. Some years after leaving service, Hennessey's wife, Linda, a native of the Republic of Balboa, and their three children were killed in a massive terrorist attack on Hennessey's native land, the Federated States of Columbia, said attack having been aided by the United Earth Peace Fleet, or UEPF, in orbit over Terra Nova. The same attack likewise killed Hennessey's uncle, the head of his extended and rather wealthy family. As his dying testament, Uncle Bob changed his will to leave Hennessey with control over the entire corpus of his estate.

Half mad with grief, Hennessey, living in Balboa, ruthlessly provoked and then mercilessly gunned down six local supporters of the terrorists. One, who survived being gut shot, Hennessey pistol-whipped to death. In retaliation, and with astonishing bad judgment, the terrorist organization, the Salafi *Ikhwan*, attacked Balboa, killing hundreds of innocent civilians, including many children.

With Balboa now enraged, and money from his uncle's

rather impressive estate, Hennessey built a small army within the Republic. For reasons of internal politics, Hennessey assumed his late wife's maiden name, Carrera. It was as Carrera that he became well known to the world of Terra Nova.

Against some expectations, the *Legion del Cid* performed quite well as auxiliaries of the Federated States. Equally against expectations, its greatest battle in the campaign was against a Sumeri infantry brigade led by a first-rate officer, Adnan Sada, who not only fought well but stayed within the customs, rules, and laws of war.

Impressed with the Legion's performance (even while loathing the openly brutal ways it had of enforcing the laws of war), and needing foreign troops badly, the War Department of the Federated States offered Carrera a long-term employment contract. Carrera, in turn, likewise offered to not only hire, but substantially increase, Sada's military force. Accepting the offer, and loyal to his salt, Sada revealed seven nuclear weapons to Carrera, three of which were functional and the rest restorable. These Carrera quietly had removed, telling no one except a very few, *very* close subordinates.

Insurgency blossomed across Sumer. In Carrera's area of responsibility, this insurgency, while bloody, was contained through the help of Sada's men and Carrera's ruthlessness. In the rest of the country it grew to nearly unmanageable levels. Eventually, Carrera's area of responsibility was changed and he was forced to undertake a difficult campaign against a city, Pumbadeta, held by the rebels. He surrounded and starved the city, letting none leave it until he was certain that every dog, cat and rat had been eaten. Only then did he let the women and children out.

After the departure of the noncombatants, Carrera's Legion continued the blockade until the civilians within the town rebelled against the rebels. Having a rare change of heart, Carrera aided those rebels to liberate their town. Thereafter nearly every insurgent found within Pumbadeta was executed, along with several members of the press sympathetic to the rebels. The few insurgents he—temporarily—spared were sent to a surface ship for *rigorous* interrogation.

With the war in Sumer winding down, Carrera and his legions were—as it turned out, unwisely—let go. When the Federated States needed them again, Carrera exacted an exorbitant price before agreeing to commit to the war in Pashtia. That price being paid, however, and in gold, he didn't stint but waged a major—and typically ruthless—campaign to restore the situation, which had deteriorated badly under Tauran Union interference and faint support.

Ultimately, Carrera's intelligence service got wind of a major meeting taking place across the nearby border with Kashmir between the chief of the United Earth Peace Fleet and the emir of the terrorists, the Salafi *Ikhwan*. Carrera attacked, killing thousands, capturing hundreds, and seizing a dozen more nuclear weapons, intended gifts of the UEPF to their terrorist allies. One he used against the capital of the major terrorist-supporting state of Yithrab. When detonated, this weapon not only killed the entire clan of the chief of the Salafi *Ikhwan*, but also at *least* a million citizens of that city. In the process, he framed the Salafis for the detonation. This ended the antiterrorist war . . . at least for the nonce.

Among the captures were High Admiral Robinson, of the United Earth Peace Fleet. His position was taken over by Marguerite Wallenstein, who had actually helped Carrera to remove her former chief from the playing board.

The price to Carrera was also heavy; he collapsed, physically, mentally, and emotionally, going into seclusion until persuaded back to active duty by Legate Jimenez and Sergeant Major McNamara. There followed a vicious no-holds-barred and little-quarter-given war with the quasi-sovereign drug cartels of Santander, along with an attempted *coup d'état*, by the treacherous Legate Pigna. In the same coup, the rump of the old, oligarchic Balboan state was reabsorbed into the rest of the country, the oligarchs and their lackeys being driven from the country or killed. The Transitway, however, the canal linking the Shimmering Sea and *Mar Furioso*, remained in Tauran hands.

An easily winnable war against Balboa on the part of the Tauran Union was precisely what High Admiral Wallenstein wanted, on the not indefensible theory that such a war would serve as a catalyst to turn the Tauran Union into a real country and a great power, which would serve to stymie the other great powers of Terra Nova. That war came to pass, though not by the high admiral's doing and not to the result she wanted. Instead of defeating Balboa and changing its regime, the Tauran forces went for high value targets that turned out to be bait for a country-wide ambush. When the smoke had cleared, thousands were dead, and almost twenty thousand Tauran troops were prisoners of the Balboans.

All was not obviously well for Balboa, however. In the course of the battle one of its double handful of stealthy coastal defense submarines managed to sink an aircraft carrier of the Navy of *Xing Zhong Guo*, New Middle Kingdom. This would have been fine, had the carrier actually been involved in the attack on Balboa. Unfortunately, it was not; it was evacuating Zhong noncombatants from the fighting. No one knew how many thousands of innocents—men, women, and children— burned or drowned in the attack. Interestingly, Carrera didn't appear to care about rising Zhong anger. One might almost have thought he wanted them to join a continued war.

Whatever he wanted, though, Carrera needed time. He'd been preparing for war for about a decade but, of necessity, many of those preparations were out of sight or not quite complete or both. He bought time for that completion by returning a trickle of TU prisoners.

There had to be a peace conference, of course, and so there was. Carrera and the president of Balboa, Raul Parilla, sent to the peace conference Carrera's second wife, Lourdes, with a small contingent. It was an unusual peace conference insofar as almost no one present had any particular interest in peace. Still, a false peace prevailed while the conference wore on. In that false peace, all the more desperately clutched for its very fragility, Carrera and his legions completed their final preparations. From all over the world, contingents of troops from allies and well-wishers, large and small, poured in to help defend Balboa. Next door, with the introduction of Tauran troops to defend a neighbor from Carrera, an insurgency sprang up, which insurgency Carrera fed. In the Tauran Union, the very lists of dead and captured were perverted and twisted to undermine the governments. Best of all was the thing Carrera had never anticipated or planned for; he acquired a spy well placed in the highest enemy camp. It was a very nice compliment to a lesser, localized spy.

Conversely, Carrera's fleet, the *classis*, first engaged a Zhong submarine flotilla, then sailed under orders to Santa Josefina, to the east, and voluntarily interned itself. This gave a much-needed shot in the arm to both the morale and the various propaganda ministries of Carrera's and Balboa's enemies. Interned, the *classis* was able to catch up on quite a bit of deferred maintenance.

With Carrera's naval power thus disposed of, the Zhong made a forced landing against the island fortress dominating the northern terminus of the Balboa Transitway. It was a move as obvious as it was necessary; without the island, the Transitway could not be cleared; without the island, no landing near the capital, *Ciudad* Balboa, could be supported. Because it was so obvious, the defenses were immense. Between those and a few secrets, the Zhong were unable to do more than seize a part of the island, and that the most easily contained and least useful part. A substantial portion—some claimed a majority—of the Zhong fleet was sunk in the attempt. What remained, with the troops not committed to the island, bounced off but then effected a landing along the essentially undefended coast east of the capital.

Meanwhile, in the city of First Landing, in the Federated States of Columbia, before the World League, Carrera's wife, Lourdes, has thrown down the gauntlet to the Tauran Union and the United Earth Peace Fleet, her speech ending with the words:

"Come on, then, you fat and lazy tyrants. Come on, then, you tools of terror and of a murderous alien whore. Come on, you political harlots. Cowards. Filth. Swine. We, the free people of Balboa, are waiting for you, side by side with our faithful and gallant allies and under the just God who stands above us all, but who stands on our side, not yours!"

To support their landing on the mainland, the Zhong, under their excellent—courageous and imaginative, both—admiral, Wanyan Liang, managed to create a limited port capability far from the impossibly dense defenses of the *Isla Real*, and to force a landing on the mainland, away from the *Bahia de Balboa*. The Tauran Union, stung by their previous humiliation and Balboan bombardment-by-drone, invaded from the Shimmering Sea side of Balboa, the territory of which was under frequent aerial attack.

With the Shimmering Sea side of Balboa's Transitway area fallen to the combined forces of the Tauran Union, the country's second city, Cristobal, was cut off and besieged. Legate Xavier Jimenez's Fourth Corps defended the city and its environs stoutly, hanging on sometimes by the skin of their teeth.

Meanwhile, barring only a number of deliberate, well-hidden stay-behinds, the scattered forces in the area under Tauran attack headed for the presumed safety of the Parilla Line. Some of them made it; others were killed or captured.

Gallic General Bertrand Janier, already humiliated by the Balboans several times, suspecting that every gain he made was a trap, was almost persuaded by his own staff and the high admiral of the United Earth Peace Fleet, Marguerite Wallenstein, that this time he really had outwitted his enemy. Still doubting, however, Janier launches a bloody, but necessary, reconnaissance in force against the Parilla Line, determining that, after all, it is facing the wrong way, that he really did outwit Carrera, and that, hence, no trap was possible.

Meanwhile, Khalid, Fernandez's tame Druze, is one of several agents funneling arms and equipment to disgruntled Moslems within the Tauran Union, even while clandestine drone launches vault high explosives into Tauran cities.

In the other local theater of war, Santa Josefina, where a guerrilla war already raged, a second Balboan regiment, made up of Santa Josefinans and masquerading as another local regiment of guerillas, has assaulted the Tuscan populated town of San Jaba, removing its airstrip from play and executing most of the town's governing body as collaborators with the Tauran occupation and enemies of the people. A similar assault saw the bulk of the United Earth embassy staff likewise stood against a wall and shot. The local fortunes of war wax and wane with whoever has sent or withdrawn reinforcements lately, as well as with which silly injunctions from the Global Court of Justice are in force, and how willing the Tauran military is to ignore them. Still, for Claudio Marciano, the Tauran

Commander in Santa Josefina, those fortunes mostly wane until he finds himself in retreat to a corner of the country where he and his small force have a chance to defend themselves.

Esmeralda Miranda, who serves as High Admiral Wallenstein's aide, her liaison officer to Marciano, and Fernandez's most prized intelligence asset, after losing a friend to the Santa Josefinan guerillas, began to doubt the morality of her aiding Balboa. Even a clandestine visit by Carrera to try to persuade her was not quite enough to keep that aid—spying—going. Later, Esma discovers that murder in revenge or self-defense isn't as hard as all that. Where that understanding may lead her even she, herself, doesn't know.

Under guard, deposed former Earther High Admiral Robinson and the marchioness of Amnesty, Lucretia Arbeit, languish in durance vile, kept out of the sun, exercised just enough to keep them from going completely to fat, and threatened with crucifixion for any failure to cooperate fully. They're still not quite sure why they've been spared, nor if they'll continue to be spared if their usefulness ever ends.

Beyond the aerial front, and the Santa Josefinan Front, past the intelligence effort and beyond even the bombardment of the Tauran Union, Carrera has opened up yet another front. Indeed, he has hired a Tauran human rights-oriented law firm and, through them, started a campaign of "Lawfare," the waging of war by judicial means. He did this more to demoralize the enemy forces than to gain any advantage over them. As it turned out, though, he achieved both effects, along with the higher and more important effect of delegitimizing lawfare, even as lawfare sought to delegitimize warfare.

A penultimate front remains to be opened; Carrera's son, Hamilcar, a key player in the operation for which Robinson is earmarked, has been afloat on the converted freighter, the MV ALTA, which has also picked up over a thousand more cadets from the refugee camps in Valdivia. Hamilcar's target is unannounced, but he knows what it is.

Finally, with the Tauran Union's forces well emplaced, deep into Balboan national territory, the beginning of the end played out. Starting with a bombardment using approximately three *thousand* guns, mortars, and rocket launchers, supplemented by enormously powerful fuel-air-explosive mines, Carrera launched his counterattack. Faced with near nuclear levels of bombardment, and that intense enough to crush morale and even send Tauran soldiers into catatonia or suicide, his infantry divisions lunged forward from the Parilla Line which was, after all, facing in the wrong direction to defend against the Tauran Union, but in a perfect direction to provide sheltered assembly areas for the initial elements of a multi-corps assault.

Though the Tauran commander, Bertrand Janier, has ordered a surrender, mopping up continues . . .

DAYS OF BURNING, DAYS OF WRATH

CHAPTER ONE

"Die hard, Fifty-seventh, die hard!"
—Lieutenant Colonel William Inglis,
Battle of Albuera, 1811

Cristobal Province, Balboa

But for the blasted skeletons of dead trees, the landscape resembled something of a *moon*scape. Fully half of the visible ground, and quite possibly more than that, was composed of craters, themselves now filling with poisoned water, seeping from traumatized soil. Repeated concussion from still impacting artillery sent ripples from the edges of the craters, across the water, to meet in the rough center and then roll back again.

Bodies and parts of bodies lay in every manner of undignified death and ruin. Some of those bodies were small, reptilian, and winged.

Carrera, standing on the lip of a large crater, closed his heart to the presence of so *many* destroyed bodies. At least, he tried to. They were just things, he told himself,

3

from which all value had been taken, except for the memories stored in the hearts of their loved ones. He closed his own heart, too, to the future wailing of mothers, once the Tauran casualty lists had been collected and sent onward. He really didn't want to think about the wailing of his own country's mothers. Instead, he summed it up, indirectly, with a well-remembered quote from a king of Old Earth: *An assegai has been thrust into the belly of the nation. There are not tears enough to mourn the dead.*

Staring down into the reeking water, he mentally measured and thought, *A one-eighty, if I had to guess.* Then he looked up at the source of the water's rippling, watching a battery of eighty-fives pounding away at some group of Taurans who simply refused to surrender, despite Janier's orders. Several large piles of expended casings grew behind the guns, far more than they had managed to carry forward with them. Streams of gunners trotted between holes in the ground and their guns, carrying at least one shell under each arm.

Awfully decent, really, for the Taurans to stand guard on the fifty or so thousand shells we left behind against this day. And I have to give Fernandez's crew credit, too, for digging into the Tauran manuals and figuring out how much "net explosive weight" we'd have to put in each dump to make it against their rules to simply blow them in place without having shelters dug for everyone. And then, after a while, I suppose they must have just forgotten about the shells, what with more pressing concerns at hand.

The gunners' ballet grew old after a time. Carrera signaled for his vehicle, an Ocelot Infantry Fighting

Vehicle, driven by Jamey Soult, to come pick him up. The driver swung around the crater slowly, careful to avoid the uncertain lips of the larger hole, though he could not avoid the stinking muck of the smaller ones.

"Where to, boss?" Soult shouted, over the roar of the engine, slowing down then to avoid covering his chief in muck.

Climbing on top, then beating his boot heels against the side of the Ocelot's turret to remove the caked-on mud, Carrera had a sudden idea. He eased himself, feet first, down into the turret, put on his own combat vehicle crewman's helmet, and said, "Take me to the FDC for that battery," pointing index and middle finger in the direction of the firing.

"Roger," Soult said, taking off gently to avoid spinning his treads and maybe becoming stuck. The Ocelot was amphibious, but not, as they said, "Mud-phibious." About one hundred and fifty meters shy of what looked to be the battery's fire direction center, the craters mostly gave out, leaving relatively smooth and firm soil for the vehicle to negotiate.

At the battery, one officer—a Tribune named Ramirez—rushed over while pulling a protective—most would say "gas"—mask away from his face. Saluting, he reported in with his own name and his battery nomenclature.

Carrera jumped from the vehicle to the ground, then asked, "Why the mask, Tribune?"

"The fumes will get to you eventually, sir. And this area"—Ramirez gestured around with a circling finger—"is already about as thick with fumes as a man can stand."

"Fair enough," Carrera said, agreeably. "What are you firing at and for whom?"

"It's a maniple-sized group of Anglians, we think, *Duque.* They're pretty well dug in and disinclined to surrender. We're shooting on behalf of a cohort from Second Tercio, Second Cohort."

"Hmmm...Jamey?"

"Velasquez's Cohort, boss," Soult answered immediately. "Want I should get them on the line?"

"Yeah, do."

It took Soult perhaps seven minutes to find and set the radio on the pertinent set of frequencies and then get himself into the radio net.

"What's the holdup, Jamey?" asked Carrera.

Frigging war on and better things for them to be doing, Soult thought. Rather than his having to answer Carrera, the Second of the Second answered him.

"Who do you want to speak to, boss?" Soult asked.

"Velasquez or his exec or his sergeant major."

Fifteen seconds after that, Soult announced, "Sergeant Major Cruz, sir. You're in the green." That last was a standard phrase for, *your communication is encrypted so you can presume to speak freely.* The warning really wasn't necessary; the encrypted radios gave off a notice that one could speak freely in the form of a *beepbeepbeep.*

Beepbeepbeep. "Cruz?" Carrera asked into the microphone, following several distinctive beeps that confirmed the encryption.

Beepbeepbeep. "Yes, *Duque.*"

Beepbeepbeep. "Who are you fighting and why won't they surrender?"

Beepbeepbeep. "Anglians, sir, and some mixed-in Cimbrians and Hordalanders, we think. Tough bastards, don't know when they're beaten."

Beepbeepbeep. "How many are there and what are you doing to deal with them?"

Beepbeepbeep. "We've got them pretty well pinned in their position with artillery and mortars. While their heads are being kept down, we're working our way around their flanks."

Beepbeepbeep. "What kind of artillery and mortar support do you have?"

Beepbeepbeep. "A battery of eighty-fives and another of one-five-twos, five sections of mortars from the cohort and another battery of heavy mortars Fourth Corps has loaned us the support of."

Beepbeepbeep. "Okay, I understand. But I put it in the order that we need prisoners, a *lot* of prisoners. Have you or anyone tried to explain to these guys that the battle is effectively over?"

Beepbeepbeep. "Yes, sir. They didn't seem interested in listening, where disinterested is defined as fired a volley over the heads of the parlimentaires we sent to talk to them."

Beepbeepbeep. "Right. Okay, tell your boss to pull your companies back and, as soon as they're back, lift the artillery and mortars. I'm heading your way directly."

Soult scowled while staring straight ahead through the windshield of the Second Cohort four-by-four he'd temporarily exchanged for the Ocelot. He muttered something unintelligible.

"What was that, Jamey?" Carrera asked, while tying a white cloth to a bark-covered pole picked up from the ground, likely the victim of some fast-moving steel shard.

Changing neither his scowl nor his focus, Soult snorted angrily and said, more distinctly, "I've seen you do some boneheaded things over the years, but this is just that one step beyond stupid all the way to insanity."

"Oh, come on; I've done dumber shit than this."

"Name one," Soult demanded.

"Flew to enemy-occupied territory to meet a girl?"

"That was defensible," Soult countered. "This is just fucking ridiculous."

Carrera finished the white flag, then stood silently for a long minute. Finally, he wiped one hand across his face, sighed and said, "This is defensible, too, Jamey. Maybe more importantly, it's for the good of my soul."

Soult shook his head resignedly, the scowl disappearing. "Still stupid," he insisted, chin down and mind expecting the worst.

Velasquez and Cruz, standing not far away, simply shook their heads, faces kept carefully blank.

Carrera pretended not to notice. Instead, he demanded, "Now tell me again what your orders are."

Velasquez, being senior and in command, replied. "If they kill you, we butcher them to a man, hacking the wounded into spareribs and tossing survivors on the points of our bayonets. If you're not back in an hour, same thing. But if they give up, you want us to stand and cheer, salute and give them an honor guard to the POW camp."

"Very good. Now have you got those half-dozen each cans of legionary rum and cigarettes I asked for?"

Passing over a satchel that looked about the right size and bulged in about the right way to be holding two hundred and forty disgustingly strong cigarettes and forty-eight ounces of preposterously strong rum, Cruz said, "The pogues I confiscated these from are *not* happy campers, but fuck 'em. I put in a couple of can openers, too."

"With luck, Sergeant Major, I'll be able to make it up to them." Turning to the cohort commander, Carrera asked, "Now, your boys are all under cease-fire?"

"Yes, sir," Velasquez answered. "But the number of guns and mortars we have to support us is going up by the minute."

"I'm sure. Jamey, how many *Cruz de Corajes* are in the case?"

"Twenty-one," Soult answered.

"That's good enough. Get about a dozen of them ready. And see if we can't get another few gallons of rum, will you?" Carrera twisted to take his pistol from its usual holster, then tossed that underhanded to Soult. "And away we go."

This is possibly even dumber than Jamey knew, Carrera thought, inching his way over the broken, chewed-up ground and shattered, fallen trees. He had to work his way around some progressivines, torn up by the barrage as was everything else, but remarkably resilient and thick.

With all the fires having lifted, those guys have got to be primed to fight off an assault. And with all the crap in the air they probably can't.

"'Alt!" said someone in some variety of an Anglian accent. "Oo goes there, friend o' foe?"

"A foe who means you well," Carrera answered. His eyes strained to make out where the voice was coming from. But whoever and wherever the speaker was, he was damned well camouflaged, indeed. "Can you take me to your commander?"

"Nao; all th' officers is dead, bu' one, and ee's bloody useless. We go' a sarn' major oo migh' wan' to talk with ya."

"Bring me to him, then, please."

"Wha's in that bag yer carryin'?"

"A gift, but it has to go to your sergeant major. You can carry it if you like."

"Roight. Ease i' off yer shoulder and pu' i' on th' ground. Gen'ly!"

"I'll do that," Carrera agreed, "and gently."

First driving the pole bearing the white flag into the dirt, Carrera hooked his now freed right thumb under the carrying strap that ran over his left shoulder, then slid it off. He clutched the strap tightly with all fingers, then lowered the satchel to the ground.

His right hand then curled around the pole. "Now can one or more of you come take charge of me?"

Two armed men in battle dress stood up warily, both keeping their rifles' muzzles pointed in Carrera's general direction.

Oh, they're good all right; I still *can't see where they were hidden.* He looked again, taking in bandages, one of them leaking a spot of red. *Both wounded, too. Tough bastards; I can hardly wait to send them home.*

The smaller of the two came forward, even as the larger trained his rifle more precisely on Carrera's head.

"'Oly shi'! Are you really . . . ?"

Carrera nodded solemnly. "Patricio Carrera, *Dux Bellorum* of the Timocratic Republic of Balboa. And we really don't have that much time. Please take the satchel—that, or let me carry it—and get me to your sergeant major.

"I'm not armed, but you can take the time to search me if you insist. However, if you're willing to skip the formalities, you and your regiment have my parole for as long as I'm here. By the way, what regiment is it, if I can ask?"

"Die 'ards, sir."

"Ah, the old Fifty-Seventh. I might have guessed."

"I think we'll accep' yer parole, sir. But I 'ave ta blindfold you."

"That's fine, go ahead. Who are *you*, by the way?"

"Corporal Cleric, sir," the Anglian answered, tying a thick-folded cravat-type bandage around Carrera's eyes. When he was done, he placed his rifle in his right hand, reached down to pick up and sling Carrera's satchel crossways, and then put his left around Carrera's bicep to lead him into the interior of the perimeter. "This way, sir," Cleric said. "Carruthers, you stay 'ere."

"Roight, Corp."

Someone was weeping, intermittently, not far away, and with the sound of heartbroken agony. A deeper voice said, "If you must die, Smithers, at least die like a man. Quietly." The weeping stopped.

"Sarn' Major," Cleric announced, as he guided Carrera down the sharp and ragged slope of a large crater, "you ain' gonna believe oo's come callin'." To Carrera he added, "You can take the blindfold off now, sir."

"Deserter is it, Cleric?" asked the sergeant major of the regiment, with disgust. "If so, he's the dumbest bastard in two armies."

"You're possibly half right, Sergeant Major," Carrera agreed, lowing himself to sit on the muddy side of the trench. "About the dumb part, that is. Indeed, I'm pretty sure that you and my warrant could agree on that completely."

Not knowing he was repeating Cleric's own words, albeit in a higher-class accent, the sergeant major said, "Holy shit!" before standing to attention and rendering a proper salute.

Not really expecting that—*Should have, I suppose*—Carrera stood again and returned it, then returned to his seat.

"Sergeant Major," he said, "we need to talk. We *seriously* need to talk." Glancing at his watch, Carrera added, "And at this point we've got a bare forty-three... no, forty-two minutes to do it in."

"If I may ask, sir; to do what?"

"Hopefully arrange some way to keep from all of us getting killed," Carrera replied, "Ummm... RSM...?"

"Ayres, sir, RSM Ayres."

"Thank you. Me, I guess you know."

The RSM said, softly, "Oh, yes, we know," and then shuddered slightly. Carrera didn't think it was about him, exactly, or even his being there, but something else, maybe something having to do with the battle.

"We're not surrendering, sir." The RSM pointed at a

radio with an obvious bullet hole in it. "Shot it myself, sir, when the order to surrender came. We're not interested."

"All your officers are dead?" he asked. *No sense saying that the corporal let that information loose.* That wasn't changing the subject; that was an attempt to figure out if there was anyone above Ayres who might surrender.

"That, or badly wounded, a couple, and unconscious," Ayres replied. "All but one, sir. Major McQueeg is in a deep bunker, playing with himself last I saw. He . . ."—and there was that shudder again—"he broke during the bombardment."

"Don't be too hard on him," Carrera said. "The Tauran Union Expeditionary Force was under a bombardment that may as well have been nuclear."

"I never thought especially well of the major, anyway," said the RSM. "But we . . . all of us"—there was a worse shudder, this time, and maybe an impossible glisten in the eye—"we mostly collapsed. For a while, anyway, we did."

"Then don't be too hard on yourselves, either. I'm telling you, that bombardment was as fierce as anyone has ever faced. There's no shame for anyone in whatever it did to them. None whatsoever. I mean that.

"And, besides, you bounced back well enough, didn't you? This will help some more.

"Excuse me a moment," Carrera said, reaching into the satchel. From it he selected by feel a can of legionary rum. This he pulled out and set on his knee, then reached in for a P-15 folding can opener.

"I've got a cup for myself," he said, genially. "You folks?"

"I do," answered Cleric. "RSM, where's yer own? I'll fetch it."

"That's the real legionary stuff?" Ayres asked, then told the corporal, "In my pack; where else?"

"We captured some early, not long after we landed, but haven't seen any in a while. It's pretty ferocious."

"It's supposed to be cut with water, yes," Carrera said, working the can opener to create two thin slices in the top of the can of rum. "And it's strong, but you could mix it in with loose shit and be sure that all you were drinking was the shit; no microscopic bugs would survive it. And it doesn't do bad things to your arteries, like the purification pills do.

"Corporal?"

Cleric who, by this time, had retrieved Ayres' enameled tin cup and his own, passed the two cups over.

Carrera hesitated a moment. "Hmm ... let me think ... forty-eight ounces ... call it about ... ah, fuck it, we'll make it healthy; there's not enough for everyone to have a decent last drink no matter how I ration it. Or ... how many men still fit, RSM?"

"I can't tell you that, sir."

"I understand," Carrera agreed, "but surely that only counts if I am going back."

"Aren't you?"

Shaking his head, Carrera answered firmly, "No. I've had enough. I've done enough. I've been at the core of wickedness beyond your wildest imaginings, always for what seemed a good reason, of course." Carrera's eyes grew distant for a moment. "Yes, it always seemed like there was a good reason." He shook his head, recovering composure. "And orders I've already given are going to add considerably to what I've already done, too.

"In about . . ." he consulted his watch, "call it thirty-five minutes, now, the bombardment's going to start again, much heavier though, this time. If you men are willing to stand it and die to the last man then I'd be proud to stay here and die with you."

"Oh, don't be silly, sir," said Ayres. "Not your regiment. Your honor isn't involved."

"It's not about my honor, RSM; it's about what I said. I've just had it. If I could have talked the Die-hards into surrendering then maybe, just maybe, I'd have brightened my soul enough. But I can see already that that's just about impossible. So here I stay."

Ayres remonstrated, "Sir, we *can't* surrender. Our colonel had us bring the colors with us here. 'Colors that aren't risked are useless,' he said, 'meaningless and valueless.' I suppose he had a point. But just surrender and give up the colors that are—at least in parts of them— over four hundred years old? That came from Old Earth with the regiment? For an enemy's children to point at and gloat over? Not a man here but wouldn't rather die than live to see that."

"I see," Carrera agreed, reaching to take one of the tin cups. Into this he poured a couple of fingers of rum, maybe two ounces' worth. He handed that cup to Ayres, saying, "Now be sure to cut it fifty-fifty or it will be undrinkable." He filled up the corporal's cup to the same level, but without repeating the warning. Then he took his own cup and canteen from their pouch, poured, put the can down, and then added a good deal of water to it.

Taking a sip he announced, "Perfect. Now where the hell, RSM, did you get the idea that we'd take and keep your colors?"

"Sir?"

"It's just not our way. There's not even a slight trace of honor or glory in humiliating a foe who fought hard, well, and bravely. It would demean us, make the victory cheap and hollow.

"No, no, RSM; if the Fifty-seventh decided to spare itself to fight another day, maybe against an enemy that *really* needs a good dose of killing, it would march out of here with its colors flying, drums beating—my warrant is trying to scare up some drums, but I can't promise—and a bullet each held in their cheeks."

Ayres looked intently into Carrera's face and saw no guile there. Without first bothering to cut the rum, he took an unhealthy slug, then began to cough uncontrollably. After a thorough back pounding from Cleric, the RSM asked, "Are you serious?"

Carrera stared him straight in the eyes and answered, "Never more serious in my life."

"So fill up your glasses," Ayres recited, softly, "And show your regard, by drinking the health of each jolly Diehard." A more gingerly sip followed that.

"Cleric," said the RSM, "round up for me the senior noncom in each company."

"Best be quick, Corporal," Carrera added. "And take the rum and cigarettes to pass out!"

To Ayres Carrera added, "There's not really enough rum to go around, but my warrant officer, Jamey Soult, should have more by the—"

"Soult, is it, sir? Soult?" Ayres began to laugh near uncontrollably. In between guffaws, he could get the words out, "Of fucking . . . course . . . it would have . . . just have . . . to a be a Soult . . . who's going to . . . watch us surrender . . . a Soult!"

One of these days I'm going to have to ask someone what's so funny about this regiment surrendering in front of a Soult.

Soult answered, "Roger," then replaced the microphone on its hanger and leaned back against the side of the Ocelot. *The fucking Pied Piper*, he thought, scowling as he leaned, arms folded, against the hull of the Ocelot he'd retrieved. There hadn't been enough room in the four-by-four for all the rum and cigarettes. He thought he heard singing, too, but, if so, it was very soft. It grew louder though, as the singers began to emerge from the sound-absorbing trees and stumps.

In the warrant's view, Carrera marched out of the smoke and mist at the head of a column of Anglians. Between the column, three across, and himself, a color guard carried and escorted two banners. The Anglian rank and file . . . *Well, them and the others who attached themselves to them, they're shot up pretty badly, a good chunk of them, but no one's letting anyone fall behind and anyone who needs help, a friendly shoulder or whatever, is getting it. And, I guess I did hear . . .*

". . . a rampart or guarding a trench
Neither bullet nor bayonet our progress retards,
For it's all just the same to the jolly Die-hards . . ."

I don't know how he gets away with this shit, I really don't. But I suppose I'd better produce the rum and cigarettes he asked for. Oh, and tell him that the package to the ALTA was delivered, safe and sound.

CHAPTER TWO

"But when Islam emerged it put slavery into order,
by limiting it to legitimate wars between Muslims
and their enemies...the female prisoners of wars
are 'those whom you own'...in order to humiliate
them they become the property of the army
commander, or of a Muslim...and he can have sex
with them..."

—Suad Saleh, Theology Professor (female)
Al-Azhar University, Cairo, 12 September, 2014

Oppenheim, Sachsen

Stomach pained and churning, as it often was these days,
Khalid stood by the main window to his small rental,
watching the drops splatter on the pavement while
runnels ran down the glass planes. He'd found himself
standing there quite a lot, of late, worried to his innermost
core.

Khalid's reflection on the glass, thin, opaque, and
somewhat indistinct and distorted, caused him to shake

his head. *So many faces now; so many identities. I wonder if I could even pull myself out of a police lineup. Surely there are people in the world who look more like the real me than I do now.*

It was a fair complaint. Since coming to work for Fernandez and the legions, when they were in Sumer, Khalid had gone under the knife more times than he cared to think about. Now, his nose thinned and shortened, his chin built up, his hair dyed blond, and blue contacts in his eyes, his own mother wouldn't have recognized him. They'd done something to his eyes, too, Fernandez's plastic surgeons; the shape and spacing seemed wrong. Hell, even his native Sumeri Arabic had acquired a Balboan accent.

"Bad enough," he muttered, "that Arabic comes harder to my mind than Spanish; at least I am domiciled in a Spanish-speaking country. But how much worse that these Sachsens' guttural *German* sounds more native to my ears than my own tongue, too?"

Those complaints really weren't at the core of Khalid's stomach issues, issues he had begun to suspect might be more than just emotional ones. No, what was killing him was the waiting.

How many more days or weeks until Fernandez gives me the word? wondered Khalid. *These people—neither of these people—are my own, but I've gotten to know them. The Moslems could fuck up a wet dream, timing-wise, and will always either strike before they're ready or delay until it's too late. The Sachsens . . . they're under the control of a political mob that seems to hate their own country, yes, but there are some stout folk, good men, brave and strong, among them, too. And even a few virtuous women, wonder of wonders. If the Moslems are held back too long, the Sachsens will figure it out. Who knows what happens then? If the Moslems strike too soon...well...maybe in this case that would be better for them. Which, I suppose would matter to me if I didn't hate their guts on general principle.*

I can understand Fernandez and his crew keeping me in the dark, me and the other agents. But it's hard to tell what I should do or when...

It's worse, too, because this isn't really my thing. Machine gun a bunch of senior Moslem leaders in the course of what's supposed to be a news interview? Just sheer fun. Blow a manhole cover through somebody's asshole? Oooo, look at the pretty colors. Cut the throat of some terrorism-supporting Sachsen bimbo? No problem. Mail a few letters, get some grids for long-range cruise missile targets? Easy can do.

Even smuggling arms was pretty easy, and pretty easy even in some very large quantities. But coordinate a bunch of Islamics for an uprising? Not really my forte; no training, no experience, no real skill...

Off in the distance, muffled by rain and window, wall, street, and tree, Khalid heard a series of pops, like fireworks. He thought little of it until police sirens began sounding, those being a lot louder and much more clear, and coming from all over.

"I wonder..."

There was really no need to wonder long; a few steps to the television, a flick of a switch, and there, on screen, was a familiar scene. It was the front of one of the mosques to which he'd delivered arms. In front of the mosque lay a pair of dead and bleeding Sachsen police officers. A lone man, bearing a Volgan-made rifle, himself black-clad and face covered, stood over the corpses.

But, to give the devils their due, they do *understand using the media to get their message across. At least, no one seems to be objecting to that camera and what I suppose must be the news team around it.*

As if to confirm Khalid's suspicion, the camera shifted to a rather pretty and admirably slender blonde Sachsen news reporter. She was standing next to another rifle-bearing man, likewise black-clad and with a scarf wrapped around his face.

I'd best report in.

Headquarters hadn't had a lot to say, really. *But they did allow that I should confirm how widespread the rebellion is. So . . . take my own rifle, put on my markers, and head on over to the big mosque.*

Khalid watched as from the Oppenheimer Mosque, in groups of ten, or twenty, or fifty, or one hundred, give or take, young men—quasi uniformed but fully armed— poured forth into the streets and began the hunt for their quarry. For the most part, this involved the police and such reserve armories as were to be found in the city. They also had lists, prepared by their imam, of those whom he considered the most depraved of Sachsen citizens to be found in the town. This included large numbers of atheists, Tsarist-Marxists, and Kosmos, to the extent those categories differed. From the point of view of the imam and his minions, their fighters would merely be purging this world of the very people condemned in Allah's Own Voice, in the Quran. From the point of view of Khalid, Fernandez, and Carrera, on the other hand, they would be purging those most responsible for the existence of the Tauran Union, as well as those most likely to object to the Union's abject surrender to Balboan demands.

Sometimes, thought Khalid, *even devout enemies can find common ground. And on that happy note, best to head home.*

Two Miles East of the Oppenheimer Mosque, Oppenheim, Sachsen

Yes, indeed, thought Khalid, glancing up at the bodies dangling by their necks from the lampposts of the town's main thoroughfare, *sometimes even the most devout enemies can find common ground.*

The scene was lit only by firelight, the fire reflecting off the smoke and clouds lingering above. There was a smell of pork on the air. *Of course, it might be pork or it might be people. If I had to guess . . . people. Lots of fires after all. Lots.*

Above the bodies and the fires, one of Terra Nova's moons—Bellona—slowly crossed the sky.

Along with the solid aroma of pork, mostly at least a bit overdone, there were screams on the air. Some, the more masculine ones, seemed to be cut short quickly. The feminine screams went on and on, so much so that they never seemed to end. In with those were what he recognized as the sounds of fighting, with different calibers and types of firearms lashing back and forth, distinct and distinctly menacing.

His eyes came to rest on the darkened and swollen face of one of the dangling corpses. He recognized the face despite the swelling, the eyes being shut, and the lips twisted into something like a grimace. Below the face the thin cord the lynch mob had used had dug deeply into the neck.

"Easy death or hard?" Khalid wondered aloud, staring up while chewing his lower lip. "Probably hard; whatever pain you felt, it must have been hard to be strung up by the very people whose cause you've championed your entire political life. Tsk; what a terrible thing it must have been to realize your mistake just *that* much too late."

Dismissing the dangling corpse with an indifferent shrug, Khalid slung his non-serial numbered rifle over his right shoulder, turned away, and set off for his apartment. It was time and past time for him to wash the dust of Sachsen from his feet and exfiltrate back to the country he thought of as home, Carrera's Balboa.

In his pocket was a safe pass, signed by the imam of the big mosque. In three languages it said, "This man is serving God by bringing arms to the servants of God. Let him pass for the sake of your souls and the advancement of our cause, and God's."

Just to make sure, for those who tended to shoot first and ask questions later, Khalid's left arm sported a green cloth armband with the words, "There is no God but God" in Arabic script on a white circle in the center of the armband. This was a sentiment with which Khalid, a

Druze in the service of Balboa, could completely agree. Islam, on the other hand, he sneered at and despised.

This had not stopped him, after the manner of the Druze, from pretending to be a Moslem. Neither had it stopped him from smuggling in arms, ammunition, and some other equipment by the ton. Virtually every rifle and machine gun used, and virtually every round fired, in this town and half a dozen others had been brought in by Khalid from freighters anchored off the coasts and in the southern ports of Sachsen. Where the freighters had acquired the arms he couldn't be sure, but the designs were Volgan. He suspected that his boss, Fernandez's boss, Carrera, had ordered them from one or more of the factories in Volga in which he had a controlling interest.

But with those two, you never really know. These things could have come from Sumer, or from any of two dozen other places that make Volgan-designed arms. Be funny if they came from the Zhong, though, all things considered. And that's not impossible; the Zhong will sell anything to anyone.

The rising had come early and, apparently, spontaneously with the news that the Tauran Union expeditionary force to Balboa had been defeated and destroyed, while the smaller one in Santa Josefina, east of Balboa, was fleeing for its life to the farthest corner of that country. *On the whole*, Khalid thought, *I doubt it will make any difference. Carrera pretty obviously—well, to me it seems obvious—wanted the uprising to completely destroy the Tauran Union once the armed forces of its member states were destroyed or captured.*

He stopped his progress to turn back to the rows of

strangled, dangling, darkened-face corpses. *I would guess that "completely destroyed" means something like that; the ruling class of the Tauran Union lynched.* He looked up again at the sky, glowing with the reflection of the many fires burning below. *And collateral damage just isn't something that would much deter him . . . or them. Both Carrera and my chief, Fernandez, are wicked, wicked men.*

He resumed his long walk home, path lit by that same reflected fire.

As am I, come to think of it, since I—

Hmmph, what was that?

Khalid stopped walking and waited, ears straining for a repeat of the sound. He thought it might have come from a human being but, if so, it was neither quite masculine nor quite feminine. *Rather, something in be . . .*

He heard it again, head snapping in the direction from which he thought it had come. There was a thin slit in the rows of buildings. *Yes, there it is again. Maybe it's a little more female than male, after all. Even so . . .*

The next sound was laughter, from at least one man, though Khalid thought two more likely.

Slipping the rifle off his shoulder, Khalid advanced cautiously. What had seemed a thin slit widened as he neared into the opening to an alley, perhaps half a dozen feet across. From its opening came more laughter, *and definitely masculine*, as well as a more or less feminine voice saying over and over, "I will not cry out. I will not cry out. I will not . . ."

Though the alley was open to the sky, the pattern of light reflecting from above mostly missed it. It was much darker than the broad boulevard.

What is happening in that alley is none of my business, Khalid tried to convince himself. It was a doomed effort; he felt his thumb flicking the safety off the rifle even as he brought it up to his shoulder.

Well, fuck, the woman is probably near the ground, whether on her back or on all fours. So I go low—he crouched down—*and aim somewhat high.*

As quietly as he could, aided by typically smooth Sachsen paving and tennis shoes on his feet, Khalid advanced toward the alley's mouth. As he did, shapes began to form outlines inside. *Four,* he thought, *plus one I cannot see who's probably fucking the girl. But this is still none of my business.*

On the other hand, I detest Moslems, so . . .

"I will not cry out. I will not cry out. I will not cry . . ."

It was the laughter, actually, that caused Khalid's finger to depress the trigger. *Bad enough to rape. Worse to gang rape. But to laugh at the girl at the same time is just too much.* He closed one eye.

His first burst ruined his night vision in his open eye, even as it lit up the alley as if by a strobe light. He shifted left and fired again, going on nothing but the memory of target placement as he'd seen it in the muzzle flash.

Shift . . . squeeze . . . *bababang.*   Shift . . . squeeze . . . *bababang.* Shift . . . squeeze . . .

He stopped then, for a moment. He thought he'd seen all the standing targets go down like ninepins. But one remained, he thought, and that one was on both knees, still behind the girl, frozen stiff with fright. If he'd been stroking he had apparently stopped with the shock.

Of all the horrors of a night like this, a woman feeling

someone die while he's inside her is just that one step too much.

Khalid arose from his crouch, padded forward and delivered a butt stroke to the right side of the head of the last rapist. That one, apparently frozen in terror at the earlier firing, was thrown to his left, head bouncing off first the wall of the alley, and then the ground. Khalid reached down, took a good grasp of the hair, and began dragging him out of the alley.

They trend skinny but this one weighs next to nothing.

Once out in the glow of the firelight, he tossed the rapist to the ground. He was surprised—*Though I shouldn't have been*—that it was only a boy of thirteen or fourteen at the most. He returned the rifle to his shoulder but hesitated for just a moment. That was long enough for the victim to say, "No, wait. Please let me."

Khalid risked a quick glance. She was tall, slender, blonde.

And apparently not a natural blonde. Not bad looking, but maybe just a little *touch horse-faced.*

"That seems fair," Khalid replied, stepping to one side and handing her the rifle. "Do you know . . . ?"

"Only in general terms," she answered.

"That's probably good enough."

"Should it bother me that he's only a boy?" she asked. "It doesn't; not a bit."

"Can't imagine why it should?"

She hesitated. "I'd like him awake to see me kill him. How do I . . . ?"

Wordlessly, Khalid walked over and delivered a vicious

kick to the boy's kidney. He screamed and then sat bolt upright.

"There you go," Khalid said, stepping back.

"Look here, boy," the woman said in German. Once she saw his eyes widen much more than the width of the muzzle, she said, "Ah, good, you do speak the language. So tell me, was it worth it?"

Tears started to flow from the boy's eyes. He shook his head frantically, opening his mouth as if to say something. No words came forth.

"You want to apologize, don't you boy?" she asked, in a sympathetic tone. "You want to convince me that it was the others who put you up to it, don't you? That it wasn't really your fault?"

The boy's head became almost a blur, so quickly and repeatedly did he nod.

"Tough shit. Apology not accepted." She gave him just enough time to realize she meant to kill him before squeezing the trigger and sending at least several of the remaining nine or ten rounds into the boy's body. The rest careened across the boulevard, striking pavement, stone, and brick.

"Motherfucker!" she concluded.

"Here's your rifle," she told Khalid, handing it back. "And thank you, whoever you are. You can bill me for the ammunition, if you like."

"That won't be necessary," Khalid assured her. "But my manners; they call me, 'Khalid.' And you are?"

"Alix Speidel, at your—but please don't take this the way *they* would have—at your service."

Something about that name. Khalid looked more

closely. The name, he face: "Alix . . . hmmm . . . Alix Spei— I know who you are! Member of the Reichstag. Most prominent voice in Sachsen for closed borders and a return to tradition."

"A lot of people know who I am," she agreed. "And, yes. I think the events of the last day argue more eloquently for closed borders than I ever have." She pointed with her chin at the alley where the cooling bodies lay in pools of mixed blood. "If these had known who I was, they'd have burnt me alive. After raping me."

"If any of the others should catch you and find out, *they'll* burn you alive." Khalid hesitated a moment before adding, "You're a much cooler customer than I expected, based on what I heard you repeating over and over."

"'I will not cry out'? Yes, well, the boy was fucking me in the ass without lubrication," she said, matter-of-factly. "It hurt like the devil. What was I supposed to say?"

"You need a safe house," Khalid announced without even thinking about answering the question. "Mine will do. And you *will* be safe there, even from me."

"Good," she said, "because I far prefer girls."

"Yes, I remember. But we'll need . . ." He began looking from one street-level window to another. ". . . a disguise. Aha; there."

Walking to one window, Khalid used the butt of his rifle to smash it in. Once he had the glass out of the way, he reached in and pulled out a long section of very dark drapery. "Wrap this like a burka. Then walk two or three steps behind me. No one will question us."

"Wait." She walked back into the alley to retrieve her

torn skirt. Seeing it would not stay up short of a trip to the tailor she let it fall back to the alley's bloody pavement. "Burka, it is." She noticed Khalid's armband. "Wait; aren't *you* a Mo—"

"No, I'm not," he answered. "My people detest Moslems more than you do, but we're not above faking it to survive and get our way."

"After this, *my way*," she said, "is likely to involve some very large gas chambers." She began to wrap herself in the length of dark cloth. "And so I, too, shall fake it. For now."

She remembered, if only just, to grab the purse that had been cast to one side when she'd been taken.

On their half an hour's walk to safety at Khalid's rented safe house, they saw horror aplenty, from gang rapes, to lynchings to apartment buildings being burned with their inhabitant still inside. Twice Khalid had to show his trilingual pass from the imam and twice he and the woman were allowed to pass. Three times she'd had to squeeze his arm to prevent him from intervening.

"What does that thing say?" Alix had asked, after the second such stop.

"I'll tell you later," he'd replied.

"You'll want to shower," Khalid said, pointing Alix in the right direction. The apartment was dark, but enough light filtered through the windows for her to see where he meant. Looking her up and down, he added, "I'll find you some of my clothes. We're close enough in size, if you're willing to make a few compromises. I suggest you hurry with the shower; the water heater is electric and it will probably be some days before power is restored, if it ever is."

"I will want to shower," she agreed, "but first I need to take a shit. That boy wasn't the first one to mount me."

"Sure. Ummm . . ."

"Yes?"

"We need to find you a doctor. There's no need to inform the police, since justice has already been done, but you might have . . ."

"Caught a venereal disease?"

He nodded, a little ashamed of his sex.

"There are two possibilities. I have or I haven't. If I haven't, there is no problem. If I have there are also two possibilities. It is either curable or incurable. If it is curable there's plenty of time. If it's not, it hardly matters when I see a doctor."

"You are—and I say this in a spirit of deep admiration—one cold and hard and *very* tough bitch."

"All my life," she replied, "all my life."

While Alix was in the bathroom, he felt his way to a flashlight he kept in the kitchen, under the sink. Once he had that on, he went to his own bedroom and rummaged through the closet for some clothes that would fit her.

Well, that will cover *her at least; fit will depend on a lot of rolling of legs and sleeves and a lot of cinching of her belt.* He thought about offering her some of his own underwear but decided, under the circumstances, that she'd probably feel better in her own skin, alone, under the too big clothing.

He thought for a moment he heard sobbing through the door to the bathroom. *Understandable, if so, but better not to mention it.*

Once he heard the toilet flush and then the shower running, Khalid went to the spare bedroom, the one he used as an office of sorts. In that room he kept a small computer with a very large battery capacity. A wire ran from it, out the window, and up to a satellite dish mounted on the roof. He turned the computer on, signed in, and checked messages and then the news.

There was only one message, sitting encoded in a draft folder that served as a message drop. Once he decoded it from a book sitting in a bookcase affixed to the wall, he read that he was to stay put in Sachsen and await further orders. *Fuck.*

The GlobalNet news gave him more useful information. It seemed that Balboa was willing to return all the Tauran prisoners of war, but only for a price. He read the price and whistled. *I guess that's how you pay for a war; you win and then present the bill to the enemy. But two million legionary drachma, roughly four million FSD, in silver and gold, per prisoner? That's got to be unprecedented, at least on this scale. And we claim to have over two hundred thousand POWs in varying stages of health. That should pay for a good deal of the war, even all of it and then some, given how we fought it mostly on the cheap.*

Shutting down the computer he gathered up the flashlight and the clothes he'd sorted out for her and went to the bedroom. There he dropped the clothing on the bed. From there he went back to the living room to wait. She was a Sachsen; long showers were inefficient and therefore out. And, if she took a little longer than most Sachsens?

Washing the memory away, I imagine, or at least trying to.

She came out wrapped in a towel. "I suppose it's silly, since there's not much of me you haven't seen . . ."

"Not silly at all. I'll sleep on the couch." He flicked on the flashlight and pointed it at the bedroom door. "You can take the bed."

"You are very kind. I have no . . ."

"Just get a good night's sleep."

Khalid was up with the sun. He was hesitant to even open the refrigerator, since the electricity wasn't on and food would begin to decompose more or less rapidly once he opened the door and let the heat in. Instead, he took a few rolls from the breadbox, some jam and marmalade from the pantry closet, and Hordalander butter that hadn't needed refrigeration, anyway.

These he placed on the now well-lit kitchen table, along with a couple of plates, spread knives, and two room-temperature beers. Then he went and knocked gently on the bedroom door. "Are you up for breakfast?"

"I could eat something," came the answer muffled through the door. "Give me a moment to dress, please."

"Sure; it's no real hurry."

When she emerged from the bedroom her eyes were red and puffy. Khalid affected not to notice. He led her to the kitchen and held a chair for her. Then he prised the tops off the beers and poured them into tall glasses, setting one down in front of her and the other on the opposite side of the small table.

"I checked the international news," he said to her. "It seems that Balboa has defeated the Tauran Union . . ."

At the mention of that last Alix stopped buttering a half a roll and spat. "Filthy fucking TU; *they're* at the root of all our problems."

He shrugged. "Be that as it may, it looks like the armies of the TU are destroyed, killed or captured almost to a man. They're offering to give them back for . . . well . . . a lot of money . . . or a lot of gold and silver, actually."

"I suppose that was at the heart of this Moslem rebellion," she said.

"That would be my guess," he agreed, more than a little disingenuously.

"We have no troops anymore," she said. "We had two and about a half divisions and sent them all to Balboa under the command of that damned frog."

"You still have people fighting, I think."

"We used to be a 'nation in arms,' with a huge slice of reservists ready to form up and fight at the call." Alix sighed, wistfully. "A lot of them had legal weapons and a lot of them had inherited weapons secreted during and after the Great Global War by their grandfathers and great grandfathers. On the face of it, we're nearly disarmed, with only one firearm for every four people. In fact, we have three times that many illegal arms hidden away.

"But conscription didn't touch the cities so much; young men there preferred an alternative to military service and were given it by a weak government and vote-chasing politicians. Most of our potential power remained out in the villages. We could have an army again, though it might be a little long in the tooth, if we had a cadre to rally around."

"All dead or prisoners, I read," said Khalid. "And how would you get them back anyway? Who knows who has control over Sachsen's gold reserves."

"Oh, that one's easy," she answered. "Whoever may have control over the gold reserves here, most of our gold is deep in a vault in First Landing, in the Federated States. It might be hard to assemble a quorum to vote on moving it, but if we could, then we could get it to the Balboans and get our troops back."

"'A quorum,' you say. How many would that be?"

"I'm not sure," she replied, shaking her head slightly. She let herself become lost in thought for a few minutes, then added, "Actually, I think it would work if we had a quorum of either the finance committee, or the minister of finance, Herr Olaf Kubier-Schmidt, acting alone. I think."

"Excuse me," Khalid said, rising. "I need to check my mail."

He hurried to his office and fired up the small computer. Encoding a message he sent it to headquarters, back in Balboa. In less than fifteen minutes—*A remarkable show of speed, really*—the message came back. Decoded, it read:

"Help the woman to do whatever she needs to do to get us sent that gold. Nothing is more important at this point than that we get the gold so we can send back their army. I am directing four other operatives to your location. They will identify themselves by the phrase, 'Saints Peter and Paul.' Expect them within seventy-two hours. They may not all make it there. F"

He emerged from the office loading a magazine, round by round, for the same rifle he'd carried last night. "So where would we find the minister for the treasury?" he asked. "Assuming he's still alive, I mean."

CHAPTER THREE

There are five normal methods of launching a
Condor, including rolling them out the loading ramp
of an airship. The other four are to a) carry or toss
them over the edge of a cliff, b) via the balloon launch
system, c) self-launching with the on-board propeller
or jet, model depending, and d) via a ground winch.
There are advantages and disadvantages to each
method.

—Legionary Field Manual 16-243 (Top Secret),
Glider Operations

SdL #1, SSK *Megalodon*

There was a strip in the Bay of Balboa, between the fortress
that was the *Isla Real* and the two not quite so large islands
to the east of it, that had never been mined. Into and
through that strip, in widely spaced columns, under the
watchful gaze of the constellation known as "the Leaping
Maiden," passed seven Meg Class coastal defense
submarines, refueled, rearmed, well-rested, and ready for
action.

First in order came the *Meg*, itself, under its skipper, Conrad Chu. The submarine was mostly submerged, leaving only the bump that passed for a sail above the water. In a square depression stood Chu, image-intensifying binoculars pressed to his eyes, scanning the shore to the west, the shore where the Zhong Soldiers and Marines of Task Force Wu suffered under a galling bombardment from what had to be hundreds of rocket launchers, guns, and mortars, some of them quite heavy, indeed. Though there were still more guns on the once poisoned landscape of the *Isla Santa Josefina*, on the opposite side of the passage, these remained silent, lest the flash of their firing silhouette the passing submarines.

Chu cursed as the binoculars' ghostly green images flared with the shell bursts, went dark, came back to life, and flared again, only to come back to life. Not knowing how much of that the device could take, Chu lowered them, being careful first to turn them off lest the greenish slow give away the sub's position.

Though no star shells hung in the air, the blasts were frequent enough to give a pretty fair view of the action ashore, as fair, at least, as the two-mile distance could allow.

Chu felt a momentary surge of pride in the men ashore, with both sides of whom he shared genes. Though Balboan by birth, by the overwhelming percent of his genetic heritage, and by loyalty, he probably felt a greater pride in the remnants of the Zhong invasion, stubbornly holding on by their fingernails and with no weapon so powerful as their sheer guts and determination.

Have I a distant and long-lost cousin there, he wondered, *another Chu fighting for his own country? Good luck to him, or good luck to them, if so.*

The *Meg* and the other six coastal defense submarines trailing it had their clickers turned off. These—sound makers that replicated the clicks of imperfectly cut turning gears—had been a method for convincing Balboa's enemies that the submarines were easy to detect, hence no threat.

And that's probably a trick we're never going to get away with again, the skipper thought. *From now on it's mostly silence, stealth, and seamanship; techno sneakiness and relying on an enemy's overconfidence are played right out. Well, not against the Taurans, anyway. We might fool the Zhong or Federated States.*

This far out from the mainland, and not being in the shadow of the directional antennas that kept the global locating system from working on the island, Chu's sub knew its location down to the meter.

At a certain point, and with the bombardment now several miles behind him, Chu ducked and slid the cover to the sail's conn over to cover the depression, then ducked down and dogged the overhead hatch behind him. The cover wasn't watertight; it merely served to limit the amount of noisy turbulence that could give away the submarine's position.

"Chill the rubbers," he ordered. "Dive the boat. Make your depth twenty meters."

Chu and *Meg* had kept the same crew for years, all good men, and smart, all graduates of the legions' Cazador School, hence reliable beyond the norm for sheer toughness and determination. Indeed, they'd been together so long on the same boat that all of them were cross-trained to do at least one other crewman's job.

Huerta, Chu's exec, answered with, "Aye, Captain, twenty—two zero—meters."

From the diving station Auletti, normally the sonarman and himself standing in for another submariner, announced, "Make my depth twenty meters, aye, sir." Aleman added, "Chilling the rubbers, aye, sir." A third said, "Helm, fifteen-degree down angle on planes. Making my depth twenty meters."

Huerta, facing forward, said, "Forward group admitting ballast, Captain . . . aft group admitting ballast."

The crew automatically leveled the boat after reaching depth. Chu then ordered that they check for leaks.

"Engineering, no leaks, Skipper . . . Power room, no leaks, Captain . . . Forward sonar chamber dry . . ."

"Head for Point Alpha," Chu ordered. This was a gap in the undersea ridge that ran from one corner of the Bay of Balboa all the way to the other. Once they crossed it, they would move to Point Bravo, not far in distance but much deeper, and then parallel the coast to the Zhong logistics base and port at the *Isla Santa Catalina*. There, four of the subs would wait until the emergence of the *classis* from internment and arrival on the scene set the Zhong to movement. The other three would advance to link up with the *classis* as near to the port of internment as possible.

Then we shall reap large, thought Chu. *Then we shall reap large, indeed.*

BdL *Dos Lindas*, *Puerto Bruselas*, Santa Josefina

"Where the hell did they get that huge band?" Roderigo Fosa asked, of nobody in particular.

His senior noncom, Sergeant Major (for the *classis* used mostly military, rather than naval ranks) Ramirez, answered, "I asked, sir; it's the Aserri Symphony Orchestra and Chorus, out showing their unquestioned and complete support for both the new regime and its chief ally." Ramirez spoke with a tone of contempt that was pretty much second nature to him.

"Then where did they get the sheet music for *our* songs?"

"That, I cannot say. All things, considered, though, sir, it wouldn't surprise me in the slightest if the *Duque* had the music printed here several years ago, against the day."

"I'll ask him, next time I see him," Fosa agreed. It wasn't, in fact, all *that* far-fetched a possibility. And if not Carrera? Well, Professor Ruiz, chief of propaganda, might have done so on his own initiative.

The orchestra, itself, along with the chorus, were giving a fine and moving rendition of the old Volgan war song, translated into Spanish as *La Guerra Sagrada*, the Sacred War:

"... let your noble wrath
Boil over like a wave.
This is the people's war
This is a sacred war."

"Nice touch, really," Fosa said. "Nice, too, that several months of otherwise carefree maintenance have our ships so ready. By the way, is the tightbeam calibrated?"

"Yes, sir," said Ramirez, "both the main one and the ones for the Crickets and drones."

"Good, I was beginning to worry."

As he spoke, two columns of ships, with two frigates and four corvettes in each column, began to steam out of the port. Both of the capital ships, the *Dos Lindas* and the heavy cruiser *Tadeo Kurita*, had already been pushed into formation by the tugs of the port. A fifth frigate, an antiaircraft ship rather than an antisubmarine ship, like the other four, was on station between them.

Not that the two capital ships didn't have impressive— possibly illegal, but definitely impressive—antiaircraft capability of their own, with, between them, five powerful antiaircraft lasers, two of them mounted high. Still, the frigate's long-range missiles, for days when the weather prevented getting much use from the lasers, were very comforting.

The crew for those lasers scanned the sky continuously for any approaching enemy aircraft, as did the radar, and several dozen men with very powerful binoculars, standing watch on all the ships.

Meanwhile, the carrier's handful of helicopters supplemented the ASW squadrons, dipping and listening, or taking more active measures, for sign of enemy submarines. Continuous sorties of reconnaissance and strike aircraft—modified crop dusters, basically—leapt from the deck to track, attack, and slow down Marciano's retreat to the corner of Santa Josefina defined by the border with neighboring Cordoba, *Lago de Cordoba,* and the *Mar Furioso.* Most of the crop dusters—Turbo-finches—carried as much as two metric tons of ordnance, generally a mix of machine guns, rockets, and bombs, however there were eleven product improved versions—called "Gabriels"— that carried twice that, at rather greater speed.

Which, thought Fosa, *may become kind of important given that most of the Tauran helicopters were faster than the older modified crop dusters. Wish we'd been able to get more of the Gabriels, but at what they cost . . . no, not until we can build our own.*

The two mixed antisubmarine warfare squadrons that had already sailed out to ping furiously for the presence of enemy submarines reported in that there was nothing out there, which pretty much agreed with Fosa's existing suspicions.

The question of what happens when a neutral power joins a war, with a belligerent fleet interned by the neutral power, has never come up before. Therefore it was never something the enemy governments even considered. Hence, nobody thought to put a couple of subs out there.

Under his command, the core of the fleet began to make way out of the port, before turning generally east, in the direction of the Cordoban border.

Among the other life-forms brought to Terra Nova by the beings called "Noahs," the most fearsome was probably the meg, or megalodon, a shark, of sorts, that could range over twenty meters long. It was believed the megs were going extinct, not least because Man had savagely hunted the whales that were the primary component of the meg diet, in some cases and places nearly to extinction.

Megs were hungry all the time, anyway, but when there were no whales around it was still worse. One such very hungry meg, patrolling the mouth of the deep inlet that led to *Puerto Bruselas*, turned into the port at the sound of the first corvette, churning the water with its propeller.

The meg, being not all that bright, became slightly confused when another propeller began churning the water. It was, at least insofar as a gargantuan shark can be, quite happy at the thought of its upcoming two-course dinner.

But then the two corvettes were joined by eight more, along with the more resounding propellers of five frigates.

A whole school of them! thought the meg. *Oh, happy, happy day.*

Ah, but, sadly for the meg, both the *Dos Lindas* and the *Tadeo Kurita* kicked in to the undersea orchestra. *Maybe*, thought the meg, *I am not all that damned bright. But, ya know, whatever those little things were, the big ones sound a little too big. Maybe better if I go find me a whale, even a small one. Or maybe a couple of seals. Yeah, that's the ticket; seals.*

The meg swam out of the inlet a *lot* faster than it swam into it.

Headquarters (mobile), Task Force Jesuit, Santa Josefina

Wounded men, dozens of them, lay in rows, perpendicular

to the inland highway. It wasn't much of a highway, to be sure, being macadamized, rather than asphalt, and not really wide enough to use as a two-lane road. This was a matter of some concern to the wounded, of course, since a bad road meant a rough ride and, for many, a rough ride meant wounds torn open, bleeding, and pain. Some of the wounded moaned with pain or delirium . . . or a mixture of both.

Along the road, three civilian Santa Josefinans with horse-drawn wagons were in earnest and loud discussion with one of the Tauran medical officers who wished to rent their carts for cash.

Claudio Marciano, commander of the task force, tried to ignore them all, not out of lack of sympathy for either but because he needed, and they needed him, to *think*.

"*I* think," said *Oberst* Rall, "that we're going to end up using this road alone, or maybe this one for the main body but with a group of engineers along the coastal highway to crater it behind us and to blow up or burn down every bridge along it."

Claudio nodded, slowly and deliberately. "I'm not necessarily disagreeing with you, Rall, but what's your reasoning? I mean, we can, after all, move our troops to our destination faster on the coast road. And, as you say, we can make it so the enemy has to crawl to pursue us. So why?"

Rall sighed, then said, "I want us to get under the cover of the rain forest, for protection from a Balboan aerial attack that I am certain is coming."

Claudio laughed, even though he understood Rall's position perfectly. Respect for the rulings of the Global

Court of Justice had almost completely stymied the air support that had been Task Force Jesuit's only real advantage over the guerillas. This, in turn, had gone a long way toward seeing them turned out of position after position until the present, which saw them no longer trying to hold but running for their lives.

"It's no protection," Claudio finally said, as gently as possible. "He"—He, in this case, clearly meant Patricio Carrera—"doesn't give a fig—doesn't give a tranzitree fruit—about any opinion emanating from the GCJ. He despises them. You've never dealt with him, have you? I mean in either Sumer or Pashtia?"

Rall shook his head in the negative.

"What would you do, Rall, if you found 'journalists' working for the enemy in a war zone?"

"I suppose I'd consult my rules or—"

Marciano cut that off. "I've worked with him. Carrera gives them a quick trial and a slow hanging. He doesn't care in the slightest—no, that's not exactly right—he takes active and serious joy out of defying and humiliating the whole Kosmo crew, from politicos, to entertainers, to human rights lawyers, to NGO and QUANGO big shots and activists, to international judges.

"So being in the rain forest, while it might have a good deal of benefit for camouflage and concealment purposes, would only draw that much more fire if we were found there."

Rall looked a bit crestfallen.

"Oh, cheer up," Marciano said. "We're going to keep using the main road along the coast, and this piece of horizontal shit, too, despite the risk from the air, because we have to move fast, to get where we're going and dig in. But I want you to start planning to use this road alone if we must. Moreover—"

A radio operator, sitting in the back of a command car, something like a Jeep on another world at another time, exclaimed, "Sir? General Marciano! Terrible news, sir! Terrible."

Marciano hurried over. "Hush, boy," he said, softly, "are you trying to start a panic?"

"No, sir," said the radio operator, "but . . . well . . . we just got word: the Balboan fleet is out of internment and sailing towards us."

"WHAT!? That's not . . . oh, shit, yes it is."

The radio operator raised an eyebrow and smiled, Marciano's "WHAT!?" had been louder than his own "Terrible!"

"Yeah, I suppose you're right, son. Rall?"

The Sachsen walked over and stood by as Marciano told him the news, preceded by a "Be very calm and quiet."

"My God," Rall said. "How? It's against—"

"No," Claudio corrected, "it isn't. It's just never come up before that a neutral power, which had an interned fleet, joined the war on the side of that fleet. At least, I don't know of any such circumstances. Nearest I can think of is a neutral power, anticipating war, that took over a ship under right of angary, and then returned it when they joined the war. And that's not quite the same."

"Oh, shit,' said Rall, "those Zhong destroyers; we've got to warn them."

"To warn them and ask them to buy us some time," Claudio corrected.

"I'll get on it," Rall said.

Marciano nodded, already distracted by what was going on with the horse-drawn wagons. He stormed over, as Rall went in the other direction, and demanded to know, "Just what the fuck is going on here?"

The Tauran medical officer—he was a Hordalander captain named Haukelid—said, with more than a hint of anger in his voice, "These peasant sons of bitches don't want us to take their horses and wagons, sir. Claim they need them."

"I see," said Marciano. "Translate for me, would you, that in the first place we must have these wagons, and in the second place we cannot leave them behind for our enemies to take."

As one man, the Santa Josefinans crossed their arms and shook their heads in negation.

"I see," said Marciano, not needing a translation for that. "Pity, really, I *like* horses. But needs must and all." He drew his pistol and walked to the foremost horse. Muttering, "Sorry, old boy, truly I am," he pointed the pistol at the horse's head and began to squeeze the trigger.

"Wait! Wait!" one of the Santa Josefinan teamsters cried.

Sadly, Marciano didn't hear him. His finger squeezed the trigger until he was rewarded with a loud *boom*. The horse stood stock-still for a moment, then its knees buckled, letting it sink to the macadamized road.

The driver, on the point of hysterics, ran over and threw himself over the equine corpse, wailing with grief.

Marciano turned to the remaining two drivers, "Are you willing now to lease us your horses and wagons?" he asked. The Santa Josefinans didn't need to wait for Haukelid's translation. Between gestures and familiar-sounding grunts they made it clear: *Take them.*

Turning his attention to the Hordalander, Marciano ordered, "Pay the first one for the loss of his horse and wagon, but do not give him the twenty percent kicker and subtract the cost of one round of pistol ammunition. Drag the horse off the road and burn the wagon. Give the other two fair rental for a month on theirs. Then load our wounded, as many of the more serious ones as will fit, and get them moving."

"Yes, sir," said Haukelid, sounding about as shocked as the Santa Josefinans.

"And next time, Captain, do not wait for me to shoot a horse to get their attention."

"No, sir. I won't, sir."

Then, feeling quite ill, Claudio Marciano walked off into the woods to find a place to empty his stomach.

**Headquarters (mobile),
First Santa Josefinan Infantry Legion**

It was an empty title but that was how they were billed, anyway: the "First Santa Josefinan Infantry Legion." It was about half true, and about half an outrageous lie. The half-true part was that, indeed, the bulk of the officers and men of two of the infantry tercios, the *Tercio La Negrita*, Legate Salas, commanding, and the *Tercio la Virgen*, Legate Villalobos, commanding, were essentially pure Santa Josefinan. Moreover, those tercios had grown to near divisional strength, themselves, by recruiting among the people of the country.

The part that made it a lie was that the Legion was under the command of a Balboan, Antonio de Legazpi, that all of the cadre and even now still a huge percentage of the rank and file were recruited and trained by Balboa, that all the equipment, less some captures from the Taurans, had been provided by the Balboans, and that the entire crew answered with alacrity to the orders of Balboa's *Dux Bellorum*, Patricio Carrera.

That the whole illusion was nothing more than a politically and diplomatically useful fig leaf didn't change the reality that they were part of Carrera's army.

And I wish to hell, thought de Legazpi, *that Carrera had seen fit to hide about five hundred trucks, a hundred of them full of engineering material, to move my legion forward after the damned Taurans.*

What brought Legazpi that particular thought were the twin factors of having to order the newly arriving troops to peel off and hide themselves in the woods to either side of the road, while his engineers figured out what to do, and the image of the bent, spindled, folded, mutilated, twisted, and utterly wrecked bridge that formerly spanned the road and now rested pretty much in the flood of the river. And it was a broad river, without a decent ford within forty kilometers. And no decent road to that.

The engineers hadn't even bothered to inspect the ruin of the bridge. One look from the bank and their chief, a junior legate, had just said, "Fuck it; we'll have to start from scratch."

"How long?" Legazpi had asked.

"Three days," had been the reply, "and that won't stand up to heavy traffic."

"Cars?" he'd asked. "Three or four tons each, loaded?"

The chief of the engineers had looked down into the stream. "You'll have to unload them on this bank, cross the vehicles, hand-carry the supplies across, and then reload them."

"Fuck."

"You said it, sir."

I suppose, Legazpi thought, *that they'll use some of the delay.* Coming to a quick decision he shouted out, "Get me the Ic, the commander of the cohort from Fifth Mountain, plus Villalobos and Salas, plus Macera!

"And I need a message sent to Carrera!"

Amidst the sounds of engineers frantically felling trees, and overlooking the ruined bridge, Legazpi gave his orders.

"We've got a problem, gentlemen. Every day the Taurans run without us pursuing not only gives them more time to dig in wherever they're going, but also more time to ruin more roads and drop more bridges.

"We've got to get something on them to pursue, but I'm badly limited in what I can supply. I sure as shit can't supply more than a thousand men.

"The Zhong lodgment still blocks the highway in Balboa, so no trucks are getting to us. I've messaged Carrera and he promises me four cargo helicopters, IM-71s. Unfortunately, at this range, two or three of those will have to be used to support one or two, but probably one. I can supply one cohort with one IM-71."

Legazpi pointed down at the river, just to the right of the dropped bridge. "So here's what we're going to do; Ignacio Macera, you're going to cross this fucking river by hook or by crook, and by God *pursue* those fuckers. Get the engineers to make you a raft or something to get at least your light vehicles across. We're going to give you a maniple of—"

"Sir," Macera interrupted, "with recent recruits, my cohort is about two thousand men strong. I need fifteen thousand kilograms of supply a day for that, fifteen tons. And I cannot carry a fraction of it even if I *do* manage to get my light vehicles across.

"That means I need probably five or—since so much of it will be food, which will cube out the helicopter before it weights out—six or seven lifts a day. Frankly I—"

"Shut up, Tribune. You'll take what food the countryside has to offer and get by on no more than nine tons, three lifts, a day. Or you'll go hungry. But you are going across the river and you *are* going to pursue the Taurans, to keep the pressure on them, so they can't fuck up the roads and bridges so thoroughly."

Macera blew air through his lips, tapped his forehead a few times, then put his palm up in an admission of acceptance.

"Now," Legazpi continued, "as I was saying, you're going to get a maniple of *Cazadores* attached to your cohort. Maybe more importantly, though, the *classis* has broken out of Bruselas; since Santa Josefina's new, revolutionary government has officially joined the war, the internment is over. What that means is that now *you* and you cohort are going to have air superiority for the first time. So along with the *Cazadores*, I'm sending my own forward air controller with you to coordinate and call for air support."

Macera whistled, then asked, "No shit, huh?"

"No shit, Ignacio."

"Well, fuck; I'll try."

**Headquarters (mobile),
Task Force Jesuit, Santa Josefina**

Marciano didn't speak a word of *any* of the languages spoken in *Ming Zhong Guo*, the New Middle Kingdom. For this he didn't really need to; the determination of the man on the other end of the radio conversation to stand and fight where he was told to came through loud and clear. Even so, he waited for the translation.

"Captain Liu says it would mean the lives of his wife and children, their children, and just possibly the lives of his parents as well, to abandon the position and mission he has been assigned, General. He says, moreover, that it would go just as hard on his officers and men, such that they would certainly cut his throat and throw him overboard if he ordered them away."

Marciano shook his head in disgust. *Fuck, to live under such a system. I wanted them to buy me some time, yes, but not to throw their lives away without a chance.*

"Ask him if there's anything we can do to help."

"He says, 'graciously, no, but thank you for the offer.'"

"Fuck."

CHAPTER FOUR

"Be extremely subtle, even to the point of formlessness. Be extremely mysterious, even to the point of soundlessness. Thereby you can be the director of the opponent's fate."   —Sun Tzu

Cristobal Province, Balboa

The prisoners of war marched into captivity with their arms, as promised, but had to deposit them at a point along the way.

As it turned out, there were a lot more non-Anglian Taurans with the Die-hards than Carrera had expected. More of them were wounded, too, than he'd hoped for. The sirens of ambulances filled the air along with the continuous *whopwhopwhop* of helicopter blades, fetching the savable among the wounded. This was still a welcome improvement over the roar of the big guns and the screams of the dying. Not that there weren't men still dying; there were. At least, though, they could die drugged against the pain.

That's something, Carrera thought.

Carrera asked RSM Ayres to send the senior medico to him. As it turned out, that was an officer, a surgeon major, whom the RSM simply hadn't counted among the officer ranks. When the surgeon showed up, Ayres was in attendance.

"How many 'expectants' have you, Major?" the *Duque* asked. "Expectant" was code for "expected to die no matter what we do so last priority for evacuation and treatment except for pain."

"Between fifty and sixty," the Anglian major replied.

Carrera nodded and said, "We're giving your wounded priority equal to our own, but our hospitals, military and civil, both, are overtasked and not as modern and sophisticated as you're probably used to. Think: A generation behind the times."

"Between ninety and one hundred, then," the major amended. "I hope."

"Amen," said the RSM, then asked Carrera, "What becomes of us now, sir?"

"You'll be going on a ship." Seeing a distressed look cross Ayres' face, Carrera hastened to assure him, "Not a prison ship, RSM, relax." On two worlds prison ships had history enough to make them synonymous with misery. "For you it will be one of the ones that brought us the supplies we'd stockpiled out of country. They're reconfiguring the containers on that one now to accommodate you and about ten or twelve thousand more Anglians. Won't have much in the way of bedding, but we can probably get you some lumber and nails to build your own. I'm not telling you it won't be crowded and uncomfortable, no, but you'll be dry and well fed. Medical care will be as good as yours and ours can provide.

"And ... ummm ... you'll have an opportunity for some education.

"Speaking again of medical care, Major, we've made an arrangement with some of the Tauran medical personnel we've captured to accept their parole and, just for the time being, work as part of our overall medical establishment, some in field hospitals and some in city hospitals. My troops are forbidden from giving their parole, with the two huge exceptions of medical and religious personnel.

"I won't ask for your answer now, but when you get to the ship, if you could tell your keeper that you would prefer to pitch in against the common disaster ..."

"I'll consider it, sir," the major replied, "but my priority has to remain my own."

"Funny," Carrera said, "the priority for my medical folks is saving human life, period. Surely we're not more civilized than you."

The Anglian medico started a retort but bit it back; there really was no good answer to that one.

"How do we get to this ship, sir?" interrupted Ayres.

"There'll be trucks within the hour. They're going to be crowded, too, what with your folks and the guards. In your case, we won't ask for your parole. However, you might pass the word that it is our fixed intention to get you all back home as soon as a final peace is negotiated. Hence, why risk the jungle or getting shot or running into a minefield? To say nothing of the *antaniae* and snakes ... oh, and caimen.

"The other thing is," Carrera said, "that I have, oh,

excellent reason to believe Anglia is going to need all her sons and daughters. And soon."

"Why's that, sir?" the RSM asked.

Carrera just shook his head and smiled, while thinking, *Because I've arranged for you to be needed soon.*

Muelle 81, *Ciudad* Balboa

Sergeant Major Kris Hendryksen, Army of Cimbria, waited under a tiled *bohio* for the new prisoners to arrive. With him stood Marqueli Mendoza, tiny and perfect, and her husband, Jorge. Behind them and the *bohio*, tied to the dock, rode MV *Clarissa*, one of the ships aboard which had been stored the carefully gathered and even more carefully hidden war stocks that had seen Balboa through a frightful war. The *Clarissa*, a container ship capable of carrying some seven thousand forty-foot containers, was still in the process of being reconfigured and reloaded with material for her soon to arrive occupants. This was a little tougher than planned, since one of the two cranes for the dock had been destroyed in the war, the remnants even now being cut away by men with acetylene torches.

Opposite *Clarissa* was another ship, the slightly smaller *Beatriz*. While *Clarissa* was being configured for English speakers, *Beatriz* was already set up for both Anglians and contingents of those reasonably expected to speak English as a second language, the Hordalanders, Haarlemers, and Cimbrians, among others. Farther down were more boats for French speakers, Italian speakers, Portuguese speakers and whatnot. A special ship, one of the two ocean liners that had been used to ferry in allied troops between the campaigns, was set aside for officers. The other, the *Mary Ann Ball*, had been set up as a hospital ship.

For everything but the hospital ship, some space had been left for future cargoes.

Most of the ships were unoccupied but for some advanced parties, from both Balboa and the prisoners, setting things up for the expected mass arrivals. The bulk of the prisoners, nearly two hundred thousand of them, by now, were still coming in, some by foot, some by truck as trucks could be made available. The advanced parties had come from those captured in the first Tauran invasion, who had been moved for their own safety to the national airport.

The road to the dock was lined on both sides with armed guards. They looked bored.

And I sincerely hope they stay that way, thought Jorge.

"And I see an old friend," said Hendryksen. "Guard? If you would be so kind as to escort me?"

The trucks pulled in en masse, about one hundred of them. The first twenty or so contained several hundred wounded, in various states of corporeal disrepair, though none urgent enough to have needed aeromedevac. Those went to the more permanent facilities in the city, in any event. One exception among the wounded was an officer, an Anglian major, confined in what appeared to be a home-made straitjacket. Someone had written on the straitjacket, in marking pen, "Do not open until Christmas."

The guard on the wounded was quite light. An MP

from the guard on the docks took charge of that section of the convoy, leading it slowly toward the hospital ship, where a couple of hundred prisoners waited to cart and assist the wounded aboard.

The next group were the officers, a dozen trucks' worth. The guard here was considerably heavier, as was the guard waiting to double search them and escort them to their new quarters. It was expected that every officer would be reasonably fluent in English, so the educational cadre for that boat was entirely English-speaking, though they all spoke Spanish as a native tongue, and had a fair sprinkling of every other language of the Tauran Union, to boot.

The last group was made up of about fourteen hundred POWs, mostly Anglian but also with the one hundred percent English-speaking Haarlemers and the nearly one hundred percent English-understanding or -speaking Cimbrians. The guard here was quite heavy, but jovial enough. Administration and logistics personnel lined the space before the ship's brow, with containers filled with supplies for the latter, including books, and cameras and computers for the former.

RSM Ayres stood by the line, along with a sprinkling of some of his fellow warrant officers, to maintain order and decorum as the men passed through. Previously taken senior POWs waited aboard ship, to ease the men into their new billets.

Ayres heard from behind, in a perfect Anglian accent, "I suspect you'll be senior, RSM, so you'll end up having to take charge of both English-speaking ships."

Ayres didn't turn immediately, puzzling, *Now where*

have I heard that voice, that impeccable received pronunciation...

He spun about. "Hendryksen! I am surprised you're still alive, frankly; surprised and pleased."

"No less than me, I assure you, RSM."

Turning to speak over his shoulder, Ayres called out a name, ordering, "Take charge of this mob until I return." Then, with Hendryksen in tow, he marched just out of earshot.

"This is the strangest thing I've ever seen, Kris," Ayres said. "They're treating us like guests, not enemies. No threats and no attempts to bribe anyone into cooperation. What the hell is going on? Is this because they think the war's over?"

Hendryksen laughed softly. "You want my personal opinion? Okay, no, they know the war is still on until its officially over. As to what they're doing...they're turning us into weapons."

Ayres' quizzical look prompted the addition, "Wait until the education sessions start."

"Aha, so it's going to turn nasty after all."

"Sadly not, RSM; you could resist that. Indeed, it will all be most civil, and in ways that are hard to resist. You won't even have to attend. And, if you do attend, you can sleep in the back and no one will mind as long as you don't snore too loudly. The only restriction is that you won't be allowed to prevent anyone else from attending and you won't be allowed to prevent those who do attend from talking. Other than that, they don't really care what you do except that they'll prevent escapes.

"Indeed, the only enticements they'll use to get people

to come and pay attention are boredom—there won't be much to do aboard ship except education, refreshments offered during the instruction and . . . well . . . turn around and look for the very tiny and very beautiful girl. That's Marqueli Mendoza. The man standing next to her is her husband, Jorge. Both fine folks and she, in particular, is both a great instructor and an extremely nice woman. Your men are going to love her more than they do the queen, and in very short order. I watched it happen with your Paras, some of whom are going to be her and her husband's assistant instructors."

"Treason," Ayres growled.

"Nope; they will never say a word against the sovereign of Anglia, the Anglian Parliament, or Anglian law, and will reserve judgment on Anglian food. Instead, they'll be talking about history, right and wrong, the Tauran Union, undemocratic rule by unelected and unaccountable bureaucrats, and against a great number of things one doubts you or any of your men swore or owe allegiance to. Moreover, if you or anyone should claim it's treason they'll simply change the subject until they can decide if it is or isn't. But that's not going to happen, I don't think. They despise traitors and have very strong—I mean absolutely frightful—laws *against* treason which they apply impartially to their own and *us*. For example, there are some hundreds of Taurans who came here trying to become hostages for the Balboans. The Balboan courts duly sentenced the lot to death and threw them out of the country with the warning that, should they ever return, they'll be stood against a wall and shot."

"Very strange people, these are," observed Ayres.

"More than you know, RSM, more than you know."

Assembly deck, MV *Clarissa*, *Muelle* 81, *Ciudad* Balboa

An open area had been left amidst the tall piles of neatly stacked containers. There were containers below it and only a tarp and a large number of large, slow-moving fans between those and the open sky, above. About a thousand folding chairs were laid out in rows, with a cruciform of wider spaces dividing the whole assembly into four parts. At the three far termini of that cross on the deck, Balboans, part of the legionary educational directorate, passed out cans of beer, one per man who wanted one, to the incoming Tauran prisoners.

Toward the front of the area, which was also toward the bow of the ship, a wooden platform had been raised by about five feet. On it were several chairs and one microphone on a stand. Behind the stand, on a wall composed of the ends of yet more containers, hung very large versions of a crucifix, a star of David, and a star and crescent.

Seeing those, the men typically moaned and said something like, "I joined the bloody army to get away from the holy joes" or "rabbis" or "imams."

It was due to the nontrivial numbers of Moslems in the Anglian forces that the first one to speak, after the RSM has quieted the men down, was Achmed Qabaash, the Sumeri sent, with his brigade, to help Balboa against the Taurans.

He wore his Sumeri uniform, the insignia of which was plainly recognizable by any Anglian. Qabaash, himself, being partially Anglian educated, simply ordered them, without the usual flourishes, to, "Take seats."

"Gentlemen," he began, "I am *Liwa* Achmed al Qabaash, commanding Forty-third Tercio, *Legiones del Cid,* also known as First Brigade, Sumeri Presidential Guard. I think this is our first chance, this war, to get to know each other, since we played in somewhat different circles during the war.

"Moslems among you, of whom I know there are some; if you look behind me you will see our own star and crescent. You may remain here, with your old comrades, and you will be treated the same as anyone else. Alternatively, I have received special permission—no, do not ask about the intricate legalities behind this and behind why you are the only exceptions granted—to sign you up with my own brigade. I have taken serious losses, so you will be welcome. However, in all honesty, I must confess that the pay is not as good as you are used to. Still, the cost of living is less in Sumer, we have a lot of fun and, after all, we were smart enough to be on the winning side."

That got a mass groan, though not an angry one, from virtually all the men in the assembly deck.

"Please make your decision quickly, for our airship home comes for us the day after tomorrow, tomorrow being our victory parade with the other tercios of the legion of which we were a part . . ."

Unheard, Marqueli quietly asked her husband, "Just what *are* the special circumstances that allow them to leave and give up on their own army?"

Leaning over slightly, he whispered, "There are two I am fairly sure of, love, along with one guess. One is that Qabaash is leaving, so anyone who crosses over won't be sticking around here to potentially have to fight their own armies. Thus, our laws against treason shouldn't kick in. The other is that nations are inherently suspect, under Islam, so the *Duque* felt it was questionable if the Moslems even *could* have legitimate loyalty to the Anglian state. The third, my guess, is that the *Duque* is planning something for which he doesn't want Qabaash here and doesn't want to ever send the Moslems back to Taurus."

"Oh."

Still at the microphone, Qabaash missed that interplay, but announced, "And so, let me introduce to you your two primary instructors for your upcoming course in History and Moral Philosophy, Warrant Officer Doctor Jorge Mendoza, and his lovely wife, Marqueli."

Jorge came to the microphone first, while Qabaash backed away, then walked down the side stairs to the back of the assembly area. About thirty swarthy men in uniform awaited him there.

"I was a healthy private once," Jorge said. "Then I was a crippled private. Let me tell you about that. I was in a tank, serving as a driver, in Sumer, during the invasion there. We were all brand new then, fighting, among others, the same man who just stepped down. The reputation of Arab armies is quite bad, of course, but there's an exception to every rule. The men Legate Qabaash fought alongside were that exception.

"My tank was hit from above by a gutsy son of a bitch with a light antitank weapon. The ammo went off; the fuel went off; and I was blown bodily out of the driver's compartment. My last sight for many years was of my own legs being snipped off as I was propelled upward on a column of fire. And that's when and that's why I went blind. There was nothing wrong with my sight; after seeing my own legs crudely sliced away my brain simply shut down and refused to admit to seeing anything my eyes sent it."

Jorge then bent over and began to roll his uniform trouser legs up, first the left one, then the right, exposing his very high-tech prosthetics, all black carbon fiber and wiring. "For a legless man, you know, I could probably outrun two thirds of the men here, today.

"I know it's going to be hard for you to believe, coming from a continent where soldiers are not only not very high priorities, but are actively despised and hated by the transnational ruling class, that a crippled soldier from a poor country like ours should get the very best in medical care and the very latest in prosthetic limbs. Well, as my wife will explain to you, there are reasons for that . . ."

Marqueli was speaking on the stage now, talking about truth in advertising, her relationship to Carrera through his wife, Lourdes, but also how Jorge's medical care preceded any relationship except that of soldier and commander between him and the *Duque*.

"You've heard all this before, I suppose," said RSM Ayres to Hendryksen.

"One version or another of it, yes. This isn't the persuasive part. That comes when they start talking right and wrong, nature and nurture, and sacrifice and power."

"Do you buy it?"

"Some of it," the Cimbrian admitted. "Okay, most but not all."

"Are the men going to buy it...no, let me ask a different question: before we speak of buying, what are they selling?"

"The short version is that service must come before citizenship, and that citizenship in the absence of service, and in the appearance of democracy, is a fraud."

Ayres digested that for a long moment, then asked, "And the men, do they buy what the Balboans are selling?"

"Overwhelmingly."

Cristobal Province, Balboa

While there has never been any such thing as the old joke about "mess-kit repair battalions," there actually were military organizations that did similar things. Sometimes called "salvage" units, of whatever size, these took damaged, lost, and abandoned equipment and supplies, inventoried them, assessed them, repaired them and issued them at need. Typically, these had a very close relationship with quartermaster laundry and bath units, because when frontline soldiers reduced to rags finally got a shower, their own uniforms were past repair and would be replaced with either new uniforms or used ones from the salvage unit.

Currently four of the five corps-level salvage maniples were busily inventorying and amassing the almost incredible haul from the Tauran Union's late expeditionary force. There were perhaps as many as one thousand armored vehicles, heavy and not so heavy, a similar number of serviceable or repairable guns and mortars, thousands, *tens of thousands*, of tons of ammunition, small arms galore, radios, wheeled vehicles, helmets, rations, medical supplies . . .

"But rounding up the small arms is the priority right now," said the commander of one such company. "Small arms and their ammunition. Oh, and the mortars, antiarmor weapons, and the ammunition for those, too."

"Kind of strange, sir, isn't it?" asked the maniple's first centurion. "I mean, you would think we'd prefer to *feed* the Taurans their own food and to use their medical supplies, but, no, we're salvaging rifles, machine guns, mortars?"

"We only serve and obey, Top."

"Yes, sir, but, you know, sir, it's going to be a while. If we put one hundred men on the small arms alone, and those just in this sector, it's going to take a month just to clean and preserve them and match them to their ammunition."

"Yeah, Top, I know. How about the containers and desiccant? Any word?"

"Just that they're coming, sir. Maybe in the next day or two. Oh, also corps told us we could coat the weapons with used motor oil in a pinch."

BdL *Dos Lindas, Mar Furioso*

It's been, thought Fosa, *a very long time since we've gone through* this *ballet.*

The dance, the *ballet*, he had in mind was the complex drill of fueling, arming, and, where needed, moving to the deck the light attack aircraft, the Turbo-finches and Gabriels scheduled for the attack on the Zhong destroyers covering Marciano's northern, seaward flank.

Though it had been months since they'd had to do anything of the kind, the crew had never really stopped practicing during their internment. As they had regularly, during the internment—standing behind Fosa, who occasionally glanced their way—the handlers coordinated—choreographed—every step, using models laid out on mockups of the flight and hangar decks.

The whole show was made more complex by the need to maintain the existing aerial antisubmarine screen even as the strike package was launched and assembled.

It's just possible that they're in the best form they've ever been.

Anyone else watching the show would have had to agree, as the ballet played out, with the elevators rhythmically lifting aircraft to the flight deck, fuel hoses dragged by men in purple snaking out to top off the fuel tanks, red bedecked ordnance crew moving, jacking up, and attaching missiles to hardpoints.

This last process was particularly of interest to Fosa, as some of those missiles cost a good deal more than the aircraft carrying them. In particular, the six Shiva-class antishipping missiles cost about two-thirds as much as all the other aircraft in the strike package, *combined*.

Part of the ballet was, of course, getting the aircraft airborne. This, given the kind of aircraft—basically derived from crop dusters—was much easier for the *Dos*

Lindas than for any other aircraft carrier afloat on the planet. No catapult was needed, only that the ship nose into the wind, that the yellow-suited aircraft handlers ensure the way was clear and give the pilots their signal.

On the other hand, even as improved, the Gabriels could only carry one missile when launched from the *Dos Lindas*, rather than the two they could have carried if flying from a fifteen hundred or so foot hard-surfaced airstrip on land. Even at half a load, and even with a strong headwind, the planes typically waddled down the flight deck, and almost disappeared as they sank toward the ocean before rising up again.

Near gives me a fucking heart attack every time I watch one of those.

Turbo-finch Number 72

Number 72, which was the tail number of the plane and had nothing to do with its serial number or the seniority of the pilot, was the command bird for the mission. As such, it carried, uniquely for this strike, in addition to the pilot, both several extra radios, a senior officer to use them, and a horribly cramped rating to assist.

It had been the first up, piloted by a Warrant Officer Valdez and carrying a Legate Third named Cortez. The rating also had a name, but nobody much cared about it except for him.

Both the Gabriels and the Finches were economic with fuel even as they carried a good deal of it. Their loiter time was impressive, at seven hours for the latter and five and a half for the former. What made that important was that even taking half an hour to form up the package, they had lots of range still. This mattered because the Zhong destroyers they were aiming at were a good two hundred nautical miles away.

Zhong Destroyer *Changsha*, Off the northern coast of Santa Josefina

A frowning helmsman kept his eyes to the front and his ship on course as his captain scanned forward over the calm sea.

There were two destroyers, only, in Captain Liu's flotilla, *Changsha* and *Chengdu*. In line abreast, they moved toward a rendezvous with the enemy fleet. Water feathered up to either side of Destroyer *Chengdu*'s bow as it sliced through the waves at about one-quarter speed. Looking at the sister ship's bow wave from the side, Liu thought, *One-quarter speed is plenty; no need to hurry to die.*

The Zhong skipper was under no illusions about his chances; they were nil. He once again glanced left from the bridge at *Changsha*'s sister ship and thought, *I could run. I could just scuttle the ships and claim we were sunk. But then someone would talk; someone always talks, and I'd be lucky if my children were not skinned alive.*

And the enemy? Yes, they're primitive, too, as much so as, or even more than, my ships. But they have the numbers. They own the water underneath me, if those Gallic reports are to be believed. Then, too, something destroyed the Wu Zetian. *My cousin, commanding the Mao Zedong, could not be very specific, but he was nearby when the Wu was destroyed and he warned me to watch out below. And behind.*

Maybe worse, they own the skies above me. Primitive aircraft? Yes. Not built to purpose? Yes. But in the kingdom of the blind . . . and we are so blind . . .

I know they're out there, both my sonar and my radar know exactly where they are, ships out of range of anything I can throw at them.

Of course, we don't *know where their submarines are. Nor will we until it is far too late. Even so, I'll make a guess that it's not submarines I have to worry about today, that those are staying fairly close to their irreplaceable carrier.*

So no, my death will come from above . . . unless they want to send their heavy cruiser to destroy me. It can; it not only outguns both my ships taken together, it has enough armor to take the hits we cannot.

I can just picture the command and staff meeting before the Balboans sailed out, with submarine captains getting into fistfights with the cruiser's skipper and the pilots, because everybody wanted the chance to kill us and any of them can do the job.

The image in his mind of that supposed argument made Liu laugh. Thought the helmsman, *If the skipper can laugh, what do I have to worry about?* His previous frown was replaced with a slight smile.

CHAPTER FIVE

No, I have no right to rank with the great captains,
for I have never commanded a retreat.
> —Moltke the Elder

Over and on the *Mar Furioso*,
North of Santa Josefina

At about fifty miles out, the package split into three, two
of six Finches, each, and one, much more spread out,
consisting of the six Gabriels. One package of Finches
circled out to sea, enveloping the Zhong destroyers. The
other did the same thing, but veered toward the land.
The Gabriels just spread out and, like the others, kept
their height over the water to about twenty to twenty-
five feet. The solitary command bird, Number 72, began
circling higher and then a bit higher, until he had not
only a clear view of the Zhong, but could see perhaps
twelve miles past them. He was well out of range of
anything expected to be on the old Federated States
giveaways.

The legate in charge, Cortez, gave the command, "Finches, start bobbing."

Those aircraft duly began raising themselves off the clutter of the ocean surface, enough to give the Zhong both radar and visual acquisition. They'd raise and then dive, raise and dive. In his very large spotting scope, Cortez could actually see the Zhong rapidly traversing their twin five-inch mounts, as well as the lighter forty- and twenty-millimeter air defense guns. The ships, themselves, also began to maneuver, or at least to zigzag. Cortez understood that this was mostly to avoid being an easy target.

This is beginning to feel like killing puppies, Cortez thought. *Oh well, mine is not to reason why . . .*

Beepbeepbeep . . . "Gabriel Six, Strike Six," Cortez sent over the radio.

Beepbeepbeep. "Gabriel."

Beepbeepbeep. "You are cleared to have one of your planes launch one sea-skimming missile, azimuth zero-one-seven."

Beepbeepbeep. "Roger, one Shiva, zero-one-seven."

Beepbeepbeep. "You are cleared to have a second of your planes launch one sea-skimming missile, approximate azimuth zero-one-four."

Beepbeepbeep. "Roger, one Shiva, zero-one-four."

"Finches, begin to close in from the sides. Don't be an easy target but keep their eyes on you."

There was a brief chorus of "rogers."

As the Finches began to veer in, Cortez saw first one, then another, Gabriel rise to launch and release a streak of flame from under its belly.

Yeah, drowning puppies.

Zhong Destroyer *Changsha*

The guns had long since been cleared to fire. The ship rattled and roared, spitting out defiance. It was a waste of ammunition, especially since the enemy aircraft were still out of range of the forties and twenties, but, *What the hell, it's not like we're going to have any use for ammunition in a short time.*

Only the five-inch guns in the three twin-mounts could even range, and they were too slow to react to the attackers' flickering in and out of view.

CIC, Liu thought, was completely confused, watching brief targets appear and then disappear only to reappear somewhere else all too quickly.

"Let's make this easy," Liu said. "Baby steps now; how many are there?"

"We don't know, sir," answered CIC. "More than a dozen. And . . . oh, shit!"

"What?" Liu demanded.

"We've got two *somethings* coming in low. Too fast, oh, *way* too fast to be one of those converted crop dusters . . . speed says . . . Shiva-class antishipping missile. The southern one is a good deal closer than the northern."

Liu felt his heart begin to pound and his blood pressure to rise.

"Shiva . . . Shiva?" he asked aloud of no one in particular. "I wonder what guidance package they have, radar or image contrast or infrared or what? Sea skimmer, though, which in some ways simplifies our problem."

We might be able to take them down if we mass the air defense.

"Bring her to heading three-five-five. Signal to *Chengdu*, cease fire, line astern, follow us, all guns that can bear to face west, oriented to engage the southern one. Fire at my command."

They didn't have long to wait. Looking through his binoculars, Liu caught sight of the first missile, heading unerringly for *Chengdu*, trailing behind. He gave orders, and both ships spat out the combined fire of twelve five-inch guns, twenty forty-millimeter guns, and a good sixteen twenty-millimeter light cannon.

Whatever the failings of the old destroyers, the crews were about as well trained as could be expected. In front of that missile *all* that firepower was concentrated. Most was, of course, wasted. Indeed, almost all of it was wasted.

Yet, still, the magic BB worked. At a height of perhaps ten feet, the missile flew into either a shell or a large fragment from the explosion of a shell. Whatever it was, it ripped the guts out of the guidance package even as it set off the fuse which, in turn, detonated the missile amidst a great flash, a tremendous roar, and a large and growing cloud of black smoke.

The crews of both vessels cheered lustily, barring only one twenty-millimeter crew that, sprayed by the fragments of the missile, screamed and bled.

And then the second missile came into view, too close and too fast for the air defense to reorient. Liu started to give an order to do just that, but then realized that, in the first place, they were no dummies and were already trying, while, in the second, they were not going to succeed. The few shells gotten off by the defenders didn't change this.

His own ship shuddered as the missile hit and penetrated the nearly unarmored hull, about two-thirds of the way back from bow to stern, right under the Number Three mount. There was a time interval between that penetration and detonation, an interval measurable only by those to whom time is about to have little or no meaning. And then the ship was gutted from the inside.

The ready ammunition for Number Three went up with the missile. Between the two, they were enough to launch the torn mount, along with a goodly chunk of the deck and a badly deformed portion of the crew, upward over one hundred feet. Still others of the crew had legs and ankles broken by the sudden thrust upward of whichever deck they stood upon. Some had feet too badly smashed to walk upon, which left them crawling, and that far too slowly to escape the almost inevitable fire. At the same time, the blast of just slightly under five hundred pounds of high explosive shattered the bulkheads and made tears in the hull of that section, next to the welding of the seams of the hull. In some places the old welding, itself, was brittle and gave way. It was close enough to the fuel tanks to tear those, releasing flammables. Most of this was not readily set off by the explosion, being a lot closer to tar than oil. However, the explosion was enough to set off all the ammunition that hadn't gone skyward with the five-inch mount, plus the not especially modest amount of gasoline carried for things like the ship's boats. And then there was the so far unexpended fuel of the Shiva.

Water poured in through rips in the welding of the hull. Of itself, at this point, it wasn't enough to sink the ship any time soon. It did, however, have the effect of lifting the bunker fuel into the ship's insulation, which had the further effect of turning the insulation into a very large wick.

When bunker oil, again, not so easy to torch off on its own, gets wicked up by insulation, and then a gasoline or other fuel fire touches it...*phoomph!*

Fortunately the screaming didn't last long.

His ship was already listing badly and down by the stern when Liu's smudge-faced, filthy, and apparently singed damage control chief reported in. He was wet nearly to the waist, which was another very bad sign.

"All the fucking hatches in the area are warped, Captain. We can't seal off enough of the ship. We're wading through burnt fetus-looking corpses and the fires are out of fucking control, too; so we can't stop the leakage at or near the source."

"And so?" Liu asked.

"Skipper, it's time to abandon ship."

Liu looked heavenward. *Will this be enough*, he wondered, *to save our families? Being sunk in action? How can it not be enough?*

He caught out of one eye a brilliant flash, presumably from a missile he hadn't seen, hitting the *Chengdu*. He looked in time to see the ship simply disintegrating.

The magazine, they must have hit the magazine. I wonder how, since the magazines are so low. Angled down a bit I suppose, or maybe some idiot failed to close an ammunition lift door or...what difference does it make at this point in time?

"Give the order," Liu said, resignation and pain in his voice. "Abandon ship."

BdL *Dos Lindas*, *Mar Furioso*

Beepbeepbeep. "They're both down, Admiral," Cortez informed Fosa. "A lot of survivors from one, but I don't think anyone got off the second destroyer. It's just an oil smudge on the ocean surface."

Beepbeepbeep. "Roger," Fosa replied, then said, "Dispatch the *Jaquelina Gonzalez* to search for survivors. Tell the *Trujillo* to cover both sectors. Then signal the fleet, heading zero-nine-zero. We're going Tauran hunting."

Some two hours later, *Dos Lindas* steamed through an oil slick and passed by the inverted hull of the *Changsha*. The *Gonzalez* was still busy picking up survivors, no easy thing amidst the thick but spreading, tar-like oil slick from the ruptured tanks.

He thought about it for all of fifteen seconds before ordering over the ship's public address system, "All hands on the flight deck not engaged in immediate launch or recovery operations, assemble to port."

Once they had, he stepped out onto Vultures' Row, a kind of balcony platform overlooking the flight deck, carrying a microphone with him. As the capsized hull came parallel to the carrier's island, he ordered, "Present...arms," before rendering his own hand salute to the ships that, however badly outnumbered and outclassed, still had bravely stood against them.

Road to Santa Cruz, Santa Josefina, Task Force Jesuit command post

General Claudio Marciano stood by the side of the dirt road, filthy, like his men. He was just as dog-tired, too, but, nonetheless, kept up a confident smile, encouraging the weary and dispirited Tauran soldiery as they trudged past, their backs bent under heavy packs. Worse than dirt and fatigue, short rations had slimmed out his once stout frame, leaving his now threadbare uniforms to hang about him, "like an old lady's loose garb." Not only had the rations grown scant but his duties had often prevented him from eating regularly.

He'd lost a great many trucks, already, or the job would have been easier and rations more plentiful. It wasn't just breakdowns, either; unexpectedly—*though I should have expected it, I can see that now*—a swarm of light attack aircraft, wave after wave of them, had scoured the road pretty much free of wheeled transport.

Some of his Hordalander-manned tanks, though, made of tougher stuff than mere cargo trucks, were still keeping up. Of course, being better suited to rough terrain, they could take the back roads and keep under trees, for the most part.

Task Force Jesuit had made good quite a bit of their loss in wheels by commandeering as many trucks and other wheeled transport as could be found, sending them well—*well!*—forward under Stefano del Collea. The sales hadn't been entirely voluntary, no, but Marciano's people had paid a twenty percent premium over the real value of the transport, so the tears from the dispossessed had been as much feigned as real.

The more genuine storms of tears, though, had come from those who had not had their vehicles seized. In most cases, for these, the Taurans had taken only the carburetors, poured sugar into the gas tanks, and set the wheels on fire, then paid the one hundred and twenty percent of that amount of damage.

The worst, though, had been the draft animals and the wagons they pulled. Some of those they'd been able to pay for and take, however, the number of Tauran soldiers who knew how to deal with animal transport had been very limited. Many of the animals, horses and oxen, both, had simply been shot and left to rot and bloat by the sides of the roads.

One such, a horse, legs up, belly burst, intestines bulging and crawling with flies, stank up the area near where Marciano stood.

I should have expected it and sunk that fucking carrier at its moorings. Did Fosa know the plan? Of course he did, that smug, smiling bastard. But he, at least, was doing his job, honorably, if sneakily, for his country. No hard feelings. Well, not much, anyway.

"What was that, sir?" asked *Oberst* Friedrich Rall, Marciano's Sachsen chief of operations. Rall was just as mud covered and sweat-stinking as his boss. "No hard feelings toward whom?"

"Was I thinking out loud?" Marciano asked. "I guess I

must have been. No hard feelings for the enemy, Rall, the enemy."

"You, sir, maybe not. But I hate losing, so I have plenty of hard feelings. Though . . . well . . . have to admire the dirty bastards even so."

"Yes . . . well . . ."

Whatever Marciano was about to say was lost under the swell of hand-powered air raid sirens. Rall instantly dived into one of the muddy ditches lining the road. Marciano scorned taking cover but just stood there and watched the attack come in.

He saw that first as a pair of aircraft, popping up over a hill in left echelon. *Those modified crop dusters the carrier was stuffed full of.*

At the first note of the sirens, a few dozen men started tossing fire at what they hoped would be where the incoming aircraft would meet it. Most of the rest of the troops lining both sides of the road dove for cover just like Rall had. Those were just barely in time to avert the twin volleys of rockets—probably seventy-six in total—launched by each of the enemy aircraft.

Some of the rockets, maybe five or six, seemed to explode in mid-air. He knew what those meant; Marciano saw a half dozen men go down, not so much bowled over as melting from the inside amidst what looked like a storm of flechettes striking the ground all around them. The rest came hard on the heels of the flechettes, blanketing the area with high explosive and whistling shards of metal. Screams and calls for medics followed instantly on the explosions.

As far as Marciano could tell, not a single bullet hit.

They turn too sharply. They don't have to pass over us except to drop bombs, and they're not dropping any bombs. All our techniques are useless. And the bastards are too daring because they know they don't have to fly over us.

I need to inflict some highly desirable caution on them, and for that I need a trap . . .

"Rall! Get your Teutonic posterior up and help me. We have an odd kind of ambush to plan."

San Juan del Norte, Cordoba

When Tsarist-Marxism and the notion of the planned economy had finally gone under, in Volga, and the Cordoban government had lost its deathgrip on the breast and nipple of international socialist aid, the government had turned to the Tauran Union as the next best alternative. The loss had been a bitter blow, for that government had only thirty or so years before been installed as a result of victory in its own revolution.

That Taurans' aid had been fairly generous, even before the troubles with Balboa. In return, when the time came, Cordoba, almost uniquely among Spanish-speaking states, had sent no soldiers nor any other kind of aid to help Balboa in its struggle with the TU.

On the other hand, Cordoba had a long memory, deeply engrained in which was the fact that they'd been under the bootheel of the Federated States for several decades over the past century, and hadn't liked it a bit. "Poor Cordoba," ran the local saying, "so far from God and so close to the Federated States."

They wished the Taurans well, both in Balboa and in neighboring Santa Josefina, but not enough to violate their neutrality in any way that risked, even potentially and even that slightly, the appalling prospect of more Federated States intervention. A good deal of that fear came from the fact that the Federated States was almost completely unpredictable; a bug or a feature, the observer could take his pick, of their peculiar political system.

But this, thought customs inspector Debayle, waving Stefano del Collea's convoy through, *is no reason for me to take note of the fact that of the fifty-five trucks, all but twelve bearing civilian license plates from Santa Josefina, and the remainder likewise civilian, every one is driven by a man wearing military boots, and assisted by one or two others, also wearing military boots.*

"Thank you, Inspector," said Collea, sincerely. "Would you perhaps accept a small gift, purely a token of our esteem, naturally, for expediting our passage?"

"I wouldn't say no," answered the inspector. He was a neat man, uniformed, short, and mildly olive-skinned. Del Collea noted, while passing over an envelope containing about two months' worth of salary for a Cordoban customs inspector that, while immaculate, Debayle's khaki uniform was also growing a bit threadbare. It was things like that, the sheer inability of a government to collect enough in taxes to properly pay, clothe, and equip its servants, that led so many of those servants to have to rely on "gifts."

"We'll probably need to do something like this a few more times," Collea said. "Will there be . . . ?"

Debayle was no fool; he knew exactly what was going on. "You want a suggestion? One that will keep my government from having to officially notice what's happening?"

"Absolutely."

"Keep the trucks," said Debayle, "and the '*civilian*' drivers here. Don't cross the border with them. You can board them at hotels. Or you can leave a few of your people to supervise and hire some of our people to drive. I can show you half a dozen spots you can use to unload near the border, safe enough from most prying eyes." He cast his own eyes spaceward, though whether that meant the UEPF or the Federated States was anyone's guess.

Collea had a shopping list to go with the safe full of money turned over to his care by Marciano. He asked Debayle, showing him the list.

"Food in those quantities . . . not local. You need to go to the provincial capital of Rafaela Herrera. There are warehouses there for what you need. Lumber . . . mmm . . . let me think. Would raw, untrimmed wood do?"

"It would be fine."

"Tapatipi, west of the capital."

"Barbed wire? I need about fifty thousand fifty-meter rolls."

"Of course, we use barbed wire, raising cattle and all. But the stuff lasts a long time and needn't be replaced often. I doubt there are fifty thousand rolls for sale in the entire country. But for what there is, look in the capital."

"I'll do that, one way or the other. How did you . . . ?"

Debayle smiled, white teeth gleaming in the olive and tanned face. "What do you suppose I did, young man, during the revolution, that got me a job at customs?"

"You know, sir," said del Collea, "that sparks a thought. Your economy is for beans, right?"

"Sadly, revolutionary promises aside, yes," Debayle admitted, suddenly conscious of his threadbare uniform.

"And you have a great many people experienced in war and even fortifications?"

The chest swelled in that threadbare uniform. "Yes, quite a few. Older now, but some things you never forget."

"I wonder if we couldn't hire about five thousand of them to help put in fortifications."

"Organization of Revolutionary Veterans, in the capital," Debayle said. "You might even get some volunteers to fill your ranks. And they won't be like the Santa Josefinans who were notionally on your side."

"More like the ones who were against us?" del Collea asked.

"Almost exactly like them."

Road to Santa Cruz, Santa Josefina, Task Force Jesuit command post

The first trick had been to figure out that there was a pattern, or at least a timing, to the aerial attacks. It wasn't necessary for Marciano and Rall to know exactly what went into assembling a strike package of converted crop dusters operating from an aircraft carrier. They only had to note that the attacks seemed to come in at intervals of either about forty-five minutes, give or take five, or about twice that. The ones that came in less frequently were invariably quite a bit larger.

The other trick was to note that, though they could have provided close air support to the pursuing tercios of former guerillas, now the official Santa Josefinan Army, this never happened. It never happened because, between seizing and destroying transportation, blowing up or burning bridges, and cratering roads, Task Force Jesuit had largely succeeded in breaking contact with their equally weary pursuers.

"And that, Rall, is why they're concentrating on trying to slow us down, to give the enemy a chance to catch up to our retirement."

Rall just nodded. That retirement had effectively stopped for a few hours, while three dozen machine gun teams formed a ring around what was hoped to be a very tempting target for the next Balboan strike, half a dozen trucks held up in column by an apparent accident between two more on the road. They were centered in an oval bowl, of sorts, of about three kilometers by four.

There were no soldiers on the trucks; at the typical range the aircraft had been using for this terrain, there was little chance of a soldier being noticed, though groups of them could be.

Marciano, about a kilometer from the trucks, consulted his watch. As he did, air raid sirens began to sound all around. "If you can't count on a Balboan air strike," he asked, rhetorically, "what *can* you count on?"

"You suppose it's something about the clockwork precision required to even operate an aircraft carrier?" asked Rall.

In reply, Marciano just pointed to his *Ligurini*—

mountain soldier—insignia. *How the hell would I know, Rall?*

"There," Rall announced, pointing at the latest attack inbound, just appearing over a ridgeline to the north. There were two aircraft coming in, as before, and, as before, they were in echelon left. This time they were closer.

The range of the rockets was actually fairly impressive, at about fourteen kilometers. The *effective* range, however, was much less so, under a fifth of that. So far, the Balboans had used terrain—*and pretty well,* Marciano admitted to himself; *I suppose being infantry-oriented even in their air crew has something to do with that*—to get close enough. They'd never before, though, had to come so close in to a target.

And that's why I picked this spot.

Marciano held out one hand, palm up. Automatically, an RTO placed a handset in the palm. Just as automatically, the general raised it to his face. He saw the first puff of smoke from the lead aircraft, a single puff, indication of a ranging shot.

Marciano pressed the key and ordered, "Fire! Fire! Fire!"

Instantly and simultaneously, those three dozen machine guns opened up, firing from all around the clock and at a combined rate of over twenty-five *thousand* rounds per minute. Following the tracers, Marciano saw an oval of glowing bits materialize all around and especially just in front of the two attack craft. The second one flashed—*probably hit some onboard ordnance*—and then began to tumble over to its left. A long burning, smoking descent followed, ending in a series of rumbling explosions, a considerable ball of flame, and then a rising cloud of oily smoke.

The lead bird, meanwhile, maybe in the hands of a more experienced pilot, jerked radically to port, apparently on that pilot's having seen the first few tracers rising in front of him. The machine guns followed, continuing to place a wall of flying lead in front of the attacker. The pilot jerked in the other direct, then apparently pulled back on his stick enough to invert completely. He jerked left again, again, and then to the right yet again. Still the remorselessly vindictive fire followed him.

And then the plane wasn't really there anymore. In its place, instead, was an aerial fireball enclosing a mass of disassociated parts.

Unconsciously, Marciano crossed himself, offering a brief and silent prayer for the souls of his enemies.

"Okay," the general said. "Now, Rall, I want the next few hours spent on getting the hell away from the roads and camouflaging everything to the Nth degree. Also get a couple more ambushes prepared, but hide the bait. If I know Fosa, and I do, he's coming back with blood in his eyes and with everything he can get in the air. They've a long loiter time, those planes, so they're going to hang around overhead for hours. Once they're gone, they're also slow, so we've got some hours to move like hell."

"Where did you learn that, sir?" the Sachsen colonel asked.

Claudio laughed slightly. "From Carrera actually. Or how do you *think* he managed to get himself whole blocks of time to deploy and support his forces?"

BdL *Dos Lindas*, off the coast of Santa Josefina

Fosa gripped the railing around Vultures' Row so hard his knuckles turned white. Over the speakers, one of his pilots reported the ambush they'd flown into in heartbreaking detail for as long as he could. "Firing from all around the clock! Trixie Two-two is down, I repeat, 'down.' Crap, where did all this come from? Dozens, anyway. Jesus, I can't dodge them forever. Bullets, not cannon she—"

The transmission cut out. For the next several minutes the bridge's radioman attempted to reestablish communications. Finally, the commander of the air wing told him, "Forget it; he's gone."

"Air boss?" Fosa called, his voice calm and even. One would have to have known him very well to detect the murderous anger within it.

The entire bridge crew, which did know him well, thought, *Oh, shit, somebody's going to pay.*

"Sir?"

"Break out a couple of the partially broken down and stored reserve planes. Hold all flights. I want to assemble a very large strike package, everything we have. We're going to go get our two lost men a *fine* funeral escort."

"Sir! Umm . . . sir, it will take until nightfall."

Fosa looked at the angle of the sun. *Nightfall, yes.* "So—barring the Gabriels, since they have integral night vision—make sure they have their NVGs."

"Sir!"

Road to Santa Cruz, Santa Josefina,
Task Force Jesuit command post

Marciano didn't know how many recon drones came in the first wave. If he were to believe the reports, there were as many as fifty. Were he, instead, to believe his own eyes, he thought there might be four or five.

But the wise guess would be that there are maybe twelve. And they're up there expressly *looking to draw fire.*

"This is exactly like what the guerillas felt like, isn't it, sir?" asked Rall.

"I suppose. So?"

"So this; if they felt anything like I feel, with those sons of bitches hunting us from the sky, we had better not surrender under any circumstances. They'll just stand us all against walls, unless, of course, they have enough rope and trees."

"And you know this because?" Marciano asked.

"Because that's what I'd like to do to them."

At this point, thought General Marciano, *I suppose he's right. We can't surrender to the Santa Josefinans, when the time comes that we can't hang on anymore. I suppose I'd best put del Collea to finding the materials to build us our own internment camp. Maybe some land, too . . . something with a beach, I think.*

"They're spotted something," Rall announced, pointing to a spot where one drone circled and to which at least two more appeared to be hurrying.

"Who's over there?" Claudio asked.

"A mess unit," Rall answered. "One set up to feed the troops passing up the road. Maybe they didn't get the—"

Suddenly, the treed area under the circling drone flashed with what seemed a mix of thermobaric, high explosive, and incendiary. Claudio looked to where the fire seemed to have come from just in time to see one of those wide-winged crop dusters ducking down behind the tree line.

". . . word," Rall finished.

Looking through his light-amplified field glasses, the general saw a fair number of his men running away from the targeted mess. That was the cue for two more of the attack aircraft to swoop in. From underneath each plane two silvery canisters dropped, tumbling end over end until they reached the ground. From where they touched down four long tongues of flame leapt out, continuing in the same direction as the plane that had dropped them, engulfing the soldiers caught inside.

He didn't need light amplification for this; with his bare eyes Marciano saw a dozen men disappear inside the curtain of fire. That was bad, but not so bad as the three human torches he saw running out of the flames, burning from head to foot, dripping fire from whatever remained of fingers on waving, burning arms. One by one the three fell, to lie writhing on the ground until death, mercifully, took them.

Shaking his head slowly in the waning light, Claudio thought, *No, we can't surrender to the guerillas at all, can we? Every one of them is going to have a memory close enough to that that they'll want to skin us alive.*

There were half a dozen more attacks between sunset and roughly midnight. Two of those were on point, and some of the men of Task Force Jesuit died under them. The rest appeared to be an attempt to spook the defenders into exposing themselves. The attackers were, in any case, few enough in numbers that Marciano took them to be stragglers or late launchers.

Marciano listened carefully for when the time came that there was no more buzzing, whether of drones or manned recon birds or strike aircraft. It came not long before midnight. At that point, he told Rall, "Turn the men out. Get them moving fast. Balls to the wall for the planned battle positions. Traffic accidents, to include fatal ones, are, at least to some extent, acceptable. We've got to move before those bastards can refuel, rearm, and come back for more."

CHAPTER SIX

The difference between stupid and intelligent people—and this is true whether or not they are well-educated—is that intelligent people can handle subtlety.   —Neal Stephenson, *The Diamond Age*

Estado Mayor, Sub camp C, *Ciudad* Balboa, Balboa

Carrera didn't really listen to the quartermaster as he droned on about how many shipping containers had been packed with which arms and what ammunition. It was too soon for it to be that many, anyway. Instead, his eyes focused on a chart behind the legion's chief quartermaster, showing ships, how many Taurans they held, how much food was aboard in tons, whether they'd taken over feeding themselves, and who, specifically, was in charge.

He held up a hand to stop the briefer, then said, "Look, I know it's too early for there to have been any real progress. So tell me, do we have enough shipping containers?"

Clearing his throat nervously—Carrera rarely asked

pointless questions or let thoughtless answers get by—the QM answered, "Think so, *Duque*. Even if not, though, we don't need the Parilla Line or the fire support area any more and there are tens of thousands of them there to take at need."

"Redeployment of First, Second, and Third Corps to face the Zhong; where are you establishing the main log base?"

"We're keeping what we have, *Duque*; it's well enough situated already."

Carrera spared those three corps commanders a set of sidewise glances. They nodded agreement.

"Fourth Corps; Xavier, how many days' food on hand?"

Xavier Jimenez, Fourth Corps commander and longtime best friend of Carrera, stood, as propriety demanded. "Days, Patricio? Tons of Tauran rations— tons? More like seven *thousand* tons—have fallen into our hands. I haven't started issuing it—hell, we've barely started inventorying it—but with that and what's left of our own, we're good for maybe two months. If you want it all to feed the prisoners, though, I've got maybe a dozen days left. More if we tighten our belts a little."

"QM?" Carrera asked.

"It's a question of transportation, sir. We've got plenty of food to feed the Taurans. Oh, it may not be what they're used to, but if it's good enough for our men . . . anyway, we can feed them from our stocks near the capital. I need the trucks we'd use to exchange food with Fourth Corps to move everything else, especially the artillery."

"Moving the artillery" really meant moving the still impressive stockpiles of ammunition. No battery or battalion in the force had enough trucks for all they might shoot. At best, they had and could carry enough for immediate needs in the expectation that more would be delivered.

Carrera nodded, answering, "Right. Perfectly sensible. Xavier, eat Tauran."

"Wilco, Patricio. I *will* ask for a couple of tons of legionary rum; most of the Taurans didn't include any with their combat rations. In fact, only the Gauls did . . ."

"QM?"

"That much we can do, *Duque*, though we may have to issue by the barrel. For some reason, though they flattened damn near everything else they could, the Taurans never bombed the distilleries."

"Professional courtesy," was Carrera's pronounced judgment. "That, and they wanted booze to celebrate victory with."

Hospital Ship *Mary Ann Ball*, *Muelle* 81, *Ciudad* Balboa

The mildly rocking ship had just as strong an odor of antiseptic and blood as any hospital Carrera had ever visited. "How is he?" Carrera asked of Bertram Janier's attending physician.

The doctor gave a shrug. "As you commanded, he's our number one priority. We've set all the bones that we could . . . some . . . well, there's no way and no point. I am worried about three things, pneumonia, concussion, and infection. He's conscious if you would like to . . ."

"Yes, I would."

"Well, as I said, I am concerned with infection. Do you mind scrubbing . . . ?"

"Does this hospital gown make me look fat?" Carrera asked of the prone and largely cast-covered Gaul on the hospital bed.

"I think you have lost weight, actually," answered Bertrand Janier, late commander of the late Tauran Union Expeditionary Force, Balboa. "What can I do for you?"

"Nothing really; just stopped by to see how you're doing?"

The briefest hint of a smile crept onto Janier's face. "Yes, of course. Nothing subtle or suspicious in that, is there? No sneaky plans hidden from view. Only the . . ."

"Tsk, Bertrand; you *wound* me."

"Not as much as I tried to."

Now it was Carrera's turn for a slight smile. "That was just business; nothing personal. I took no offense, of course."

"Of course. But you still haven't answered me. Or, at least, you haven't answered me honestly. You are here for something and I'd like to know what it is."

"Really, Bertrand, no subtlety or obfuscation here; I wanted to see for myself and hear your prospects from your doctors with my own ears."

"'Infection, concussion, and pneumonia,'" Janier echoed. "Well, for that, I *do* get a little nauseous from time to time. I don't think it's from the big bomb you set off more or less under my feet. What are they called? And how did you set them up?"

"They're called 'Volcanos,' and they were on a seismic trigger with a timer to prevent them from going off prematurely."

Janier nodded. "Ah. Well, that turned out to be clever. I've heard there are Tauran POWs who are *convinced* they've got radiation sickness from artillery-delivered nuclear weapons. I don't suppose . . ."

"We have no artillery-deliverable nuclear weapons," Carrera answered, careful to keep his voice completely without inflection.

"Interesting how you phrase that and what you don't say," Janier observed. "In any case, I think the concussion is from landing on that lake and being skipped like a flat stone for a quarter of a mile . . . or however long it was.

"Pneumonia? My lungs feel fine, really. Oh, it could happen, but so far it doesn't seem likely.

"Infection? Your country is a cesspool of infection for those who are unlucky or not careful. Careful I was, but lucky I was not; I may succumb to that. Some of my broken bones, after all, did break through the skin."

"I remember. I also remember you refusing care so that your troops would be taken care of. The citation will follow but . . ." Carrera reached into his pocket and withdrew a silver cross on a ribbon and hanger. This he clipped to Janier's pillow.

"I might be a whore," Janier said, glancing at his newly awarded *Cruz de Coraje en Acero*, "but I am not a *cheap* whore. It will take more than a medal to buy me."

"Then call it a down payment," was Carrera's retort. He began to turn to go, then thought better of it. "I'll have one of my personal staff check on you daily. For reasons I don't think you need to know yet, it is very important to me that you get healthy again."

"Why does this newfound care and concern for my person not fill me with joy unstinted?" Janier asked rhetorically, as Carrera actually did turn to go.

"Probably because you're a bloody frog," he answered over his shoulder. "Be seeing you."

"Before you go, could you check on the disposition of my aide?"

"Malcoeur, wasn't it?"

"Yes."

"I'll see what I can do."

It was dark by the time Carrera left the *Ball*. Already, three moons were showing and the constellation of the Tap was filling the Beer Glass Galaxy, overhead.

"Where to, boss?" Soult asked as Carrera reached the sedan he used for the city and highways.

"Let's go back the *Estado Mayor*, Jamey. Kuralski and the Ia are supposed to have a plan for dealing with the Zhong out on the island."

Headquarters, Task Force Wu, *Isla Real*, Balboa

A medal hung on a concrete wall in between two citations. One was personal, to the Zhong commander, for leadership and valor. It shook with the concussion of a near impact. The other, a unit commendation, was addressed to and covered the entire command.

The Zhong lodgment on the fortified island was thin.

In no place was it more than three kilometers deep and it was less than one deep for more than half its length. Of course, at the ends it trailed off to nothing where sea met shore. Indeed, sometimes the tides made the troops on the very edge of the shore displace inland.

It was also crawling with *antaniae*, the septic-mouthed winged quasi-reptiles that fed on the young and the weakened and the foolish. Though they looked reptilian, the Mandarin name for them translated out to, "Genetically engineered murder pigeons."

Maybe worse, the air was alive with mosquitoes, their numbers swollen beyond reason by the stagnant water collected in innumerable shell craters. While there hadn't been an outbreak of the worst Terra Novan jungle diseases, a good quarter of the Zhong ashore had malaria.

After the pasting they'd taken the previous night, the men of the task force, mostly Zhong Imperial Marines, breathed a sigh of relief that the shelling had dropped to nothing more than an occasional bit of harassment and interdiction. Some of those shells were monstrous so the sense of relief was limited. They were entrenched, of course, and had been since shortly after arrival. A shallow, scraped out trench was fine for the snipers their enemy used so plentifully. For a nearly three-hundred-pound shell—as many of the mortars on the island fired—with a payload of seventy-five pounds of high explosive, the shallow and thin trenches were fairly useless for anything like a near miss, let alone a hit.

The headquarters itself was not in a trench, nor in one of the ramshackle bunkers the Marines had thrown together using whatever local materials could be scrounged. Instead, former Major—now Colonel and perhaps soon to be General—Wu had taken over one of the very stoutly built bunkers the Balboans had so liberally dotted the landscape with. The redundant tank turret above even worked, after a fashion, though it had had a rough enough time that the mechanism squeaked and screeched outrageously whenever anyone tried to move it.

Outside, a handful of simple wooden crosses, tied together with communications wire, marked where most of the previous occupants, a few boys with Down Syndrome, had been buried.

Wu's senior noncom, though in practice something more like his executive officer, Sergeant Major Li, shook his head every time he passed those simple grave markers. More than once Li had stopped to render a hand salute.

There wasn't any time for any such dramatics at the moment, though. Li burst into headquarters carrying a parcel of newspapers from the Federated States. Some Balboan had passed them over under the protection of a white flag.

"It's true," Li announced, tossing the papers on Wu's makeshift desk. "The Taurans have been knocked out of the war. We're on our own."

Wu picked up the first of the papers and read the headline. *Good thing I studied English in school.* He wasn't actually surprised at the news of the crushing of the Tauran Expeditionary Force. Though the lodgment was blocked from a direct view of the mainland, they'd all been treated to the sound of what was probably the greatest artillery bombardment the planet had seen since the Great Global War. There had been some doubt—*be honest*, thought Wu, *a lot of wishful thinking*—that maybe it had been the Taurans pounding the Balboans.

But, no, not a chance. The Balboans are the only ones who use artillery like that anymore. As we should well know from our own reception here.

"Maj . . . uhh, Colonel?" asked Li.

"Yes, Sergeant Major?" Wu was pretty sure he already knew the question that was coming. He'd been asking himself the same thing.

Li hesitated, then asked, "Can our country take these people on, on our own? Can we fight the war to a successful conclusion on our own? If not, what's the point of sacrificing the boys who've done so much already?"

Ordinarily, Wu and Li would have worried about one or another of the three branches of the secret police, and especially of the *Juntong*. There *had* been members of that organization in the landing. Somehow, none of them had seemed to survive.

"Are you counseling surrender, Sergeant Major?"

"No, sir. I'm really just asking what we should do?"

Wu drew in a long breath of air tainted with too much high explosive. "Top, I just don't know."

Estado Mayor, Sub camp C, *Ciudad* Balboa, Balboa

It was cool down there, in the thick-walled concrete of the briefing room. Even so, it smelled musty, as if some of the jungle fungus was preparing to colonize, or had already colonized, the nooks and corners of the place. A thin whine told of filtered air being pumped in from above.

Even filtered and chilled, the air was damp.

Above the stage was a screen showing what those in the business called a "TPFDL," or "Time Phased Force Deployment List," matching troops to be moved with assets anticipated to be available to move them, over time.

Carrera had left his staff out of the briefing, for the most part. They were all busy as could be just redeploying troops to face and eliminate the main Zhong lodgment in the east. The only man in the audience besides the *Duque* was Omar Fernandez, the paraplegic chief of intelligence. And he stayed on a landing in the back where his electric wheelchair could safely travel.

Dan Kuralski turned away from the slide showing on the glowing screen behind him and continued, "... so, in summation, Patricio, we can move two infantry legions to the island over the course of about a week, minus a good deal of their heavy equipment, but add to their artillery all the heavy multiple-rocket launchers. Can probably knock the Zhong into the sea in maybe a day, two at the most. They're not really dug in especially well."

"The fortifications they've captured all face the wrong way, and they're on the thin edge of survival anyway. By the time that's done, we'll be about two days shy of ready to eliminate their lodgment east of the capital. We can redeploy one of those legions back in time to participate, too."

Carrera placed his left hand on his right bicep, then proceeded to stroke his chin with his right hand, thoughtfully. "There's one problem with that, Dan. Just like I didn't want to exterminate the Tauran troops here, I want the Zhong available as a weapon to use against their government. I was hoping you would have some means to induce surrender..."

Kuralski shook his head. "They're not the surrendering kind, really. We get a deserter or two every now and then—well, maybe every few days—but, in the main, they're hanging pretty tough...admirably tough, really."

"Any chance they'd accept a cease-fire until certain other matters"—Carrera's eyes shifted heavenward—"are resolved?"

Kuralski shrugged. "Wu might...or might want to. He's got nothing to reply to our heavy artillery with, poor bastard, and is losing at least a hundred men a day to it. How long he'd survive the attentions of the *Juntong*, though, is anyone's guess."

"There probably aren't any *Juntong* on the island, except for three we're holding as POWs," Fernandez piped in. "Those three and the deserters we've interrogated made it pretty clear that the Zhong troops have taken every possible opportunity to get rid of anyone they suspected of being in the secret police. Indeed, that's how we got those three; they were fleeing for their lives from what was pretty obviously an existential threat."

"Any of the other deserters *Juntong*?" Carrera asked.

"I doubt it, *Duque*. Those three made it very clear who they were, right up front, and begged not to be tossed in with the general population."

Carrera leaned back in his movie theater–style chair, clasped hands over his belt, and began to twiddle thumbs.

He once again cast his eyes generally skyward. "Is Flight Warrant Montoya, perchance, still alive and available, Omar?"

Headquarters, Task Force Wu, *Isla Real*, Balboa

"You want *what*?"

A parlimentaire from the Balboan Fifth Corps, Rigoberto Puercel, commanding, stood blindfolded inside the concrete bunker where Wu made his headquarters. The poled white flag under which he'd approached the front line stood propped against a corner.

The young Balboan tribune—short, brown, and stocky—answered through a Zhong-descended Balboan interpreter. He was as level-voiced as possible given the stresses inherent in his very vulnerable position. "A very important person—no, sir; they didn't tell me who but my guess would be the corps commander—wants to talk with you under a flag of truce with an eye to negotiating an end to this battle."

"We will *not* surrender." That was a surprise to Wu, himself, because he had been contemplating just that for some time. When faced with the reality, though, *I just can't; my men deserve better than to march into foreign captivity.*

"They didn't tell me to ask you about surrendering, sir," the Balboan replied, "just to enquire whether you would or would not see our man."

"A trap?" wondered Sergeant Major Li, aloud.

Wu laughed at that. "Top, we've been in a trap since

we boarded the landing craft to get here. What's one more?" More seriously he said, "Relax; they've played it amazingly straight, so far. I don't see them tossing that away for a trivial advantage. And besides, Sergeant Major, it's not like we're hurting them any here. If they had them they could use nukes to obliterate us and all it would matter to them is that they'd have to decontaminate that part of the island we hold to use the beaches for tourism someday."

"So you will see our man?" asked the tribune.

"Sure; what's to lose? Let's work out the details."

"Dea' Buddha," Wu said, "it *you!* Your messeng' did'n give hin' . . ."

"He didn't know," Carrera said. "My intel chief insisted on keeping it to ourselves. Silly man thinks it might be worth risking having your troops massacred to the last man to get rid of me."

Wu smiled, chewed on his lower lip for a moment, then answered, "A' one time . . . migh' 'ave been, to terr tluth. Now? I no see rot of diffelence now."

"See? That's what *I* said."

"I no sullend' even so," Wu insisted.

Carrera shook his head. "Not going to ask you to. Oh, hell, no; the courage of your enemies honors you, so the gallant stand of Task Force Wu is going to enter the ledger of *our* national mythology, too. Surrender would ruin that. But we're also not going to give you back any of the trickle of deserters who've been feeding us intelligence, either. That's all very fair, isn't it?"

"So you wan'?"

"A permanent cease-fire, in place. We'll even stop shelling the shit out of you nightly. But no improvement of position. No bringing in ammunition. Medical supplies unlimited.

"We won't dig in further, not that we need to, and you don't dig in any more than you have. No sniping. Prisoner exchange but not to include deserters."

Carrera decided to toss in the sweeteners, the things he was pretty sure Wu couldn't turn down. "Since it would be safe enough to do so, I'll move a couple of four-hundred-and-fifty-bed field hospitals up to the front. You can send your men to be treated and they'll be allowed to go back to you unhindered. Oh, and we'll give you enough oil and poison to take care of the mosquitoes. They're a plague on us, too. Plus we can give you quinine or an equivalent prophylaxis for the malaria, and a flock of trained trixies to start to get rid of the *antaniae* that are probably plaguing you."

"I nee' as' mah boss," Wu said. "This no' smarr t'ing."

Carrera nodded. "If he accepts and you accept, send a parlimentaire under flag of truce to this spot. I won't be here, but a messenger will. The local corps commander has my authority to end the fighting."

"Why you do t'is?" Wu asked.

"I'm sick of killing people whose only fault is being born to a hostile government," Carrera answered with an unfeigned sigh. He didn't say, but thought, *Especially if I can save them to use as a weapon against that hostile government.*

"If no aglee?"

"I'm either going to have to destroy you to free up my

troops here for something else or destroy that something else to free up troops to deal with you. Please don't make me do the former. Maybe then I won't have to do the latter, either. I certainly don't want to."

"Me," said Wu, "I jus wan' go home wife."

Carrera had his driver take him to a particular fortified position, a concrete hangar, of sorts, carved deep into the central massif of the island. He was met, just past the entrance, by Tribune Aguilar, the commander of the most deeply held secret of the entire Balboan war effort. Aguilar was shorter than Carrera, and much darker, but also broader in the shoulders and with arms that were about the size of most people's legs.

"We're fucked, *Duque*," were Aguilar's first words. "The fucking shuttle won't work anymore and we don't know why. And the goddamned ex–high admiral and that cunt of a marchioness of Amnesty don't have the first clue, even after I tied them to crosses and left them for a day and a half."

"Lead on while we talk," Carrera ordered, then, when they'd resumed their march into the bowels of the island, he asked, "What are we doing to get it up again?"

"Even the fucking commander of the island doesn't know about the project," Aguilar replied, "so we can't go to him for help. I've actually had the boys kidnap one software guy, and we've hijacked both a fuel truck—the thing can get by on helicopter fuel or gasoline, in a pinch—and a mobile machine shop. Oh, and an aircraft mechanic who works on the corps' remotely piloted vehicles. I figured that, as long as there's no chance of them getting out—and

I have them sleeping in cells—I could read them in partly on the shuttle, if not the mission."

"They have any clues?"

"Not really. I took the fuel on principle, but it has an almost full tank. The software guy says it's a physical issue; the machinists and mechanic say it's software. Me, I wonder if it isn't both with one covering for the other."

"Shit, shit, *shit!* I can't even begin to tell you how important this is, Aguilar."

"*Duque*, my men and I have given *years* of our lives to this, years without women, years without rest. You don't *have* to tell us how important it is."

"What can I do to help?"

"Scientists? Do we have any scientists that might know about this kind of thing?"

Carrera shrugged. "Honestly, I don't know. Fernandez will know, though; I'll ask him to find us somebody. For now, though, show me what we've got?"

"Inspect the troops, sir?"

"That, too. I want to look at everything."

The twenty-four space suits hung in a row, each on its own special rack. The base material was a kind of off-white. That could only be seen in spots, though, as each was covered with some black silk for camouflage's sake.

Carrera walked down the line, fingering here, poking there, and generally trying to look like he knew something about the suits.

"We can barely move in them," Aguilar offered, "and we're not weak men. We have to load the EVA modules on the shuttle, then load ourselves, and then rig up for extravehicular activity under low gravity. It's a massive bitch, like inflight rigging for a jump, only worse. But, once we're inside we can dump most of the weight."

"Best we could do," Carrera said. "I sure didn't trust the Federated States to sell us any and keep quiet about it. Show me our weapons."

"Yes, sir. Over this way, please."

Aguilar led the way to a set of weapons racks. Inside them, secured with chains and a rotating irregular bar, were more than a score of shotguns.

"The trick," Aguilar said, "is in the ammunition. We don't really know what the hull can take, up there, so we figured lighter-weight projectiles were inherently better. Not good at range but the range is going to be measured in mere meters, and not many of those. So these are underpowered, can carry a double load of shortened flechettes, thirty-eight of them, of about half a gram, each. We've had all the guns tested in zero gravity . . ."

"How did you manage . . . ?"

"Firing out the rear door of the plane we used to get used to it, ourselves. We were high enough up that we needed oxygen, so we think they'll operate in vacuum, too."

"Fair enough. You have enough of these and enough ammunition?"

"More than enough, *Duque*."

"All right; take me to meet the troops."

Flight Warrant Raphael Montoya sat just off the small runway—more of a clearing really—where his Condor rested. He had his back against the auxiliary propelled stealth glider, enjoying the shade and the cooling sea breeze that was one of the few perks to being stationed on the island fortress. He found himself getting weary with boredom and . . .

"Enough slacking off, Montoya," came a roar from the strip. Montoya was young and nimble enough to snap straight to attention.

"On your feet, son! We've got places to go and people to see!"

Task Force Jesuit, Cordoban-Santa Josefinan Border

From where he stood, Marciano could see a battle position being built, a long, snaking line of Cordoban laborers—very well-paid laborers, by their own lights—bringing forward the construction materials the men of Task Force Jesuit were turning into their own little Maginot Line in the jungle.

The corner of Santa Josefina Marciano had picked for his last redoubt was comparatively quiet, but for the whine of saws, the smack of axes and picks, the scraping of shovels, and the ever-present complaints of dirty, sweaty, exhausted, and still cursing men.

"No goddamned bombing, at least, Rall," Claudio observed.

The Sachsen nodded, afraid of jinxing things by openly commenting. Even so, he wondered aloud, "Is it because they're getting ready to hit us hard, because they're moving their fleet on—west would be my guess, to take on the Zhong—or because we're so close to the border they're on weapons hold lest they add another enemy they don't currently need."

"All of those," agreed Marciano, "individually or together, in any imaginable part. How long do you think, Rall?"

"Before the former guerillas of this place catch up to us, invest us, and overrun us?" The Sachsen looked skyward, thinking hard. "The points of their columns will be here in three or four days, I think. They may have eyes on us already. Another week after that . . . no, make it ten days, before they're completely present here in full numbers. Artillery sufficient to deal with the kinds of field fortifications we'll have put in by then? Two months after the Zhong landing goes under, and not a day less."

"Less, I think," Marciano said. He chewed his lower lip, contemplatively. "Or, at least, it could be less. The Balboans only have to clear the main highway of the Zhong; then their artillery and, more importantly, the trucks with the ammunition, can pass more or less freely. I'd say two to three weeks after they begin the attack to pinch out the Zhong lodgment, we're toast."

Rall considered that then answered, "No, it's even worse. I forgot for a moment—no, I don't know how I could have, given the bombing we've suffered recently— but now *they're* the ones with air supremacy, not us. They can use either their own or hired airships to move as much artillery as they want, even before they clear the highway of the Zhong. We may have as little as two weeks."

"Two weeks," Marciano echoed.

Both men grew silent then, contemplating what was likely in store for them in two weeks' time. They stayed that way, standing in dread silence, until a familiar set of booted footsteps and a familiar voice interrupted them.

"Sirs," said del Collea, "I have some really…no… appalling isn't strong enough. I don't know a word or phrase strong enough. I bear news from hell." Without another word, he proffered several local newspapers.

"Just give us the gist of it, Stefano," Claudio ordered, ignoring the newspapers.

"The gist…the gist…oh, sirs; the Moslems have risen back home. Tuscany and Sachsen, Anglia, Gaul, Hordaland, Haarlem…they're all in flames. The police are routed. It's murder and plunder and rape from one end of the Union to the other. Our women and girls are being auctioned off on the open market. The pope's been hanged inside the New Vatican."

"Shit," said Marciano.

"On the plus side," said Rall, with a Teutonic shrug, "the pope was more an enemy of Catholicism than the Red Tsar, in his day."

"You always have to see the bright side of things, don't you, Rall?"

Rall didn't answer right away. Instead, he seemed to be listening, to be concentrating on his listening. And then the sirens began to kick in.

**Former United Earth Embassy,
Aserri, Santa Josefina**

As the revolution had advanced, and the capital had fallen to the guerillas, most of the embassies had remained open. Even the Taurans' embassies had usually retained at least a token presence of locals. One embassy, however, was completely closed, with the legation burnt and most of the workers, even locals, killed. That was the embassy of United Earth.

Fortunately, a couple of outbuildings, to include the ambassador's residence, a sprawling twenty-thousand-foot mansion, still remained. It was in this that Carrera met the three main commanders of his Santa Josefinan arm of the legions: Villalobos, of *Tercio la Virgen*, Salas, of *la Negrita*, and their chief, the Balboan, Legazpi, normally commander of Fifth Mountain Tercio.

"In numbers," said Legazpi, "we're growing stronger all the time." His two main subordinates nodded at that. "But in combat power, we are, if anything, shrinking."

"Why's that?" asked Carrera.

"The new men are untrained, mostly unequipped—we don't even have enough rifles for every man, not by a long shot—and we're having to detach experienced cadre to train them."

"We're also having some trouble feeding them whenever we move them away from the main highways," added Salas.

"Uniforms and field gear are completely unobtainable," said Villalobos. "We're doing well with finding enough insignia and pieces of recognizable equipment to keep our boys within the laws of war."

Carrera thought about this information, then nodded in such a way as to convey he held none of them responsible. "Have you managed to reestablish contact with the Taurans?"

Legazpi answered, "We've got eyes on their battle positions, yes—and, by the way, they're digging in furiously and don't seem to lack for building materials—but it will be another—what do you think, Jesus—six days before the point of your tercio reaches them?"

"At least that, yes," Villalobos replied. "We have little motor transport, and not even much animal drayage, while the Taurans wrecked the bridges and a good deal of the road network behind them to slow pursuit."

"And as for how we're going to dig them out…" Legazpi let that thought trail off.

"You're not," Carrera said. "Just between us three, I just want you to reestablish contact and dig in around them. They don't leave, except into Cordoba for internment or…maybe by sea. And that's plenty. No sense in throwing away lives on a cause we've already won."

"Then should I dismiss the new recruits?" Legazpi asked. "I mean, if we won't need them to fight."

"No," Carrera said, "for Santa Josefina will still need them to *vote*."

CHAPTER SEVEN

All action takes place, so to speak, in a kind of
twilight, which like a fog or moonlight, often tends
to make things seem grotesque and larger than they
really are.   —Clausewitz, *On War*

**Santa Cruz, Santa Josefina,
by the Cordoban Border**

"Sir . . . sir . . . I think they're *gone.*"

The speaker was *Oberst* Rall, gently nudging the body
of his napping commander, Claudio Marciano, with the
toe of his boot. Some generals might have taken offense
at that. Marciano was, Rall thought, as Sachsen as a
Sachsen, no matter that he was a Tuscan. He wouldn't be
upset by the familiarity in the field.

"Wha' . . . what's that? What time is it?" Marciano asked
needlessly; he'd already bared his sleeve to consult his
watch. He was dimly aware of three things. One was the
sound of saws, mattocks, picks, and shovels coming from
all around. The other was the absence of both the drone

of aircraft engines and the pulse of explosions, coming from anywhere at all. The third was the rather pleasant aroma of terribly deadly tranzitree fruit, hanging from the trees overhead.

"You've been asleep a grand total of three hours," said Rall, equally needlessly. "And the reason for that, the reason you were able to sleep, is that the aerial attacks appear to have been called off. The observation posts you left behind to keep us informed also report that there's none inbound. I *think* they're gone."

"Okay . . . okay, good. Now what else have I missed?"

"The Cordobans appear to have put two battalions in on our flank, between the lake and the border. They're digging in like busy little beavers. I had a chat with their commander, across the border, and he says he's purged his regiment—yes, there's a third battalion coming, plus an artillery battalion, an engineer company, and a battalion of air defense—anyway, he's purged his regiment of the few veterans of the legions it contained. So that flank, at least, we don't have to worry about."

By this time Marciano had sat up straight and cross-legged, rubbing sleepers from his eyes. "Any chance of—"

"Absolutely none," Rall replied. "The commander of that regiment, a Colonel Alfaro, said, and this is exactly what he said, 'Not just no, but fuck no. I'll defend my own country's borders and turn a blind eye to the smuggling you're going to have to do just to stay alive. At least I'll turn a blind eye until the legions turn on me, at which point you're on your own. But start a fight? Not in my portfolio.'"

"He sounds like a sensible man," Marciano observed.

"Yes, far too sensible for our good. On the other hand, though, he struck me as someone we really *can* count on to make sure the enemy doesn't outflank us through Cordoba. Have to take the bad with the good, I suppose.

"And speaking of the good, Stefano . . ."

"Yes?" Claudio asked, suddenly alert and tense.

"He gave me the report. He's come through, everything we asked for except barbed wire, either here, stockpiled on the border, or enroute. Oh, he has some wire, a few thousand rolls of single strand, zinc-coated, and maybe twice that on order. It will help, at least. But what he has brought or assembled is better than I really hoped for: rations for twenty days, lumber enough to dig in everyone to the Nth degree, medical supplies, fuel, mostly in drums. He's even managed to come up with a few thousand rifles, surplus to Cordoban military needs, and a couple of million rounds of ammunition. Plus some mortars and ammo for those. I understand the arms and ammunition came pretty dear, mostly because of bribes.

"We're shunting it from the places he's stockpiled it, right by the border, and distributing it where needed.

"Also . . ."

Something in Rall's tone brought a glare and raised eyebrow from Marciano.

Rall continued, "There's a small delegation that wants to see you, Santa Josefinan politicians and such. They want to leave and cross the border to safety."

Marciano, fairly neutral at first, had acquired a considerable distaste for Santa Josefinan politicians, for Santa Josefinans, generally, in fact, over the course of the guerilla war there.

"Fuck that," he said. "They're our only rationale for still staying here, to protect a government in being inside the country. Put the lot of them under arrest and under cover. They speak to nobody."

Rall, sharing his general's feelings on the matter, simply gave a broad grin, raised and lowered his eyebrows a couple of times, and said, "Already done."

The two heard the sound of cows, mooing as they were herded down the road.

"I did mention, sir, that Stefano has found us twenty days of rations."

"Yes," Marciano agreed. "Now, if you would, take over the command post. I am going to go back to seeing that the troops are digging in properly. That, and thank God for the breather."

Marciano turned away to go, then twisted back. "How close are our pursuers now?"

"At this point still maybe three or four or even five days until the points of their main columns close with our forward trace. They don't have enough vehicles to really move any faster, not with everything we did to the roads and bridges as we passed."

"Good."

BdL *Dos Lindas, Mar Furioso*

The ship churned through the water at a fair clip. Under the figurehead, a representation of Carrera's first wife, Linda, murdered, with their children, by terrorists, the bow wave was barely noticeable. This was the result of the retrofitted bulbous bow, unseen under the water, put in when the ship was retrofitted by the legions' *classis*, or fleet. That retrofit had included the addition of nuclear power and AZIPOD drive, which had made it, in the first place, of nearly infinite operational range, while the second had given it a maneuverability pretty much unknown among surface warships of that size on Terra Nova.

The retrofitting had not stopped there, with renaming, figurehead, bow, nuclear power, and drives. Oh, no; in addition, the far-in-excess-of-needs nuclear plant also powered three quite powerful lasers, one each forward and aft, and another above the island.

She'd carried different armaments loads over the years, too. Initially, she'd been more of an amphib, carrying a demi-cohort of commandos and the helicopters needed to move them to shore to combat pirates, to ferret out their nests, and destroy their infrastructure. Since the infrastructure was almost entirely blood-based, this had meant virtual extermination of the clans engaged in piracy. The lesson was not lost on any other clans that might have been thinking about it, either.

Along with the helicopters and commandos, back then the ship had carried only enough fixed-wing aircraft for reconnaissance and close support, a bare twelve of the latter. Later, the pirates pretty much extinct or having acquired a new and profound sense of caution, she'd lost her infantry back to the ground forces, and picked up more significant antisubmarine and antisurface capability.

Fosa, standing on the bridge of the *Dos Lindas*, kept his eyes on the computer screen. This, continuously updated, showed the plots from the reconnaissance screen spread out forward and to starboard of the *classis*, at a range of a couple of hundred miles.

The nearest segment of the screen consisted of one modified Cricket, an extraordinarily effective STOL bird, essentially hovering above and five miles to starboard of the carrier at an elevation of twenty-four hundred feet. The Cricket was linked to the carrier by a tightbeam, along which traveled information garnered from the drones. Those, an even dozen of them, were flung out in an aerial picket line forward of the *classis*. The drones flew a preplanned course, though one which could be, on a case-by-case basis, modified in flight by the Cricket.

As the drones passed over the shore inside the Zhong lodgment, over the channel between *Isla Santa Catalina* and the mainland, and over the island, itself, and the mostly artificial port, one thing became clear:

"Where the fuck is their fleet?" Fosa fumed. "Have we been able to get anything on satellite?"

Balboa owned no satellites, but did have a very limited ability to tap into and use the satellites of others. The ship's communications intelligence officer shook his head no, then said, "Against people who aren't looking or don't care we can sometimes get in, Skipper. But whatever the merits and demerits of the Zhong political system, sir, give them their due; they've got no masters at fucking with satellites and shutting us out."

"Yes, yes; the dirty bastards." Fosa scowled, then said, "And, of course, they've got the fucking Peace Fleet on their side, the best satellite reconnaissance system in existence that we know of. We could fool it on land, and the *Duque* has, several times. Not so much at sea. They know exactly where we are, all the time, on visual. Only reason even to try to hide ourselves is to make terminal guidance for a missile tough. But where we are, generally? They know that, and in real time."

"So where do you think *they* are, Skipper?" Comms asked.

Fosa filled his cheeks with air and blew them out, in exasperation. "They went to sea, maybe not so much to get away from us as to get away from land-based air, now that the TU is out of it. They may even be headed to Atlantis, though I doubt it."

"So what are we going to do?"

That took all of three seconds' thought: "We're going to entice them back in by bombing the shit out of their lodgment and anything that supports it."

Fosa chewed his lower lip for a bit, then ordered, "Orient our screen out to sea two hundred miles. Pass to the *Kurita* they're to take point. Also shunt them control of four drones. And send the all clear to raise the submarine fleet."

"Skipper!" Intel exulted, pointing at the screen. "The Zhong fleet isn't entirely gone. We've got visual on two freighters, one airship, and a bunch of lighters."

"Ready a strike. But not until *Kurita* has done for their air defense umbrella. Ops?"

"Yes, sir?"

"Recommendations on strike composition in twenty minutes. Oh, and coordinate with the Legion Jan Sobieski to provide cover for the strike, again, after *Kurita* takes out the air defense."

SdL *Megalodon*, off Santa Catalina Island

Extremely low-frequency communications had never been on Balboa's wish list, even though it might have allowed communications down to hundreds of meters of depth. The problem was just too hard, and the soil of the republic too conductive; never mind the unfortunate side effects. Instead, the *classis* had opted for a very low-frequency system, supplemented by an acoustic system and some prearranged codes. The very low-frequency system, or VLF, was based on the mainland. VLF was slow, though, very slow. And, while it could retransmit *Dos Lindas'* messages, the simple act of sending that message was a potential risk from a radiation homing missile.

Or—fuck, I don't know, maybe a homing torpedo if we responded. And homing pigeons are right the fuck out, thought Chu, commanding the *Meg* and the squadron. *Pity no one's yet come up with homing mackerel. Salmon . . . note to self, see about homing salmon.*

They'd heard the Zhong fleet depart, generally to the north, half a day or so ago. Chu had eaten his own guts out over the question of whether he should attack on his own ticket, even without the presence of the *classis*. Standing orders for the squadron had been that, if one of the seven engaged, they were all "weapons free."

Ultimately, he'd decided against. *And, sure, maybe I'm a little skittish after sinking a Zhong carrier I wasn't supposed to, loaded with civilians, mostly women and children, when we weren't even at war. Would anyone blame me if I were? But, no; it was because as far as I could tell the other six weren't in position to engage, and the* classis *wasn't remotely near.*

The Zhong had left half a day ago, but then they'd heard the approach of a similarly sized fleet. Acoustics in the shallow, island-rich waters off Balboa's and Santa Josefina's northern coasts were difficult. It was only four hours ago that Sonarman Auletti had been able to confirm, "Those are the AZIPODs of the flagship and *Kurita*."

That the fleet approaching was friendly didn't necessarily mean that there were no enemies about. Chu waited until . . .

"Underwater explosion, Skipper!" Auletti announced. A minute passed. "And another." Another minute passed. "There's number three, all timely."

"Wait for it," Chu ordered.

"One . . . two . . . three . . . four. I have four bangs in rapid succession," the sonarman said. "A delay . . . nothing . . . another bang . . . I mark two minutes . . . another bang . . . one-fifty-nine . . . another bang . . . another . . . another. That's the signal, Skipper: be ready to surface in five hours."

Santa Catalina Island, Balboa

Fleet Admiral Wanyan Liang had been aboard his flagship for several days, ever since the Balboans had appeared to have knocked the Tauran Union right out of the war. Long before that, the admiral, currently ordered away with the remnants of the fleet, had demanded that sixteen pyramidal flak towers be built. This was not so much to raise the guns and missiles above the clutter on the ground, though that mattered, nor to extend their range, though that mattered, too, as to make them relatively immune to any incoming fire that wasn't a direct hit.

Since Wanyan had left, Marine Lieutenant Colonel Ma Chu, the admiral's aide de camp, had served as the admiral's "eyes on the ground" of the whole effort, island, port, and mainland, all three. Ma was outranked by any number of people, ashore and afloat, but, as the admiral's eyes, his "I suggest" or "I think" or "Why don't you?" had the effective force of coming from the admiral, himself. Ma had tried not to abuse that and, it had to be said, generally succeeded. He'd only had to say, "Let me consult with the admiral" twice to bring some hardheaded sailor or soldier around.

Being driven in the admiral's vehicle by the admiral's driver, passing between two of the air defense pyramids, the two nearest the port, Ma thought he spied a small aircraft, briefly visible before disappearing into the clouds. The view was gone so quickly, and the air defense people seemed so oblivious to it, that he was inclined to discount his own eyes right up to the point that he saw half a dozen bursts of smoke suddenly spring into existence above and to the east of the pyramids. The shell bursts—for he knew instantly, from hard-won experience, that that was what they were—were followed by the sound of their own explosions, the freight-train racket of their passage, and the sound of heavy steel rain pattering down to the ground.

Just under seven seconds later, the same pattern was almost repeated. This time, though, some of the enemy's guns—*A single turret, I suppose*—must have been aimed a little off, because the steel rain came down all around Ma. One ball went through the hood of the admiral's vehicle with a sound of tearing sheet metal and the clang of steel off an engine block. That ball then came up through the hood again, through the windshield, and then went right through the driver's head. Ma was spattered with blood, brains, and bits of crimsoned bone.

With the driver no longer in control, the wheels straightened, letting the car run off the road. Too late, a shocked Ma grabbed for the steering wheel. The vehicle went nose-first into a freshly carved drainage ditch, hit the far wall, and stopped.

Ma, however, did not stop. There were no seat belts in a Zhong military car. He was thrown forward, over the frame of the shattered windshield, and past the ditch. He hit, rolled, bounced, and finally came up, gut first, against the stout trunk of a tree. His lower ribs cracked on the bark. The pain was intense but, *Thank you, ancestors. If it didn't hurt, it would mean I'd been paralyzed.*

Ma wasn't paralyzed but he was hurt. Slowly, gingerly, feeling cracked ribs grate inside him, he turned himself over and got his back to the trunk. There he saw that the salvos—*about nine or ten per minute per gun, I suppose, if it's their cruiser*—were no longer bursting in air but coming in to strike at or below the ground. He saw one air defense gun simply lifted into the air on a cloud of dirt, rocks, sandbags, and angry black smoke, men and parts of men falling away as it arose.

I know the admiral understood and intended that they come for this place, but I wonder if he understood how quickly they would trash it. I wonder, too, if her imperial fragrant cuntedness will let him come back to save us.

I wish we'd had some of the same class of cruiser when we went for their Royal Island . . .

Standing, rather, using the tree to pull himself to his feet, Ma Chu gasped at the agony radiating from his shattered ribs. He felt light-headed and found himself swaying side to side and back and forth, swaying, indeed, in something of an oval.

Concussion? Internal bleeding? Both I . . .

BdL *Tadeo Kurita*, East of Santa Catalina Island

Naval guns will often confuse a landlubber. In part, this is because, for a given shell's caliber, the shell itself will be much more powerful than its land-bound equivalent. In part, too, it is because it is often much longer ranged than a similar land caliber. In part, too, rate of fire can vary dramatically. The reasons for the difference were largely that weight of gun made a great deal of difference on the land, but ships weren't much bothered by weight. In the case of the dozen six-inch guns mounted in *Kurita*'s four triple turrets, the range was roughly sixty percent greater than for a similar land-based system, while the shells—which could be armor piercing, enhanced armor piercing, shrapnel, high explosive, or illumination—were a quarter heavier. Moreover, while a land-based but similar system might fire two and a half to three and a half rounds per minute, maximum, and temporarily, these particular naval guns could fire nine, in the first minute.

Kurita's skipper, Legate Cristóbal de Carvajal, down in fire control, watched four salvos of six come in atop one of their first two targets, one of the curious pyramids the Zhong had put up. The first dozen were shrapnel, followed by another dozen of straight high explosive, with point-detonating fuse. The latter exploded on the flat surface atop the pyramid, sending clouds of razor-sharp, smoking hot metal in all directions. Zhong air defense troops, running for their lives to the shelters, were cut down in swaths. One fairly dense group, clustering at the entrance to a shelter, had the misfortune of having a shell detonate in their midst. The bodies, parts of bodies, and bodies still shedding parts were flung away from the blossoming yellow, red, and black flower.

It somehow still surprises me, thought Carvajal, *that you can actually see a shock wave in the air.*

"I think we can call Target Two Alpha 'destroyed,' Skipper," Gunnery said. "Shifting X and Y turrets to Three Alpha."

"Ammunition?" asked Carvajal.

"We'll be ceasing fire after this target to restock the turrets," Gunnery said.

"Very good."

Santa Catalina Island, Balboa

Every breath was a struggle, every movement of his chest, whether internally or externally driven, sent waves of agony coursing through Ma Chu's body and mind. He found crawling was better than trying to walk since, when the pain put him into unconsciousness, he didn't have as far to fall.

The ambulance crew found him like that, facedown in the tire-spun muck, still trying to rise to all fours to move himself forward.

"The admiral," Ma Chu whispered, "...the admiral must be told...it cannot wait..."

Bridge, BdL *Dos Lindas*, Heading west toward Santa Catalina Island

When the sea was smooth, as this one was, on a ship the size of the *Dos Lindas*, even at her top speed of twenty-seven knots, the ride was as smooth as the sea. At her current speed of about fifteen knots, only the natural vibrations of the ship and the passing of the land to port told of any movement at all.

"Okay, *Meg*," replied Fosa to the news. "Go back on down and spread your squadron out to screen us if they start heading back."

Beepbeepbeep. "Wilco...Meg, out."

Fosa walked—it was only a few short steps—to the chart table laid out centrally to the bridge. He sensed someone, his ship's chief noncom, Ramirez, he thought, take a position just behind and to his left.

"What are we going to do, Skipper?"

Yep, Ramirez.

"They've got nearly ten knots on us, Top. We couldn't

catch them if they had a head wind and we had a hurricane-force tailwind. So...I'm kicking this one upstairs."

"Makes sense," Ramirez agreed. "But..."

CHAPTER EIGHT

Whoever makes me unhappy for a day, I will make
suffer a lifetime.   —Empress Dowager Cixi

Task Force Macera, surrounding Task Force Jesuit

He'd given it his best shot, Macera had, but his best hadn't
been good enough. Oh, he and his tercio-sized, reinforced
cohort had pursued long, fast, and hard. They'd gone
hungry as many days as not, and still kept it up. Through
darkest, slipperiest night and hottest, muggiest day,
through rain and high winds, shedding weight with every
forward step, they'd tried to grab hold of the Taurans' tails
and slow them down before they reached a defensible
position.

And all for nothing, Macera cursed his luck. *Here they
are and here they are digging in like beavers.*

Macera could hear the sounds, actually. It should not
have been possible at this distance but, *When you've got
nine or ten thousand people cutting trees and shoveling
out dirt, I suppose it can carry.*

Food had been pretty much catch as catch can during the pursuit. Oh, the helicopters had tried but, as the distance from their base areas increased, the helicopters had been forced from using two to support Macera and two to ferry support to the helicopters, to one and three, and then, for the last hundred miles, to just about three sorties every two days. Since arrival here at the doorstep of the Taurans, even that had proven impossible to keep up.

Macera and his men were borderline starving.

Estado Mayor, Sub camp C, *Ciudad* Balboa, Balboa

There was no longer a security or survival need for the General Staff and Carrera to operate out of the cramped and uncomfortable, but happily fairly bomb-resistant, camp.

"On the other hand," observed Carrera, "the other one is flatter than a pancake except where a piece of the former wall looks like it was chewed by a Meg, so we really have nowhere else to go for now. And probably not for a while."

Soult shrugged; none of his business and he didn't really care where the *Estado Mayor* hung out, his concerns were with the care, feeding, and transportation of a Carrera. The latter, though he wasn't drunk, or not yet, had put away a few. He might get drunk, too.

"And why not?" he asked Soult, rhetorically. "Pretty much everything is out of my hands and has been since the Die-hards surrendered." Soult started to object but Carrera shushed him. "Pour yourself a drink and have a seat, Jamey; I'll let you in on a secret."

Soult did pour himself one, then, though he was a lot less generous with his own drink than he had been with Carrera's. He took the bottle with him.

Once he was settled in, Carrera said, "You know, the history books are going to say all kinds of interesting things about me. Most of it will be lies, some good, some bad. Among the lies the biggest will be that I was in control start to finish, here. This will be closely followed by the idiot notion that I never made a mistake.

"To take the latter first, Jamey, I've made plenty of mistakes, from fucking up my own logistics in Sumer, back when we started . . . well, let me tell you, if Adnan Sada had had his brigade within twenty miles of where our point finally stalled out in the desert—you remember that sandstorm? Jesus!– he'd have beaten the shit out of us. And that wasn't the only one. Oh, no.

"Dropping the bridge outside Ninewah under the nose of that asshole, Lamprey? We're lucky we didn't end up needing the Federated States' help, just sheerly lucky. That fuckhead is pretty well-placed now to have sabotaged everything if we'd asked for help. And he can hold a grudge as well as I can, too.

"Humiliating Pigna in public to the point where he joined the opposition and launched a coup? Well . . . I already paid for that one, maybe in a couple of ways.

"The fleet action Fosa has upcoming? He's on his own; he's going to be out of range of anything I can send him. The Moslem rebellion in the Tauran Union? Bastards couldn't wait for the fucking signal, oh, no. Control? Hah! My ass!"

Carrera held out his glass for a refill.

"There is no justice, Jamey, none whatsoever. Speaking of which . . ." Carrera hit his intercom button. "Is Captain Gold here yet?"

Came the answer, "Yes, *Duque;* he's been cooling his heels for fifteen minutes."

"Send him in."

Turning back to Soult, Carrera said, "Oh, there are still a few things I can do."

A few silent moments passed before a knock on the door announced Gold's presence. He was a tall, slender, mustached merchant skipper, though not in uniform at the moment. As a member of Balboa's merchant fleet, Pedro Gold was also part of the hidden reserve. As such, he'd made two supply runs before the main Tauran invasion, then hightailed it for a neutral port to await being called forward again.

Carrera gestured at an open chair. "Have a seat, Gold. Jamey, get the captain a drink, would you?"

"Ice, Skipper?" Soult asked.

"Please, Mr. Soult. Much ice; I'm not a heavy drinker."

"So how's the *Alberto Helada* at the moment?" Carrera asked.

"Fine, *Duque.*" Gold gave a little shrug. "She's sailing up under my exec. Per orders, I flew up here on my own.

"She's supposed to hold prisoners, right? I've got the food, some bunks, stoves, porta-potties . . . basically everything for ten or twelve thousand men. It's for the POWs, like the others, isn't it?"

Carrera gave a wicked, somewhat whisky-fueled smile. "Well, no, not exactly. You see I have this odd kind of mission . . ."

When the mission was explained, in full, Carrera added, "He's going to say, '*et dona ferentes.*' I can hear him saying it as if I was standing there."

Walking to his desk, Carrera picked up a sealed envelope. "When he says it, give him this. My penmanship is awful, so there's a typed transliteration."

"He's a madman, you know, your boss," Gold said to Soult as the latter drove him to an ad hoc heliport not far from the city.

Soult might have taken umbrage except that they were, after all, on the same side. *And, besides*, "Oh, Skipper, you have no fucking idea how much of a madman he can be."

Reaching the heliport, Gold noticed a series of pallets being loaded aboard one of the helicopters. "And those, I suppose, are the small boats and motors he spoke of."

"I'd be guessing if I said, Skipper. In any case, that's your chopper. You can ask the crew. I will say that, at about a sixth of a ton, each, that helicopter is probably going to be carrying between twenty and twenty-four of them."

Oppenheim, Sachsen

Khalid was surprised at how quickly two of his fellow agents showed up, knocked on his door, and announced, "Saints Peter and Paul." He didn't know either of them or, if he did, plastic surgery had done for any chance of recognition.

One was tall and blond, blue-eyed, too, and looked so

Sachsen he could have passed as Alix's brother. That one answered to "Fritz," though privately he said his name was originally "Abdul." Another, slender, swarthy, and decidedly Arab-looking, answered to "Tim."

"It's what my friends call me," said Tim.

Fritz added, "I've been Fritz so long it's what I've gotten used to answering to. And, before you ask, I was born here, to revert parents, and rejected the whole 'submission' thing as a boy. I'm an immigrant to Balboa, like you.

"There were supposed to be two of us," Fritz said, "but the other never met me at the rendezvous point."

"You're Balboan?" Alix asked. "What are you doing here? What..." She had a sudden glimmering of a horrible truth.

Khalid sighed. This moment had always been, after all, inevitable. "We're officially enemies, Alix. I've been working for Balboa, to include delivering arms to the Moslems in Sachsen, for a number of years now."

"Then you..." Her fist flew to her own mouth. She bit down hard on it.

"We all follow orders, Alix," Khalid said. "Yes, you ended up in very unfortunate circumstances because of those orders. You also, please note, ended up saved from very unfortunate circumstances because of those. And because we follow orders, you've a chance to get your army back to undo some of the damage we've done you because of the damage your country helped bring on mine."

She dropped the fist. Her eyes flashed and her lips curled into a sneer. "That's what you call 'unfortunate circumstances': finding myself with my bottom bare, facedown on the cobblestones, and a string of scum taking their turns sticking their cocks up my ass?"

"It would be hard to call them 'happy circumstances,' now wouldn't it?" was Khalid's retort. "You can dwell on that to your heart's content, Alix, but, longer term, if we don't get you your army back, there are going to be a lot more Sachsen girls experiencing the same thing you did. Indeed, it will be the rare one who doesn't experience it— no pun intended—in *full*.

"Take your pick of what you want. But do it quickly because once we're assembled, we're going after your Minister of Finance. If you want your country back, you'll forget about resenting people doing their duty."

"It wasn't your duty to get me gang-raped," she said, calming slightly.

"It wasn't my duty to save you from it, either, but I did. And it wasn't *me* doing the raping."

Tauran Union Defense Agency Headquarters, Lumiere, Gaul

The uprising in Gaul had followed a different pattern from Sachsen. In Gaul, precisely because the Moslems in Sachsen had risen first, the authorities had had a modicum of warning, enough to call out and form something like a militia, to drag in and organize food, and to expel likely fifth columnists.

What that meant was that instead of a sudden takeover, the capital of Gaul, Lumiere, had found itself besieged.

One peculiarity of that was that, as the ad hoc militia folded in key places, the largely military contingent of the Defense Agency headquarters had found themselves not only on the front line, but a key component of the frontline defenses.

"Now meself and Turenge," said Major Campbell, lightly, to the Anglian twit, Houston, "if they capture us, we'll probably be raped in a place reasonably well-suited to the purpose. On the other hand, you, Major Houston, will be raped in a place very poorly suited to the purpose. And, yes, they do prefer boys, many of them."

Her two main bits of muscle, Corporal Dawes and Sergeant Greene, snickered at the sudden pallor that took over Jonathan Houston's face. The rest of Campbell's direct-action team, seconded to her from the Anglian Special Air Service, likewise snickered, but lacked enough of the detail Greene and Dawes possessed to make a very enthusiastic show of it. They simply enjoyed Houston's obvious discomfort.

The whole Anglian crew, nine members of the SAS, Campbell and Houston, plus the lovely, albeit thin, Gallic captain, Turenge, occupied one corner of one floor of the headquarters. Turenge, though armed, was away from the windows, listening into an earpiece attached to a small portable radio. They were all armed. Unlike the Anglians, whose insular histories tended to deprecate and discount both domestic violence and the means of violence, the history of Gaul had been almost unremittingly violent since inception. As such, they tended to expect disaster and likewise to prepare for it. In this case, preparation had come in the form of an arms room and ammo bunker, in total with enough arms and ammunition for a small war.

There was also enough food for several weeks, over and above what the city authorities had collected.

These factors had both proven to be important, though the food was less so, so far. Whereas the Moslems in Sachsen had been more or less integrated inside the cities, hence had found it fairly easy to take them over, in Gaul they'd generally been banished to towns outside the major cities. This had had two effects. One was that it had been easier to smuggle arms to them, by Khalid's French-speaking colleagues, meaning they were also somewhat better armed. The other was that taking the cities had been much harder, since they'd had to work their way in from the outside, and the Gallic civilians had turned out to be a lot better armed than Gallic proponents of gun control had imagined, with a surprising number and amount of arms and ammunition left over from the Great Global War, generally hidden in a closet, or up in an attic.

The headquarters had been among the first places to stand like a rock, as the men and women—to include a goodly number of civilians—had flocked to the arms room and then, the armorer having given up on getting signatures, raced to man the windows and doors. A substantial number of Moslem rebels lay in various postures of undignified death in the streets around the building.

So far, the Moslems hadn't asked for a truce to recover their dead, while the Gauls and other Taurans in the building hadn't been especially eager to offer one. Instead, as they'd organized their numbers, they had simply sat back for a siege of the place. This didn't prevent a certain amount of psychological warfare from continuing.

Jan and her people were better placed than most to see where the screaming was coming from but they still couldn't see it. They were also better placed to hear what the screaming was, and couldn't do anything to stop it. It went on for a long time, several hours, from at least two tortured throats, before anyone had a clue what it was.

They found out when two poles were erected over a wall on the other side of the boulevard. The poles hadn't been screaming, of course. Instead, the sources now hung by their wrists from the poles. Jan took a set of binoculars, dialed the focus in, and immediately pulled them from her eyes.

"My God, how could anyone . . . ?" She had no answer, though she had a strong urge to retch. Greene borrowed the binoculars and looked for himself. It took about half a minute for his mind to believe what his eyes were seeing.

"They skinned them," he said. "Obviously alive . . . they're still alive . . . the bastards fucking skinned two people alive and then hung them up on display."

"Braiden?"

"Yes, Sergeant?"

"Put them out of their misery."

Two shots rang out. Everyone could hear those, too, and, by that time, understood what was going on.

Ten minutes later, Sergeant Pangracs came calling. He was the senior medic at the headquarters, and more used to passing out pills to snivelers than to field expedient surgery. He was, however, picking up the latter rather quickly.

He'd already been a deft hand with psychological issues. That was why he materialized at Jan's corner with a bottle of brandy and a fistful of paper cups.

"I figured you guys might need this."

Santa Cruz, Santa Josefina, by the Cordoban Border

"The patrols all say the same thing," said Rall to Marciano. "The enemy is thickening by the day. One group managed to get eyes on a particularly nasty-looking artillery group, about ten kilometers from our forward trace. It looked, the squad leader thought, like Balboan regular artillery, well trained, and digging in fast."

"They're not even bothering to hide it," Marciano observed.

"They don't have to, anymore, sir. They've won. They've won more completely that I ever imagined they could have."

"How long do you think we have before they've brought up enough to stomp us out of existence, Rall?"

"Less time than I thought initially," the Sachsen answered. "Do you think it's time for us to get interned in Cordoba?"

"No . . . we've got to get back home intact. And soon. We are needed there. Internment would last until a peace treaty was arranged, and there can be no peace treaty while most of our government—our govern*ments*—are on the run from or captured by the Moslem rebels."

"It would be a worthy goal, getting home to fight for our own again," Rall agreed, "but, I confess, I haven't the slightest idea how to do it."

"An airship, maybe?" Marciano suggested. "We have enough in the treasury to charter one."

"No . . . no," said Rall, "the range is so short the Santa Josefinans will shoot it down. And we can't cross into Cordoba to get out of range because they'd have to intern us. They were terrified of the Balboans before, but now . . ."

"'And now Carrera, too, is running on the mountain, with no more between him and his will than a wolf has.'" Marciano quoted.

"Where did that come from?" Rall asked.

"Book—*old* book—from Old Earth; *The Last of the Wine*."

"Ah. Someone predicted the son of a bitch that far back?"

"In a way."

MV ALTA, *Mar Furioso*

A single Condor, one of the stealthy gliders developed by *Obras Zorilleras*, had come in the night before, carrying a heavy package for Hamilcar Carrera. Opening it would have been a chore, the package being three Faraday cages, one inside the other, with directions not to open them until the very last possible minute. Given that Ham knew what was inside the last cage, those were instruction with which he fully agreed.

This morning, a two-man Condor sat on the deck, with eleven more resting behind it. The gliders sat on lightweight rolling frames. The frames might be recovered, when the gliders launched, but they were just as likely to go into the sea. No matter; they were cheap and easily replaced.

The Condors were highly stealthy auxiliary propelled gliders developed by the Legion's *Obras Zorilleras*. Stealthiness, in this case, was not achieved with precision manufacture, based on advanced engineering, itself derived from complex calculations. No; stealth here was acquired randomly.

Of the three normal primary factors that affect an aircraft's radar, cross section, size, materials, and shape, the Condor made little deliberate use of the first and the last. True, they were not large, and that helped. It was also true that they had no sharp edges and no flat surfaces. These, however, were incidental. For size, although it is the least important factor, if two aircraft have exactly the same materials and shape, but are of different size, the larger will have a greater radar cross section. For shape, the important things are to have no sharp edges, no flat surfaces pointed toward the radar. These things, however, accrued to the design by virtue of them being gliders, and had little deliberate stealth to them.

Instead, it was in something of a perversion of the normal rules for materials that the Condors acquired their stealthiness. The short version was that they were built, at core, of a radar-absorbing carbon fiber and resin shell, around which had been built up a thick layer of decreasingly dense foam in which were suspended hundreds of thousands of tiny, radar-scattering concave-convex chips. The shell, being "lossy," absorbed incoming radar and converted it to heat. The chips either scattered incoming radar or concentrated and then scattered it. Very, very small percentages of the radar energy would ever return to the sender.

So far, whether in scouting or bombing the tactical enemies, carrying messengers and senior leaders, bombing the Tauran Union on their home turf, bombing Cienfuegos, killing foreign dignitaries and even chiefs of state, delivering a nuclear weapon, or, indeed, scouting the United Earth Peace Fleet's Atlantis Base, the amount of radar returned had never yet been enough to permit detection. Moreover, since the process of applying the foam was random, every Condor was tested for radar return and then assigned to a particular duty based on mission, with the most stealthy being used for the most important missions, and the least as throwaways for less important ones. A lot of very expensive missiles could be expended on birds before a first-class Condor was identified and engaged.

It didn't go without saying, because it had never been so much as whispered outside of the most secure facility in Balboa, or aboard a ship, that the twenty-four crew and four standbys selected from the Fourteenth Cazador Tercio for the mission were among the most capable, more determined, gutsiest men in Balboa. Moreover, they'd been preparing for years.

Awaiting launch, two of those men sat in the lead

Condor: Tribune Cherensa, the mission commander and one of the oldest still active Cazadores in the Legion, plus the pilot, Cazador Sergeant Leon. Both wore combination intercom and oxygen masks.

The launch method had been a subject of much thought, as had the payload. For the latter, it had been argued that two five-hundred-pound bombs would have been more effective against a block in the UEPF's perimeter defenses than three hundred pounds of men and two hundred of equipment and ordnance. The question had never gone up to Carrera. Instead, Omar Fernandez and the legate of Fourteenth Cazador had decided, together, that a bomb was good for one place and one time, if everything went right, but that men, good men, were flexible enough to deal with anything.

To amuse himself while waiting, Cherensa mentally recited the legion's definition of Special Operations: *"Special operations are those small unit actions, the geopolitical, strategic, or operational importance of which, and the price for failure in which, are so high that they justify the early identification and special training of extraordinary human material and the continuing expenditure of relatively lavish levels of money and materiel."*

Well, thought the tribune, *this being the first blow in the "First Interstellar War," it probably counts as* special *enough.*

Cherensa's reveries were interrupted by one of the deck crew, holding out an inquisitorial thumbs-up, head half turned away. The pilot, sitting up front, returned it. The deck crewman made a kind of "after you, madam," bow. The Condor began to thrum and vibrate as Leon started the small jet engine and fed it fuel. The engine also gave off a whine that Cherensa found distinctly annoying.

The Condor also began to move, slowly at first, and then picking up speed. Still, it was all very gentle. Between the wind coming from the bow, half natural and half from the forward movement of the ship, it seemed to be mere seconds before Cherensa felt the thing lift off the cradle. He didn't have the chance to see deck crew race out to drag the cradle out of the way.

The ship wasn't pointed quite at the target, so almost immediately after takeoff, Leon had to veer a bit to keep the glider between the island, and any thermal detecting defenses it might have, and the engine.

"Is number two behind us, yes?" Leon asked.

Cherensa turned to look. A curse died unspoken as he saw the other glider rise to take up position behind and to the right of his own. "They're in place," he answered.

"Okay, increasing speed, sir. Please let me know if they start to fall behind. Also, if you can tell me about number three?"

"Wilco . . . there's three."

Leon kept track of altitude as the Condor arose. At twelve thousand feet he reached over and turned a dial to provide one liter of oxygen per minute to each mask. Cherensa didn't consciously notice any change.

Shortly after turning on the oxygen, Leon announced, "Sixteen thousand feet, sir; I'm killing the jet and leveling off."

After the long climb, leveling off felt like falling to the

tribune. "Roger," he said, then asked, "how long before the engine gets cool enough to retract?"

"No more than twenty minutes, but I'll give it thirty to be safe."

"Good. I like safe."

"Me, too, boss; me, too. Is number two conforming? Number three?"

Again Cherensa twisted about and watched the trail gliders for a few moments before reporting, "Yes."

Condors, especially when purely gliding, were slow. They were also, absent turbulence, extraordinarily smooth riding. In other words they were . . .

Boring, boring, boring, thought Cherensa. *I'd probably go to sleep except that we have essentially no idea of what's waiting.*

Cherensa pulled out the target folder from its pocket on the front of his silk and liquid metal *lorica*, the legions' standard torso armor. He turned a page and looked at a map on the left and a photo on the right thinking, *Defenses. All strategic recon could figure out was that there were domes around the perimeter of Atlantis Base. They're well positioned to be defenses, but we don't know what kind, or even if they are. Fernandez's best guess—and I agree with him—is that they're probably antiaircraft and antimissile defense, mostly with the Federated States in mind.*

The next page was labeled "Landing Field Conditions." Sadly, it was blank except for a photo that was too fuzzy to be remotely useful.

He turned another page and scanned for the umpteenth time for "Enemy Personnel." *Not like it's going to have changed since last night. Vehicles were spotted carrying people to and fro, but what they did there or how many were stationed there . . . no clue. We could make an educated guess about how many might be stationed on the single visible floors below the domes— maybe six or seven, not more than that—but we don't have a clue how many floors deep down into the ground they go. We don't know how well trained they are. We don't know how they're armed. We don't know if they have defenses for poison gas. We have an idea of how long it will take to reinforce them, because we think there are company-sized barracks, maybe five kilometers away from the four we're going after.*

On the other hand, if we and the other three mission packages succeed in taking out the defenses, those reinforcements won't matter, because the ALTA is going to pour missiles through the gap and obliterate anything that looks like a possible defense or barracks within minutes of our reporting in.

But, for that to happen . . .

Cherensa's thoughts were interrupted by a clank and a shudder.

"Tell me, Leon, that that was just the jet being retracted."

"Yes, Tribune, just that."

"Great. In the future, let me know, okay?"

"Yes, Centurion. Sorry, Centurion."

"How long until we hit now?"

After a brief delay, Leon answered, "About an hour and ten minutes."

CHAPTER NINE

When one would make a surprise attack on the enemy, he should avoid the major roads and seek out the lesser ones. Then attack. —Takeda Nobushige

UEPF *Spirit of Peace*

Ensign Esmeralda Miranda sat on a chair in a corner of the high admiral's plush quarters; plush, at least, by the standards of the United Earth Peace Fleet. Xingzhen, empress and de facto, if not de jure, ruler of the Zhong, lounged against pillows piled against the bulkhead that did double duty as the head of the bed. The empress was covered only by a light sheet that came no higher than her waist. Not young and yet still aetherially beautiful, she enjoyed the effect her half nakedness had on the high admiral, who was also her lover. Also in the suite were Commander Iris Khan, the fleet's sociology officer, plus the high admiral herself, the tall, blonde, and svelte Marguerite Wallenstein.

"They did *what*?" demanded Wallenstein, slamming

153

her hand down emphatically onto the top of her Silverwood desk.

"They've declared war on us, war on the Earth," answered Iris, also known as "Commander Khan, female" or "Commander Khan, wife." "That barbarian Carrera's wife announced it in the World League. Formally. In the middle of the battle they assembled a quorum of their senate and got a formal declaration of war. Ordinarily, I'd say we could just blow it off, a little pissant country declaring war on a planet they can't even get to. But . . ."

"But, no, not in this case," said Wallenstein. "In this case, if they say something, we need to take it seriously. Where's your husband?"

"Hunched over a monitor, scanning inputs from every ship, every skimmer, every embassy . . ."

"The embassies!" Wallenstein's blue eyes flashed. "They can get to us through those!"

"He's also had his assistant ask all the host countries down below with help providing security, from the ground and the air. They've put out a general alert for all our personnel planet-side to get to the nearest embassy or, at least, to vacate their normal quarters, if they're not staying inside an embassy, and to go hide somewhere."

"That's sound, I think," Wallenstein agreed. "How long before our local security is augmented?"

Khan sighed, looked away, and then returned her gaze to the admiral's face. She shook her head slowly, then said, "A day, say most of them. But a surprising number of the barbarians down below refuse to answer. Some have answered and said, 'no.' How did we sink so low that the ground-dwellers down below can just tell us, 'no'?"

I know the answer to that, thought Marguerite, *and so do you*.

Khan, female, not normally the boldest among the Peace Fleet's officers, still found it within her to ask, "What are we going to do now, High Admiral? The Taurans are gone as a power. The Federated States hate us beyond words. The Spanish-speakers will probably follow Balboa's lead from now on."

"We still have the Zhong," Wallenstein said, firmly, casting an adoring gaze at Xingzhen. "As long as we have them then we are not without friends."

"I am with you, as always, *baobei*," the empress assured the admiral.

Marguerite nodded gratefully. Then, turning to Esmeralda she said, "Esma, honey, go find Commander Khan, husband, and tell him I'd like to be briefed on the security down below at his earliest convenience."

"Yes, High Admiral," said the girl, standing and hurrying from the room.

Condor One, Over the *Mar Furioso*

A small string forward of the cockpit told Leon something of the wind direction and speed. It was quartering, from ahead, and not too bad. But, with every meter the Condor descended, the nature of the ground got a little more plain . . . and he didn't like it. He didn't like his options, either.

Try to pick up a thermal? A quick glance around suggested not, and pretty strongly. *Extrude and crank up*

*the jet for another go-round? No, noisy and, frankly, we're
already too obvious. Another patch of ground. No, too low.
So all I can reasonably do is . . .*

"Hang the fuck on; this is going to suck Meg cock!"

The glider touched down, Rather, it should have.
Instead of touching down, however, Leon discovered that
"solid ground" was, in fact, "tall grass." The glider went
past the heads of that and kept on sinking. Indeed, it sank
deep enough to completely obscure any view of the
ground. Then it hit bottom and bounced several feet in
the air.

It didn't bounce up evenly, though. Instead, the
portside wing came up a lot higher then the starboard one.
That meant that, when they came down again, the
starboard one hit the ground, first and *hard*. The Condor
began a clockwise spin.

"Shiiitttt!" screamed Cherensa and Leon, together, as
the world spun around them. Leon had a vision of the
starboard wing snapping off, and then they were back
down in the grass, acting for all the world like a very large
lawn mower, but spewing great swaths of grass in all
directions, rather than through a chute.

"Ffffuuuckckck!!!" Leon screamed, as the Condor
bounced up again, this time letting the port wing down.
It sheered off, too, leaving them wingless but at least
killing their spin . . . in one direction.

"Ohjesuschrist!" Cherensa managed to pray—it was
clearly a form of prayer—as the glider's tail hit ground and
broke off about a meter from the end. All things
considered this would have been a non-event, except that
the main body was descending as the remains of the tail

bounced upward. When that main body hit it was nearly nose on.

Fortunately, the manner of building the things, thick foam over carbon fiber and resin, allowed the nose to absorb the impact. The glider hung in that position, almost vertical, as if deciding which way to fall. It finally did fall, and backward, so that its belly ended up more or less on the ground with the canopy facing roughly skyward.

After several long moments of silence, Leon asked, "T-t-t-Tribune, i-i-is there an-an-an-ny ru-ru-rule against ha-ha-having-ing-ing hav-ing having... having a fucking drink?"

"None that comes to mind, Leon. Just one though; just one."

Two and Three had a somewhat easier time of it, Two coming in uneventfully and Three careening into a hidden ditch before coming to a complete stop. Leon was still choking down his one permitted drink as he raced for Three, Cherensa double-timing for Two.

It was the pilot of Three, Moya, who first voiced the common reason for jubilation. "They didn't blast us out of the sky. Right up until we landed I was *sure* we were all dead men. But..."

"Yeah, I didn't let myself think about it," said Leon. Despite—or because of—the one drink, his voice was steady now. "Come on now, out we go. Cut some camouflage for the Condor then follow my trail to One. Give me the extra pack; I'll carry it."

Moya's passenger, Carrasco, undid his restraining

harness and leaned down. When he straightened up again, he had a pack frame to which were strapped a number of the components of a demolition kit, to include a very large shaped charge. Leon took it, pulled the straps over his shoulders, and began to trot away.

Both Moya and Carrasco then unloaded their packs and personal weapons, a suppressed submachine gun for the former and a suppressed sniper rifle in Hush fifty-one for the latter. Within a few minutes they had cut enough brush and grass to cover their glider from casual observation. Then, the pair of them headed in the direction Leon had followed. By the plan, their extra equipment would be there but Leon and Cherensa would be forward, reconnoitering the target.

"Nothing," said the tribune, looking through his field glasses at what appeared to be the entrance. "No sign of life. Well, no sign of *recent* life anyway. And not even a fence around it."

"You figure it's automated?" Leon asked. "Maybe no fence because it's mined?"

"Mined? That's not how I'd bet it, no. Why not? Because mines *especially* have to be fenced. As for manned or automated, my gut tells me the latter, but we're going to treat it as the former.

"Go get the others. I want the M-26 machine gun, the demo kit, the flame thrower, the sniper rifle, the Pound submachine gun, and two F-26s. Also the radio."

"Roger," said Leon, who them snaked backward on his belly until he was out of sight of the white—*and that's a little strange, too; why white?*—domed tower. It wasn't much of a tower, either, at about five meters across and maybe eight high.

Leaving the M-26 light machine gun and the sniper rifle in overwatch from his previous observation point, Cherensa and the remaining three men, one bearing the demo and another the flamethrower, crawled on their bellies through the grass, long and wild, that grew in the flatland between their observation post and the UEPF tower. Leon trailed a little, partly for carrying the pack frame loaded with demolitions and partly because he couldn't help himself, every minute or so, from probing the ground ahead of himself with a stick he'd cut and sharpened.

About halfway to the UEPF's position, they came upon a small stream, running low and with tall grass to either side. Thought Cherensa, while waiting for the glider pilot, *If this goes where it looks like it does, it will get us close to rush range for the entrance. And then fucking Leon can stop probing for the mines that aren't there.*

Two minutes after the tribune and two of his men reached the stream, Leon showed up, looking apologetic. Before he could say a word about being slow, Cherensa hushed him and explained the new plan. Then, without another word, crouching low, the men began to splash their way—splashing at little as possible, actually—up the foot-deep stream. Finally, they came to a one vehicle–width bridge, from which a trail led directly to the tower, to the left, and off somewhere into the interior, to their right.

"Shaped charge ready?" asked Cherensa of Leon.

Leon was already taking off the pack. He leaned it against the stream's steep bank, then knelt down in the water to undo the straps holding the shaped charge on. It was a twenty-kilogram version, with what someone on Old Earth, centuries prior, might have called "Octogen." Explosives are ordinarily fairly cheap for the work they do, but the twenty kilos in this shaped charge had cost the Republic on the order of fifteen hundred legionary drachma. That was about eight times a private's monthly screw.

There was also a covered ring around the diameter of the shaped charge, fixed with the best adhesive the legions could find. Leon slung his rifle across his back, checked that the two fuse igniters, their fuses, and the nonelectric blasting caps were all in place, removed the cover of the ring, and announced, "Ready."

Cherensa spared a glance for each man. "On three," he said, then began counting, "One . . . two . . . three; Leon and Moya, go, boys, go!"

Like gazelles, the men fairly erupted from cover. Legs churning, each expecting to be mowed down like weeds by the presumed defenders. Thus, each was totally shocked to reach the door to the tower unharmed.

They'd rehearsed this part a thousand times over the previous several years. While Moya scanned left, right, and left again, Leon did a quick check, visual and by touch, of the door. *Clean and smooth enough for our purposes.*

The Cazador threw all his weight and strength against the shaped charge, obliterating the weak seal over the adhesive, thus spreading it out and squashing it between wall and charge. He held the charge in place for the full minute recommended.

"Get ready, Moya," he said with more nonchalance than he felt. Reaching down he pulled first one igniter, then the other. He was rewarded with two bubbling fuses, one of which ruptured to let smoke escape.

"Let's get the fuck out of here!"

Huffing and puffing, both men raced back to the stream, and rather faster than they'd raced up to the tower. Moya almost overshot it, but Cherensa reached up to snag an arm and spin him into cover. The wait while they hugged the bank nearest the tower was short, and then *Khawaam!*

"Wait! Wait!" Cherensa reminded them. "Let the debris fall."

After a slow count of ten, by which time Leon had the pack frame with the rest of the demo back on his back, Cherensa ordered, "Let's go!"

All four jogged forward in a shallow V. Leon went to the door and began to affix to it a large charge of plastic explosive, but flat this time, rather than shaped. Cherensa watched over him as he made his preparations. Meanwhile, Carrasco shone a light into the hole made by the shaped charge and determined that it had, indeed, gone completely through the wall. Dropping the light, he put the nozzle of the flamethrower into the ragged hole, braced himself against the long, slow, but hard recoil, hit the electric priming trigger, and fired. He gave everything the flamethrower's two tanks had to the tower, and only regretted he didn't have four more tanks, just to make sure.

From inside came a horrible heartrending screaming, as

if from dozens of damned souls. Some of it came through the hole and around the nozzle, but more of the sound seemed to come through the very walls of the tower.

"Poor bastards," Carrasco muttered, with Moya nodding silent agreement.

Fortunately, the screaming from inside died quickly, presumably from lack of oxygen.

About the time Carrasco's tanks were exhausted, Leon gave the thumbs-up. Cherensa looked around, to determine Moya's and Carrasco's locations, then told Leon, "Blast it."

"Fire in the hole! Fire in the hole!"

The tribune waited for the two fuses to begin to bubble. Then, grabbing Leon by his pack frame, he physically pulled him away from the door and around the tower until they were safe from, at least, direct blast. The whole time Leon counted down, "Fifteen thousand . . . fourteen thousand . . . twelve thousand . . . two thousand . . . one . . ."

Khawaam!

That rocked them all.

"Come on! Form up! Monocles down. IR flashlights on."

Running to flatten themselves against the tower wall to either side of the blasted door, Cherensa took point on the right, and Moya on the left, with Leon and Carrasco behind them. Reaching up to his harness, the tribune pulled off a fragmentation grenade and flicked off the safety clip. He held it up for Moya to see, but Moya already had one out.

"On four," the tribune mouthed, holding the grenade to chest level with his left hand and putting a finger through the ring from his right. "One," he and Moya both pulled their rings. "Two," they let the spoon fly off so the striker could impact on the cap to start the fuse. "Three," they waited to let the fuse burn down slightly. "Four," both grenades went flying through the smashed door and into the room beyond.

Whawham!

Then Cherensa and Moya, crouching low, burst into the room, screaming and firing like maniacs, with Leon and Carrasco standing tall and doing the same until . . .

"Cease fire! Cease fire!" Cherensa had to practically scream to be heard after the beating all their eardrums had just taken. Looking around he said, wonderingly, "Moonbats; just fucking *antaniae*." The *antaniae* were winged, genetically engineered, septic-mouthed reptiles, left by the Noahs who had seeded the planet, and hated by every intelligent being on Terra Nova.

Through their monocles, in the scene illuminated by the flashlights, the foursome saw hundreds of burnt, blasted, shot *antaniae* . . . and nothing else. If any of the creatures were still alive, they gave no sign, not even their characteristic cry of "mnnbt . . . mnnbt . . . mnnbt."

"What the . . . ? Carrasco, Moya, find the door down and *clear*. Leon, follow me."

All that led up was a ladder that reached to a simple square opening. Cherensa again pulled a grenade from his harness, flipped off the safety clip, and pulled the ring. This time he didn't count aloud, *no real point to it*. Instead, releasing the spoon, he mentally counted off to three, then tossed the grenade overhand to sail through the opening and past into the dome. A muffled *wham* followed and then echoed from the walls. At the ladder,

Leon bent and cupped his hands together. Cherensa slung his weapon into the crook of his arm, grabbed the ladder, and put his right foot into Leon's cupped hands. The junior stood and lifted, even as the senior pulled with both hands and explosively straightened his leg. The result wasn't so much a lifting as a launching, with the tribune disappearing into the dome almost in an instant. A long flourish of automatic fire followed, then devolved into single shots. As Leon hurried up the ladder, he heard more muffled shots and explosions from below.

What he saw, though, at the top of the ladder, was stunning. Beyond some number of dead and dying *antaniae,* there were two cranks, large, though looking hand powered. In the middle, on a kind of crude stand, was a large pipe. Yes, it may have looked like a weapon at a distance, but it was only a pipe. A smaller crank on the stand may have been connected to the pipe; Leon couldn't be sure without closer examination.

"Fake," Cherensa judged. "The whole goddamned thing is fake. This is not high-tech defense against the Federated States missiles; this is a fucking bluff."

As if to prove the point, the tribune went to the smaller of the wheels and began to turn. Slowly, with much squealing and creaking, a straight crack appeared in the dome's face. The more Cherensa turned, the wider the crack grew, until eventually it was about a half a meter open at the bottom. That let in enough light to see a piece of glass, a lens of sorts, in the end of what was still, after all, only a pipe.

"Let's get the fuck out of here. We need to report to the ALTA."

Barco de La Legion ALTA (Armada Legionario Transporte de Assalto), Mar Furioso

The Ic, or intelligence officer for the missions, said, "Two were fake, two were real, but only one seemed to be powered and capable of working. The other had obviously not been maintained in a long time; it was loaded with *antaniae*."

"How do we know the one they said was working was actually working?" Legate Terry Johnson asked.

"The team said, 'It looks like it would work; it had power; and it was manned with seven Earthpigs, five of them among the recently deceased and the other two insisting it was real.'"

Johnson shrugged an eloquent *maybe*.

"That doesn't really help us that much, does it?" asked Hamilcar Carrera.

"No, we still have to blast all the towers. But, then again, we always intended to do so, the same as we're going to blast everything that remotely resembles a military installation. Unless the fakes were a trap and they've got hidden defenses we might not be able to deal with . . ."

Ham thought furiously. It wasn't like Johnson to hesitate or equivocate. But he had a point, even if he wasn't stating it. If they lost here, ultimately the war, the important war, was lost as well. *I'm glad this is his job, though, not mine.*

The operations officer for the mission, currently down below with the landing troops, was David Cano. He was married to Alena, the beautiful, green-eyed "witch," so called.

Alena the Witch then spoke up. "No. That's not what's going on."

Johnson directed her an inquisitive glance.

"If they had better defenses, they'd almost certainly not have bothered with weaker ones like those domes that ring the island and have had both the Federated States and everyone else, including us, bamboozled since the Great Global War."

"But what if they have them hidden, rising from the ground, maybe?" Johnson asked.

"No," she insisted. "The defenses of Atlantis Base were never meant to defeat an attack so much as deter one. If they'd intended to defeat an attack all those towers would have been capable, manned, and ready. On the other hand, when you want to deter, you put it all on the line. Even—no, especially—if it's a bluff."

"She's right, Legate Johnson," said Hamilcar. "But you know what? Even if she's not right, I know my old man. He wants this done. This *must be done*. At any cost. Now will you do it?"

Johnson nodded, solemnly. Then he repeated, "It must be done."

"Captain, are the rockets unmasked?"

"Yes, sir, unmasked but still under the tarp. Shall I have the tarp pulled back?"

"Do it. And bring her around to fire."

The tarp wasn't set up to be withdrawn mechanically. Erected by the men, it also had to be taken down by the

men. Even the ship's gantry crane was useless, rolled back
as far sternward—against the superstructure, actually—
as it would go.

To this end, several times more "sailors" than a
container ship ought even to have had swarmed on deck
to begin pulling on the ropes that furled it. Meanwhile,
the ship, itself, began to swing in a wide arc to starboard
to bring the port-facing rocket launchers generally to bear.
There were over seven hundred long-range rockets, in
clusters of twelve, carrying a mix of warheads: high
explosive, sub-munitions, fuel-air explosive, and mines. As
the tarp pulled back, these were revealed, in several
banks, elevated to as much as twenty-eight degrees,
though the bank of launchers farthest from the ship's port
side seemed to be raised to no more than perhaps twenty.
The launchers twisted, indeed, almost writhed, as they
changed azimuth and elevation, under the control of
gunnery, in order to bear on their assigned targets.

"This is the only part that actually frightens me,"
Johnson admitted, still standing on the bridge, along with
his immediate and primary staff as well as the necessary
naval crew. "Once we launch then either the Earthpigs'
defenses are destroyed or we guessed wrong and we get
destroyed. Both of those are out of my control, so no need
to worry about them. Sort of like whether Valparaiso
commits some of their air force to us. I can't do a damned
thing about it except make sure the airfield here isn't
attacked or mined by us."

"Firing solutions set," announced the ship's gunnery
officer.

"We'll zigzag," the captain said, "with the rockets firing as they bear . . . ummm, when they're pointed in the right direction. Guidance only carries us so far."

"Standing by to fire."

"No!" shouted Alena. She raced to the launch control station as if physically prepared to stop the firing button from being pushed. "Hamilcar must fire! It is written . . . was written, long, long ago. One of the seven signs . . . 'Iskandr shall strike the snake in his den.'"

Gunnery looked at the captain, who shot an inquisitive glance at Johnson.

"Wouldn't do to mess with old prophecy, especially when it's been scarily accurate so far. Hamilcar?"

"Yes, sir."

"Stand by at the launch station. Gunnery officer?" he asked, further, as Hamilcar walked the deck.

"Yes, sir."

Anything special he has to do?"

"No, sir, it's all automated from here."

"Show him what to push and explain when he's to push it."

The gunnery officer simply lifted a green plastic cover from over a red button and turned a dial to an engraved number "1." Pointing, he said, "You'll push this, son. I'll tell you when to fire . . . and . . . ready . . . FIRE!"

Ham's thumb mashed the button, In that instant the ship began to belch flame and shake like a whale in a meg's mouth, as the rockets of the starboard-most battery all launched themselves at the nearest targets and at a combined rate of a dozen every second.

Blow-out panels on the starboard side of the ship flew

off wildly, spinning through the air before slicing into the sea with enormous splashes. Flame and smoke, bright orange and red and dark gray and black, shot out that side twenty meters or more.

Gunnery removed Ham's thumb, then twisted the dial to "2." "Fire now, Ham."

CHAPTER TEN

Many intelligence reports in war are contradictory;
even more are false, and most are uncertain.
                                        —Karl von Clausewitz

UEPF *Spirit of Peace*

The door to the intelligence shop opened automatically.
Esma, always polite, half leaned in and rapped her
knuckles on the inside of the bulkhead. Inside, she saw at
least half a dozen men and women hard at work, scanning
intently or calculating the unknown. Otherwise, the shop
was an antiseptic gray.

Looking up from his monitor, Commander Khan,
husband, smiled brilliantly—it was always a thing of joy
to see the most beautiful ensign on two worlds and one
fleet—and said, "Come in, Esma, please. Have a seat?
Coffee?"

"Thank you, sir, but no. The high admiral sent me to
tell you she would like to be briefed on security down
below at your 'earliest convenience.'"

"It actually isn't very convenient," Khan said. *Which*

is likely why she sent you, rather than use the intercom, so I wouldn't have to make public excuses. "Right now I am . . . well, see for yourself."

Khan gestured at the monitor embedded in the workstation. Esma stepped over and looked down. There seemed to be, faint through the clouds, a large ship, turning hard to its right and leaving behind a churned sea.

"What is it?" she asked. "I mean, yes, I know it's a ship but . . ."

Khan explained, "It's a freighter, a good-sized one, though they use some much bigger down below. We noticed it a little less than an hour and a half ago—as soon as it looked like it would breach the forty-kilometer exclusion zone—and have been tracking it ever since. Waste of time and effort, though, as it turned out, since it's veering away from Atlantis Base at something like full speed."

"Why forty kilometers?" Esma asked.

"Funny," Khan chuckled. "I wondered about that, too, when I first was posted here. Turns out it was the limit of naval cannon gunfire when we dropped nukes on the Federated States, toward the end of the Great Global War they had down below. The dozen or so lasers we mounted to defend the base from aerial attack were sufficient, but no laser in the inventory could stop a thirty- or forty-centimeter spinning steel shell, so we concentrated on bluffing the barbarian states that had battleships and heavy cruisers. We declared the zone then, except for the regular freighter service from Valparaiso, and it was never updated, especially since naval cannon fire, down below, was mostly dispensed with. Anyway, you can stay here, young ensign, if you like. You may learn something useful to you. Meanwhile, I'm going to my day office to get ready for my chat with the high admiral."

Esma nodded, saying, "Yes, I'd like that. Thank you, sir."

Khan turned to go and had actually taken several steps past the hatch when Esma turned and shouted to him. "There's something wrong with that ship! It looks like it's blowing up and burning!"

BdL ALTA

"Holy shit," Ham said, shocked from the shaking, the roar, the fire, and the smoke. Alarms, too, were going off on the bridge as, apparently, there were some uncontrolled fires raging on the starboard side of the missile deck. Ham looked up and, mesmerized, saw a massive cloud of smoke rising ahead.

"Fire now, Ham," the gunnery officer repeated.

"But the . . . yes, sir." Again, the boy looked down and mashed his thumb onto the firing button. Again, the ship recommenced spewing the heavy long-range rockets at a rate of a dozen per second. The color of the flames shooting out to starboard changed slightly.

"They're carrying melted steel and maybe even some burning ferric oxide with them," Gunnery shouted over the incredible roar. "Pay it no mind."

He gave the dial another partial twist, to "3," and then said, "Fire, Ham."

"What if there's a misfired missile with an unexploded warhead?" the boy asked.

"Worst case? Probably the flames torch off the rocket and it at least goes somewhere besides here. There are baffles and barriers, too, to keep it from doing much damage if it explodes on the ship."

"Okay." Again, Ham mashed the button. It all seemed fine until, maybe ten seconds into the salvo, there was an explosion, a very large explosion, in the middle of the port-side array of missiles. That one was quickly followed by two more, and then one more, and a number of smaller ones.

The first blast cracked the glass of the bridge. Alena cried out then moved like lightning, sideways, to put her body between Ham and the blast. The glass of the bridge shattered a fraction of a second later. She cried out again, this time in pain, as one piece sliced her scalp and another embedded itself in her abdomen. She clutched herself and sank to the deck, a long, low moan of agony escaping her lips.

The captain of the ship shrieked as a storm of thin slivers lanced into his face and eyes. He clawed at those, while continuing to scream.

Johnson was more fortunate; whatever any of the smaller fragments might have done, one large piece of glass sliced through his neck, cleaving his jugular. He fell as a kind of blood fountain, spraying a crimson spiral across the bridge as he twisted to the deck. He was either dead or soon to be.

Ham had heard ships alarms before, but nothing like this. There seemed to be half a dozen, all of different quality and frequency, all demanding attention from somebody who knew what he was doing. He heard through a loudspeaker the call for damage control parties to control flooding on one of the lower decks, and an equally insistent call for firefighters for the deck below the missile deck. The missiles—those that had not exploded in their launch racks—continued spewing forth at the same rate of a dozen per second.

There was also an insistent searing pain over Ham's right ear. He ignored that, running around the gunnery station to his "mother in all but womb," Alena.

She looked pale and ghastly but was still awake and alert. He gasped at the blood flowing down her face, coloring her emerald green eyes red, and seeping through the fingers clasped over her abdomen.

He forced tears from his eyes. *No sense in letting her see how bad it looks.*

"Iskandr," she said, "do not worry for me. This ship must survive and the attack must go on. Legate Johnson?"

"Dead," said Ham, after glancing at the still corpse in a pool of blood.

"No one else can do this, then, but you, my lord. Use my husband as your executive, but *you* must command the attack. It was written."

"I will."

Two of the ship's corpsmen, along with a not terribly senior naval officer, a lower grade, and correspondingly short, tribune by the name of Campos, suddenly appeared on the bridge. Already smoke from the successful launches, the resulting fires, and the unplanned explosion was drifting in through the shattered windows.

Gingerly, Ham bent over to kiss Alena's forehead. Before he stood he had to use a sleeve to wipe blood from his lips.

Ham gave an order he had no legal right to give. "Take command of the bridge and the ship until relieved. Keep her afloat. Move us in closer to shore with whatever speed you can get consistent with the damage control effort. I am going to go below and take command of the landing force."

Whether it was the blood dripping down the right side of his face or not, Ham never knew, but whatever it was, the tribune saluted, said, "Yes, sir," and took over the captain's station. As he did, the corpsmen split up, one going to the captain and the other to Alena.

Ham ran to the ladder but stopped, sparing one glance, maybe a last one, at the woman who had, as much as his mother, raised him. Turning away he practically flew down the ladder, then used the ladder as an anchor to spin around to the next one down, and flew through that, too . . .

. . . and entered a kind of hell on earth. There was hot smoke floating in the passageways, and men . . . oh, and boys, too . . . were crying out for help from somewhere deeper in the ship.

He found David Cano, Alena's husband, in consultation with some member of the ship's crew.

"How bad is it?" Ham asked Cano.

"Not as bad as it looks. One maniple of cadets was assembled in one of the corridors under the explosion— what the fuck was the explosion, Ham?—and they're . . . well, not many survivors and those few are too badly hurt. The hovercraft, the tanks, the helicopters, and the Ocelots are all fine. But instead of a dozen maniples of cadets, we have eleven."

"It was one of our own rockets' warheads that went off, David," Ham said. "That set off two or three more. From up top it looks bad, but that's only the top. Ships don't sink from the top up."

"Where's Legate Johnson?" Cano asked.

"He . . . he didn't make it. I am taking command."

"Alena told you to, didn't she?"

"Yes. You would know, if anyone would. She's hurt, by the way. As her husband you've a right to know."

"Will she live?"

"I'm not an expert. She's lost some blood, but she was conscious and alert when I left her. I do think she'll live."

Cano breathed a heartfelt sight of relief. "Thank God for that. As for how I knew, she said that it should be you, if things went to crap. I trust her judgment, even though she is biased where you are concerned. I will follow. Some of the others might have trouble taking orders from a boy, after all. I'll keep them in line."

"Thank you. I'd hate to have to face your wife after she recovers if I hadn't obeyed her orders."

At that, Cano, despite the circumstances, laughed. "You *or* me. Thataboy! Now what are *your* orders?"

"I'm going to go look over the damage. While I'm gone, first, I want . . ."

UEPF *Spirit of Peace*

The ship was already engulfed in smoke by the time Khan returned to the monitor. Sudden eruptions of fire illuminated the smoke inside, flashing like lightning inside a storm system, first here, then there, and then somewhere else.

Khan scrolled in to bring the ship into greater focus. It was only then that he caught the waves of foot-wide somethings surging out from the ship toward the island base.

The blood drained from Khan's face, leaving it a ghastly white. "Oh, shit! Oh, fucking elder gods! The base is under attack!"

There were no other officers present in Intelligence. *No, wait, young Miranda, here, is commissioned.*

"Esma?"

"Sir?"

"I want to you take charge here. Forget the embassies we've been watching. Split your efforts between that ship—dirty bastards waited until they were just about in range before they declared war!—and the island. I've got to go see the high admiral now!"

"Yes, sir! I will, sir."

"Call the high admiral," Khan yelled over his shoulder. "Tell her Atlantis Base is under attack and that I am coming to her quarters!"

BdL ALTA

Ham pressed himself against a bulkhead to allow two men carrying a stretcher to pass. The bearers wore masks. The undersized form on the stretcher, he saw, was blackened and charred over a good part of the body; in places it was impossible to tell what were scraps of burnt cloth and what were strips of skin. Somehow the poor boy on the canvas still hung onto life, whimpering softly into arms crossed over his face.

Taking the implied hint, Ham took a mask from a dispenser and put it on. No more stretchers came. *I wonder why just the one? Maybe they did well getting the wounded out.*

With the stretcher having passed, Ham continued onward. Farther ahead he found the answer to the stretcher question: men and boys, but more of the latter by a factor of twenty, lay, fully equipped but heaped and tangled with each other. The corpses made a solid carpet. Nowhere could Ham see a piece of deck to place a foot; he had to step not just over but onto the bodies to keep going.

Carrera's son shuddered, then muttered, "Dead, all dead; an entire maniple of dead." He was too much his father's son not then to think, *And how do I find replacements for them? For they must be replaced. That, or the plan must change and in a hurry.*

Smoke poured overhead, hugging the top of the passageway, while water—deeply red-tinged, to be sure, with odd bits of solid black in it—eddied around the bodies. Ahead, Ham heard cursing and the sound of high-pressure hoses.

He steeled his heart and soul to what he had to do. Whispering, "Sorry, friends," he stepped onto one of the bodies. That done, the next was easier, and the next easier still. At length, he came to a naval noncom, directing the crews of two hoses. They all wore silvery suits.

"Status?" Ham demanded, briefly lifting the mask off his face.

The noncom didn't turn to look who had asked. Nor did he seem to notice that the asker's voice was young. Lifting his own mask, he leaned sideways toward Ham and shouted, "Iffy, sir. We've got the fires mostly contained down here, but the real problem is up on the missile deck above us; we don't know how many rockets and warheads failed to launch and are still unexploded." The sailor replaced the mask, took a few deep breaths, and continued, "The division chief took himself and another man in fireproof suits to inspect but they haven't come back yet. I'm starting to worry."

Suddenly two men emerged from a side corridor. They moved awkwardly up to the noncom, one man leaning heavily on the other. On closer inspection, that one being half carried had blood seeping through some tears in his silver firefighter's suit.

Said the one helping to carry the other, "No more rockets unexpended, but I think there's a warhead—writing's all burned off so no idea if it's mines or high explosive or FAE or submunitions—sitting on the deck. It's hotter than Hades up there; we've got to fight our way to it and cool it down!"

"Great, sir," said the noncom directing the hose parties.

"Can you do it?" Ham shouted.

"That or die trying," answered the division chief.

"Not good enough. I repeat, 'Can you do it?'"

The division chief answered, "We partly did, using handheld fire extinguishers. Then some little goddamned bomb went off and tore up my sailor, here. I'm going to grab another man, and four more extinguishers. Then we're going to try to get it to where we can shove it over the side. Big gash in the hull, up there, so we might be able to."

Ham felt in the air several noticeable concussions.

"What the hell was that?"

The sailor answered, "Bomblets. Well . . . big bomblets. One of the warheads that went off must have been carrying submunitions. Not a danger to the ship, but it's a danger to the people trying to save the ship."

"Is there anything anybody can do to help you?" Ham asked.

"If you believe in God, pray for us and for the ship!"

"I'll do that, but God helps those who help themselves . . . hmmm, I might have an idea."

"What's that?"

"If we use some demo to open more holes . . ." Ham let the thought trail off, suspecting, even before the division chief said anything, that it wasn't such a good idea.

"Nah, forget it. Explosions sensitize other explosives. A bang near the warhead might be enough to set it off."

"Shit."

"Shit. By the way, son, who are you?"

"Carrera's son. I'm in command—at least now I am— of the landing force."

"Then go worry about that. I'll buy enough time, at a bare minimum, to get the landing force off. But maybe better hurry."

UEPF *Spirit of Peace*

Wallenstein was sitting at her own desk, stunned and even paler than usual, when Khan, the husband, burst in. His wife, Iris, stood behind the high admiral, her hands on the senior woman's shoulders and her head shaking in denial.

Still on the large bed and still showing herself naked from the waist up, the Zhong empress's face had turned to stone.

"Why?" Wallenstein asked, her voice tremulous and unsteady. "Why our base? It has ... no ... well, no serious ... military potential. So *why*? Why this ... this little country? Even the ... the Federated States ... they never dared ... dared to attack us there."

"They probably don't know there's no real military potential," Iris Khan said. "And some people are not rational, thus cannot be deterred."

"And some people," said the stone face over the bed, "simply hate with an inhuman hate, a hate they can never let go. You know, *baobei*; we've spoken of it. That man hates you as I would hate someone who took you from me, or as you would hate someone who took me from you.

"Now you must rise above this, collect yourself, and defend what is yours."

Slowly, Wallenstein nodded. Then, looking up at the male Khan, she asked, "What can we do? Can we sink their ship?"

"We have nothing guided aboard except for the nukes," Khan said. "And those ... well ... we already know the weapons are unreliable ... worse than unreliable, really. I am not too sanguine about the guidance systems, either. And the cost of either aspect failing ... High Admiral, it would not surprise me if the Federated States went fully nuclear on us simply for launching a weapon aimed at their planet."

Marguerite looked imploringly at Xingzhen.

"It would be," said the old-ivory-skinned empress,

"anywhere from a day to several days—I am guessing even as much as a week—before the Celestial Kingdom can assemble and move forces to defend Atlantis Base. Virtually every strategic asset we have has been supporting our enclave in Balboa.

"They *are* coming, love, but it will not be immediate."

"What have we below?" Wallenstein asked.

Khan, the husband, replied, "With the battalion we sent to secure the embassies, there is about one more battalion on Atlantis but...oh, shit...excuse me a moment, High Admiral."

Moving to an intercom, Khan raised his own shop and asked to speak to Esmeralda. "Ensign," he asked, "what's happening on the base?"

Von der Leyen Barracks, Atlantis Base

Show any military veteran with two spare brain cells to rub together a map of a town in which there is a military garrison and ask him to find the barracks. He'll pinpoint those in anywhere from minutes even down to seconds. There are simply certain common features, common anywhere and any-when man had set up a concentrated military presence, that screams, "Here sleep the soldiers." It is partly a question of size, partly of relative positioning, partly of regularity, and partly other, more subtle, indicia.

Thus, when Fernandez's organization had analyzed Atlantis Base from, among other things, photographs brought back by aerial recon flights, there had never really been a moment's doubt but that the barracks—they had no clue about the name—was the major military installation on the base.

As such, literally dozens of heavy rockets had been scheduled for it.

The barracks were not, as it turned out, as well manned as Fernandez's boys and girls had thought. Indeed, there was space enough here for more than twice as many security personnel, here at the Consensus's main base, as it currently held. The rest were either securing embassies, the sixteen deemed most at risk, or in one of the three platoon-sized reaction forces set out to the same end, or out in one of the five small camps a few kilometers inland from the coast. In the barracks themselves, exclusive of dependents, clerks, and cooks, were a scant six hundred and twenty-seven black-uniformed men and women, officers and enlisted, both.

With klaxons sounding from every quarter, and lasers criss-crossing the sky, overhead, the scene outside the buildings was chaos, with near riots breaking out at the doors to company arms rooms, people pushing and shoving, half-naked personnel trying to pull on boots or combat harnesses.

Virtually all the personnel stopped as one as, from off in the distance, there came the sound of masses of very large explosions. The sounds all began and ended in the space of under half a minute. Spontaneously, the frenzied attempts to get ready for action resumed. Ten seconds later, someone—several someones, actually—shouted as one of the parade fields to the south erupted with what looked to be the equivalent of between sixty and eighty sixty-millimeter mortar shells.

But those had to have come from somewhere. Eyes began scanning the skies. It wasn't long at all before one of the security men pointed upwards to several newly forming dark clouds.

That man hardly had time to shout, "Look! There!" before the clouds descended. Von der Leyen Barracks was shortly engulfed by a storm of shells, little just under four-pound bomblets, that rolled across the scene like a wave. In places, standing or running troops found themselves in the middle of the shell storm, buffeted by concussion from all sides, their bodies likewise perforated from all sides by the masses of average seventy-grain splinters each bomblet threw out.

Oddly, there were still men and women standing, unharmed or only slightly hurt. They stood unsteadily, swaying to and fro, uncertain whether to be grateful or not that they still lived. But around them, whole sections and platoons writhed and screamed in agony or bled silently in death.

The question of gratitude was moot, as it turned out, because the next salvo consisted of a mix of unitary high explosive and fuel-air explosive warheads. With terrible accuracy, the high explosive hit the roofs and upper walls of the old barracks, drove in, and then detonated. Light shards and heavy sections of masonry burst outward from the blasts. More Earthers fell under that hail.

The fuel-air explosive, on the other hand, seemed to have been aimed for open areas. Anyone unfortunate enough to be found still alive and conscious quickly found themselves amidst clouds of explosive aerosol and then in the middle of quasi-nuclear explosions. The lucky died soonest, the unlucky got to experience both massive overpressure, massive burning, and then minimal enough air pressure that their lungs were literally ripped from their chests and, in some cases, halfway through their mouths. They didn't really need their lungs anymore, anyway, since the FAE warheads had ensured a level of oxygen in the area less than sufficient to maintain life.

Miniature mushroom clouds began rising all over the caserne area, "almost a half dozen of them," later said one of the few survivors in a position to see. And then came the last rockets, the ones bearing a mix of antivehicular and antipersonnel mines.

CHAPTER ELEVEN

Land the landing force. —Traditional

BdL ALTA

An IM-71 shuddered and hopped on the pickup area of the rear deck. Into it shuffled a short line of cadets with one or two adults for leadership. Another waited at the top of the ramp that led down to the helicopter storage and maintenance deck, while a third had just taken off. Toward the shore, the peaks of the island just now becoming visible, seven attack helicopters, Volgan-built IM-53Bs, screened inward. If there *were* hidden laser or missile defenses, these would have a chance, at least, of taking them out.

"Turns out we lost the drone crews from the intelligence platoon," Cano told Ham once he had navigated his way back to the stern. He could only be heard over the loading, taking off, or winding up of helicopters by shouting at the top of his lungs. "I didn't know before because they weren't part of the landing force. We're going to be going in blind."

Oh, joy, thought Hamilcar. He felt, however, the same mental and emotional detachment that he'd had when thinking about replacing the lost company of cadet infantry. "Are the drones, themselves, all right?"

"Yes," Cano said, "and the launch crews are fine, too. It was the operators who got caught in the blast. Well, them and the control station."

"Is there a backup control station?"

"I don't know. Johnson or the captain would have known, I suppose."

"Where do I find the launch crew?"

Cano pointed to the superstructure, forward of the helicopter loading deck. "They're up there. One deck down. They lost a lot of friends and are pretty dejected."

Carrera found them where he'd been told. These were adults, rather than cadets, full members of the legions.

"We don't have a lot of time for commiseration," he said. "Yes, I'm sorry you lost friends. I've lost friends, too. But we have a job to do and we need to do it. Now is there a backup control station for the drones?"

The half dozen men of the launch crew looked pained. None of them said anything at first. Then one spoke up. His name tag read "Wilson," which Ham took to mean he came from Cristobal.

"Not as such," Wilson said. "But there is a simulator about five layers of containers down. Maybe we could rig something up with that. It's got everything we need *except* wireless."

"What do you need for it?" Ham asked.

The crewman considered. "A frequency-hopping radio, AM. Some wire. Some time."

"We don't have a lot of time," Ham said. "Who can fly a drone?"

Everybody looked down, sheepishly. Finally, the same man put up his hand and admitted, "Probably any of us. We weren't supposed to but we used to use the simulator whenever the regular flight crews weren't using it."

The hand was still up. When Ham asked who was senior, it stayed there. "But that's not much. I'm a private first class and the rest of these shitheads are privates. That's how we ended up on the launch detail."

"How many drones can the simulator handle?"

"No more than two."

"Two is better than nothing. Here's what I want you to do. First, I want you to get out and set up two recon drones . . . no, make it three in case we crash one. Second, though preferably simultaneously, I want that simulator modified or whatever needs to be done to it so it can control two recon drones. Third, I want them in the air, over the sea, above the island, and feeding us intel. Oh, and you'll need another radio for that and another antenna, and the radio has to be on our hopping schedule, our code."

Nobody moved. They all just sat there.

"Umm," said the man who had been the only one to speak, so far, "just who the hell are you, sonny boy?"

"I'm Hamilcar Carrera, son of the *Duque*, and right now . . ."

He never did get the sentence finished, as the launch crew, like a single man, exploded into action.

And still I find I'm dependent on the old man's name. Someday I'll have my own name to reckon with.

UEPF *Spirit of Peace*

Wallenstein seemed to wilt in her office chair, to sink in upon herself. On the desk's monitor, little mushroom clouds spouted over craters, large and small, over ruined buildings, and over smashed and bleeding bodies.

Now where, she asked herself, *just where have I seen something like this before?* Aloud she muttered, "Be all my sins remembered. He, at least, has never forgotten them."

"We have skimmers from the base over the enemy ship now," Khan, husband, announced. "Putting it through to your monitor, High Admiral."

Wallenstein looked at the screen and gasped. True, the enemy ship was still smoking and, in a few places, burning. But the smoke seemed to be lessening even as she watched, while one section of flame disappeared over the course of a minute.

They're not going to sink now.

The damaged ship, though, wasn't the cause of the gasp. Rather, it was the steady stream of helicopters, hovercraft, and smaller amphibious vehicles departing the ship for the shore. Indeed, already some of the helicopters seemed to be on the return trip.

"How many?" she asked Khan, male.

"Hard to say, High Admiral, but there are at least twenty cargo helicopters and some of what they call 'gunships,' six or seven of them. That's a one-lift capability of six hundred or so. I would think the hovercraft could carry two hundred men, each, though these seem to be each carrying a brace of armored vehicles instead. The little ones that plunged into the water . . . there are twenty-four of those we've seen and they can probably each carry eight men. So they can put in about a thousand men or so per lift. Now as to how many are *aboard* the ship; that I can only guess at. Several thousand, anyway, I would think. And quite possibly a lot more armored vehicles. Maybe artillery . . . well, probably artillery, given their national taste for it."

"And we have what to resist them?"

Khan scrunched his eyes, as if thinking and remembering hard. "Stretching a point, after the destruction of von der Leyen caserne, maybe two hundred men and women, most of them more on the order of a police force or gendarmerie than a combat organization. They probably don't have anything—yes, I have one of my people trying to find out—to fight a tank or even a lighter combat vehicle. Against Balboa's—I assume these people must be from Balboa; anyway, against Balboa's hardened regulars they won't stand a chance. They probably wouldn't stand a chance if the Balboans were using spears, and they most certainly are *not* using spears.

"These are not, after all, real Marines; those are almost all at the embassies or were caught at von der Leyen caserne."

As if in punctuation, on Marguerite's monitor the first of the hovercraft ran itself up on the shore, coming to a fast stop amidst a cloud of sand, and dropping the ramp. Within mere moments, all securing straps apparently undone, two tanks slithered down the ramp, then churned sand to take up station facing inland. The hovercraft then lifted off, again in that huge cloud of blown sand, twisted around its axis, then moved back to the shoreline. Its only obstacle was a second hovercraft, for which the first yielded right of way.

Khan, the wife, corrected her husband. "They're not regulars, actually. Or very few of them are. They've mostly reservists and cadets. Their leadership tends to be regular."

Marguerite had a sudden thought, prompted by Iris's mention of cadets.

"He's used children to humiliate our allies down below before. What does it do," she asked, "to your estimate of the enemy force, if most of it is composed of kids?"

Khan, the husband, looked down, plainly thinking hard. After that moment's reflection, he raised his head and answered, "Maybe increase it by a quarter or so, High Admiral."

Wallenstein wilted internally still more. *All my sins remembered and the punishment poetic in form. In aiding Martin to help Mustafa attack those buildings all these years ago, I indirectly killed children. Some of them were Carrera's children. Now the child cousins of those murdered children come for me and mine and the families of mine.*

It would be so comforting to just surrender, but I can't. It isn't in me. I must still try—I have to—even when the odds are, as they are now, all against me. And even when I deserve what I'm getting. I deserve it; my people—most of them, anyway—do not. Their families surely do not. So I will try.

Where for a moment she had been a wilted flower, Marguerite seemed then to grow in her chair. "We fight," she said, as if answering a question someone had actually asked.

"I want three things to happen. First, loot the ships of the fleet's arms rooms and cannibalize ship's personnel. Second, use the landers to get as many down to defend the perimeter of the base as we can get down there. Third, get our ambassador in Hamilton, in the Federated States, to request an emergency meeting with their president. Tell him I will speak to their president via communicator. Fourth, get three nuclear weapons—who's in the best launch position?"

"*Spirit of Brotherhood*, I think."

Wallenstein buried her face into cupped hands. *It had to be; elder gods, why did it have to be Battaglia? No help for it now.*

Looking up again, she ordered, "Get Battaglia on it, then, tell him to get three ready for launch. Pick the ones most likely to have a reliable guidance package. They are not to be armed. I'll explain to the FSC that this is an attack in defense of our homes and families . . ."

Quarters Twenty-one, Atlantis Base

A maid, now in middle age, scrubbed a polished marble floor on her hands and knees. Sometimes, in the course of her lowly duties, the maid wept.

Once upon a time, Irene Temujin had been an important functionary in Amnesty Interplanetary, a subsidiary of the Marquisate of Amnesty, based on Old Earth. Then she had been tricked and publicly humiliated, so publicly that her value to Amnesty had been reduced to, essentially, nothing. Following that, after a series of very pointed and utterly credible and totally frightful *promises*, Irene had asked for sanctuary from the UEPF. She'd gotten that but, rather than being whisked off to a life approximating the one of privilege in which she'd grown up, she'd found herself deposited on Atlantis Base as a mere *menial*, indeed, legally an indentured servant, one step above a slave. Her immediate family, likewise, had been found work, and that no better than her own. She saw them only on her one day a month off, and then only when schedules coincided.

She never saw her husband. Indeed, she avoided seeing him. In the first place, unlike her, he had some skills considered valuable by their owners. Hence he had a much better job at an office building on the base. She found this humiliating, for she had always been the major breadwinner for the family. Far worse, though; as an indentured servant, she had lost the right of refusal, hence had to accept the sexual advances of anyone on the estate who outranked her, which was almost everyone but the outright slaves. She'd tried to refuse, at first, but the subsequent whipping had also beaten any sense of defiance out of her completely. When she let her guard down she could sometimes still feel the short whip the house overseer had used on her naked, lacerated, bleeding flesh, as she hung by her bound wrists from a hook set in a basement ceiling.

She could not bring herself to face her husband after so many violations.

Her daughter, much younger and also rather prettier than Irene had ever been, never talked about her life as a servant. Irene assumed, correctly, that the daughter's life was even more degraded and degrading than her own.

Worse, one of her sons, Arpan, having seen what the system of Atlantis Base really was, and understanding what that said about old Earth under the Consensus, had spoken a little too freely. *Him*, she had not seen in two years, ever since his indenture had been converted into actual slavery. Her last, tear-filled glimpse of her boy had been as he was led from the auction block in the center of town. It was then that she'd realized that old Earth's masters, the high-caste sons and daughters of the Consensus, didn't keep slaves because they needed to; they kept them because they *preferred* to.

If I had known then . . . what? This: If I had known then what I know now, when Esterhazy came to see me and threaten me, I'd have joined forces with the mercenaries— or "auxiliaries," as they insisted they were—to fight old Earth and Amnesty to the death. It would be better than this living death.

Feeling tears begin to form, Irene wiped her eyes with the sleeve of her shapeless, coarse garment. *Esterhazy was right*, she thought, *right to threaten me and even mine then, for I was a pompous, self-important ass, serving evil and hiding from my sight the evil I served, so long as I was admired and my life very, very comfortable.*

And then she heard something unlike anything she'd heard since leaving Sumer under a cloud, years ago. *It's not a shuttle, not even the high admiral's barge. I wonder . . . it's a rocket, a war rocket.*

She gasped and caught her breath. *What could it mean, a war rocket here? Is the place under attack? Be still my heart. If it is, I must find the attackers and offer them my aid, whatever little bit an indentured servant can hope to give.*

BdL ALTA

A small group of soldiers, some adults, some cadets, some bearing radios and others only small arms, clustered about Ham, waiting for the currently loading chopper to take off and the next one, refueling at a pad a bit forward, to come over. The helicopters were moving as much logistically now as they were in terms of tooth. Long lines of sailors pulling loaded carts waited for the helicopters to come for their loads.

Up the ramps also came the first of two SPLADs, Self-Propelled Laser Air Defense systems, plus four of the nonlaser-armed versions, the ones with the quad cannons and radar. These began to take up stations around the ship.

Inside the circle of men and boys about Ham, a package sat on a light amphibious vehicle, a Volgan Model 967, from which both the roll-guard rails and windshield had been removed. It was almost exactly sixty centimeters across and close enough to one and one-third meters long. Silvery steel in color, it bore both markings in *Hangul* as well as two symbols indicating radiation danger. The yield wasn't listed but Ham knew that it, and its brother device, were rated for at *least* one hundred and sixty-five kilotons.

Next to the nuclear weapon sat a small metal box, a Faraday cage, about the size of a box of heavy machine gun ammunition.

"That's half the force ashore," Cano said to Hamilcar. "Time for you to go, too. I'll see things from here."

"I'll go with this first bomb," Ham said, "next chopper. Send the second right after. Also . . ."

"Yes?" Cano asked.

"I want the wounded evacuated to shore. Moreover, I want your wife moved soonest."

"I can't argue with those orders."

UEPF *Spirit of Peace*

"I have no choice, Mr. President," High Admiral Wallenstein said to the image on her monitor. She'd delayed the call for the few extra minutes it had taken her communications people to set up a teleconference. "Those people are attacking our base, our families, our innocent noncombatants. Every minute I delay means more of them get ashore. I cannot delay much."

The face in the monitor, that of the president of the Federated States, Walter Madison Howe, seemed quite serious, indeed. Marguerite couldn't tell that crossing his mind was the key and critical thought, *I wonder if she swallows.*

Whatever he might have been thinking, Howe's answer was fairly rote, "I cannot permit . . ."

Wallenstein's blue eyes flashed. "Let me make this clear, Mr. President, I am not asking you to permit a fucking thing. I am going to drop three packages on that ship. If you want to make war over it, be my guest, but Earth and the Consensus can build a new fleet. Where are you going to find a new country?

"Now, if it's any consolation or help to you, they're going to be inert. My people are taking the nuclear weapons out of the shells now and filling them with scrap to increase the kinetic energy. So you won't have to worry about trying to explain away three large mushroom clouds to your constituency, nor why you didn't go to war over them. But I *am* launching and I am putting my fleet on alert to turn your cities into green glass if you attack us over it."

Except for his harridan of a wife, Howe was *used to more compliant and submissive females than this high admiral chick.* His earlier thought changed to, *I wonder if she bites. Best not to find out the hard way, no pun intended.*

Howe turned his attention to his military aide, Major General Jeff Lamprey. Lamprey, who had reasons for detesting Carrera that went way back to Sumer, and was a petty, priggish sort, even before that, wrote down, *This doesn't threaten or damage us. I think you should let them do it.*

Howe read the note and then said, "All right, Admiral Wallenstein, three inert packages delivered to the vicinity of your base, in self-defense. I'll stand our forces down."

Lamprey thought, *And I finally get to pay that motherfucker back. Sweet!*

Wallenstein cut the connection, then said to herself, *All that acting practice fucking my way up the chain of command seems to have paid off. How many lies was that I told? Three? One thing's not a lie, though, those things* are *going down inert, if only because I don't want the Federated States sending one of their submarines to recover them. Who knows what one of them might tell about whether the rest are likely to work or not?*

Of course, armaments are among the weakest departments in the fleet. Nobody's taken them all that seriously in the last seventy years. I don't know . . . hmmm . . . as a matter of fact, I don't *know . . .*

"Computer, get me Captain Battaglia on *Spirit of Brotherhood*."

"Calling."

A distracted-looking face appeared on the screen. "Yes, High Admiral?"

"What's the status in getting those packages ready to fire?"

"I'm not sure . . ."

"Never mind. Put me through to your gunnery officer."

There was a brief delay before a lieutenant commander's face showed on the monitor. Behind him some sweating, cursing noncoms and yeomen could be seen trying to crack open a metal casing. The lieutenant commander seemed terribly flustered.

"Yes, High Admiral?"

"How long before we're ready to launch?" Wallenstein asked.

"I could launch now," said the officer, "except you want the nuclear packages removed and we're still trying to figure out how. They were made to be maintained *in situ*, and apparently nobody ever considered we might want to send down the shell alone."

Shit.

"Keep me posted. Indeed, keep me posted directly."

Marguerite broke the connection, then ordered the computer, "Get me flight operations."

The monitor changed scene to the flight deck of *Peace*, where a couple of dozen nervous-looking crewmen were lined up to board one of the landers.

"High Admiral?" answered one of the hangar deck crew.

"Have we any weapons we could mount on a lander to provide ground support?" she asked.

"Nothing comes to mind. We have some machine guns on the ship, yes, but there are no mounts and, even if we had something like that, no controls that penetrate the hull and nothing I can think of for remote control that wouldn't take a couple of days to gin up and test. Why do you ask, ma'am?"

"There's a delay in rendering the nuclear packages inert. I need something to attack that ship."

"We can land on it."

Now why didn't I think of that?

While a good many of the members of the crews of the Peace Fleet looked in their twenties and could measure their years in centuries, Spaceman Bethany Wallace, brunette and a bit too thin for current tastes, really was in her twenties. Following orders to draw a weapon—but no ammunition—from the arms room and report to the hangar deck, she didn't expect to get much older, either. She was also one of those pulled by High Admiral Wallenstein from the academy, back home, to fill up the ranks in the Peace Fleet.

"Wallace; over here," said Petty Officer, Third Class Christopher Robin, light skinned, bearded, and a little bit stout. Robin was fortunate that no one on Old Earth even remembered the stories of Winnie the Pooh anymore, nor had for generations, or his childhood, over a century ago, would have been a misery.

The gravity on the hangar deck was paltry, but she had magnetized shoes to let her put one foot in front of the other and join him. It was an awkward kind of walk, and especially so for those, who, like Bethany, had little cause ever to go to the hangar deck.

"You're in my group for this," Robin announced. He reached into a bag slung over his shoulder and passed her several hundred rounds' worth of preloaded four-millimeter ammunition.

"Chris," she said, holding up her carbine, "I haven't touched one of these—I haven't so much as *looked* at one of these since my first year at the academy. I don't know what I'm doing."

Robin sighed. "Almost nobody does. We have to hope that what's going on down below doesn't take Marines to handle."

"Hope's not a plan," she replied. "I remember that much from first year, at least."

Beach Red, Atlantis Island, ten kilometers north of the base

Both bombs were ashore now, with a platoon detailed to prepare them for sling loading under one of the helicopters and guard them until the slingload was in the air. Their control boxes were with Ham, on one of the two 967s that had come in with the bombs.

All the troops were ashore now or enroute, along with eight Jaguar tanks, two dozen Ocelot Infantry Fighting Vehicles, plus one short battery of light artillery.

Ham reached for a radio handset, passed over by an eager young cadet. This was for the general push, so every maniple and cohort would hear it.

The basic plan was Johnson's. Ham hadn't written it, but he knew it. They'd rehearsed it verbally and on map exercises so much that every man and boy knew it.

"All stations, this is headquarters. Commence Operation Roundup. I say again, commence Operation Roundup."

BdL ALTA

While the dead and wounded on the bridge had been taken away, shattered glass still littered the deck. Along with the shards of glass, the deck was also liberally covered with sticky, drying blood.

Tribune Campos would have had to stand on a crate to see properly, except that the blinded skipper's chair could be elevated. He sat on that, watching as little by little the smoke from the fires disappeared and the flames feeding that smoke went out.

Fortunately, the comms had never gone out, except in some of the forward sections that had been blasted by the rockets' warheads. For those, he had radio communications.

He also knew that the officer in charge of damage control outranked him, rather badly, and should have taken command. But that officer had judged, perhaps rightly, that getting the fires under control and unexpended ordnance over the side was more important.

Fat lot of good if we all get court-martialed.

The problem was that, while the ship was naval, the crew and officer arrangements had been, more or less, mercantile, with only minor increases. The extras who had come aboard had mainly been for the mission, not the ship. There were officers in plenty—*well, as plenty as the legionary system allows, anyway*—from the tribune commanding the helicopter squadron to the one in charge of the hovercraft to the commanders, executive officers, platoon leaders, and staff of the landing force. But plenty hadn't meant an increase in naval crew beyond what they'd set out with.

And so this devolves on me because, as it happens, I can command the ship better than I can do damage control.

Now Campos *had*, at least, been able to scrape together a replacement bridge crew, someone to steer, someone for communications, someone to keep the tactical map ashore updated, that kind of thing.

"Message from damage control forward, sir," said the sailor in charge of communications.

"Campos, here."

"Campos, we have something of a problem. We got the warhead that was on deck cooled down enough to try to push it over the side."

"That's great, sir!"

"You would think so, wouldn't you? But here's the

problem one of the party pointed out to me. We still don't know what it is. If it's bomblets and they go off underwater they probably won't hole the hull. Mines? Meh. Fuel Air Explosive . . . key word there is 'air,' and there isn't any under the water.

"But if it's HE, high explosive . . . and if that HE goes off next to the hull . . . well . . . five hundred pounds, give or take of high explosive, while we're passing over it? Might as well be a torpedo."

"Could use the bow thrusters," Campos offered.

"Coanda effect."

"Shit, yeah," Campos said. "No use even trying if we're doing even three knots. So what do we do?"

"For what I'm thinking, I think I'm crazy, so I want a second opinion."

"Shoot, sir."

"The gantry crane. It doesn't look to have taken any damage. We roll it up to where the bomb lays and lift it. But before we lift it we wire the bomb for sound, then set it off when it's as high as we can lift it."

"Wish we had a rotary crane," Campos said.

"Yeah, but wish in one hand and shit in the other . . ."

"I know; see which one fills up faster. But wait; I just realized; yes, you're crazy."

"How so?"

"What if it *is* an FAE?"

"Shit, I must be getting old. That would be very bad, son, very bad indeed. Much worse than HE going off overhead, though not as bad as HE going off under the keel. Right, no controlled detonation for us. So what then?"

"You want my opinion, sir? Pack it carefully so it won't

roll. I'll do everything possible to keep the ship steady until you relieve me. And then I'll go down to the containers under the bomb, with whatever manpower we can scrape together, and sort out key supplies and get them ashore."

"Yeah, okay. Just do our best to live with it, huh? I think you're right . . . okay . . . I'm on my way."

Latifundia Mixcoatl, Atlantis Island

The former ambassador to Santa Josefina, Claudia Nyere—despite her name, as white as any Nordic—was at loose ends. She'd had a job until recently and had rather enjoyed it; it, and the prestige and perks.

Not that she harbored any ill will toward the high admiral, oh, no, *But for Wallenstein's intervention and buying me back from the barbarians who'd captured me, I have absolutely no doubt they're have dismembered me and sent me back a piece at a time . . . and in not very large pieces.*

Imagine treating a well-connected and properly credentialed Class One like that! Barbarian scum!

Of course, there were compensations to being out of a job; Nyere had always had to put on a friendly and caring face before the Santa Josefinans. She'd had to treat the embassy staff, the local elements of it, with consideration, too. That had been galling—treating lowers as if they were real people rather than highly expendable, individually unimportant, organic machinery.

She didn't have to treat the slaves of her *latifundia* well, though. If any of them had had any doubt of that, the one hanging from a cross by the slave barracks would have reminded them.

She looked at the writhing almost man, occasionally howling with agony from pierced and shattered wrists and heels. At the foot of a cross wept a young girl, perhaps his special girl.

Claudia nodded with approval. *It's better when slaves understand that their actions cause pain not just to themselves, but to those they care about. As to what to do about the slut . . . maybe nothing except to turn her over to the field hands.*

Raising her eyes from the brokenhearted girl back to the victim, she thought, *Not much more than a boy, really.* He, *certainly, won't be inciting rebellion anymore.*

She wasn't sure of the victim's name—*who bothers to learn the names of any slaves they're not using for sex, anyway?*—but she remembered him as the offspring of one of the locals, some woman who had once figured prominently in one of the front organizations the fleet and the Consensus maintained on the planet. He'd only gone up on the cross that morning, so would likely last as an excellent example to the rest for at least another two or three days.

A waste, in a way, when I could have sacrificed him to Mixcoatl, but that's altogether too quick, painless, and honorable for a disloyal slave.

Ambassador Nyere—she was still entitled to the title, even though out of a posting—turned her attention from the slowly expiring boy, who certainly didn't matter, anyway, when she heard explosions—some loud and near, others distant and weak—coming from just about every direction.

She rang for her majordomo, a portly and unusually dignified slave, older and balding, and dark like almost all her human chattels.

"What are those noises?" she asked, when the majordomo arose from his proskynesis.

"I don't know, mistress. Shall I find out?"

"You shouldn't have to ask," she informed the slave. "Your duty is to anticipate my wishes and meet them in advance."

The majordomo didn't point out that he'd heard the explosions at the exact same time his owner had, so could hardly have anticipated anything, and had spent the intervening time running to her summons. Instead, bowing deeply, he backed away.

Trotting to the slave barracks, the majordomo summoned two of the drovers for the property, both, like himself, slaves, and both, like himself, trusted. "Take a horse each," he ordered. "You, Pablo, follow the north road. Francisco, go south. When you see anything unusual, turn around and report back."

"Unusual like what?" Pablo asked.

"If I knew *that*," said the chief slave of the property, "I wouldn't need to send *you* out, now *would* I?"

"Fine," said Pablo, "we go. Any problem we put little weepy girl, whose boy we nailed up, on all fours and arse to the sky when we get back?"

"I don't see a problem. Only hurry; don't take over an hour."

"Yes, boss."

CHAPTER TWELVE

It's a Vietnamese soup that answers the question, "What happens when a former child soldier pours hot rain water over fish nightmares." It's delicious and I can't stop eating it, that's what happens.

—Kyle Kinane

BdL ALTA

Air Defense Station Number One was just a reinforced spot on the deck next to a hatch up which ammunition could be passed, and from which a normally ground-based air defense weapon could command a significant arc of fire. To its right and slightly forward, the SPLAD—Self-Propelled Laser Air Defense—likewise sat. Number Two had no hatch for ammunition, but did have a connection for the system to hook into ship's power rather than relying on its own. Three was a mirror of One, currently sweeping from about one hundred and thirty-five degrees sternward to just past the bow. The cannon for One and Three were water-cooled, a necessity given their caliber, rate of fire, and design.

It was Number Two, the laser, that first picked up the incoming targets. Rather, what it picked up was bounceback from its detection and timing laser, which bounceback, given the speed of light, meant that a) there was something there worth shooting and b) *oh, frabjous day, you can shoot it, o machine*.

Unfortunately, the main laser wasn't powerful enough to do anything to an aircraft, itself. Instead, it was intended to blind the pilot so that he lost control of his plane to that agonizing blindness, then crashed, and died. Proven quite effective in the air war over Balboa, when facing Tauran Union jets, it did absolutely nothing to the UEPF's incoming landers. Rather, if it had any effect, it was tolerably hard for the crew to see any.

The commander of Number One, tracking the incoming lander with binoculars, also found it tolerably hard to see after the bounceback from the main laser assaulted his eyes. Fortunately, it was only painful, causing him to swear and see spots. If he'd been on the brunt of it, blindness, total and permanent, would have followed.

If the SPLAD proved useless, not so, however, the gun-armed models. Left and right of Number Two's laser, boxy turrets, each mounting four small-caliber cannon and a radar emitter, automatically elevated the cannon and slewed around. Number Three fired first, though, right on its heels, Number One continued the burst into one long one of exactly four hundred rounds, fifty each from each barrel from each system, in a mix of three high explosive to one armor piercing.

No one knew how many hit. The chief of Number One

estimated something on the order of eighty hits before the target literally disintegrated in the air. But then, he thought he saw some of the pieces of the lander waving arms and legs and clawing at the air in what appeared to be desperate attempts to fly.

The chief blinked his eyes, which hurt like the devil, actually, from flashback from Number Two's laser. "Must have been the laser fucking with them," he thought. "No way anybody survived those hits."

He radioed to Number Two, "Hey, your laser isn't doing a damned thing. How about turning it off until we have reason to expect a target you can deal with?"

"Roger," came the reply.

Already, the crew of One and Three were feeding the next four belts of fifty, in expectation of another target.

UEPF *Spirit of Peace*

Marguerite watched the lander disintegrate in midair. She cursed herself, specifically for, *Thirty irreplaceable crewmen, gone for nothing.*

"Call off any further attempts to land on the ship itself," she ordered. "Send the forces to defend the base." *Shit; I should have known my enemy would not leave his weapon vulnerable to anything so predictable. And I wonder, now, why I didn't think of* that, *either.*

Switching channels, rather, having the ship's computer do so for her, she asked once again for the lieutenant commander in charge of gunnery.

"We've got one nuclear package pulled, High Admiral.

The next two should go a little quicker now that we know how."

"Ten minutes? Twenty?" she asked, impatiently.

"Maybe a little longer; I think I can promise disarmed, loaded, and ready to fire in thirty."

"Thirty," she agreed, while wondering, *Do I demote or get rid of this guy, for not being ready, or promote him for figuring it out? Probably promote, because we're probably going to have a do a crash program to get our nukes on line again, if they* can *be brought on line again.*

The second lander in order of march was the one holding Bethany Wallace. She watched the point lander on the screen as it disintegrated. She saw crewmen, too, seemingly trying to fly as they fell to certain death in the sea, below. She stuffed her knuckles in her mouth to stifle a scream, then began praying silently to whatever she hoped might be out there and concerned with human events enough to save her.

With relief she saw on the screen and felt in her guts and inner ear the sharp turn that brought the lander around and the sudden thrust that pushed her back against the seat.

I am NOT trained for this! Not! Not! NOT!

Still in intel, where she'd effectively attached herself since the beginning of the crisis, Esmeralda was still following the ship-to-shore attack on the base. Khan, husband, asked her for a progress report.

"They seem to have all their men ashore," she answered. "Supplies, too, I'd guess; at least enough of them. Their helicopters, the bigger ones, began to fan out across the island a few minutes ago carrying soldiers."

"Heading for where?" Khan asked.

"No*where* in particular, sir. If I had to guess . . ."

"Go on, Ensign; what would be your guess?"

"Well . . . I followed a few of them. They're flying low, hugging the ground . . ."

"They call it 'Nap Of the Earth,' or 'NOE,' down below."

"All right, sir, 'NOE' works for me. Anyway, they're following . . . NOE, so they're changing direction so much that none of them appear to have a particular target. But—remember, sir, I am *guessing*—I think they're heading for the *latifundia*, or for about half of them anyway.

"Why would they do that?" Esma finished.

The latifundia . . . *the ambassador to Santa Josefina . . . we sent her back to hers after our embassy in Aserri went under . . . and she was . . . oh, fuck.*

Khan didn't answer, directly. Instead, he cursed and then asked the computer to call directly to Wallenstein.

The high admiral's lover answered, "Xingzhen?"

"Your Imperial Majesty, this is Khan, male. I must speak to the high admiral."

After a short delay came the words, "Yes, Commander?" Wallenstein spoke with a calm she didn't feel. There was something at the heart of this attack, something unspeakable, and she had the unshakeable conviction that it had to do with her and her actions under her predecessor.

"I know . . . I *think* I know . . . what this attack is about. All praise to your girl, Esma, for figuring it out; at least figuring out a key part. But High Admiral, the barbarians are going for *hostages*."

"Are you certain?"

"It all makes sense. Think about the damage they did to von der Leyen caserne. With everything else, they could have as easily obliterated the base for the use of that much firepower. If they'd wanted just to hurt us, they didn't need to land ground troops, no assault guns, no tanks, no helicopters or hovercraft.

"But they sent all those things. They sent them despite the greater security risk that kind of force represented. Why? It's as clear as a bell: they intend to take hostages."

"Why?"

"Our nukes," Khan answered. "They're afraid we'll use our nukes on them to settle the problem they represent. Hostages prevent that."

"But our nukes . . ." Wallenstein let the thought peter out.

"Yes," Khan said, "our nukes are terribly old, hence unreliable, and probably, in fact, do not work. But they don't *know* that."

Esma, unnoticed at her desk, kept her face carefully neutral while thinking, *Oh, yes, they do. So they're taking hostages, Commander; you're right about that. But they have another purpose in mind for it. I wish I understood better how Carrera really thought . . .*

Beach Red, Atlantis Island

The helicopters could normally carry twenty-six soldiers and their equipment. The cadets who made up most of the maniples weighed rather less, though; thirty-seven were stuffed onto each, along with one or two fully grown adults.

It was cramped, of course, but comfort counted for little—less than nothing, really—under the circumstances.

The platoons of cadets were odd in one particular way. No one had had any idea what language or languages would be spoken by the Peace Fleet personnel or their staffs actually on the base, so each platoon carried on its rolls at least one English speaker, one French, one German, one Russian, and one Italian. *Everybody* spoke Spanish. Chinese and Japanese? There just weren't enough of those in Balboa to have made a difference.

One of the first helicopters to have carried a platoon out came back, having dropped its load of infantry onto what appeared to be the headquarters of a large farm. With the rotor churning the air overhead and raising a choking cloud of dust, a singing platoon hustled aboard, the cadet noncoms prodding and even kicking the younger and junior boys into their places. Ham watched them fill the cargo deck. Even after that, many had to stand, grabbing whatever handhold could be found.

Over the sound of rotor and engine, Hamilcar heard a familiar old song:

"In the morning we rise early
Long before the break of dawn,
Trixies screeching in the jungle,
Moonbats scurrying from the sun.

Now assemble, *mis compadres*.
Gather, boys, and muster, men,
Hand to hand with butt and bayonet,
Let their blood across the homeland run.

And you are welcome, *Balboenses*.
Side by side we'll make our stand
Hand to hand with butt and bayonet.
We'll rise up together with the Legions then
Rise up together with the Legions then . . ."

The platoon sergeant was a senior cadet rather than an adult. He was also an old friend and comrade. Cadet Jorge Rodrigues, black and very, very slender, waved from the helicopter's ramp, smiled happily, then stood to attention and saluted.

Still skinny as a rail, Ham thought, *even though you can eat enough for three boys.*

For his part Ham likewise stood to attention and solemnly returned Rodrigues' salute. Then he returned the smile as well, giving a thumbs-up and pointing inland, roughly in the direction he knew the chopper would go. Jorge nodded, then turned back to his platoon.

Ham turned around to find a mixed journalism and long-ranged communications section standing by for instructions. "Just keep close," he said. Then he opened a metal box about the size of a heavy machine gun ammunition can and withdrew from it a very futuristic-looking communications device. He turned it on and deposited it in a breast pocket.

Jorge felt his stomach sink down about to his knees as the helicopter pulled pitch to spring into the air. It went up only about fifty feet, he judged, before swinging around to face generally in the direction of their target, something labeled on the maps as *"Finca* 42."

What was there neither Jorge, nor the platoon leader, Centurion Vicente, really knew. Certainly it had *looked* like a ranch, not really different from back home, except there was somewhat less mechanization than one would expect from a similar operation in Balboa.

From where he stood, Jorge could watch progress through the windscreen in front of the pilots. He watched, with his rifle slung over his shoulder and both arms raised to allow a grip on a strap hanging from the perforated metal that made up the ceiling of the cargo compartment. First the chopper aimed for a pass between two hills. He felt it rise slightly, to stay above the ground and scattered trees.

On the other side, where he had felt his stomach sink before, now he felt it try to crawl out of his mouth when the IM-71 dove low into a narrow valley. They followed that for a while, then veered hard to port to lunge through another low pass between hills. From there, the ground leveled out enough that Jorge felt comfortable letting go with one hand so he could turn about to see the lay of the land generally. He saw a great many farm workers simply stop what they were doing to stare at the passing bird.

Funny; I'd expect them either to wave or to run, but, no, they just watch. Simply not very curious people? Or have they no idea what a . . .

The chopper began a rapid rise again, causing Rodriquez to have to scramble to get his double handhold back. He turned his attention back to the front. Over another ridge the helicopter went, then down again.

Through the windscreen Jorge saw a set of buildings, white stucco–covered, mostly. They'd built a model of the target, from the map and the aerial photographs, back aboard ship. He was pretty sure it was a target match.

The nose lifted slightly, though enough for the collection of buildings to disappear. Jorge saw the two door gunners, integral parts of the helicopter's crew, take a more determined control of their machine guns and begin scanning the ground to either side closely. The descent then became relatively steep, with the pilot slowing down only in the last few seconds before hitting down with a considerable shock to the passengers.

Jorge wasn't sure if he was the first man off the chopper, he was sure only that he was the first one off the rear ramp. When he turned, Centurion Vicente was already on the ground, out the left-side door, and already pointing the squad leader for first squad in the right direction.

When Jorge looked to the other side, he recoiled. There, nailed to a cross, was a young man little older than himself, with a young woman, more a girl really—dirty faced, ragged, and underfed—standing defensively between the cross and the helicopter. She was somewhere in color between his own black and the light-skinned victim on the cross. Past the dirt on her face, Jorge thought she was probably pretty.

Too skinny, though, way too skinny.

There were four more uprights, these not surmounted by a crosspiece, next to the one occupied cross.

Jorge keyed his Red Fang communicator.

"What is it, Rodrigues?" asked Centurion Vicente.

"There's some kid—young enough, anyway, no older than us—over here crucified," Jorge informed him. "We need cooperation from the locals, don't we? So how about if I take a couple of men and get this kid down? Bet he'll be as helpful as can be."

"Good thought," agreed Vicente, "Do it. Steal no more than one man each from second and third squads, plus I suppose you'll need the medic. Nailed or tied? If nailed, how are you going to get him down?"

"Figure that out when I get there, Centurion."

Jorge reached out and grabbed the last cadet storming out of the back of the helicopter on the right side of the ramp. A couple of shuffling steps and he likewise caught one from the other side. Keying his Red Fang again, he announced, "Second and third, this is the platoon sergeant. I've taken Lopez and Navarro. You'll get them back when I'm done with them. Until then, make do."

"Roger . . . roger."

The chopper was already leaving when Jorge ordered, "Follow me, you two. And MEDIC!"

"Here," answered a boy even younger than Rodrigues. A tape on his chest said his last name was Parilla. He was the great-grandson of the president. "But I'm not a fully trained medic; I was just a member of the medics club at the school. That's something I wish you and the centurion would keep in mind."

"Best we have. You come, too."

The four trotted to the girl standing defensively in front of the cross. Rodrigues gently pushed her out of the way before he noticed she was speaking Spanish.

Well, sort of Spanish. I can recognize about half of it but the other half seems a little strange. Short words and simple sentences time.

"Miss, who are you?"

That brought a flurry of words, again only about half comprehensible.

Jorge sighed. *Simpler still, I guess.*

"Who you?" Pointing at the thing of pain on the cross, "Who him?"

"Me Miriamne. Him Arpan. Him MINE!"

"Why there?"

The girl's eyes flashed purest hate, so pure that the next words hardly mattered. "Mistress angry. Punish. Order. Evil bitch . . ."

A single shot in the distance caught Jorge's attention. He held up a palm to tell the girl to be quiet for a moment. Vicente's voice came over the Red Fang, "Some old, bald fool, carrying an ancient shotgun. He's down. Continue the roundup."

Jorge pointed at the nails holding the boy up by wrists and feet, then used the bent index fingers on his right hand to mime pulling a nail from his left wrist.

"You help?" the girl asked.

He pointed at her, then said, "Get help. Get tools."

She nodded eagerly. "I get. Oh, please, oh, *please*; I get." Then she took both of Jorge's hands in her own, kissed each a half-dozen times, quickly, and ran off toward what appeared to be barracks.

"Nice girl," Jorge muttered.

"She is . . . a very . . . nice girl," said the young man on the cross, in what appeared to be only slightly accented but otherwise perfect Spanish. He'd raised his head to speak, then let his chin sink back onto his heaving chest with an audible groan.

Jorge heard a rumbling. Turning in that direction, he

saw two dozen or so badly dressed and poorly fed workers—*slaves; I suppose they must be slaves*—dragging a wagon that looked to be of about the right size to stand on to pull the nails. The skinny, but still maybe pretty, brown girl jumped and danced excitedly in front of them, beckoning them to greater speed.

The crew wasn't stupid, Jorge saw. Though it seemed unlikely they'd ever pulled a live victim from a cross, they knew to pull the wagon up and pull the spikes from the boy's heels first. He screamed as the first spike was pulled and wriggled out, followed by a well of blood. For the second he'd fainted dead away.

Just as well, Jorge thought.

The crew rested his feet on the wagon bed, then climbed aboard to start worrying at the spikes through his wrists. The whole time Miriamne keened, pressing herself against him and stroking his face.

First one wrist spike came out, which caused his body to twist and interfere with removing the other. The girl held him up as best she could until the other slaves joined the effort, straightening him up until the final spike could be removed. Then they gently lowered him to the wagon bed. This was made a little harder by the girl, Miriamne, refusing to be parted from him by so much as a millimeter.

"Doc," said Rodrigues, "I think you had best turn her into an assistant, because she's going to be in the way unless you do. Oh, and small words, simple sentences."

As it turned out, while there were very close to even numbers of men and women, only one woman was well dressed and healthy-looking. The others all stood in a circle around the former oppressor and recent chief liberator.

Claudia Nyere, also former ambassador to Santa Josefina, twisted and squirmed while being held by her arms by two of the largest liberated slaves on the ranch.

"You can't do this to me, ground-bound scum! I'm an ambassador, hence inviolable, and a Class One of the Castro-Nyere clan, rulers of TransIsthmia, on Earth!"

Centurion Vicente nodded solemnly, then from a standing start, without windup, backhanded her across the face, loosening teeth, ripping lips on those teeth, and causing blood from the torn lips to fly through the air before splashing onto the gravel.

"Shut up, bitch. My orders are to take you alive but I'm close to retirement already so I have come to consider orders not much more than a basis for discussion. And, ya know, no one back home would really mind if I turned you over to the men and women here for their justice. I understand the nails from the cross came out straight, too.

"In fact, the only reason I'm keeping you alive at all is that, if I let them tear you apart, I might have trouble finding someone else as monstrously guilty as you are."

I don't believe that, really, Vicente thought. *The air of this whole place* reeks *with the odor of the monstrously guilty.*

Rodrigues was close enough not to need the Red Fang. "Platoon Sergeant?" shouted out the centurion.

"Yes, Centurion?"

"That kid who was crucified, he alert yet?"

"He was in a good deal of pain, Centurion, and weak. Doc gave him an injector of morphine, but I think he can answer questions."

"Very good."

Turning his back on Nyere, Vicente took long steps to get to the wagon upon which Arpad's tortured body still lay, his girl, Miriamne, in attendance on him. The centurion didn't climb onto the wagon. Instead, he stood beside it and reached out one hand to twist the boy's head to where it faced him.

"I understand you speak real Spanish rather than the pidgin most of these poor folks manage."

"Yes, sir," Arpad said, slowly. "Pretty good . . . anyway."

Vicente nodded. "Yes, 'pretty good.' Okay. We've got the cunt who calls herself 'Claudia Nyere.' She'll face justice in God's good time. Maybe sooner than that. Now is there anyone else here on this ranch who would matter to the people in space? Let your imagination run free: spouses, children, sex toys, official aides or secretaries from Old Earth; anybody like that?"

Arpad said something to the girl in that almost-but-not-exactly Spanish. She answered, at some length and with a few unusual punctuations, like spitting on the ground, and forming her fingers and thumbs into a ring that she slowly closed, and grinding her foot on the gravel.

"'No,' she says. She also says . . . that everybody here . . . would really like . . . to tear . . . the bitch limb . . . from limb. I don't suppose . . . ?"

"Sorry, no, orders. Or, at least, not yet."

Miriamne then said something else, pointing to the south.

"She had a kid, sir, not here but in boarding school. My girl can show you where."

"Excellent." Vincente consulted his map. "We didn't know about the boarding school."

CHAPTER THIRTEEN

De Oppresso Liber
—Motto of the U.S. Army's Special Forces

UEPF *Spirit of Peace*

At another station, Xingzhen angrily berated someone down below in her ministry of defense. A long cursing session ended with something that, even in Mandarin, sounded a lot like, "Make sure you do."

"Just what the *fuck* are they doing?" Wallenstein asked. "Some kind of hostage catch-and-release program?"

"It's a new wrinkle," Khan, the husband, admitted. "We've seen them do something like this before, at Pumbadeta, in Sumer." He began chewing his lip and pacing, as if seeking an answer to a problem that was somewhere in his mind, but coyly hiding.

Marguerite thought back. *Ah, yes, push the civilians in and keep them there; then let no food until they surrender. Cheap and easy, just takes a little time.*

"And the ship . . ." Khan continued.

". . . is," the high admiral finished, "to complete the ring and, based on what that lander reported before they blew it out of the sky, they have some laser capability to prevent aerial resupply or reinforcement."

The empress reported, "It took threatening to extinguish several gene pools down to the last generation, *baobei*, but two battalions of paratroopers, with a few medium vehicles, will take off in four hours. They'll have to refuel at Wellington, but those people can hardly restrain themselves from fawning, cringing, and begging to please us. The rest of their brigade will follow in another six hours and the division within twenty-four to forty-eight."

"And they'll arrive, that first group?" Wallenstein asked.

Xingzhen rocked her head from side to side, twice before answering, "Twenty-four to twenty-six hours. Sorry, love, but even *I* cannot move them faster than the planes will go."

"Computer," the high admiral ordered, "get me Battaglia on *Spirit of Brotherhood*."

The answer came very quickly, "Ready to fire at your command, High Admiral."

"Wait!" Khan interjected. "Wait! I've got it! Wait!"

"Why?" Marguerite asked.

"When the enemy is seen to be making a mistake . . ."

". . . don't interfere," finished his wife.

"I don't . . ."

"High Admiral, the enemy doesn't know we have help coming and has every confidence that their ship can close the ring. If we destroy the ship their—what did you call it? Their 'hostage catch-and-release program'?—will come to a screeching halt.

"So let them continue. Leave their ship alone. Maybe even call Carrera to try to start negotiations. By the time Her Majesty's paratroops arrive, we'll probably have every potential hostage the Balboans could have taken, safe in our own hands. *Then* we destroy the ship, just before the Zhong come in, in ever-increasing numbers.

"At that point, we can supply to our heart's content. We can defend the base. Meanwhile the Balboans will have lost their main source of supply. *They'll* be on the wrong side of the logistic stick."

Wallenstein, though not a ground-combat officer, was also no dummy. "So why are they leaving the *latifundia* slaves behind?"

"I'm guessing," Khan admitted, "but my guess is that they've somehow figured out some of our more, mmmm . . . cosmopolitan trends, which is to say that, for certain among us—the neo-Azteca spring instantly to mind—those slaves are not people who will suck up food; they *are* food."

I had hoped to save my planet and its system, Wallenstein thought. *It could be so much better a system and so much better a planet than it is. But very nearly at the top of the to-do list for that was exterminating the slavers, the neo-Azteca, and the Orthodox Druids. No matter, I think Khan has the right of it.*

"Battaglia?"

"Yes, High Admiral."

"Minor delay in plans. Do not fire. Stand down for now. I'll let you know when."

"Wilco, High Admiral."

Breaking that connection, Marguerite told the

computer, "Connect me to the communicator I gave to Carrera."

Beach Red, Atlantis Island

Before the thing had beeped three times, Ham had it in his hands. "Hamilcar Carrera speaking. May I presume that High Admiral Wallenstein is on the other end?"

There was a long silence on the other end. Finally, High Admiral Wallenstein identified herself and asked, simply, "How and why?"

"Did this end up in my hands? My father sent it to me. Can your ship identify where I am? I imagine so. No matter. He sent it to me because he was quite certain you would be calling..."

UEPF *Spirit of Peace*

"...and wanted you to know, in no uncertain terms, that the person you were dealing with was even more ruthless than he is. And I am."

The voice seemed a little high, perhaps, but not unsteady. It didn't break, at least.

Where? Marguerite mouthed to Khan.

Khan took over the workstation occupied by Xingzhen, gently nudging her away. After some frantic checking, he turned to the high admiral, wide-eyed, and mouthed back, *Atlantis*.

Khan then turned back to the station and began pulling

up what little was known about the boy. This he forwarded to the high admiral, who began reading as she was talking.

"I see you are a god, Hamilcar."

"No, I am not. There are some devoted but deluded people who think I am. These are not the same things."

Crap, not vain . . . no vanity to play on.

"And you are on our base, I see." *Let him get the feeling for my presumed omnipotence. Maybe it will help me bluff him, later.*

"I've already suggested, did I not, High Admiral, that you can track this? Of course, you can't tell if I am speaking directly or if the communications are being remoted, can you?"

Bloody damned smart little bastard, isn't he?

"And, no, High Admiral, my father wanted me to assure you that he and my mother beat me to the altar, if not, perhaps, by much. Now, pleasantries aside, what can I do for you?"

"You can call off your attack."

"No, and if that's all you wanted to ask, you'll forgive me if I get back to my duties."

"The link has been broken," announced the computer. "Shall I try to reestablish it?"

Wallenstein shook her head, *no*, then remembered the computer couldn't see that. "No," she said, "just keep track of where that comm device is."

Turning her attention to Khan, the husband, she said, "Now tell me everything we know, everything we can suppose, and every educated guess we can make about that boy."

"Yes, High Admiral," Khan said.

Xingzhen then piped in, "The base is not our only problem, *baobei*. That fleet that hid under a false banner of internment and which is now at large? I need it tracked and the information sent to my commander below, Admiral Wanyan. As a matter of fact, I need a line to tell Wanyan to move our fleet out of danger."

"Khan?"

"I'll get someone on it, High Admiral, along with trying to shut the Balboans out of the satellite net."

"Don't worry about shutting them out, Commander," the empress said. "We can shut down all the satellites over that part of the world easily enough. That leaves this fleet alone able to scout below."

"*You* can, Empress," said Khan. "If we tried it would be instant war with the Federated States. It might, even if it's your people doing it. Please, *please*, just shut out the Balboans but not the FSC."

Beach Red, Atlantis Island

"Can we get through to my dad, yet?" Ham asked one of the commo rats, a short and dark sergeant.

"No promises; I can try."

"Do."

The old man had set Hamilcar to studying war since he'd been a very little boy. However, high-tech communications were not among the things he'd been taught in any detail. Instead, all he'd learned was what they could, with a little luck, do. Thus, the various whistles, beeps, crackles, and sound tones meant nothing to him. He hoped they signaled progress. He stared at the directional satellite antenna as if hoping to see a message coming out.

The commo rat handed Ham a handset. "Your father's on the line. It's secure, so you can speak freely, but it's iffy, so speak quickly."

The old man sounded very chipper, saying, "Hello, Son, how goes the battle?"

"A little iffy, so far, Dad. We're ashore and driving civilians toward the base or dropping them off nearby, if they're too far out. The Peace Fleet seems to be reinforcing, but the rocket strike on their main barracks, well . . . I've seen what the drones saw and there's not much there but the bodies of the dead and dying. No . . . likely all dead by now. The ship had a misfire on one of the rockets . . . and . . . well . . . I don't know how to tell you this, but . . . well . . . Legate Johnson . . . I know he was one of your oldest friends . . . and . . . I'm sorry to say . . . he didn't make it."

Carrera the elder whispered something into his own phone, at the far end. Ham wasn't quite sure but it sounded a lot like, *De profundis clamavi ad te, Domine . . .*

That doesn't sound chipper at all. But he had to know so he can decide if he should relieve me and put Cano in charge,

Ham continued, "I've taken command, which was not in the plan. Seems to be working so far but I'll credit that mostly to Alena's husband, who's been running interference and kicking ass for me. He deserves a nice promotion, Dad.

"We haven't had much in losses—hardly anyone—once ashore, Dad, but we lost over a hundred cadets on the

ship from the explosion. Yeah, I don't envy you telling
their parents . . .

"Right. Now what about the Valpo air force. Are they
coming or . . ."

Ham heard another series of clicks and tones, and then
the connection dissolved in static.

"We've lost it," said commo. "Shall I try again? I can do
better, I think, once we get out of this bowl of a beach and
onto some high ground."

"We'll wait," said Ham. "I told the old man everything
he needs to know for now. Pass on to all cohorts and
maniples, 'charlie mike'—continue the mission. And the
rest of us, prepare to displace closer to the base."

Latifundia Amistad, Atlantis Island

The platoon had spent the whole night rounding people
up, pointing others in the direction of the base and
sending them off under guard, liberating slaves. All of
that, while tiring, hadn't been especially dangerous, a
matter of considerable relief to Centurion Vicente and of
considerable disappointment to his cadets.

Now, with orders received over the radio, the platoon
would soon be going into action. Two helicopters were en
route for the platoon and the few special prisoners it had
taken. Ambassador-without-portfolio Claudia Nyere was
one of these, though her daughter and those other upper-
crust children seized at the boarding school near *Finca*
Mixcoatl were not.

This last one, before the choppers showed up . . . *Odd,*

damned odd, thought Vicente. *Most of the shitheels in charge of this place deserve everything that's coming to them and more. But there are a few... Well, five exactly, by reports... whose slaves vouched for their kindness, sympathy, and humanity. And this one...*

He'd been skeptical at first, but no matter how much he dug, there were no crosses, no gallows, no whipping or branding posts—no whips or branding irons, for that matter—and no barred pits in the ground. The slaves looked a lot healthier and vastly happier, too. Those slaves, a dozen of them, clustered around the woman as if shielding her.

"I am Centurion Vicente, Timocratic Republic of Balboa. You? Why are you different? Why do your slaves care for you?" the centurion asked, speaking over the small crowd of clutching men, women, and children, all with fear-filled eyes.

You know, I think these people will fight for her if we try to take her.

The owner, a woman, Esther Shazli—*Damned fine-looking woman, too, if you ask me*—said, "I know what the system is that I was born into, Centurion. I know it's rotten and that so are most of the people in it. I am only one; I cannot help what others do. But I am still one and must do what I can."

She really was good looking, too, especially for a woman probably about two hundred and fifty years old. Tall, slender, huge brown eyes. She was shapely if perhaps a bit small breasted, a fact easy to see since, like most of the women of old Earth, she was, as usual, topless.

Vicente considered what she'd said, then answered. "I am only one, too, and under authority, to boot. But I will do what I can. You hide, stay hidden. Dress like your slaves . . ."

"Servants," Esther corrected, "and friends."

"Who gives a shit what you call them; dress like them anyway. And stay low. If I can, I'll come and tell you when you can come out. If I never can come . . . think twice before revealing yourself."

He heard the insistent whine of inbound helicopters.

"And now, madame, I must go."

"I'll consider what you've said."

"Consider my ass," Vicente answered. "Get your shapely posterior hidden!"

The helicopter that picked up Vicente, Rodrigues, and their platoon of cadet infantry skimmed the ground, wheels low enough to snag the odd bush. It wasn't the most fuel-efficient way to travel, wing-in-ground effect or not, but it had the distinct virtue that should one of those laser defense towers still be operational it would be unlikely to spot and engage them.

The island wasn't all *that* big, really. The trip to the foot of the ridge half encircling the base took less than twenty minutes. The helicopter made one quick stop at a holding area still being formed, where Claudia Nyere was unceremoniously booted off—literally. Vicente had her dragged to the rear ramp and then planted his boot on her posterior and kicked her off face forward into the dirt, before tossing to the MP on station a brief list of her more obvious crimes.

After that, the chopper cut to port and scaled the slope. There, still keeping low, it made three touchdowns on the exterior slope—exterior to the base—before letting the platoon off, in a great cloud of dust. It made two more touchdowns after that. The last the platoon had seen of it, it was flying low still, skirting around the three-quarter circle of a ridge line before skipping across the waves to the ALTA, there to be refueled and rearmed, rather than drain the small FFAR point ashore. Still more pairs of choppers, raising dust all over the plain, swooped in- or outbound, ferrying in more units and more prisoners.

GLS worked here. Checking his map and deciding the chopper had dropped them off to perfection, Vicente directed his platoon up the slope to an assault position currently marked by a brace of Ocelots.

Even as he hustled the boys along, Rodrigues pushing them from the back, he mused, *Damned fine-looking woman. Maybe if . . .*

From behind, the landing force's sole artillery battery, eight of the eighty-five-millimeter jobs, pounded frantically, the pounding punctuated by brief lulls as they shifted targets. Their shells' passage overhead was marked by a freight-train racket. *Another damned good reason for the helicopters to stay low.* Mortars, too—and there were a lot more of those, likewise kicked in. The fragmentary order they'd been given by radio had promised a smoke screen to cover their approach down the slope and into the town. He expected it would be damned thin and damnably iffy.

Finca Mixcoatl

There was a dirt road from the *finca* to the main road that ran north and south. This was the road taken by Pablo and Francisco. It was also the road they'd met at on the way back. From there, having seen little but strange flying machines, the occupants of which ignored them, they trotted their horses.

There were reasons—very good reasons—that the majordomo had chosen Pablo and Francisco to ride out to scout for danger. As he, himself, had been, those two were true, eager, and willing stakhanovites. This, among other reasons, was why they'd been trusted with horses.

They're also been trusted with punishment. Indeed, it had been those two who had nailed young Arpad to the cross beam, then lifted and fixed the beam to the top of the upright, the *stirpes*, and first tied his ankles to the upright, and then nailed his heels to the wood.

"Hey, Pablo," Francisco said, "I bet we get a lot more willing and eager cooperation from little weepy girl if we hurt her boy first and threaten to do more if she doesn't cooperate."

"We can do her in front of him," Pablo added. "The mistress will appreciate giving him more suffering."

They'd had a little fun with Miriamne, afterwards, but that was just part of the compensation package. The fun had been an additional reason for the girl's weeping at the foot of Arpad's cross.

Neither Pablo nor Francisco had any particular reason to fear their return. The *finca*, after all, was peaceful, as a general rule, with the majordomo's *escopeta* to back up the orders of the more privileged among the slaves, the stakhanovites like themselves.

The several hundred slaves who worked the land and

provided domestic services to the mistress all turned out to meet the two. They were formed in a kind of loose crescent, with the thickest part in front of the punishment area.

As Pablo and his pal rode in, chatting with each other amiably, they failed to notice immediately several important changes. One was that the cross they'd had the disloyal slave on was empty. Another was that two different crosses were filled. A third was that, a few rows of people into the crescent, the majordomo's *escopeta* was in the hands of someone new.

They also failed to notice as the arms of the crescent began to fold in behind them. Indeed, their first realization of change came when the cry arose—was it a young woman's voice?—"Get them!"

Pablo was pulled from his bucking horse almost immediately. Francisco managed to strike some heads and faces with his short whip, but his resistance didn't last very long, either. Once on the ground, both tried to cover their heads against the kicks aimed their way.

"Too quick! Too quick!" Miriamne cried above the exultant shouts. "No beat. No!" She pointed and demanded, "To the crosses with them!"

Outside Atlantis Base

Lying side by side in the brush, Vicente and Rodrigues alternated watching through their single pair of binoculars as some thin traces of a smoke screen appeared. Overhead, the freight-train-rattle of 85mm artillery sounded, low and menacing, accompanied by the softer sounds of mortar shells cruising at a higher altitude. The explosions to the front, being just light artillery and mortars, were nothing like the gut-rippling catastrophes of heavier shells.

"Wish to hell we had the cruiser in support," the cadet said.

"Wish in one hand and . . ."

"Yes, Centurion; I know, 'shit in the other.' But I still wish we had the cruiser in support."

"For smoke?" Centurion Vicente asked. "They don't make a smoke shell for that. For high explosive I feel the same way."

Rodrigues shrugged. "Just a thought."

"Was never practical," Vicente said. "Having the cruiser in range to get in range to support us would have given the game away. And if that had happened, we were deader than chivalry . . . hmmm?"

"Yes?" the cadet asked.

"We're getting mixed HE with smoke now. The order will be coming down in a few minutes to move out. Go check that the machine guns are ready, then get behind the platoon to kick asses."

"Yes, Centurion," the cadet answered, before beginning to slither backwards to avoid silhouetting himself to the defenders below.

"Rodrigues!"

"Yes, Centurion?" the cadet asked, his slithering coming to a temporary halt.

"This will only be your second time in action, right?"

"Yes, Centurion."

"First time in a position of responsibility?"

"Yes, Centurion."

"Scared?"

"A little," the boy admitted.

"Don't bother; you're going to be too busy to be scared once we get the order to go in."

Rodrigues thought about that for all of half a second, then answered, with a smile, "You know what, Centurion? I think that's right."

"It was right when Sergeant Major Mac gave the advice to Sergeant Major Martinez, and right when Martinez gave it to me, more than fifteen years ago. The world hasn't changed since. One other thing, too: those guys and gals waiting for us down there are sailors, and space sailors at that. They've never been in action and, I'll guarantee you, if the shells hitting amongst them don't impress us much, *they're* so impressed their trousers are brown. Now go on."

"Yes, Centurion."

Rodrigues continued down the slope, knocking the odd pebble loose to roll down, until he judged he was low enough that he could rise to a crouch without being seen. That happened to be about where Parilla, the medic, was waiting. Giving the medic the thumbs-up sign, Rodrigues arose, cut left, and paralleled the crest of the slope to just behind the weapons squad.

The machine gun crews were in defilade, with only the squad leader looking out over the town via binoculars. Rodrigues passed those at a duck walk, then fell to the prone and crawled up.

"You're a noisy crawler," said the squad leader, a cadet

named Negrón, who was also the lightest-skinned member of the platoon, man or boy.

"Odd layout," Rodrigues said, "with your machine guns that far back."

"They can be up here in about two and a half seconds," Negrón replied. "And engaging targets half a second after that. I've brought the gunners up one at a time to show them what I want suppressed.

"You know, it's funny, Jorge."

"What is?"

Negrón gestured in the direction of the base. "Those Earthpig shuttles that have been landing? They've been avoiding the ship, probably to avoid the guns, and flying very low nap of the Earth. I see the same six hull numbers, over and over, plus any number of other numbers that only show up once. I think they're trying to bullshit us as to how many people are down there to defend."

"Now *that* is something Hamilcar needs to know! Good observation."

Jorge immediately began to slide back, to make his way to the platoon radio.

CHAPTER FOURTEEN

Carpe diem, quam minimum credula postero (Seize the day, put very little trust in tomorrow).

—Horace, *Odes*

Atlantis Base

Turning away from the window at which she stood, Bethany asked her leader, Christopher Robin, "Why do the shuttles keep coming down? I've seen the one that brought us come in at least six times."

"Probably to try to bullshit the Balboans into thinking that there are a lot more of us than there are, get them to take more time getting ready, expend more ammunition, which they can't have an infinite supply of, while other shuttles really *are* bringing in reinforcements.

"It's clever of the high admiral, if she's behind it, but clever doesn't mean it will work. Okay, now back at your windows. You're firing . . . you're firing . . . and damn! Clear a stoppage again."

Wallace went through the drill for what seemed to her

the fiftieth time, slapping her top-mounted magazine down, jerking the charging hook, releasing the hook, hitting it forward, and then resuming her aim. The unexpended round flew through the air to clatter on the tile floor. The other few members of the team did the same, their own rounds likewise hitting the floor.

Robin's small crew were in a large room in the basement of one of the public buildings of the town. They'd come in through a side door, though, and none of them had the slightest clue what the functions of the building were, beyond a general idea that it housed some of the inevitable bureaucracy. Her occasional shore leaves had never brought her to this part of the town, the government area north of the central park.

There were windows in the basement, but all were above, well above, shoulder and eye level.

Thus, the first thing Robin had done was have them push tables under each of the windows, then mount the tables to see if they could see out. It wasn't perfect; the men had to scrunch down while Bethany had had to pile several flat monitors to see out. It was an unstable platform.

But best I get used to it.

The Balboan artillery fire, which the crew could hear and feel but not see, seemed to be coming in a fair and even safe distance away, somewhere—some on the edge of town, some inside it—where Bethany couldn't see. She could see, from time to time, tracers lancing upward from positions near hers.

"Trying to keep the Balboan drones off our backs, I suppose," had been Robin's judgment. "There really aren't enough of us to hold the base if—when—they attack, not unless they're very, very cautious. They won't be cautious if they know where we are."

At his temporary command post, on the reverse slope east of Atlantis Base, Ham studied the map, worrying in turn about the oncoming Zhong Paras, the defense he might be facing ahead, and what had to be admitted was the fragility of both his own command and his state of command over it. With one ear he listened to the radio chatter, as well.

"And there goes another fucking one," came the curse over the radio. The voice was familiar, if only from recent acquaintance. "Tell Carrera's kid that at this rate, we'll run out of drones before we get anything worthwhile."

"Carrera's kid"? thought Ham. *Well, I am, of course, or Mom would have a good deal to answer for. But is that all I am? I suppose the next couple of days will tell.*

"Tell Seaman—hell, what was his name?—oh, yeah, Wilson. Tell Seaman Wilson to pull back the drones."

From an entirely different radio, the intelligence net's, came the words, "Flash! Flash! Flash! For the commander; the Earthpigs are sending in empty shuttles to try to seem stronger than they are!"

Well, isn't that interesting. Explains the effort they put into driving back the drones, too, doesn't it? But what does it mean? *And what do I do about it? Well, first off, ammunition isn't unlimited so,* "Have the artillery and mortars cease fire."

"Wilco, Ham."

One: they're weaker than they're trying to look; that

much is obvious. Two: they're either trying to bluff us into not attacking at all or to buy time for more help to arrive so that we'll be too busy fighting them off to attack. Three: eventually they will get stronger. They may even have time to call in their Marines from around the world when they just might become too tough a nut to crack. No, I don't think they'd be that tough, even so, but I could be wrong. So, "Fire support?"

"Here, Ham."

"Smoke screen, as thick as possible, northern edge of the base, from the shore to as far in as we can go and still make it thick. How long to prep for and lay the screen?"

"Top of my head, twenty-five minutes. But we can't keep it up long; not enough ammunition unloaded."

"That's good enough. Ops?"

"Yes, Ham," David Cano answered.

"Have all the armor back off and shift around to the northern edge of the ridge—a caldera, I suppose it must be—to support the two maniples up there. Once the screen is in, they go in to grab the northern edge."

"Ocelots, too?"

Ham thought, *As tanks go the Ocelots aren't. Lightly armored, they still carry a decent gun. So "boot, don't spatter."* "Ocelots, too."

"And then?"

"Once we have the northern edge of the base, we'll peel from that, working north to south and bringing the rest in as the way becomes clear."

"Roger," agreed Cano. "Intel was silent on this, but they've probably got thermals integral to every rifle and machine gun. They *ought* to be advanced enough for that, anyway. The smoke won't do that much good."

"It will worry them. Doubt they've ever seen smoke up close and personal before. Even so, the second we have a good screen established shift fires slightly southward and inward and make it high explosive. We'll see how well they can use their thermals when they're shivering and shitting their pants."

Not every firearm in the legions had a thermal imager, not nearly; they were just too expensive for the budget to support. Instead, snipers had them and one or more machine guns per weapons squad had them. In the case of Negrón's squad, he had control of their one thermal imager, though some other weapons squads had two. One thermal, of course, wouldn't do for three machine guns. *What to do; what to do? Well . . . maybe it will do, at least for a while.*

Negrón knew what he wanted his guns to suppress, so, once the smoke had built up enough to obscure the edge of the base, he called the first gun forward.

"Set up your tripod *here*," he said, pointing at a spot on the ground, "oriented there." His finger gave a general location to the south. The crew, who hadn't had a lot to do on their long voyage *but* gun drills, set up the gun on the tripod with a minimum of fuss. Thereupon, Negrón slapped the thermal onto the gun, ordered the gunner away, and got behind it himself. He set the range on the thermal, then elevated the gun until the sight was on the building—indeed, on the particular window—he wanted suppressed. Then he locked the gun into place on the traversing and elevating mechanism, telling the gunner,

"You're on now, close enough. When we begin to engage, I'll give you the thermal back for ten seconds or so, so you can make fine adjustment."

"Works for me," the gunner agreed, before turning to curse the ammo bearer for being just that bit too slow in bringing up the heavy boxes of ammunition.

Negrón then took the sight back, stepped about five paces to the left, and called up the next gun.

With an Ocelot infantry fighting vehicle serving as an assault gun to either side, Vicente's platoon walked toward the topographical crest, the very top of the ridge, shrinking their posture as they neared it. Several meters before reaching the crest they dropped to their bellies to crawl over it, to avoid being silhouetted. This took longer, of course, causing the boys to bunch up a bit while they were still in defilade and while it didn't much matter.

Even so, Rodrigues, taking up the rear, with the forward observer team and the medic, Parilla, worried. *What if we take some mortars or artillery? What if they have some air capability beyond just shuttles? What if… what if… what if…*

What if I stop worrying about things I can't do anything about? Yeah, what if that?

"Hey, Third Squad; keep your bellies to the dirt as you go over that crest."

Off to the left Negrón's crews had begun a desultory prep. *Though it sounds funny*, thought Rodrigues. The implied question wasn't answered until Rodrigues, himself, crested the ridge. Then he could see Negrón, trotting from gun to gun with his thermal in his hands, letting the gunners see potential targets through the smoke—potential because no one was actually shooting back yet—and write down the data from the traversing and elevating mechanism to find those targets even without an imager.

Maybe fifty meters down the forward slope, and with his elbows beginning to feel the scraping from the long crawl, Rodrigues arose to his feet, though still at a crouch.

To Rodrigues' right, one of the Ocelots' ten-centimeter cannon blasted. The shell was a low-velocity high explosive—and probably high explosive dual purpose; there was no way to tell without asking the crew—hence he could follow the round by eye until it disappeared into the smoke.

The explosion, when it came, told everyone—not least the boys and girls of the United Earth Peace Fleet, the UEPF—that, no, it was neither antiarmor nor high explosive nor dual purpose, but a thermobaric warhead, several times more powerful than anything of the same size involving conventional high explosives. Whatever had been on the receiving end, none this side of the smoke screen who lacked a thermal imager could say. But the sudden brilliant flash could be sensed, even through the smoke, while, above the screen, the rising mushroom cloud spoke of much greater destruction than mere high explosive would cause. Even before that, the thump in the chest felt by every man and boy in the assault told of something unusual.

Can only imagine what that thump felt like on the receiving end.

★★★

Perched on her unstable platform of monitors, the whole assembly sitting atop a table of no great strength, Bethany Wallace peered out through the narrow basement window. She glimpsed the smoke screen building up, but had no idea what to do about it. Over the relatively soft thumping of the smoke shells, she heard something she suspected were heavy engines.

"You've got the ability to see through the smoke," Christopher Robin shouted to his team. "Your scopes can do thermal imaging. Look for the green button on the left side. Push it."

Bethany did—*I should have remembered on my own*— then peered through her scope. Her heart nearly stopped at what the scope revealed. Rising from the ridge outside the base were a dozen armored vehicles she could see. They moved forward, right across the sharp cut, until their centers of gravity caused them to flop downward from the front, a move as menacing and frightening as anything she'd ever seen.

A dozen? Gods alone know how many I can't see. Following those behemoths, scores of—*"Infantry," I suppose they're called, or "Marines"*—likewise rising from the earth to follow the armor. She wasn't experienced enough to say how good those foot troops were, less still the armored vehicles.

But I am pretty sure they're better than we are.

There came in her view a sudden flash from the muzzle of one of the lesser vehicles. Given the angle, and the low velocity, she had no trouble following it for most of its flight, right up until it disappeared behind a building which, almost immediately after, disintegrated. The shattered roof, itself, flew off in pieces, giving birth to a rising mushroom cloud.

And my building's not a bit better built than that one.

Bethany let that sink in. *I'm going to die. We're all going to die. There's nothing we can do. We have no defense. I'm going to . . .*

And then she screamed, dropped her firearm, and leapt from her precarious perch, screeching for the door.

Rodrigues could still hear the tanks and the ocelots, even after they passed the smoke screen. He watched the last of the platoon disappear into the same screen before plunging into it himself. There weren't very many shots from the main guns, but the coaxial thirty-millimeter light cannon and the thirty-caliber machine guns kept up a fairly steady chatter.

Return fire was . . . not all that impressive. I don't know what they're thinking, in that base, but the tanks and assault guns can't really take the place. We, on the other hand, can . . . even if we're at best half-trained for this sort of thing. But they're concentrating on the armor that they can't hurt rather than us whom they could. I wonder . . . yeah, makes sense. The couple of buildings the armor destroyed caught all the attention they have to give.

He keyed his Red Fang to contact Centurion Vicente.

"Yeah, what is it, Rod?" the centurion asked.

"If you've got good commo with the armor," the cadet answered, "ask them to blast a couple more buildings. We haven't taken any serious fire—no casualties, anyway, that I've seen—because what the Earthpigs has is all concentrating on the tanks and Ocelots. I don't think it's a coincidence."

"It isn't," Vicente agreed. "Against well-trained troops, they'd have butchered us and that would have stopped the armor. These are not well trained, maybe not trained at all."

"Makes up for a good deal of our own deficiencies, Centurion, no?"

"We'll see when we get inside. You out of the smoke yet?"

"Not quite, but I can see some outlines of buildings and even of some of our Ocelots."

"Anyone fall behind?"

"Not that I've seen, Centurion, but it's possible. Someone could have gotten himself lost in the smoke, maybe not even on purpose . . . hmmm, let me check with the squads . . ."

"Present or accounted for," answered first squad, just as an Ocelot or tank fired a main gun round. "No casualties. Second, present . . . third, all present or accounted for, one casualty not to enemy fire . . . weapons, good to go."

"We're good, Centurion," the boy reported back.

"Fine, the tank gunners are"—there was another organ-churning report from a main gun—"doing their part."

Bethany was frantically tearing away the office furniture piled in front of the door when Robin tackled her from behind, pulling her away and to the floor with as much gentleness as possible, then sitting on her and pinning her arms until she quieted down.

"What the fuck were you doing?" he asked.

It all came out in a rush: "We've got to get out of here! We're going to die! They're going to kill us all! I *saw* it, a building just disintegrated! We don't stand a chance! We've got to—"

That last sentence was interrupted by Robin's right hand slapping her across the left side of her face.

"What we've got to do," he said, still as gently as possible, "is calm you down. Yes, we've got problems, but we've also got a job to do. The Peace Fleet depends on this base . . ."

She filled her lungs as if to scream, but calmed immediately as he released her left shoulder and showed her his open palm.

"And the families of most of the crews, to include the crew of our own ship, are here, with no one to defend them except you and me.

"We don't have to hold on forever. The Zhong are coming to our rescue, I've been told. We need to hold on until they get here. Do you understand?"

She didn't trust herself with full lungs. Instead, she nodded, three or four times, shallowly and quickly. She felt calm returning to her mind and body, but it wasn't the calm of confidence. Instead, she found she had surrendered to the calm of resignation and helplessness. *We don't stand a chance, not a chance. I'm going to die— we all are—and there's nothing any of us can do about it.*

Robin mistook it when he felt her muscles relax and saw the look on her face. "Go on," he said, "get your carbine and get back in position."

★★★

We were never really trained for this, thought Rodrigues, not for the first time. He rested his back against the white stucco wall of a two-story building, looking left and right as second and third squads piled inside through smashed windows, boosted up by first. There were muffled explosions and the distant staccato of automatic fire coming from inside.

A club, a city-fighting site at the academy we used maybe two or three times a year, some very quiet lectures and walk-throughs aboard ship; those don't make us experts in city fighting.

That doesn't mean we're going to lose; only that we're going to lose more boys than an equivalent platoon of trained men would. And all of them are my friends. Damn.

"Casualties coming out!" shouted one of the team leaders from third squad, Cadet Corporal Franco, his head sticking out a broken window. "Sitnikov and Mendez."

"Medic!" Rodrigues shouted. "First squad, help our boys down." Turning back to Franco, he asked, "How did it happen?"

"You don't want to know, Rod." Seeing a look cross Rodrigues' face that insisted he very much did want to know, Franco said, "Friendly fire. Grenade. Mendez threw it so hard into a room it bounced back and went off under him and young Sitnikov." Franco and someone else Rodrigues couldn't see began smashing out the remnants of glass jutting inward from the window frame.

Rodrigues nodded, thinking, *"Friendly fire . . . isn't."*

Both boys were conscious, he saw, as they were lowered out the now cleared window. Both were also bleeding from maybe a dozen wounds each to their legs and abdomens. Both, too, were trying very hard not to scream as their comrades' hands grasped those wounded legs to help them down.

As soon as they were flat on the ground, the medic, President Parilla's grandson, took their ponchos and spread them out, side by side, with a couple of flicks of the wrist. With the help of a couple of other boys, he got them lifted and placed on the relatively clean ponchos. He then proceeded to draw a scalpel and begin cutting their trousers away. *Good,* Parilla thought, once he was able to see, *you didn't get your balls or dicks blown off. If my grandfather is to be believed, that will matter* overwhelmingly *in the not-too-distant future. Now let's look for lesser damage.* "Hey, you, get your canteen out and start pouring water to wash away the blood. I need to *see* what I'm doing." *Even if I have only half an idea of what I am supposed to do.*

From inside came the voice of Centurion Vicente, loud, sarcastic, and *angry.* "Look, goddamit; grenades *bounce.* The enemy, if he's ballsy, can pick them up and throw them back at you. Once you let the spoon fly off, count to three thousand, and *then* throw them. And don't mention quality control at the factory; I know all about it. But you still need to cook them off!"

Now *you tell us,* thought Rodrigues, along with Parilla, Franco, and, not least, Mendes and Sitnikov.

"And don't say I didn't tell you before," continued Vicente, "because I did. Not my fault that for you youngsters some safety regs crept in about cooking off grenades. And Sitnikov"—here Vicente raised his voice a good deal to be heard clearly outside the building—"don't forget that it was *your* old man who was running the academies all these years, either."

Well, maybe you did. Shows the limited power of talking as opposed to doing, I suppose.

Bethany heard voices she couldn't understand, shouts that held no meaning for her. The screams, though, of pain and fear, those she understood well enough.

They're coming to kill me. I am going to die in agony. And no one will care.

She saw through the broken, ground-level window a small knot of her enemies, pounding across a street. She donated them a burst but hit, so far as she could tell, nothing. Nothing, at least, came of it except that she lost some of her hearing for the nonce.

I'm going to die in agony, no one will care, and it will be a completely useless, pointless, wasted death, too.

Professionals would have not only knocked out the window, they'd have put up some kind of wire, chicken wire in preference, to keep unfriendly objects like grenades out. Sadly, the crewmembers sent down to the base to buy time were not professionals in ground combat. The cadets, of course, weren't either, but they didn't need to be.

Two objects sailed in through the window almost simultaneously. One went past Bethany, leaving a thin trail of smoke, then hit the floor and rolled across it to the pile of furniture by the sole door. The other hit the light armor over her breasts, bounced away, hit the desk, then fell behind her precarious perch of tottering monitors.

She had just turned and asked, "Petty Officer Robin, what's . . . ?" when the thing exploded.

The shrapnel from the grenade actually didn't do much. But the one that had struck Bethany shattered the monitors, and sent a good deal of plastic and glass into her legs. It also rendered one eardrum insensate for the time being and burst the other. She screamed and went down.

The other grenade was, perhaps surprisingly, only a hexachloroethane-zinc smoke grenade. It burnt, rather than blasting, but in the burning it filled the room with hot, toxic smoke.

Recognizing the danger, Robin ordered, "Clear away the door, we've got to get out of here!" Then, holding what remained of his breath, he crawled across the floor to where Bethany lay. He grabbed her by the collar of her uniform and began dragging her across the smooth tile.

By the time he reached the now open door, the other members of his fire team were gone. He heard firing from outside the basement.

"Don't shoot," he cried. "We're coming out. I've got wounded! Don't shoot!"

Irene Temujin caught a glimpse of the familiar—and once hated—uniforms and came running out of Quarters One dancing, jumping, twisting in air for sheer joy at the prospect of liberation. *They seem so young . . . have I truly gotten so old?*

The cadets had already gotten the word: *If they look poor and bedraggled, they're probably on our side.* No one, in any case, took a shot at her.

She brought herself up short at the first cadet she came

to, dropped to both knees, and then took the cadet's hand and began covering it with kisses.

"Thank you! Thank you! God bless you. God bless all of you for coming."

"Miss . . . madame . . . I think maybe we have a case of mistaken identity. You probably want to see our commander."

"Yesyesyes! Where is he? Who is he? Where can I find him? Oh, tellmetellmetellme! Where can I find him?"

The cadet took his firing hand off his rifle and jerked a thumb over his left shoulder in the direction of the central park for the place. "Command post's back that way. Ask anyone for Hamilcar Carrera."

UEPF *Spirit of Peace*

On the big Kurosawa screen in the ship's main conference room, Marguerite Wallenstein watched the planet spin below in the center, while the left-side quarter showed the entire island of Atlantis, annotated for the tactical situation on the ground, and the right showed in much greater detail the progress of the Balboan boys through the base, itself. She wondered if the boys were bothering to take prisoners, or just butchering the crew she'd sent down to try to buy some time,

She could see on the left screen that every *latifundia* on the island, too, was surrounded with a black circle, indicating that there was no communication with it and that the owners were likely either dead or in Balboan custody.

And, since the helicopters have stopped landing at the Class One and Two schools, I assume that all the children are in custody, too.

She gave a command and the left-quarter images dissolved, to be replaced by a close-up from a recon skimmer of the *latifundia* of the former ambassatrix to Santa Josefina. A large circle of poorly dressed people, thin, dirty, and not very healthy looking, watched two better-fed and better-dressed men writhe on crosses. Long lines of mostly women and children snaked from the *latifundia*'s mansion to the crowd, bringing food and drink looted from the main house's cellars.

I was going to get rid of slavery, here and on Earth, too, as soon as I had the power. I couldn't get rid of it until then, though. I couldn't even give a hint that I wanted it gone by freeing my own or I'd have killed the chance to ever get the power. Slavery, especially for sex though not just for that, is too much beloved by the Class Ones to expect them not to destroy me if I showed I wanted to destroy it.

Another verbal command and the scene shifted back to the island as a whole before dissolving again to show an extremely detailed close-up of the base. Marguerite could see tracers slashing back and forth as boys in small groups dashed across streets and alleys. Windows blew out into the streets. There were also scattered small knots of her own people, under guard, being hustled to the northern edge of the built-up area, there to join a larger group under armed guard. She couldn't be sure, but she thought two of the guards, seated, lacked trousers.

A third of the way through already. We're not even slowing them down.

Two of her own black-clad people sat down instead of proceeding to what was plainly an ad hoc POW holding area. That little knot of prisoners began moving again, and quite briskly, as soon as one of the guards shot both of the sit-down strikers, and without any obvious hesitation.

Fanatical, ruthless, vicious children. None moreso than his son. Elder gods, what have I created? What have I let loose on the galaxy?

Wallenstein buzzed her own quarters. "How long until your people arrive on the island?" she asked her lover, the Zhong empress, Xingzhen.

"There was a delay. I am sorry, *baobei*; but I believe them when they say they're moving as fast as they can."

Should I call them off? No, if they can grab the island outside of the base it's a bargaining chip—no, don't pretend you know things you don't—it could become a bargaining chip. Let it ride.

By that time the base was effectively all in the Balboans' hands. If there were any holdouts, nothing her ship or the skimmers could sense indicated they were doing anything but trying to hide.

At the same time, from the large collections of noncombatants that had been held outside of the ridge encircling the base from the land, steady streams began moving inward. She watched the progress for perhaps twenty minutes before she identified for a certainty that the civilians—*And no, now the prisoners, too*—were being marched to the large central park inside the base. She didn't notice that two small vehicles likewise began moving toward the base's park. She certainly didn't have the kind of resolution to see that Hamilcar had likewise shown up at the park.

Still, she was unsurprised when she asked, "Where's the communicator I gave to Carrera right this minute?" to receive the answer, "At the central park."

"Put me through to him."

Atlantis Base

"Hello, High Admiral. How can I help you this fine day of liberation?"

Little bastard sounds smug enough.

"What do you want?"

Hamilcar glanced over at Irene Temujin, about whom he knew nothing beyond the spiderweb of scars she'd shown him across her back. "After what I've seen and been told here, High Admiral, I want your flayed hide nailed to a wall. I will settle, however, for what my father demands: your unconditional surrender and the unconditional surrender of the entire Peace Fleet, your holdings on the planet, your files, your embassies, and all of your personnel."

"I think that's a little ambitious, young man."

"Is it? Is it once your crews know that if those ships do not surrender, I will, if necessary, set off one or two large nuclear weapons and kill their families here, in toto?"

"That's nons—"

Impatiently, Ham interrupted with, "Hajar, High Admiral. You know, if anyone does, who destroyed Hajar. You know why. And you know where the nuke we used came from. Lastly, you know we have more.

"Of course, we'll only use the nukes if we're rushed. Hmmm...you get visual on this thing, right? Yes, of course you do. Watch this, High Admiral."

Ham turned the communicator around to one corner of the park. Two men and one woman had been stripped of their clothing and now lay down atop hastily constructed crosses, bound at the wrists and feet to those crosses. He walked forward, to give the communicator a better angle. Then he focused on the woman as a burly centurion took a hammer in one hand and a large nail in the other.

The hammer blurred. There was a loud clang of metal on metal. Blood welled up around the nail. A heart-tearing shriek followed instantly, then grew louder—impossibly loud—as the centurion drove the spike in with another half dozen solid hits.

We have a lot to do, quickly, thought Ham; *this is only a part of the play.*

UEPF *Spirit of Peace*

Marguerite wanted to wretch as she saw the nail driven into Claudia Castro-Nyere's right hand, just outward from the wrist joint. She ordered the Kurosawa to silence as she could not bear the sound of the screaming.

I wanted the evil bitch dead, yes, but not like that.

"You can be as much of a murdering little barbarian as you think you can get away with, young Carrera, but I still will not surrender and, if my people's families come to harm, your country will be slagged."

"You sound very confident for something we both know is bullshit, High Admiral. Still, I'll let you stew for a while, contemplating all the worst we can do. And, you know, while you're stewing, your crews can stew, too. Carrera the Younger, out."

What did he mean, "something we both know is bullshit"? What does that little bastard know? And how could he know it?

"Khan, what did that little monster mean about 'bullshit'?"

"I'm guessing that he means we both know the Federated States would go to war, without any restrictions, if we use nukes anywhere on the planet."

"But he knows about all the nukes we sent down to the Salafi *Ikhwan*. We sent them because ours didn't work."

"Sure, High Admiral, but there's another and more plausible explanation for our sending them nukes from down below: to, again, keep the Federated States from blasting us."

"Maybe that's it," she tentatively agreed. *But I'm not sure of it. Could we have a spy aboard?*

Atlantis Base

The crowd—half in stunned silence and half weeping—gathering in the central park was on the order of ten thousand or more, between spouses and children, ground crew, grounded pilots on crew rest, administration, etc. It was important to the plan that they be separated out by their connection to the Peace Fleet.

"Shut the fuck up!" The speaker, an intelligence warrant named Robles, stood with a handheld megaphone atop a hastily piled mass of office furniture. "It is critical, both to our purposes and your own continued good health," the English-speaking warrant said, "that you be segregated by ship and ground function." He jerked a thumb at a place behind him where the last of three crosses was being erected, each with an agonized Class One nailed to it.

"Don't fuck with us. We don't care about your special status; you have no special status. You have no rights. You have no privileges. You do what you're told, when you're told, and you need not—you and your children—end up on one of those. If you don't cooperate, however..."

He consulted a clipboard listing the name of every ship in the Peace Fleet. It had never been secret.

"Very good. Now all people connected in some way to the ship UEPF *Spirit of Brotherhood*, come forward to me with any bags and children you may have. Quickly now, we don't have all fucking day..."

UEPF *Spirit of Peace*

Shorter than Wallenstein by nearly a foot, Xingzhen was still the dominant one. With Marguerite slumped in a chair, head resting on arms crossed on her desk, the Zhong empress stroked her back and whispered words as soothing as she could come up with. Under the circumstances, these were probably not as soothing as one could have wished for but, for all her flaws, lying was not something Xingzhen generally permitted herself.

"I've asked my general staff back home," she said. "There is a way to save your people and your base. Yes, we can do this."

"How?" Wallenstein asked, without raising her head.

"I've ordered a holdup of the two battalions I was sending. Within two days we will have almost a full division of parachutists assembled on Wellington."

"I'm surprised it isn't a full division."

"It was going to be, but some has to be left behind to make room for a special regiment."

"Special?"

"Very special. Our army is huge, and our military personnel very high quality. They're not as well armed as some, but the quality of the people is still the best.

"Even with that, though, some are better than others. This special regiment is a little under a thousand men and has the highest quality manpower in the entire Zhong Empire. It is trained to attack and render useless nuclear facilities: missile silo farms, submarines, air bases; all that kind of thing. The airborne division will land and form up to attack the perimeter of the base. While they are landing, the specials will jump with—do I have to say 'special' again?—parachutes that will allow them to glide a long distance. They could go further, I'm told, but they tend to get disorganized and dispersed, so they'll jump at about sixteen hundred meters and about five kilometers from Atlantis Base. Their jumping will be covered by the mass jump of the airborne division. When the Balboans rush to defend the perimeter, the special regiment will swoop in."

"They'll be seen, won't they?"

"Probably not; they'll go in by night and, yes, before you ask, we expect ten to fifteen percent casualties from the jump and landing *alone*."

"It won't work," Marguerite said. "What if they get fighters from somebody? Any fighter aircraft and they'll smash your planes in the air."

"No," Xingzhen said softly. "No, they won't. I have ordered the carrier and the remnants of the fleet to abandon our lodgment—abandon the men in our lodgment—and sail for Atlantis at what they call 'flank speed.' If fighters show up, they'll be met by a fighter screen of our own."

"But the men in the lodgment . . . ?"

"That war is lost beyond recovery. I'm going to give them permission to surrender, but if and only if the Balboans forgo their demand for ransom."

Slowly Marguerite raised herself. "But . . ." she began to object.

"I'm not sure you understand," the Zhong empress said, bending over at the waist to bury her face in Marguerite's fragrant blond hair. "And I know I haven't been good at showing it—part of the game we play—but I love you and would do anything in my power for you. I think you're the only one I've ever loved. I would do anything."

"Thank you," whispered Marguerite, before adding, more loudly, "you must know how terribly I love you, too."

CHAPTER FIFTEEN

The punishment for those who fight God and His Messenger, and strive to spread corruption on earth, is that they be killed, or crucified, or have their hands and feet cut off on opposite sides, or be banished from the land. That is to disgrace them in this life; and in the Hereafter they will have a terrible punishment. —Sura 5.33, *The Table*

Oppenheim, Sachsen

It was all very Teutonic, really, the way Alix Speidel was able to suppress her personal feelings in order to save her country. *And, to be fair, it doesn't hurt any that he did in fact save me from another several hours of taking it up the ass, likely to be followed by a short time of bleeding out after they cut my throat. Unless, of course, they'd realized who I was and decided to take their time over it.*

They might, indeed, have taken their time over it.

"So what now, then?" she asked.

"Now we have to find your minister," answered Khalid. "Any ideas?"

"Not really," she answered. "He was a Kosmo, so could not normally bear even to say hello to me. I understand he had a wife in the capitol, Potsdam, and a mistress in Leinenfeld."

"I don't believe that," Khalid said. "Leinenfeld doesn't even exist. I mean, have you ever been to Leinenfeld? Do you even know anyone from Leinenfeld? Have you ever met this supposed mistress from Leinenfeld?"

"Aha," she accused, "so you take this Leinenfeld conspiracy seriously."

"No," Khalid answered, smiling, "but I figured you could use a good laugh."

"We Sachsens have no sense of humor," she answered primly. "It is a well-known fact."

And then, remarkably, she began to giggle. The giggle transformed into a single laugh which she tried to suppress. Failing in that, she had to let the next laugh escape. From there, there was no holding it back. She ended up rolling on the floor, repeating, over and over, "Do you even *know* anybody from Leinenfeld?"

After rather a long time—and whether it was because the humor had worn out or because her sides began to hurt rather badly—the laughter subsided.

"Thank you," she said. "I needed that."

"Figured. Now if you were the minister of finance, and you were running for your life, would you run to your wife or your girlfriend?"

"Well, I, of course, have superb taste in women, so as far as that sort of thing goes, either would do." This time she was able to kill a fit of laughing before it could take her over.

A good sign, thought Khalid, *that she can crack a joke, too.*

"However," she continued, "wives are at homes, with known addresses. In his shoes, *that* is absolutely where I would *not* want to be. So the mistress's place, I would think."

"How would we find her name and address?"

She thought back. "Well, let me think; how did *I* find out about it? Mmmm . . . it was from one of my colleagues and *she* got it from a scandal sheet. But which one? I can't recall."

"The global net, then," said Khalid. "But my power won't last indefinitely. Sure, I have a hand generator to charge it, but that takes time. Let me compose and send a message home."

Khalid emerged from his own room chuckling, lightly. "How far does this conspiracy go?" he wondered aloud. "Fernandez answers, 'Leinenfeld? We don't think it exists. But we'll see what we can do. Save your battery. Check back in six hours.'"

"Wait!" Alix said. "Your own chief of intelligence doubts Leinenfeld exists?"

"He must be serious, too," said Fritz. "If you think Sachsens have no sense of humor, you haven't seen anything until you've seen Fernandez."

"Merest truth," Khalid confirmed. "Maybe Leinenfeld really doesn't exist."

"Oh, of course it does," said Alix.

"Have you ever been there?" Khalid asked, again.

"Do you know anyone from there?" Fritz added.

"Do you even know anyone who's been there?" asked the third of the Balboan agents.

That set Alix to another round of uncontrollable, painfully side-splitting laughter. When she'd recovered a bit, she said, "The chancellor, the *Reichskitzler*, once said she'd been there."

"Ah, but she's a well-known liar," said Khalid. "What more proof do you need?"

"Stop, dammit, stop!" Alix rolled onto her side, her arms gripping her sides, in another fit. "Bastards!"

At the proper time Khalid rebooted his computer. There was, as promised, a message there. Decoded, it read:

"The name of the girlfriend is Ann-Marie Maybach, aged twenty-four. Though we still harbor our doubts about the existence of Leinenfeld; if it does exist, there are three women with that name in a certainly forged and fraudulent telephone directory for this town that probably doesn't exist. One of them is seventy-three. One we do not know the age of. The third is thirty-two. If the last isn't lying, and what woman of at least twenty-one lies to make herself older, then it's the second. Her address is Two Brunnenstrasse, Leinenfeld. There is a parking garage across the street and the town's main theater half a block east. We are arranging on-call transportation—a helicopter, or possibly two, with one to refuel—for a pickup in the swimming pool park six hundred meters southwest. It will not show for at least two and a half hours after you call. Good luck.

"Further, we have reason to believe the other two agents we sent you are not coming. Act accordingly.

"PS: If you have the opportunity, please confirm if Leinenfeld University is, in fact, a disguise for a hidden UEPF base."

This Fernandez is pulling my leg, thought Alix. *He's got more of a sense of humor than these two give him credit for.*

"And now," Khalid observed, "the big problem is getting there. All the highways run through or at least close to cities. The cities are where the Moslems are. They will control ingress and egress."

He looked very pointedly at Alix. "We have what amount to vouchers and passes from their local religious leaders. We have guns. We have gold to bribe. The problem is you."

"Me, how?"

"How much do you know about Islam?"

She shrugged with indifference. "Essentially nothing."

"Then you wouldn't be one of them. A good deal of what they think they know is nonsense, theological balderdash, picked up from barely literate imams who don't really understand their own holy book. But there are a number of things they'll agree on: the five pillars of the faith, some of the history, that kind of thing.

"If you don't know any of that, and if we're stopped by a checkpoint and you're asked, it could get ugly."

"Okay, I can see that," she agreed. "What do you suggest?"

"Defense in depth," Khalid replied. "We shall put you in a burka, which will discourage anyone from trying to question you . . ."

"And?" She wasn't fond of the idea of being wrapped in a black sack, but she suspected it could be worse. *Hell, I know it can be worse.*

"And you will be presented, if necessary, as our slave. Or my slave."

"You mean sex slave, right?"

Khalid looked somewhat embarrassed as he admitted, "Well, all slaves are potentially sex slaves, so yes."

"Okay, what do I care what they think?"

"Well..." Khalid hesitated, before continuing, "if you're a sex slave they may offer to buy you, which I can refuse without suspicion until the price rises to a certain level, when it would be very suspicious if I didn't sell."

Her face suddenly lost its color. "You wouldn't sell me?"

"Couldn't possibly; we need you. There's one other possibility, if that should arise," Khalid said. "I could *rent* you."

"*Rent* me?" Alix's face grew paler, still. "You mean like a whore?"

"Yeah. Look, it may not come up but..."

"But we'd best be prepared." She thought about it for a moment, then said, "Won't work. I don't think I can. I'm lesbian, I don't even know *how*. If I tried to fake it, they wouldn't suspect us; they'd just flat *know* I wasn't anybody's sex slave...or slave who's also available for sex...or whatever."

"Right," Khalid agreed. "Screws that theory up. Anybody?"

Fritz looked carefully at Alix. "You already have kind of a deep voice. Are you willing to give up your hair?" he asked. "I mean just about all of it?"

Her hand flew defensively to her golden locks. "Why?"

"Because, with a few shouting exercises to blow out your vocal cords, and a little dirt rather than makeup, we can make a boy out of you. I have an extra rifle in the trunk of my car, too."

"You want to make a *boy* out of me . . . a *boy*?" The giggles took up where they'd left off, in long-lost and highly doubtful Leinenfeld. "A *boy*? Hey, look; if we stop at a whorehouse, can I have a girl, too?"

"Let me go ransack my closet," said Khalid. "How are you with a needle and thread?"

"My cover was as a tailor," Tim said, before Alix could answer. "I can do for that. I even have the needle and thread."

"Just as well," said Alix. "I'm utterly incompetent with needle and thread."

Gasoline was more or less impossible to obtain from a filling station, what with the loss of the electric grid.

While Tim did some important modifications by hand to some of Khalid's clothes, Khalid and Fritz drained both Fritz's and Tim's autos for more gas. They still didn't have quite enough for a full tank.

"And we may just need that full tank," Khalid said.

Fritz looked up and down the street. "We're 'Muslims,'" he said. "At least everyone thinks we are. These cars belong to 'infidels.' We'll just take what we need."

"Works for me," Khalid agreed. "Go back to my place and get us a few containers. Anything that we can seal and that can hold more than a couple of liters will do."

Without another word he walked to his own car and removed a jerry can, crowbar, and a short piece of hose from the trunk.

They met again next to a large black sedan, a Sachsen luxury model. Fritz dropped about half a dozen small plastic containers on the ground.

"Can we burn premium gas in your car?" asked Fritz, doubtfully.

"It will be diluted by normal gasoline, I think," replied Khalid, slipping the end of the crowbar into a crack between the car and the filler cap cover. "I think we could run it anyway, even if all we had was the high-end stuff. Not my forte but, from what I understand, the only problem with premium in a car that takes regular is that premium is actually less powerful."

A Sachsen man, older, going to fat and balding, came storming out of a house very near to the big black sedan. The man's eyes widened when Fritz unslung his rifle and took aim at him, saying, "Go back inside, old man; the gasoline isn't worth your life. And neither is the little bit of damage we'll do to your car." The Sachsen bolted back into his home.

"We can get away with that here," Khalid opined, while pushing on the crowbar to tear open the cover, "with the pussified city folk. But there are people out in the country whose fathers and grandfathers picked up everything imaginable from the battlefields of the Great Global War and stashed it away against a day of need."

"Yeah, I know."

Khalid fed the hose into the car's now open tank, then bent and applied enough suction to start a flow. Spitting out a small quantity of gasoline, he fed the hose into his jerry can and waited while the fuel transferred.

"I think there's enough here to fill my can, at least twice over, and those containers."

"Wow," said Khalid, when he saw Alix dressed out properly in men's clothing. "I'm impressed."

The woman's hair was cropped off much shorter. And the clothes were masculine. It helped that she didn't have a lot in the way of breasts that needed hiding. But the big difference was in what she'd done to her face. That was amazing.

The only serious flaw in her disguise was her feet; she was still wearing the office pumps she'd had when she'd been grabbed.

"I didn't really know what I was doing," Alix admitted. "I'm already kind of horse-faced..." Seeing Khalid was about ready to argue that, she went on, "No, I am and I know I am. But I figured thicker eyebrows couldn't hurt. For those I had my regular makeup pencil. The scruffy beard won't bear much scrutiny; it's just boot black stippled on with an otherwise dry sponge. Well, that and some hair from...well, I'm not a natural blonde as you may have observed...once. I'll probably have to reapply it twice a day but what I have on now ought to get us out of the city."

"We're still missing something...something...aha! We don't have a pass for you."

"Can we forge one?"

"Maybe. Not my forte, but..."

"I've had the basic course," Fritz said. "And half these motherfuckers are barely literate in their own languages."

"Okay," Khalid said, "You get to work on that and I'll try to scrounge something that will do for a *keffiyeh* for her. I think I've got a tablecloth somewhere."

The trunk could have held the packs well enough. Instead, they'd put in more food and a couple of twenty-liter bottles of water, then half buried Alix in the back seat under two of their packs plus one they'd made up as her own.

Everybody had their rifles not only in plain sight but to hand. That wouldn't be remotely suspicious to the people they were trying to avoid. The roads were surprisingly clear of burned-out automobiles, given that burning cars had become the explicit expression of Muslim loathing of Taurans and everything they stood for and believed in.

The answer as to why the roads were clear wasn't long in coming. Khalid, who was driving, had to stop to allow a large gang of male slaves to pass under guard, with their flabby and pale bodies exposed to the weather. An overseer, who could easily have passed for one of Khalid's cousins, before his first visit to the plastic surgeons, pointed. Instantly, a dozen of the slaves trotted over and began pushing a wrecked car off the road.

"Remember," said Tim, "most of the Muslims here aren't Arabs, but a mix of people from Noricum, from Anadolu, and even home grown. Not only do they have a different work ethic from Arabs, they're also much more inclined to tidiness, even when they have to do the work. Better beep, though, or they'll start to suspect you're an unreverted Sachsen."

Khalid duly *did* beep, repeatedly and impatiently, causing the crowd of slaves to part ways to let the car through.

He called to the overseer, in passing, "Brother, are all the roads clear or are there some I should avoid?"

"I can't speak to very far outside of town," the overseer shouted back, "but until you reach the outskirts just stay on the main roads and you should be fine."

"*Il hamdu l'Illah!*" Khalid returned, then returned his attention to the road, lest he run over some of the newly minted slaves.

Looking at the broken-spirited, terrified slaves, Alix muttered, "Is it any wonder I'm a lesbian when the men of my country are such pussies?"

"It's not all of them," Tim opined. "Some remain pretty tough."

"Yes," she sighed, "but they're all prisoners in Balboa or penned into one corner of Santa Josefina . . . which is why we're trying to get the finance minister to release the gold to free them."

She had a sudden horrid thought. "But what if the swine won't?"

"Not a problem," Khalid said. "I've had *that* course."

"You've had the interrogation course?" Tim and Fritz asked together.

"Just the truncated one—no live subjects—but it was taught by Mahamda, himself."

"Live subjects?" Alix asked.

All three together answered, "You really don't want to know."

The car continued on until reaching downtown. There,

Alix noted two popular lesbian spots, *Sappho* and *Chapstick*, had been gutted and burnt. She pulled the *keffiyeh* Khalid had found for her over the face, put her head down, and did a pretty fair job of not showing she was crying. Except for her shaking shoulders, the others would never have known.

The woman stayed like that until, after the cart had rolled another mile or so, she heard Fritz say, "Jesus, it's a slave auction."

That was enough to bring her head back out of the *keffiyeh*, though she kept low, watching as the car passed what appeared to be several hundred women and girls— and some of the girls looked young, indeed—standing on various platforms while prospective buyers wandered around, inspecting the merchandise. The inspections tended to involve the girls and women having to show off their wares, to disrobe, on demand. Many, Alix saw, not allowed to keep their bodies covered, instead covered their faces out of shame.

"Didn't take them very long to set things up," Tim said.

Fritz replied, "It wouldn't; they already had the blueprints for this kind of thing."

Perhaps five miles outside of the city, they came to an apparently abandoned town, Dudenhausen, which was right down the road from Babenhofen. There was no bypass; the road ran right through the middle of town. They could see damage on the outskirts, a bunch of blown out, shattered windows, a number of burnt-out homes with fires that were still smoldering.

There'd obviously been some fighting there but just

how much they couldn't say without entering it. And Khalid especially didn't want to drive into a town where the occupants might just shoot first and ask questions later.

"Tim, take over the driver's seat and wait here. Be prepared to run for it with or without us," Khalid said. "Fritz, come with me. Alix, keep your head down; we haven't a clue what's in there."

Warily, with one man on each side of the main street taking turns overwatching each other, the pair moved from house front to house front up *Hauptstrasse*. At any second, each of them expected to be met by a hurricane of fire, based on both the bullet holes and the damage, which grew more serious the deeper they passed into the town. Instead, a steady breeze blew from behind them.

Finally, at the last house—rather the burnt-out ruins of the last house—before the town square, they stopped. They had to stop, after all, Fritz was vomiting and Khalid felt like it.

The town square was piled deep with corpses, four or five hundred of them, Khalid suspected, maybe more, and with flies buzzing and lapping at the blood from innumerable wounds. There were buildings around the square, some damaged and some not. To the exterior walls of each, corpses had been nailed through the wrists and the feet. There were several dozen shot dogs, as well.

"They were alive when they went up there," Khalid judged, pointing with his chin at one of the victims. "Wounded maybe, but alive."

"All men," Fritz noticed. "I wonder where . . ."

"Slave market," Khalid answered. "I suspect some of

those women and girls we saw on display were from here. Come on."

They walked around the pile of bodies to the burned-out church that stood on the other side. The wind mostly kept the stench of the bodies away. At least it did until they reached the church. There they stopped, taking in the nailed-shut main entrance, the collapsed roof, and the walls from which the stained glass windows had somehow burst.

"I suppose we have to look, don't we?" *But I think I already know what we're going to find.*

Rather than try to pry off the bar that sealed the main door, they walked around the side and scrambled up to where they could peek in. What they saw . . .

"Dear God," Fritz said, tonelessly.

What they saw were several hundred small to tiny burned bodies, twisted into a fetal position, piled like the charcoal they resembled, deep on the floor of the church. Some *antaniae* were tearing burnt strips of meat from the corpses.

Khalid let himself fall back to the ground. It was then that he noticed the bullet marks that scarred the stone frame of the window.

"What . . . who?" Fritz wondered.

"Some of the women, I suppose," Khalid replied. "The older ones who weren't worth the trouble of trying to sell. Boy children who weren't quite pretty enough for the market. Herded in, then burnt alive, with rifles and machine guns posted to drive back any who tried to escape.

"Come on, let's go back to the car."

The way out was quicker than the way in. Khalid was pretty sure there was no one left alive in the town to worry about.

"Switch off, Tim," he said. "I'll drive."

With a shrug, Tim got out of the car and walked around to the other side. Khalid got in around the same time, and, seeing everyone had settled in, began to drive. Once past the first block, instead of following Main Street, he cut right, went two blocks, and then left to parallel Main Street and avoid the scenes at the town square.

Even more than his normal very Sachsen appearance, Fritz was ghastly pale, Alix noticed. She also noticed that Khalid's route made essentially no sense whatsoever.

"What are you trying to keep me from seeing?" she demanded.

"The road up ahead isn't suitable for vehicles," he lied.

"Bullshit! Take me there!"

"Alix, you don't want to . . ."

"Take. Me. There."

Crap. If I don't take her she'll assume it's even worse than it is. I suppose I'd better. Shame she's too bright to fool.

Reluctantly, he turned the wheel to head toward the town square. Once there, he stopped but left his motor running.

At first, the big pile in the center made no sense to Alix. She had no frame of reference for it. Then she made out a pale arm, maybe beginning to turn a little greenish. Leaving her borrowed rifle behind, she opened her door and jumped out of the car. Suddenly, the whole scene became clear. She saw the bodies. She *smelled* the bodies. She split the air with her scream.

At her scream, Khalid, Fritz, and Tim likewise exited the vehicle.

She turned on them. "You bastards did *this!*" Alix exclaimed. "You . . ."

"No, they didn't," Khalid said. "Oh, *I* had a part in it, as I already admitted, but Tim and Fritz had different jobs."

"I did targeting, actually," Fritz admitted. "My tailoring shop was useful for keeping tabs on your military," added Tim.

"And you?" Alix accused, turning her full fury back on Khalid. "How many guns did you smuggle to my country?"

Khalid didn't answer right away, thinking on it. "Two or three thousand, I suppose, to Oppenheim and its environs—"

"And . . . ?"

"Maybe seventy thousand, all told, here and there. Well, maybe eighty thousand. Hmmm . . . are we counting hand grenades, machine guns, and mortars?"

"Bastard!"

"How many tons of bombs did your *Luftstreitkraefte* drop on *our* country?" Khalid asked. "How many piles of dead did your bombs leave?"

"That was *different*. That was—"

Khalid cut her off. "That was using the means at your disposal to win a war. So is this. And so was my smuggling arms. The difference is that your planes were dropping bombs in an optional war in support of aliens and a homegrown, bureaucratic tyranny, while this was necessary in order for a genuine republic to survive.

"So tell me, how hard did *you* fight against the invasion of my country?"

Alix looked at the pile of corpses, buzzing with flies, and thought, but did not say, *Pretty obviously, not hard enough.*

"What is your country?" she asked, trying to change the subject. "Are you not Moslem?"

"No, I am not," answered Khalid. "I told you when we first met that I am a Druze."

"What's the difference?"

CHAPTER SIXTEEN

Our greatest foes, and those we must chiefly combat,
are within.
        —Miguel de Cervantes Saavedra, *Don Quixote*

Tauran Union Defense Agency Headquarters, Lumiere, Gaul

Though two of Terra Nova's three moons provided close
to half illumination, the office suite, itself, was near
enough to pitch black as, indeed, were the entire
headquarters and, except on the streets, the city in which
it found itself. It was believed that the main power plant
for the city had fallen. Into this pitch darkness, Jan
Campbell had awakened with a start from a fitful and
miserably uncomfortable sleep, back propped against the
wood paneling lining the dressed stone wall of the
building. She thought it was raining.

"Wha'... what?"

She'd taken the pitter-patter of bullets striking exterior
stone for rain, for a moment, as she'd taken the reports of
far-off rifles and machine guns as some kind of thunder.

"Here they come again!" repeated Corporal Dawes, raising his rifle to his shoulder after pulling a careful nighttime watch from a partially blocked, glassless window. His shout was loud enough to wake the dead, in the confined spaces of the headquarters building, which was just about enough to get the other Anglians and the Gallic woman, Turenge, on their feet and racing to their firing positions.

Is this the fourth attack or the fifth? Campbell asked herself. She didn't remember. Shaking her head to clear it, she shouldered her own rifle, then used the muzzle to push aside the ad hoc curtain stretched across the window. She could hear bullets impacting the stout and solid stone of the place. Some even entered the long-since-destroyed windows, flying across the office space to bury themselves in the wood of the opposite sides. She'd have been frightened of the bullets, perhaps, but for two things. One was that she was an officer of the Anglian Army, hence had traditions to uphold. The other was . . .

Silly turds still cannae shoot fer shit.

In her night-vision scope, sadly only an image intensifier and not a thermal, Jan could see some dozens, maybe even scores, of the enemy charging across the broad boulevard, leaping over their own dead to reach the protection of the lee of the building. She took aim at one, squeezed off a round, then cursed the miss.

Calm yerself, woman! she told herself. *Calm!*

An easier target appeared, three men struggling with what she thought was a medium antitank rocket launcher or recoilless rifle.

Now that *can fuck us up. Bloody tube's longer than 'ee*

is. Quickly, dammit, decide quickly; the one man carrying the launcher or the two with a shell each on each shoulder? The launcher!

This time Jan took her own advice. Forcing herself to calm, she breathed deeply, once, twice, partially exhaled, and then began to squeeze the trigger. The Gallic rifle she used—unfamiliar, yes, but not in principle very different from her own army's—bucked against her shoulder. She was rewarded with the image of her target falling forward and the antitank weapon going flying.

Now who ... aha, one is going for the launcher and had to put his ammunition down. So the one with the ammunition ...

Again she fired, missed, and fired again, this time with better luck. Clutching his throat, which was probably where the bullet had entered, he sank slowly to his knees, then flopped over face-first.

That'll do for ye, ye damt dirty bastard.

The new gunner got into a firing position, then swung around, probably to call for someone to load the thing. Apparently, he didn't like the implication of the other ammunition bearer being down, too. He hesitated for a moment, then threw the large launcher away, before getting to his feet to flee.

Oh, no, ye howlin' dobber; get away so ye can come back with friends? A thin' no'.

The rifle bucked. Though her fleeing target fell, he rose again to all fours, trying to crawl off.

Were A the cruel sort, A'd put one up yer arse ... that, or shoot yer balls off ... well ... maybe A am.

She wasn't entirely sure if she'd actually hit either his

rear end or his testicles. Didn't matter, she put three more rounds into the body, just to make sure, making it shudder with each impact.

"Bastard!"

Giving the area to her front a quick scan, Jan saw nothing worth her immediate attention. She let the rifle rest on the thick sill, then looked around to see how the rest were doing.

The first thing Jan saw was Captain Turenge and Corporal Dawes counting off together after each pulled a ring on a hand grenade. Amusingly, Dawes counted in heavily accented French and Turenge in equally accented English. On each's equivalent of three, the grenades went out the window—well, technically Dawes bounced his off the frame—to fall to the street below.

The twin explosions that followed were to be expected, though one seemed louder than the other. *Maybe it went off just a bit below the window,* Jan thought. Whether that was true, the screams that came through the window were *most* gratifying.

There was another explosion from somewhere outside, one that made the building shake, ever so slightly. It worried Jan a bit. *If they had one antitank launcher, they might well have had another.*

"*Bâtards!*" exulted Turenge, over the screams. On the spur of the moment, she lanced her arm out to grab Dawes's shirt front. Quickly, she pulled him in and up for what one might have thought to be a kiss, both pure and chaste. And so it would have seemed, except for her, "We'll continue this later . . . if we can." She released him as quickly as she'd grabbed him. "Now, more grenades."

"Wait!" ordered Sergeant Greene. "We don't have an infinite supply. Dawes, watch my post."

"Aye, Sarn't."

Without another word, Greene bolted out of the room. He returned in a few minutes with a slick, red-dripping hand clutching a half a dozen shards of government-provided toilet mirror.

"Use these to check the base of the building," Greene said, as he passed the shards out. "Only risks a hand and not a whole head!"

"How many grenades *have* we got, Sergeant Greene?" Jan asked.

"Four cases of twelve, ma'am," the sergeant replied. "Forty-eight—well, forty-six now—sounds like a lot but it's really not much."

"Do we know if the arms room has more? Any kind of reserve?"

Shaking his head, unseen in the deep darkness, Greene answered, "No; they issued everything they had to whoever would take it. I took as much as I could carry, along with everything else."

Greene was a pretty stout lad; "everything else" included one recoilless rifle with four not especially light rounds for it. Turenge had said she knew how to use it, so there it sat, to the left of the window she and Dawes had tossed grenades out of.

Greene was also an inventive sort, as witnessed by the mirror shards he'd brought back. He lifted his arm over a window sill, holding one of the fragments gingerly between thumb and his first two fingers. With the mirror at just the right angle he scanned the street below, with especial care for the line where the building met the sidewalk.

Nothing, thought Greene. *Bloody odd. I'd have sworn I saw at least a dozen of them charging across the street.* He looked in the angled mirror again. *Strange.*

"Major Campbell?"

"Yes, Sergeant Greene."

"I have a very bad feeling. Permission to take Corporal Dawes and check out the lower floors."

"I'll go with you," Jan said. "Turenge? You're in charge here."

"Got it."

There was a complex system of stone walls, glass walls, and doors inside the headquarters. Added to that was a good deal of effort having been put into muffling sound. It had also been hard to hear much while firing outward; the muzzle blast inside the room and ear plugs stuffed into ears working together. The net result was that, while inside the cocoon of their own office, they hadn't heard anything particularly untoward.

Once they stepped out of their room, though, they heard—at least felt—sounds of firing, explosions...

And maybe the odd scream, too, thought Jan. *Maybe...*

"Corporal Dawes, go back and get everyone but one man to stay with Turenge. Bring them here."

"Yes, ma'am."

Once Dawes had gone back, Jan said to Greene, "Sergeant Greene; I'm a pretty good intel type. And I can hold my own in fighting off a small band of Hibernian bandits. But this is out of my league.

"I *think* the bloody wogs got into the building somewhere. What do we do?"

Greene smiled, unseen in the darkness. Softly he said, "You're a bloody jewel, ma'am, you are. Not one in... well, never mind. I think..."

"Yes?"

"I think we need to get closer. If you're right, and they're inside the building, we need to figure out where, facing in what direction, then come in behind them—there are enough staircases here; hell, with enough balls we could use an elevator—and hit them in the arse. I don't think there's many, if they are inside. Just a small group that somehow cleared a room from outside and slid in. We'd be hearing a cosmic catastrophe if it was more than a squad or two. And we'd probably see all kinds of pseudo-soldiers and sailors running our way to get away from them."

"Right, we'll do that as soon as Dawes—"

"'ere, ma'am. Wit' everyone bu' Trooper Proctor and t'e captain."

"Very good," Jan said. "Sergeant Greene, lead the way."

"Right. Monoculars on. Dawes on point. Spaced-out column of twos, staggered. Make it so."

Dawes said, "'ope ya don' min'. I ha' every man draw four grena'es. I bough' another couple for you and t'major."

"Right," said Greene. "You did well. No sense hoarding ammunition only to leave it to *them*. Now move out."

Mostly by touch, sense, practice, and long drilling, the men did.

Then Greene ordered, still quietly, "To the next division of this floor, quietly, move."

Jan took up the rear. As the men moved out, she marveled at just how quiet they were. *And A'd better be as soft-shoed, for all our sakes.*

Dawes, on point, stopped at the first division of the floor. This one was glass, which meant he could see past it reasonably well. Using first one hand, then the other, he physically prodded two men into taking up positions on either side of the glass door, and a third to hold the door open for him for a moment. Then, squatting low, he duck-walked himself through the door.

The sounds on the other side sounded a lot more like fighting.

Getting down to his belly, Dawes kept his head up, while pulling his lower body along the polished stone floor. He went to a narrow staircase, one intended only for the maintenance crew who swept and mopped the building on ordinary nights. He stopped and listened a while, then slid forward so he could both look down and hear in stereo.

Dawes lay there for several minutes before sliding back, getting back to his feet, and padding back to where the others waited.

"I can 'ear fightin'," he whispered to Greene and Campbell. "But it's no' a' the base of those stairs. I think we can use them to ge' to whatever floor it's on."

"Ma'am?" Greene asked.

"Do it."

Greene added, "I suspect that, with our monoculars, we'll have a huge advantage over any intruders."

"I believe you," Jan said. "Doesn't even really matter. If we can't get rid of them, now, eventually there'll be so many of them that they'll simply overwhelm us. So let's get on with getting rid of them."

Dawes took an approach Jan found, frankly, bizarre. At the head of the stone stairs, he dropped to the floor, rolled over on his back, and, with rifle to the front, slid down the stone risers that way, letting his head fall back with each riser encounter to see the way ahead. If he made any sound doing so, she couldn't hear it.

Greene and another soldier—she wasn't sure in the darkness or the grainy monocular which one—kept to their feet, following Dawes a bit more slowly. Spaced out, the rest of the party went down the same way, except for one man who, apparently without being ordered to, nudged Jan to start descending while he took up the rear.

With each step downward, Jan felt her stomach tighten and her heart begin to pound just that little bit more. *This is definitely* not *what I signed up for. "Oh, young miss," the recruiting sergeant told me, "why you'll be sticking pins in maps and drawing on plastic with a colored pencil. No risk for you at all." What a lying asshole!*

It was a bit easier for her than for many, as she'd been under fire before, not least to include the disastrous battle between the Balboans and the Taurans in and around Balboa's Transitway Area. But that relative ease lessened that little bit more with each step, as the sounds of fighting and screams grew louder.

She didn't notice the little column had stopped until she nearly ran into the man ahead of her. In about a minute, Greene was there, too, along with Dawes.

"The corporal tells me they've coming out of one room,

a couple at a time. He says bullets are flying in every direction down on the ground floor, but that the first floor is quiet. My guess, from what he's seen, is that they took out one room from the outside with a heavy weapon, stormed it, then fanned out."

Jan shook her head. "Can't be. To have a chance of getting to one room, they'd have to have knocked out several near it *and* several overhead on the upper floors."

"Fair enough," Greene agreed, thinking, *I wouldn't ask this of any old female major. Nor of a male major, come to think of it. But this one deserves the chance so*... "Your orders, ma'am?"

"*We'd be'er nae just caw canny.* Rather, we need to hit 'em with everything. Send two men out onto the first floor, with orders to seal off the breached area by fire. They're first to find out where the heavy weapon is that cleared the rooms up there. The rest of us...we're gonna get behint 'em and fook 'em in the arse."

"Suggestion, ma'am?"

"Aye."

"How about if the rest of us spread out in good firing positions? Then, when the two upstairs start cutting off reinforcement, and the rest boil out to head upstairs to take them out, we can reap large of the ones who start heading that way."

She considered it seriously. "Nae," she said before correcting her girlhood accent to, "No, there's too many rooms they might be in, and too many ways up for us to cover and have some mass. When they open up, we have to get surprise, some shock, and a little terror. We need to get them running and keep them running. So let's get down there, identify the best rooms to hit, then hit them. Keep the thought, though; when we get down there, we might find a good opportunity to leave a couple of men to guard our rear."

"As you wish, ma'am."

There was an undertone in his voice that made her ask, "You think I'm wrong?"

"No . . . I just don't know if you're right. Even so, better to have an officer who'll make a decision than someone like that dithering, plump, caterpillar-mustached dolt, Houston."

With that, Greene turned away and, *sotto voce*, gave the orders, pointing where useful. The first two men he addressed took off as quickly as they could for the first floor, while still being quiet.

As the men moved out, he waited behind until Jan came up. "You can't be seen or heard," he said, matching her pace down.

"Why's that?"

"Because it's not hard to make the wogs run or surrender, ordinarily, but if they think they're facing women, they'll do neither."

She considered that for all of three steps, realized it was true, also realized her little command was just that, *little*, and agreed . . . reluctantly. "I'll keep quiet and stay out of the way."

"God bless an officer who knows what's what."

While the upper floors were subdivided, the ground floor, what Americans of the twentieth century would have called "the first floor," had been left open to provide

an impressively broad vista for visitors. At the moment, as
seen through the monoculars, what was most impressive
were the dozen and a half or so bodies bleeding out on
the stone floor.

When they reached that floor, it wasn't hard for Greene
to listen for all of thirty seconds, then whisper, "Dawes,
you and Jones will seal off where they're coming in from.
Everybody else, except the major, will come with me.
Major Campbell, in thinking about it, the most important
thing we can do is to seal off anyone else from getting in.
That is probably where you should be, ma'am."

"I agree."

"Let's do it, then. I'll not start our clearing until we hear
that you've begun yours?"

"Correct," Jan said. She'd been a noncom, herself, long
enough to recognize when a fine NCO is playing straight
man and feeding an officer his or her lines. "Corporal
Dawes; lead on."

Unerringly, Dawes went right for the room from which
he'd earlier seen the enemy coming. He wasn't worried,
overmuch; he could see them through his monocular; they
were *most* unlikely to be able to see him.

About halfway there, he reached to his belt and
withdrew a bayonet. It was a Gallic thing, long and
wicked, and perhaps the only thing Gallic of which he
approved besides Turenge. His wingman did likewise,
with the two bayonets clicking into place almost
simultaneously.

Jan was a bit slower.

As he was drawing and fixing the bayonet, Dawes
automatically picked up the pace. Once it clicked, his long

stride—very long for such a short man—turned into something of a gallop. His wingman matched his speed.

How the hell do *they manage to run so quietly?* wondered Jan, lagging behind.

One of the rebelling Moslems—he answered to "Farid" and thought of himself not as a rebel but as a holy warrior, a *mujahad*—came out of the targeted room. He was wary but, having been told the coast was clear in the corridor, he didn't expect much. As dark as it was, he saw literally nothing. There'd been a little light in the breached room, moonlight leaking in from outside. But here in the broad open corridor? Nothing.

The other reason for his wariness had been that he was almost completely untrained. He'd never so much as fired his rifle before this night. The men of his squad hardly knew each other. Of even fairly mundane military techniques, if he hadn't seen it in a movie he had no clue. And if he had it was almost certainly silly.

Farid sensed someone approaching fast. He was about to call out the agreed upon challenge, *Mubarak*, when he felt something long and sharp slide into chest, just under the sternum. He was pushed backwards in an agonized instant.

Farid screamed and dropped his rifle, hands reaching for the pain and to stop the blood that welled out from the now vacating bayonet wound. He felt the horrid thing twisting inside his body as he fell and his assailant passed over him. He hit the stone floor and bounced, adding to the pain and drawing forth another horrible, agonized shriek.

From somewhere above his head, as his head was now oriented, he felt as much as saw a burst of automatic fire, followed by several more. He didn't see the other one, from Dawes's wingman, coming, exactly. Instead he was suddenly able to see his surroundings clearly in the strobelike light, even as he felt three or four new entry wounds being created.

The bullets entered his torso, then tumbled, passing on energy and shredding organs. Continuing on, they passed through his back, except for one that lodged in his spine. The three still in progress then ricocheted off of the stone floor, passed through the flesh of his back a second time, but at a new angle. They continued, tearing up one lung, his esophagus, and a rib. The one that hit the rib basically stopped there, after breaking it, while the one that slashed through his esophagus burst out the left front of his neck. The lung-wounding one exited from his chest.

Worse, through all that the man—no, not a man, but a mere thing of pain—still lived conscious of nothing but agony such as he'd never even imagined.

He wasn't other than a man merely for the mind-wrecking pain he endured, but also because he was but fifteen years old and was never going to see sixteen.

Lying, bleeding... too slowly dying, the boy Farid began to cry.

Jan leapt over the still-living body of some one of the enemy. She didn't notice his age—the monoculars were not that good—but did note he was alive. The bayonet had never been her thing, but, turning, she put the muzzle of her rifle to the top of the victim's head and fired once.

She thought, before she pulled the trigger, that he'd spoken two syllables, something her sound-assaulted ears still vaguely heard as, "*Shokran*."

She smelled the stench of burnt hair.

As Jan fired she became aware of several more things at once. One was that, a ways off to her right, as she faced, Greene had begun his attack. Her ears were sufficiently beaten that she didn't hear the grenades going off as much as felt them. The other was that some very bright flashes came from somewhere below the windows, which were quickly followed by what seemed fairly mild blasts. The third was that there were a number, *nine*, she thought, of bleeding bodies on the floor, of which four seemed to be uniformed Taurans. The last was that she could see tracer fire coming from above and lancing down into the boulevard and beyond.

But the important thing, the really important thing . . . she had to practically scream to make herself heard, "HAVE WE IDENTIFIED AND TAKEN OUT THE HEAVY WEAPON THAT OPENED UP THIS ROOM?"

"MAYBE," Dawes shouted back. "*T'EY GOT ONE FROM UPSTAIRS BUT I DON' KNOW IF I' WAS T'ONLY ONE. T'EY ALSO TOOK OU' ABOU' HALF A DOZEN OF T'DIRTY BAS'ARDS THAT TRIED T' RECOVER I'.*"

"FAIR ENOUGH," she replied. "GUARD HERE; I'M GOING TO CHECK ON SERGEANT GREENE."

She took a quick look out the window, hoping to spot any more of those nasty rocket launchers. She didn't see one, but she did catch the first faint rays of the very breaking of dawn.

CHAPTER SEVENTEEN

All action takes place, so to speak, in a kind of
twilight, which like a fog or moonlight, often tends
to make things seem grotesque and larger than they
really are.   —Clausewitz, *On War*

Atlantis Base

When you use terror on someone, thought Ham, *when you
support terrorists in using terror on someone, you have to
expect that the people you used it on will lose their
objections to using it back on you. I wonder, High
Admiral, if, when you used my father's first wife and
family as stationery, to send a message, did it ever cross
your mind that you had some stationery available to send
messages on, too?*

*Now, me, I think the old man had the instincts and
ruthlessness for it, anyway, even without your help. But
why, in the name of God, would you ever want to give
someone like him reason to go with those instincts? It was
a terrible mistake . . . as I am sure you will come to agree.*

Thirty-one representatives of the ships' families, the twenty-seven of the geosynchronously orbiting ships, plus four of the five colonization ships Wallenstein had taken over to move support from Old Earth to the fleet, stood around two large nuclear weapons. They'd been chosen partly based on spousal rank and partly on their demeanor after having seen their base overrun by those they had to consider feral barbarians. The calm demeanor was important, because it was terribly difficult to get a message through to someone who is shrieking at the tops of their lungs. For the nonce calm held. The hostages, for that's what they were, just stared, as one of the men in charge of the bombs—and they were all adult warrant officers—explained the bombs and the power they had.

"The very short version," the warrant said, "is that if the Peace Fleet does not surrender, you and your families will all be killed, incinerated, disintegrated, when we set one of these off."

That was Hamilcar's cue. "Which we will do . . . unless you can talk your spouses' ships into surrender. So now I am going to send you, two guards each, to your homes where you will call your husband's or wife's ship and tell them what you have learned here today.

"I caution you—turn around and see where those three unfortunates are dying in unspeakable agony on crosses— that if you try to convince those ships not to surrender, you and your children, if any, will be nailed up. Do I make myself clear?"

It seemed impossible to the prisoners selected for this duty that one so obviously young could be so ruthless and brutal. Ham could see that in their eyes and on their faces.

"I sacked and burned my first set of villages when I was ten," he said, "killing all the men—more than a thousand of them—and taking the women and children as slaves. Don't try my patience.

"Guards, take them to their homes and have them call the ships. Make sure that they say the ships are to blink their lights and send down two shuttles to *Ciudad de Balboa* if they surrender."

Hamilcar then turned on his heel and walked off toward the execution spot, the place where the crosses stood.

More crosses—many of them—were going up near the site of the three already in use. The newer ones, though, were of the more traditional sort: an upright *stirpes* to which a cross piece could be attached once a victim was nailed to it.

Crucifixion hadn't been an especially uncommon sentence since the revolution that brought Parilla and the legions to power, overturning the old corrupt oligarchy of the families and instituting a republic. Even so, not everyone could look on the process with equanimity, could watch the slow dying by inches, over days, of someone pinned like a bug to a display board.

The newscaster—Diana Balbo, tall, surprisingly blonde, and photogenic—brought along on the ALTA, could not. She was visibly upset, shocked really, at the spectacle. Had she been witness to the actual nailing and raising of the crosses she'd probably have fainted. As it was, she had to turn her back and face the camera so she couldn't see the suffering souls. She was still a little shaken, truth be told, by the unexpected explosion aboard the ALTA, the fires, and the screams of the dying and burnt.

And I can still hear them. All of them.

That's how Ham found her, facing away and rehearsing into the camera. He approached from the side, thinking, *Nice profile*.

"Miss Balbo?"

She knew who the boy was; everyone did. She had not known he was capable of this kind of atrocity.

"Yes . . . ?"

"I have no official rank beyond cadet," he said, sensing her confusion. "'Ham' will do well enough. Are you set up to broadcast?"

She nodded, then said, "We have a satellite link back to Balboa. From there the news will go out . . . but . . . Ham . . . are you sure you want people all over the world to see what you've done here?"

"Doesn't matter a bit what I want," he answered. "The old man, though, it matters what *he* wants. And he doesn't care in the slightest what the world thinks. He cares that those people upstairs"—Ham pointed skyward—"are thoroughly convinced we are all bloodthirsty maniacs who can be neither defeated nor reasoned with, but only bribed and surrendered to."

"I see."

"Good. When will you be broadcasting?"

"Will ten minutes do?"

Ham consulted his watch, then added a couple of time zones for Balboa. "Make it fourteen. You can tack your broadcast on to the regular news."

UEPF *Spirit of Brotherhood*

Among High Admiral Wallenstein's most keenly felt failings had been her inability to get rid of John Battaglia, duke of Pksoi. It hadn't mattered too much to anyone outside of his own ship, which ship tended to hover on the edge of mutiny at all hours, anyway. But he was next in command after her, and the prospect of his taking over the entire fleet again, even if, as last time, only temporarily, was enough to put anyone in the Peace Fleet into a state of depression.

Happily, that was most unlikely to happen now, as the ship broke down into fistfights, club fights, and, once the galley was raided, knife fights. And then the mutineers seized the arms locker and the two and a half dozen firearms still held there.

"What is happening?" Battaglia, clueless, asked from his bridge.

The chief of communications looked up from a screen on which he'd been scrolling through communications activity. He leaned to his right to consult with another crewman.

"It seems, Captain, that we've gotten both a lengthy private call from down below and some newscast from our own base."

"Put it on screen."

The bridge's main screen refocused and settled on an impossibly young boy in battle dress, standing in front of three victims of death-by-torture.

"That's the uniform of the secondary enemy, down

below, secondary after the Federated States, Balboa," announced intel. "And...yes, it's the son of their war chief. I don't recognize the other two, but that middle one on the cross is Claudia Castro-Nyere."

"Sound? Where's the fucking sound?" demanded Battaglia.

"...and so," said the boy, "either the Peace Fleet surrenders unconditionally, or every civilian hostage in our hands goes up on one of these crosses"—he gestured toward a veritable forest of *stirpes* going up in the park— "or they try to rescue them, in which case we either defeat them, and their families go up on crosses, or they win, or appear to be winning, in which case I set off one of the two nuclear weapons we have here, and their families die by nuclear fire. Those are the only options."

"How can people believe our little country has nuclear weapons?" asked a female voice, off screen.

The answer was accompanied by Hamilcar's best, most practiced, sneer: "Because we took them from the Earthpigs, in Pashtia, where they were trying to give them to the Salafi *Ikhwan*. It's common knowledge in certain circles. Among those circles are the command of the Peace Fleet, since their high admiral was up to her ears in the plot."

The first sounds of fighting came through the bulkhead and hatchway separating the bridge from the ship's central, hollow spine. Several hard *thwapthwapthwaps* told of some kind of high-velocity projectile stinking that bulkhead.

The bridge crew began to murmur among themselves. Battaglia didn't notice his aide edging herself away from his command chair.

UEPF *Spirit of Peace*

Richard, earl of Care's voice sounded strained. "High Admiral to the admiral's bridge. High Admiral to admiral's bridge. This is not a drill. This is not a drill. High Admiral to the—"

Wallenstein was out of her cabin and rushing for the spine before the call could finish. She called behind her, to Xingzhen, "Stay here; it's as safe as anywhere."

Even as she entered the spine and began kicking and pulling herself sternward, she thought, *I don't use that bridge much, hardly at all really. Why did Richard direct me there?*

The exits from the spine went by in a blur. When she emerged feet first from the one that opened directly onto the admiral's bridge she found both Khans waiting for her, along with all the staff from Ops to Comms.

"What the hell?"

Nobody wanted to be the first to speak. Finally, Khan, husband, took it upon himself. "There's no way to make this gentle, High Admiral: we've got active mutiny on three of the ships of the line, *Brotherhood*, *Annan*, and the *Margot Tebaf*. I think we've also already lost two of the colonization ships we've been using since you came back from Earth. I would suspect that mutiny is brewing on every ship in the Peace Fleet."

Marguerite shook her head in disbelief. This just wasn't possible but . . . "How? Why?"

Khan, wife, filled in those details. "It's that little bastard down below. He put wives and husbands and kids on phones to the people aboard the fleet, letting them know that their lives depended on our surrender to them. And then..."

"To prove his point," Khan, husband, continued, "he put himself in front of three of our people that he'd had nailed to crosses and explained what was going to happen if we didn't surrender. The attack on Atlantis is the biggest news going on below, bigger even than the Moslem rebellion in the Tauran Union, so everybody on the planet was carrying it. And..."

"And?"

"Our intel shops monitor the news down below diligently."

"Oh, shit," Wallenstein said, flopping into a seat as her knees gave out from under her.

I can just picture it: news hit the intel offices and became instant rumors. Then, or at the same time, maybe even before, the phone calls hit personal comms and that news began spreading from there. They probably met somewhere in the middle, fucked wildly, and had instant quinto-septo-octuplets, which then ran wildly themselves... spreading... mutiny. There's never been a mutiny before on a Consensus ship. Never. And now...

Marguerite's personal communicator beeped with the code for Xingzhen. She answered it, but without giving her lover a chance to speak. "Just stay in our quarters, *baobei*. We have a huge problem now, all across the fleet. You'll find my sidearm in my upper-left desk drawer. Take it. Arm it. Defend yourself. Now I have to go. Remember, I love you."

Turning back to her staff, she said, "Okay, we're not surrendering a thing. Instead, the first thing I want to happen is for every ship's captain to identify two or three dozen reliable men and women and issue them arms. Then I want them to secure their bridges, life support, and engineering..."

High Admiral Wallenstein had gotten the process of how the mutiny had started almost right. On most of the fleet both newscast rumors and personal comms rumors had met somewhere at random and propagated still other rumors which, themselves, begat conspiracies and plots. That, however, had happened only on the ships of the line that hadn't risen—or not yet, anyway—in mutiny.

A slightly different process had taken place on those ships of the line that had. This was when the personal calls had been received by either someone in an intel shop, already or about to watch the worldwide newscasts, or someone in comms doing much the same thing. In either case, the two hitting together, at about the same time and place, had meant no need for propagation, mere seconds for consultation, and then a rapid rise into a family-saving surge to take over and surrender those ships.

Still another set of circumstances had caused the defection of the two repurposed colonization ships. This was that they were huge ships, with very small caretaker crews, who were very close and who tended to watch the local entertainment and news together because there wasn't another elder gods–cursed thing to do, most of the time. In those cases, there was no violence whatsoever, just a collective sigh and a rapidly and peacefully reached agreement, "Fuck the Peace Fleet, fuck Earth, and fuck the high admiral, too. We surrender."

There was a fourth process, too, though only a single member of the fleet knew it yet . . .

Sitting in *Peace*'s intel shop, Esmeralda knew momentous events were taking place all around her, all across the planet and fleet, but didn't know her place in them.

She watched Hamilcar's broadcast with considerable interest. *Better looking than his father, if not so full of . . . character. I wonder how he smells in person . . .*

Oh, my, what's he saying? Surrender or they'll kill the hostages? Now that *sounds like his father or, at least, the army his father raised. But surely . . .*

Slowly Esma became aware of another conversation going on in the intel shop, that between one of the mid-grade officers and someone below. She also became aware of whispering and had the distinct sense that a number of pairs of eyes were on her.

Now why would they . . . oh, oh.

She bolted a split second before the other crew present lunged for her. One managed to wrap his hands around her leg even as she dug her own fingers into the bulkhead around the hatch. She kicked down with a booted foot, landing a solid blow on the other's face, then pulled and pushed herself through the hatchway.

The hatch was normally sliding and electrically powered but there was an emergency hatch plus an override on the bulkhead. She hit the override, which, since there was no emergency, caused the hatch to slide shut with a sigh before half opening again. Then, after a slap to a restraining latch, she slammed the emergency hatch shut in the faces of her pursuers. A spin of the hand wheel dogged it temporarily from the outside. She couldn't know it, but what actually gained her a few moments' time was the other half dozen crew getting in each other's way.

Whatever the cause, she had a few seconds to run down the passageway until gravity dropped to where she had to mostly pull herself along. Then she disappeared into the spine of the ship and kicked off in the direction of her own quarters.

The sections flashed by until, nearing her own, she used light finger grips to slow herself down. Then, at the proper spot, she grabbed a rail tightly, causing her body to do a one-eighty before slinging her lower half through the hatch that led to the low-gravity portion of her next section.

She almost missed the exit nearest her own cramped quarters, catching hold of a passing rung, and half jerking her left arm out of its socket. Gingerly—*That hurt!*—she pulled herself through the exit, hanging onto the sides of the hatchway while the microgravity pulled her lower half down to proper orientation. Then she let go, sank slowly to the deck, and began to pull herself along to where the gravity was greater and she could walk.

Once at her cabin, she practically dived through, then slammed and dogged the hatch down. She rested her back against it, waiting for her pounding heart to slow enough to hear herself think.

They came after me. They came after me! *But why? I'm*

nobody . . . well, I'm nobody in my own right but I suppose I seem like somebody because I am close to the high admiral. They figured I would be on her side.

Okay, that means mutiny starting right in intel. Sure . . . if it were going to start anywhere, that would be the place.

If this is happening, he *planned it. If he planned it, what can I do to help? Because, yes, whatever* he *wants I will do.*

She gave off trying to hold the hatch shut with her back, plopping down on the thin but adequate mattress.

So what is going on and how can I help? Obviously enough, one, they have the base below. Two, they are holding the families and ground crew hostage and will kill those hostages if the fleet doesn't surrender. So, three, the surrender of the fleet is their goal.

"How did he know that grabbing the families and base crew would cause mutinies?" she wondered aloud. Then she thought back to the book Cass Aragon, her handler, had given her. *"When a group uses terror, even though it doesn't work on the targets on which they use it, it is generally because they do not understand why it isn't working, because it would work on them. Terror works best on terrorists."* Yeah, of course. *I know the high admiral was involved in the attack that killed his first family. I've heard her weep over it. Though . . . was she weeping because she was involved and it was wrong, or because it didn't work? The answer's not obvious to me.*

More obvious, though, if I hadn't gotten out of intel when I did the others would have taken me prisoner, maybe made me a hostage in my own right, for leverage over the high admiral and Richard. Why? Because it would work on Marguerite and Richard, and they knew it because it would work with them.

I'm guessing, of course, but . . . the more I think on it, the more certain I am it's a good guess. So . . . if I help him, use terror in my own right to help him . . . it's likely to work.

She felt a momentary but strong pang of guilt. *Marguerite has treated me like a daughter and I owe her my life. Richard . . . poor Richard, I know he loves me but I simply cannot feel the same way. I never could have, but after meeting him I can hardly even pretend anymore.*

So . . . questions but no qualms; ungrateful bitch that I am, I am going to betray both of them.

She stood up and thumbed open her locker, rummaging around inside until her hand fell upon the pistol given her by Claudio Marciano, down below when she was the high admiral's messenger and liaison. It was a Helva 21S, an elegant nine millimeter, with Silverwood grips over a single stacked magazine, well suited to a dainty girl's hand.

Will your grandmother be proud of me now, General, I wonder?

Fortress *Isla Real*

You never knew from the deep inside, not without consulting a clock, what time of day it was outside. You also never knew, when you asked a Latin mechanic to fix something, just how he would fix it. Coat hangers and baling wire could generally be expected, though. Along with those you could reasonably expect that he *would* fix your problem.

In fact, it was day. Inside, a very pleased Tribune Aguilar congratulated a rather proud mechanic because, also in fact, the problem *was* fixed.

"Proud of you, son," said Aguilar. "Damned proud of you."

As the tribune spoke, the shuttle hovered three feet above the concrete floor, magnetically suspended, with a pilot inside, grinning from ear to ear.

"Now, *how* did you do it?"

After the briefest of hesitations, it was the mechanic who answered, not the shamefaced software gweep standing nearby. "I rebooted it."

"What?"

"Well . . . it *was* more complex than that, Tribune. The computer was covering up for a mechanical problem, a defective fuel pump, but it also had a problem of its own, in the control application. By rebooting it, the latter problem was fixed and we could see the former. The mobile machine ship produced the part we needed for the fuel pump, and . . . well . . . there she is."

"Ever think about maybe bucking for warrant or even officer?" Aguilar asked.

The mechanic shook his head. "I'm here because my country called me. But, no offense intended, I hate this shit. I just want to get out and go back to my own little garage in *Valle de las Lunas* . . . if it's still standing, that is."

Aguilar turned to his senior noncom, Centurion Martin, who was also grinning from ear to ear. "Tell the men we start countdown procedure in half an hour, and launch in accordance with the timetable."

"Roger that, sir."

Martin Robinson's smile was positively beatific as he thought, *Then it will be the nails, but on a low-gravity part of the ship . . . I'll move my own quarters down there so I can hear her scream for days or maybe even weeks. I wonder how long someone could last on the cross on the hangar deck. Could be weeks. Wouldn't that be nice?*

Robinson's reveries were interrupted when his cell door opened, followed by the entrance of his chief keeper, Tribune Ernesto Aguilar, plus his physical training instructor, and the chief tailor for the base and fortress.

"Time to get dressed, High Admiral," said the former, using a title that was, at best, a courtesy for the nonce. "We have places to go and people to kill."

"Yes," said the former and perhaps future high admiral, without specifically agreeing to get dressed or that there were, indeed, people to kill.

In the event, it didn't matter. The tailor had brought with him Robinson's bespoke uniform, black silk with his old insignia, the latter salvaged from the threadbare uniform in which he'd been captured.

With the tailor's help Robinson put on the form of the uniform he hadn't been allowed to wear since shortly after his capture.

It feels good to be in command again, he thought, even though he was not and likely never would be.

Uniforms had been made for both Robinson and his cocaptive, Lucretia Arbeit, the true marchioness of

Amnesty. She wasn't going on the shuttle, though; hers had been made in case Robinson had died. Instead, she looked out through the bars of her cell and said, "Get the bitch for me, too, Martin. Make the lower-class cunt suffer for everything we've suffered."

"Shut up, woman," commanded Aguilar. "There's a cross"—he pointed at two that had been erected outside the cells—"waiting for you, if we need to use it."

Wearing the look of a trapped animal and giving off an inarticulate cry, the former marchioness slid down, away from the bars and out of view behind the cell's thick door.

"Come with me, High Admiral," Aguilar ordered, then led the way down a long corridor to a thick-walled concrete hangar bay.

Inside the bay masses of sandbags—insurance against a near miss or minor penetration during the attack on the island—were piled against the walls. Robinson didn't know, but guessed, that they'd once been piled around the shuttle—his personal pinnace—the Balboans had captured in Pashtia and for which they'd found a control model in a storage closet of an old museum.

The shuttle, itself, looked different. It took Robinson a moment to realize why. *They're added extra armor to it, ceramic plates I suppose they must be. Well, given that the ships are not completely devoid of some self-defense capability, this makes a certain sense. And, since I am going up on this one, I'd just as soon that we not be shot to bits by one of the antimeteor cannon.*

There were also, in an adjacent area cleared of both shuttle and sandbags, twenty-two men, two pilots and twenty strikers, donning fairly advanced space suits. He didn't know, but could guess from their glum expressions, that the other men, the ones helping those twenty-two, had been trained for the mission but not chosen to go on it. The suits were Volgan-manufactured jobs, Model SPM-7b, with their extravehicular activity modules already stowed aboard, and almost as advanced as anything produced on the world of Terra Nova. The Volgan suits' off-white material was hidden behind black silk little, if at all, different from Robinson's own uniform.

While some were putting on their suits, still others, those not selected for the mission, loaded various incomprehensible items aboard the shuttle. Given the time between the items being carried aboard and those who did the carrying emerging, Robinson figured they were probably stowing the things inside with some care. Some, too, he noted, were very heavy, requiring anything up to four men to port them about.

The suits were generic, but had the means, pressure sensors and inflatable bladders, to be fitted to the individual wearers. This Robinson discovered when Aguilar led him to his own suit, which was then fitted to him. He noted the name on the suit wasn't "Aguilar" or "Lopez" or "Ruiz" or "Velez," but said, simply, "Earthpig."

Because they couldn't know in advance, I suppose, if they'd have to crucify Lucretia or myself to get the full cooperation of the other. That, and to let whoever ended up wearing this suit know in full that they despised us.

There were other differences: the others had various weapons and other paraphernalia attached to their suits, where Robinson's had none, while each of the strikers mounted a substantial module on the back, where

Robinson's and the pilots' were much smaller. On the other hand, his and the pilots' modules had a couple of D-rings attached that the others' did not.

"There was no real need and no good way to train you," Aguilar explained, "nor any particularly good reason to trust you. Once they put on the EVA modules, my strikers will have the ability to maneuver outside the shuttle. You, on the other hand, we'll just haul over by rope once we have a secure area."

'I see."

"Do you? Do you understand your part in this?"

"My part is mostly done with teaching your pilots to fly the shuttle, with making a recording, and with showing you how to tap in to the internal systems of the *Spirit of Peace*. I don't really even understand why you want me along."

"Me," answer Aguilar, "I *don't* necessarily want you along. But Carrera thinks that, if there are any holdouts in the Peace Fleet, then seeing you transmitting a surrender order on the bridge will persuade them. Maybe he's right, too."

"And I, of course, will transmit that order because . . ."

"Nails," answered Aguilar, simply.

"Ah, yes; I had almost forgotten." *Not for an instant.* "Nails."

Everyone was seated, helmeted, and strapped down. The great steel doors opened with the shriek of rust and not enough lubricant. As they did, they exposed a long tunnel with a glimmer of light at the end. Through mystical and arcane manipulation of the controls—

something Robinson understood and mentally *tsk*ed at— the pilots lifted the shuttle about two feet off the ground and started in on a slow course down the tunnel.

The shuttle lacked windows but the forward display was a very high-resolution screen. It had an airlock that was too small for the suits, so the cargo hatch had been left open. Air pressure would drop inside as it did outside. All the men were connected to a life-support system that wasn't integral to the shuttle.

Aguilar watched the view screen as the thin glimmer of light became larger and brighter with each forward meter. Finally, the walls of the tunnel disappeared, to be replaced by a mix of shattered jungle and man-made moonscape, together with a good deal of jungle still standing and even some fair number of cows grazing amongst some cleared areas or drinking from shell craters.

As soon at it emerged, the shuttle nosed up and began building speed for space. A couple of unanticipated coughs and shudders in the system set everyone's—in this case to include Robinson's—heart to racing, but these settled out into a fairly smooth flight.

It was smooth, that is, except for the weightlessness. Yes, yes; the men chosen for the mission had all done a good deal of freefalling and training in a zero gravity plane during its unpowered phase. It was always a little different, though. At least one of his legionaries, thought Aguilar, was bent over slightly as if ready to hurl.

"Don't even think about it, Velez," the tribune said into his comms. "Remember you can't use a barf bag."

"Yes, sir," said the half-stricken trooper.

"Eighteen minutes out, Tribune," the senior pilot,

Lopez, announced, turning his head over his right shoulder. "Give 'em the message?"

"Do it."

Lopez turned a dial and pressed a button. Instantly, the message went out, "This is High Admiral Martin Robinson, the true high admiral of the Peace Fleet. Having been betrayed by the current imposter, Marguerite Wallenstein, I am only now able to return to you. Your bridge crews can check my transponder easily enough and prove it is my shuttle.

"I hereby order the arrest of that same traitor, Wallenstein. I have also agreed to the surrender of the Peace Fleet in order to preserve the lives of our families and other noncombatants on Atlantis Base. Once again, we will save our people at any cost. Once again, the traitor, Wallenstein, is to be arrested or, if she should try to escape, shot. I am coming, with an escort. Let none of the minions of Wallenstein resist, they will be killed."

Without let up or break, the message repeated, "This is High Admiral Martin Robinson, the true high admiral of the Peace Fleet . . ."

UEPF *Spirit of Peace*

Esma played with the hammer of the pistol while she tried desperately to think. *And so I have the means to do exactly what? I am one girl. I cannot be in two places. So, go to the ship's bridge and take it over or go to the admiral's bridge and take that.*

I can't, I just can't, do the latter. Richard I can betray and face him as I do it. At least I think I can. But Marguerite? I cannot face her. Richard, I care for but do not love. My mother in all but name, the high admiral, I do love.

Besides, she thought, *from the ship's bridge I can isolate the high admiral from the rest of the fleet, while from her bridge I cannot control the ship.*

She chambered a round in the pistol, just as *Maresciallo* Bertholdo had taught her, back in Santa Josefina. With a little more rummaging she found the spare magazine and tucked it into a pocket.

Esma took a deep, steadying breath, then undogged the hatch and stepped through. The red alert lights were still flashing and the sirens now blaring, but there was something else. Following some squelching, some squealing, and a good deal of static, over the public address system came a voice she'd never heard before: "This is High Admiral Martin Robinson, the true high admiral of the Peace Fleet . . ."

CHAPTER EIGHTEEN

Men should be either treated generously or destroyed, because they take revenge for slight injuries—for heavy ones they cannot.

—Niccolo Machiavelli

Revenge is a moral obligation of the first water.

—Patricio Carrera

UEPF *Spirit of Peace*

Esma thought furiously. *What does it mean...the implications...of the old high admiral coming back, seemingly from the dead? Now that's one my high admiral never let me in on. But what ship is he headed to? Don't be a ninny, Esma; this is the flagship; he's coming here.*

When he gets here, I think she's a dead woman, one way or the other. The only way to save herself would be to have the ship use its antimeteorite cannon to destroy the shuttle and *order the fleet to surrender to save the people on Atlantis. And she cannot do the latter.*

Even so, she'll try the former if only to save her skin. So . . . the controls for the cannon are on the bridge. And, since that's where I'm going anyway, since he *ordered the shuttle here—of this I have no doubt—then I am going to make sure it gets here.*

Though the crew in intel had tried to take her, the crew she passed on her way inward to the spine and forward to the bridge ignored her. *Just as well; I really* don't *want to kill any of my shipmates if I can help it.*

Once again she ducked into the ship's hollow spine through the asynchronous open hatchway and then kicked her way forward to the bridge. As usual, she had to apply a degree of main strength to kill the limited Coriolis force she still had from the low-gravity deck.

On her way forward there were, so it appeared, half a dozen pairs fighting or trying to. She passed two bodies, locked in a death grip, one with a crowbar driven through his sternum and the other with a knife buried in his belly. Blood seeped out before separating as individual droplets floating around the cylinder. These she tried to avoid but it just wasn't possible. A few hit her uniform and a few more touched her hair and spread out from there.

Madness, she thought. *But . . . then . . . they're fighting for opposed principles, aren't they? Save their families on the one hand; defend the fleet and the Earth on the other. I suppose I should know about opposed principles if anyone does.*

Again, sections flashed past. She paid them no mind; her destination was ahead and only ahead. The whole trip the message echoed in her ears, "This is High Admiral Martin Robinson . . . they will all be killed."

She finally reached the airlock for the bridge—it was rarely needed as an airlock but was there anyway, against the day—and found it locked. *Never before but, of course, with the mutiny . . . shit.*

Keeping her pistol carefully out of sight of the camera, she pressed the buzzer for admittance. In the small screen she caught a glimpse of the bridge. It was chaotic, but at least nobody was fighting. *Yet,* she cautioned herself. *Yet.*

She heard Richard's voice. "Who, what is it? Esma? Elder gods, what happened to you?" This was followed by, "Open the door you fool, open it now."

I suppose he's seen the blood and thinks it's mine. She quickly opened her tunic to push the Helva in and then resealed it.

The wheel on the hatch spun and then the hatch swung outward. A strong pair of hands gripped her and pulled her through, before pulling the hatch shut behind her and spinning the wheel to dog it down, again.

She found strong hands replaced by strong arms wrapped around her, while Richard whispered in her ear, "Thank all the gods that ever were or might have been that you're safe."

"It was close a couple of times, Richard," she answered, without elaborating.

He nodded, though what he was agreeing to wasn't clear. *Maybe that I'll give him a fuller explanation later. That's probably it.*

"The blood isn't mine, Richard," she informed him.

"Thank them for that, too."

Letting her go, Richard pulled himself back to his command chair. "Can't we do something about that damned message?" he asked.

"If we still had communications we could, sir, but it's either abandoned or in mutineers' hands. We're stuck with it."

"Shit. Guns, have we got the antimeteorite cannon on-line yet?"

"Online, yes, Captain, but we don't have one that can bear on the shuttle yet."

"How long?"

"A little over a minute."

Oh, hell, thought Esma, *now or never.* Unseen, behind Richard's command chair, she opened her tunic, pushed herself back against the hatch she'd just come through, and pulled her pistol out.

"Get away from the controls, Guns! Everyone, get your hands up."

At the tone of her voice, full of desperate purpose and infinite menace, with just a hint of hysteria for ambience, all eyes on the bridge except for the captain's turned to her. For Richard, earl of Care's part, he swung his chair one hundred and eighty degrees around before asking, "What are you doing, Esma?"

"Just keep your seat, Richard," she ordered. "I don't want to hurt you."

He smiled slightly, certain that his lover couldn't hurt him. He began to stand.

"Stop, Richard. Just stop."

He ignored her, continuing to rise and then to push himself forward.

With an inarticulate scream, half of anger and half of despair, Esma pointed the Helva at him and pulled the trigger, once, twice, a third time. Each shot pushed her back against the hatch while driving her hands and arms upward. There was a slight delay between shots as she recovered and took aim anew.

The frangible ammunition Bertholdo had procured for her was somewhat irregular and unpredictable. The first bullet entered his abdomen, fragmenting into hundreds of smaller bits and dumping all its energy into collanderizing his lower intestine. This begat the beginning of a scream from sheer agony. The second hit him over his right lung, but did not disintegrate before passing through. This one broke up on the inner bulkhead above the main screen. The third shot took Richard in the right shoulder, breaking up on the shoulder cup and doing incalculable damage to muscle, tendon, and bone.

Each shot pushed him back toward his command chair. The last one pushed him into it. He sat there a few moments, uncomprehending. He looked down and saw blood pouring from his body. *Where did that come from? Is Esma all right? I cannot see her. I cannot look up to see anything.*

Slowly, so slowly, he raised his left arm. For some reason, he couldn't move the right. As he raised his arm he forced his head up again. *Ah, there she is ... safe. So beautiful. Such a wonder. When we are married and settle down here ...*

Slowly, with the image of the girl he loved engraved on

his eyes, Richard, earl of Care and one of the few decent Class Ones to be found anywhere, let his lids relax and sleep take him.

Esma, watching her lover die, screamed his name once. But she could not go to him, not yet. Gulping, taking her nonfiring hand off the Helva to wipe her eyes, she ordered, "Now pump out the hangar deck and open the doors."

Ex-Admiral's Barge, astern of the *Spirit of Peace*

"Tribune, the hangar doors on the target . . . sir, they're opening them up."

Aguilar cocked his head inside the helmet, staring at the screen with a cynicism born of many years with the legions. *I wouldn't trust that if they baited it with a piece of cheese.* "Ignore it, Lopez. We proceed as per the plan."

While the hangar bay was stationary relative to the shuttle, the exterior of the *Spirit of Peace* chosen for touch down spun at about ninety-two feet per second. Long, many long, hours had been spent aboard the shuttle by Lopez and his copilot, just learning with the simulator program to match velocity while maneuvering inward to touch the hull.

But, thought Lopez, *simulators never quite give you all the answers. On the other hand, we didn't train to enter the hangar at all, so . . . hmmm . . . on the other hand, the prisoner.*

"Sir, we could have the high admiral pilot us into the bay."

"No, Lopez. It could be a trap. It's too convenient not to assume it's a trap. So we go in as we planned, the hard fucking way."

"Yes, sir."

Lopez applied retros to slow down, stop, spin the shuttle on its axis, and then begin to match the rate of spin of the ship. This was complex and difficult, because the shuttle insisted on continuing in a straight line, while the pertinent par of the hull kept turning away. Finally, he admitted defeat: "Tribune, there's no way I am going to be able to touch down where we planned. The simulator just didn't prepare us for this; it's a lot harder than it looked."

"High Admiral?" asked Aguilar. "Your recommendations?"

"My first one was to take the hangar bay but you're right; it's too convenient while Wallenstein is nothing if not sneaky and treacherous. You have a way to affix the shuttle to the hull?"

"Yes, we've got adhesive stanchions. Peel 'em; slap 'em to the hull; wait nine seconds, and they stick. Then we could lash the shuttle to them. And we know they work because we have six of them stuck to the hull of the shuttle and they wouldn't budge a bit when we tried."

"How much cord do you have?" Robinson asked.

"Shitloads, why?"

"Send the strikers down to affix the stanchions and tie themselves down, then we can match speed and haul the shuttle in."

"Lemme think . . . Sergeant Ruiz?"

"Yes, Tribune?"

"Can your team tie the shuttle down, then move forward of it to blow the hull?"

"Maybe better to move forward and counterspin-wise, Tribune, to keep from having the piece we take out smash the shuttle."

"Okay, fine; the key question is can you do it?"

"Probably."

"Fucking *'probably'?* What the fuck is 'probably'?"

"Life's a gamble, Tribune. We can probably do it. But sure as shit we can't stay out here indefinitely."

God save us from philosophical sergeants, thought Aguilar. "Yeah, yeah; all right. Are you ready?"

"As much as we're going to be."

"Lopez?"

"Yes, Tribune?"

"Take your orders from Ruiz."

"We need a short period of no spin relative to the ship, Lopez, while we're over our breach point. Can you do that?"

"Give me . . . twenty seconds."

"Roger."

"Okay . . ." said the pilot. "Get ready . . . four . . . three . . . two . . . go!"

Ruiz was first out of the cargo hatch, as was only appropriate. He trailed a thin cord behind him as he progressed, the cord running back to the shuttle. Using his right hand to manipulate the little joystick that sat on an arm jutting forward from his maneuver pack, he directed himself to the ship, thin and faintly visible streams of fire coming from the back and sides of the pack. In his left hand he held a stanchion that was already peeled and tied off, with an elastic cord running to a D-ring on his suit. His feet hit the hull a glancing blow, which twisted him to where he was facing away from it off into outer space.

"Shit!" For a brief moment, facing infinity and having temporarily lost his bearings, Ruiz almost panicked. The key word there, though, was "almost."

Forcing himself to calm, with a little more manipulation of the joystick he managed to turn himself around to where he was facing the hull again. A bit more and he began to move in closer... closer... closer.

"Got it!" Ruiz exulted, as his left hand smashed the stanchion's adhesive side against the hull, breaking the thin plastic film and letting the adhesive reach the hull to stick. With a well-practiced set of motions, he untied the cord he'd trailed from his own suit and then reattached it to the stanchion.

"Come on down," he ordered his team who, one by one, appeared in the cargo hatch, attached themselves to the cord, then moved themselves down to the hull. There, at the hull, five more stanchions were stuck on.

While that had been going on, two more men crawled out onto the exterior of the shuttle. Working from rear to front, each tied off three color-coded cords to three stanchions that were attached to each side of the shuttle. As soon as they saw that the six stanchions had been affixed to the ship's hull, they tossed down the free ends of the cords.

Total gaggle fuck, thought Ruiz, watching his men try to scramble for the cords. That was bad enough, but still they got them. It was when they tried to tie off the shuttle so they could haul it down that the real problem arose.

Neither the men nor the adhesive nor the stanchions were strong enough for the task.

"Goddammit, grab Velez," Ruiz shouted, seeing one of his men torn off the hull and heading into space.

"It's not going to work, Tribune," Ruiz said, "Got a better idea?"

There was a long pause before Aguilar answered, "Yeah ... maybe. Can you tie off some cords to the five remaining—"

"Four remaining," Ruiz corrected.

"What the fuck ever; *four* remaining stanchions. Can you get some cord on them and run the free ends to the cargo hatch?"

"Think so."

"Good, because we're going to burn our boats and just let the shuttle go."

"Guts move, Tribune."

"That's what I get the big drachmae for."

Crewmen Steven Smith and Gaige Mosher, having seen the chaos into which the ship had descended, had decided they wanted no part of it. Rather than be caught up in the mayhem, they'd decided to find a nice safe spot, only diverting long enough to hit the crew's bar and grab a couple of glasses, a bucket of ice, and a bottle of, it must be admitted, not very good scotch on the way.

With glasses and booze and ice in hand, they'd gone as far from the sound of anything resembling excitement as they could, finally finding themselves in a large storage compartment just off the ship's full gravity gym. There, having piled some boxes into makeshift chairs, and dogged the hatch from the inside, they'd proceeded to crack the bottle, add some ice to the glasses, and wait things out in a degree of style.

They were on their third round when Gaige asked, looking down, which is to say, outward, "Steve, did you just hear something?"

Exterior hull, UEPF *Spirit of Peace*

From Ruiz's point of view, the slowly receding outline of the shuttle disappeared behind the spinning hull. It would come back into view in about two hundred seconds, though it would be farther away and even less likely to be recovered. The shuttle kept the same orientation to the ship as it floated away.

I hope to hell Carrera's got a sense of humor about that shuttle, thought Aguilar.

Meanwhile, through a combination of maneuver packs and belay lines, the rest of the force—one commander, Aguilar, one assistant, Centurion Martin, two pilots, one former and future high admiral, and nineteen strikers— assembled on the hull, securing themselves either to the previously anchored stanchions or adding new ones.

"Breach it, Ruiz," ordered Aguilar, while Martin made sure everyone else got as close and low to the hull as humanly possible.

"C'mon, First Squad; let's make us some hole."

Following Ruiz the other five and he formed a loose circle. Each man had taken out and carried in one hand a folded and curved section of something that looked rather like door weather stripping on steroids. Each also had an adhesive stanchion attached to a bungee cord, itself attached to their suits.

Ruiz was the first down. He gave the joystick for his maneuver pack a little extra oomph, then released it and took the stanchion in that hand. A bit more experienced now, he waited until the hull was less than an arm's length away and . . .

"Got it." Calling for "Number Two," he unfolded his section of presumed weather stripping, held it onto the hull, and hit the top of one end *hard* with his right fist.

Yeah, fucking yeah, he cursed as the blow drove him away from the hull until the bungee cord caught him short and pulled him back. *Every action has a reaction, equal to . . . and fuck it. It's just going to take more time.*

He struck the strip again, a little bit away from his first blow. The same thing happened but, since he was more ready for it, the third blow came quicker still. By that time, number two was nearly beside him, unfolding his own section after slapping his stanchion down.

Number three followed . . .

"Are you people done yet?" Martin asked, possibly only to break the monotony of the group being nagged and cajoled by Aguilar.

"Few minutes, Top. Almost there."

A few minutes passed with both Aguilar and Martin ready to apply a little more verbal encouragement when Ruiz and his five came floating back on maneuver pack power. Hands reached up and pulled them down, close to the hull.

Ruiz started to turn the detonator over to Aguilar. "You want the honors, sir?"

"Nah; your crew did the work; you can have the honors."

"Yes, sir. Fire in the hole! Fire in the hole! Fire in the hole!"

"What, you think some space monster's beating on the hull to get in?" Smith ridiculed.

"I don't know what it was, Steve, but *something* was beating on the hull."

"Drink more," Smith suggested, proffering the bottle. "At least then we'll have an excuse for . . ."

Suddenly flames jutted into the compartment, a circular wall of them, rising about six feet high, surrounding Mosher. The instant overpressure burst both sets of eardrums. The flames then disappeared, as did Mosher and a circular section of the hull. As that section went, so went Smith, initially because he lunged to grab Gaige but then unwillingly following Mosher as he was pulled out of the compartment with the escaping air. His hands' attempt to gain purchase on the rim of the newly made hole proved sadly futile.

Both men had screamed, soundlessly, in stark terror. This had its upsides and its down. In the first place, screaming emptied their lungs, which saved them from rupturing. But in the second place—the down side—it roughly doubled from fifteen to thirty seconds the amount of time it would take them to lose consciousness before dying. And those seconds were going to be long seconds, indeed.

Three effects hit both Smith and Mosher close enough to simultaneously that they couldn't have told the difference even if they hadn't been in utter mindless agony. First was the sun which, without an atmosphere, was intense, causing extremely serious sunburn on all exposed skin as that skin rotated with the bodies. Second, the moisture in their eyeballs and nasal passages evaporated, causing freezing of both. If that wasn't quite shitty enough, each got an instant and agonizing case of the bends.

Ah, but there was more. In the hard vacuum, the moisture on the tongues began to boil, even as the pressure differential between inside the skin and outside caused the skin to puff up, especially the extremities. Mosher's hands, for example, just before he went blind, looked to him to have grown to four or five times their normal size. It is possible that this effect was exaggerated in his mind; we'll never know for sure.

Finally, mercifully, after those long, long seconds, both Smith and Mosher lost consciousness. They were unaware of it, then, when paralysis and convulsions took turns sending them into something remarkably reminiscent of an Old Earth entertainer's dance routine or, rather, several of them.

"Holy shit," said Ruiz. He wasn't the only man to make the sign of the cross over his suit and helmet as the two twisting, writhing bodies sailed off into space behind a circular section of the hull.

"First squad, in," ordered Aguilar.

"Follow me," said Ruiz, flailing doomed bodies

forgotten. He carried with him one of the cords—a white one—that he would tie off inside.

"Second squad, follow me," Aguilar continued, as the last of Ruiz's squad disappeared into the hull.

"Third squad," said Centurion Martin, with the high admiral and the pilots in tow, "in you go, after the tribune. The rest of you, follow me. Just haul yourselves along the white cord."

Nobody lost their grip as they moved along the exterior of the hull and into the compartment, though Centurion Martin was poised and ready to retrieve anyone who did. When Martin reached the hole, he looked up to see that half of the force had already dumped their maneuver packs and the rest, less third squad, were being helped to do so.

Aguilar looked down at the gaping hole and ordered, "Third Squad, seal it."

The assistant squad leader unrolled a six foot in diameter sheet, woven carbon fiber backed up by an aramid fiber, sandwiching a thick layer of mylar between them. The six members of the squad each took a portion and stretched it over the hole the shaped charge had cut, rhythmically punching the edges to release the adhesive and then running palms over those to create a seal.

"Looks good, sir," third squad leader, Sergeant Padilla, announced.

"You have the spare if this doesn't work, right, Padilla?"

"Yes, sir."

"Okay, everyone find something to grab . . . and . . . pressurize."

Every member of third squad pulled out a red metal

bottle topped by a valve. All together they turned the valves, releasing enough air to form a normal atmosphere. The bottles soon misted as their temperature dropped well past icy. While Martin kept an extremely close eye on the seal, Padilla and Aguilar, both, watched their pressure gauges until, "We're at one atmosphere. First squad to the left, second to the right, take your posts by the hatch."

On the bridge, Esmeralda and her pistol were in effective command. Even so, she couldn't bring herself to unseat Richard's corpse. Instead she kept her spot, by the hatchway, where she could keep the bridge crew covered. Nothing but microgravity held her in place.

A new alarm sounded, as a computer voice began to complain, "Hull integrity compromised vicinity deck uniform, section sixty-four. Repeat, hull integrity compromised vicinity deck uniform, section sixty-four. Air completely lost from one compartment . . ."

Every set of eyes turned to look at, first, Esma, then her pistol, then her again.

"We need to dispatch a damage control team, Ensign Miranda," said the chief of engineering. He eyed the pistol warily, before continuing, "There's no telling what other damage has been done."

"Do it," she ordered, in her best imitation of the high admiral.

The chief turned around instantly and began giving orders.

It took time, amidst a riot amounting to a mutiny, for a damage control party to be assembled. In one case, a chief had to drag two combatants apart physically and slap some sense into them to get them to understand, "You fucking morons; there's nothing worth fighting about if the ship loses its air!"

In the event, a twelve-man team was assembled with a mix of vacuum welding equipment, temporary patches, both metallic and magnetic, as well as fiber based, some lumber, and in vacuum suits.

These waddled, as quickly as they could, to the spine, then pulled themselves to section sixty-four. There was confusion at the exit as too many men and women tried to push through the relatively narrow opening, while avoiding being chopped by the asynchronous exit.

Finally, the chief got them assembled in the passageway, then ordered, "Follow me," leading off at as brisk a trot as the low gravity on this deck allowed. As they moved, the damage control team made sure to dog shut every hatch behind them. They arrived at the location of the breach, therefore, and were surprised to find that the gauge on the friendly side showed no loss of pressure. The chief picked up a phone from a compartment on the bulkhead and said, "Bridge? Yeah, there's nothing wrong here . . . no, I can see it on the gauge . . . yeah, yeah . . . sure . . . of course we'll look . . . oh, *shit!*"

At that moment, the hatch to the supposedly breached compartment flew open.

"Go! Go! Go!" shouted Aguilar, as soon at the hatch was opened. Nobody went anywhere, even so, since the passageway on the other side of the hatch was full of enemy personnel. Instead of moving, the lead two men started blasting with their shotguns, sending clouds of flechettes to tear through uniforms, skin, and vital organs.

The sound and blast would have been dangerous in such cramped quarters but for the insulation of the helmets and suits.

Seen but unheard, the UEPF crewmen and -women went down with shrieks and cries that were hardly human. Only when their bodies, dead or dying, had carpeted the deck of the passageway did anybody move.

There were three survivors among the damage control party, one fleeing sternward and two towards the bow. More clouds of flechettes sailed down the almost straight and flat passageway, catching the refugees before they had crossed even half the distance needed to get to cover. It took many more shots to bring them down than one might have expected. They went down in a slower motion than the gravity would have suggested, landing somewhere to the right of where one would have expected them to have landed.

"Remember the Coriolis force," Aguilar cautioned.

As the force piled out, about a third of them fired a shot downward into the damage control party, making sure. Those flechettes passed through, hit the deck, usually broke, and then bounced back up, tearing still more flesh and spilling still more blood.

Quickly scanning the prone and helpless bodies, Aguilar asked himself, *If any live, are they going to be a danger to us or our mission?* He shook his head, taking in the pool of spreading blood and thinking, *Not a chance.*

As they took off, in a column of twos, Centurion Martin looked at the seal they put over the hole they'd blown, and then dogged the hatch behind them. *Because me, I don't trust the promises of chemists and engineers.*

CHAPTER NINETEEN

Those wars are unjust which are undertaken
    without provocation.
For only a war waged for revenge or defense
    can be just.   —Marcus Tullius Cicero

The fair Ophelia!—Nymph, in thy orisons
Be all my sins remembered.
    —Shakespeare, *Hamlet,* Act 3, Scene 1

Bridge, UEPF *Spirit of Peace*

"Stop!" Esmeralda ordered. "Stop the cameras . . . no . . .
go back . . . back . . . there."

Where the internal security cameras had been flashing
from one scene of mayhem to another, now the view
screen showed just one image, that of fifteen or sixteen—
it was hard to be sure—armed, armored, suited men, with
huge, spherical helmets, storming up one of the full-
gravity corridors, leaving a trail of broken, ruined bodies
in their wake.

The attackers began to disappear from the screen until one of the bridge crew shifted to a different camera.

If they're interested in prisoners it's tolerably hard to see exactly how, thought Esma. *What to do? If they come onto the bridge they're going to kill everybody. And I know some of those bodies were women; so they won't stop just because I have tits. I need time to talk to them.*

But how do I get their attention? How do I get them to slow down long enough to talk?

Damn, I am an idiot. "Put me on the PA set."

"What the fuck was that?" asked Aguilar, his audio pickup being temporarily overloaded by massed twenty-gauge fire. "Cease fire! Cease—"

The sound came from everywhere, a female voice, decidedly so, and a *most* pleasant one. Moreover, the accent spoke strongly of home. "...alda Miranda, from TransIsthmia, on Old Earth. Please stop killing the crew. They have no means to resist you, to speak of, and you are going to need them later on. I repeat, *please* stop killing the crew. They can't hurt you and you will need them.

"I am going to order them to assemble on the hangar deck, right after I finish talking to you and..."

"Shut the hangar deck doors," Esmeralda ordered, pointing her pistol at the bridge crewwoman responsible. "And then pressurize."

Esmeralda continued in English, the language of the Peace Fleet and the common tongue of the educated, upper classes on Old Earth. "Crew of the *Spirit of Peace,* our ship has been taken by forces from down below. We cannot resist. Stay away from Corridor G-27 and move to the hangar deck, if other than medical personnel or wounded. Medical personnel and wounded go to sick bay. I cannot emphasize this enough, stay the *hell* away from Corridor G-27. These are apparently very dangerous people who have boarded us; stay *away* from them.

"We can all come through this alive but we have to remain calm, surrender in absolute good faith, and—once again—*stay away from the boarders.*"

Marguerite Wallenstein alternated between fury at Esmeralda surrendering her flagship, pride that she had done so decisively, and sheer terror for the future. Her terror redoubled when she remembered that Xingzhen, the love of her life, was still forward and not that far from where the boarders were.

She said over her shoulder, "Wait here, Khan and Khan; I'm going for the empress."

"Aye," answered Khan, husband. "We'll keep tight. I'll commence a remote start-up prep on your barge."

She stopped and turned. "What point?"

"That was Robinson's voice we heard earlier. Never mind why and how he's alive when he was supposed to be dead. *You're* dead if he catches you. Your only chance is to get off here, get to one of the colony ships, and run for Earth. The wife and I"—they exchanged glances and nodded at each other—"have worked for both him and you. We'd rather work for you.

"For that matter, your barge could make the trip on its own if there are only the three of us."

Marguerite herself could only nod, before running off

to the central spine. Her progress was delayed by a veritable sea of refugee crewmen and -women, heading to the stern per Esmeralda's orders.

Aguilar looked at the corridor marking and made a decision. "Centurion Martin?"

"Sir?"

"Can you find the high admiral's quarters from here?"

"After all that VR? All those rehearsals?" Martin snorted. "In my sleep."

"Well . . . do be awake for this. I'll continue on to the bridge with everyone but second squad. Take it and try to grab the high admiral. Kill or capture; but I'd prefer capture."

"Wilco, sir; second squad, on me."

The six men of second squad immediately trotted after Martin as he went forward a few paces, then cut to antispinward, or port, or left, cultural frame of reference depending, and jogged toward the high admiral's suite. On the way, dozens, scores of crew ran away or hid themselves as they passed. Martin took a look around and saw that, indeed, they all headed sternward as soon as the squad had passed.

The corridor was entirely on the exterior of the spinning starship, so gravity remained normal. Walking while taking account of the Coriolis force, however, remained a little awkward, with the steps, when moving in this direction, seeming to be just that little bit more ground-covering than they should have been.

When they reached the high admiral's suite, the door opened automatically and instantly.

A design feature, wondered the centurion, *or our little girl on the bridge overriding local controls? No matter because* . . .

Xingzhen, tiny and perfectly beautiful, whatever her age, stood next to the bed and waited, with Marguerite's own pistol clutched tightly in small, delicate, and elegant hands. Her heart raced as her temples throbbed; for perhaps the first time in her life, the empress was terrified.

What do I do? Where is my lover? Will she come for me? Should I try to go to her? What if . . . oh, Gods, does she know how much I love her?

Suddenly, the hatch flew open as a monster entered; such an apparition could not be a man! Xingzhen pointed and fired four times. One of those—she didn't know which—staggered the monster, knocking it back. She sensed the hit had been effective, drawing blood and doing damage. Yet there was another behind the first and . . .

Centurion Martin saw that the first man to enter went down, a bullet hole in his chest. The second one instinctively blasted in the direction from which the shot had come, then fired again and yet again, the undercharged shells of the heavy shotgun keeping on target as he pulled the trigger.

Xingzhen saw the flash of the muzzle. It was less intense than she might have expected, had she been thinking about such things. She didn't see that first cluster of flechettes coming toward her. Still, she certainly felt them as they made at least a dozen and a half red-leaking pinholes in her torso and upper legs, tumbling and slicing through her organs before making just as many, and larger, on the way out. The pain was bad enough that she lost control, flopping back against the bulkhead. Two more shots came, loud and terribly final. Those two held her there, as if pinned. After that, though she wasn't aware of it, two more men likewise fired a single round each. After that, the target was so obviously dead that it would have been an embarrassment to have shot again. The woman slid down to the deck, leaving a bright red splotch on the wall behind her.

The net result, in any case, had been to turn what had been an absolutely stunning beauty into an obscenity of a shredded corpse. Martin thought that, of the one hundred and ninety flechettes that had been fired at her, at least a half and maybe as many as two-thirds had struck home.

Her face, though . . . her face is still very beautiful, even in death. What a waste.

"Tribune, Martin here. We took the high admiral's suite. She was a no-show. Lost one man"—Martin shot an inquisitive look at the legionary tending the downed man, who mouthed, *Need a medic, pronto*—"Estavez, who may make it if we can get him to the medico.

"Oh, and it seems we killed the Zhong empress."

Aguilar answered, "Roger. Damn. I have no idea what the fallout of that will be. Carrera could have traded her for so much. Oh, well; bring the wounded man to the bridge."

Martin considered taking the gun but, *Fuck it, I don't need a souvenir and wouldn't know how to use it anyway.*

Marguerite ducked back into a side exit when she saw the first of the men in their outlandish space suits enter the spine. Though she thought one of them glanced sternward, they paid her no attention. She also saw two of them helping—carrying, really—a third who leaked crimson that floated in the microgravity of the spine.

They went to my quarters. If they captured her, Robinson can have me; I will never leave her. But . . . She deliberately forced that thought down. There could be no "but."

Marguerite let a few seconds pass, then risked sticking her head out for another quick glance forward. *Nobody. Bet they realized that, unless you're used to it, moving in zero gravity is harder than it looks.*

Deciding to take the risk, she hooked an ankle around a ladder, her hand into the same, and swung herself out. Then, grabbing the ladder with both hands, bending her knees, and resting her feet on a rung, she kicked and pulled herself off, shooting forward rapidly until she had almost reached the level of her own quarters.

Normally, she enjoyed this passage and the speed. This time she was simply desperate to get to Xingzhen. Gentle fingers and toes dumped her forward momentum until she found herself at the proper asynchronous exit. She would normally have dived through. This time she stopped herself and looked forward for any sign of the borders. *No, they probably went outward again for more gravity.*

She maneuvered herself down to the low-gravity deck, and outward under increasingly greater gravity. At the final exterior passageway, she bolted for her own suite before drawing herself up short.

She saw blood on the deck, which set her heart to racing and gave her an ill feeling in her stomach. Still, since she hadn't seen any sign of the boarders having taken her, assumed it was one of their own.

They wouldn't just leave her behind, though, would they? She had my pistol; she had to have used it and if she used it...

Marguerite forced herself to walk through the, in fact, automatic door.

She stopped. She looked. She drew in a breath and then expelled it in a single cry of utter despair and psychic agony. Another breath followed, to be followed by another heart-torn shriek.

"Oh, no...elder gods, oh, no, please no."

She ran, heedless of the blood spread across the deck. Falling to her knees in the crimson pool, she reached out to the cooling corpse. A gentle hand brushed away a lock of hair, before moving to behind the dead woman's neck. Another, scorning the red flowing down all sides, grasped Xingzhen from the back.

Half pulling the corpse to herself and half bending inward, Wallenstein alternately crooned and begged, while rocking the empress's corpse, "Please, oh, please, don't be dead. You cannot be dead, *baobei*. You cannot be. Don't leave me. Please, don't leave me...please..."

Khan, the wife, found her like that; the high admiral, or perhaps effectively ex–high admiral, cradling the bloody corpse of the Zhong empress, alternately moaning, sobbing, and keening, her knees wetted in the broad pool of blood spilled from the tiny and now pale frame of Xingzhen.

Khan made a small fist and, for a moment, just stood there, biting down on it. *You poor thing*, she thought, *she was all you ever really loved, wasn't she? Or almost all. Poor thing.*

Finally, unable to deal with even one more heartrending shriek, Khan paddled forward and knelt down to Marguerite's left side, putting her right arm out and around her to draw the high admiral in. The pale-skinned corpse of Xingzhen came with her.

"High Admiral? *High Admiral! MARGUERITE!*"

The last attempt to capture her attention worked. "You have to come with me," Khan said. "My husband has your barge prepared. You cannot stay here. You will be killed if you do, crucified most likely."

"I . . . I don't want . . . to . . . live," the high admiral sobbed.

"Yes, I understand that," Khan agreed. "But—trust me on this—you don't want to be nailed to a cross, either. And Carrera, if he has the first glimmering that you had anything to do with the loss of his first family, *will* nail you to that cross."

"I did, you know," Wallenstein said, beginning to recapture some small measure of self-control. "I was in it up to my eyebrows. It was just an order . . . a problem . . . a way to get myself ahead. I never thought . . . I never imagined . . . and now . . ." Again, she broke down in deep sobbing, pulling away from Khan and resting her shaking face in the bloody crook of Xingzhen's neck and shoulder.

"Then, yes," Khan continued, loudly enough to get through to her. "He's going to avenge himself on you if he gets hold of you. And if he does that, then who will avenge your love?"

That got a response. Releasing her death grip on the corpse, Marguerite rocked back until her back was straight. "Yes . . . yes, I must avenge her. I must make him suffer as I will be suffering. *He* found another family. I never will; I never could. We'll go..." She stood and began to try to pick up Xingzhen's tiny body.

"We can't take her with us," Khan said. "The barge can make food, but it cannot refrigerate. Do you want to watch her beauty corrupted? To smell her stinking as she rots and melts away? For eighteen months? Better to keep your memories intact."

"But Carrera...her corpse?"

She's too lost to remember we're going to take a colonization ship if we can reach one. But the empress's corpse doesn't belong there, either.

"He won't do anything to her corpse except give it back to the Zhong," Khan insisted. "She never hurt him personally. She was a political and military enemy, but not a personal one."

"All right," Marguerite said, weakly. "Let's go, then. But wait; what about my Esma, my child?"

Khan couldn't bring herself to say what she'd been able to piece together about the admiral's treacherous aide de camp. Instead she said, "She'll be all right. She's on the bridge and already their prisoner."

Bridge, UEPF *Spirit of Peace*

"I've seen you before, miss," said Centurion Martin. "Well, after a fashion I have."

"How's that?" asked Esma, in an accent that fairly reeked of Balboan Spanish. Her pistol was out of sight in its holster now, what with having twenty-two armed men on the bridge with her.

"Well . . . see . . . we have this aircraft carrier; the *Dos Lindas*. I served aboard it when we were dealing with the Xamari pirates, oh, a *long* time ago. Anyway, the ship has a figurehead; looks exactly like you. Weird, really."

Martin didn't bother to tell Esma that the ship's figurehead was topless. This was probably just as well. She didn't bother to tell him why she thought the figurehead resembled her.

She was about to ask about the figurehead when she caught on screen two familiar images leaving the high admiral's quarters. "Excuse me," she said, before twisting one dial and hitting another button, which shifted the image on screen to an empty passageway on the other side of the ship completely.

Rather, the passageway was almost empty. There was one apparently badly shot-up crewwoman crawling in the direction of the hangar deck.

"Do you mind," she asked Aguilar, "if I order some medical personnel to retrieve the wounded you left behind?"

Aguilar had good reason to trust her commitment, perfect evidence of which still sat strapped to the captain's chair. "Is there any way for someone to take control of the ship from anywhere but here?"

"No," she replied, "I locked out the alternate bridge."

"Okay, do it, then. Where is your sickbay?"

Esma took control of the view screen again to bring up a large, three-D diagram of the ship. She directed Aguilar's attention to that.

"How good are the medical facilities aboard ship?" Aguilar asked.

Esma shrugged; young and healthy, with no basis of comparison, she really didn't know.

Aguilar looked for someone more experienced on the bridge. His eyes came to rest on someone he took to be a senior noncom or warrant officer equivalent.

"They're very good," the Earther admitted. "Much better than anything below, outside of Atlantis Base, which has better."

"Centurion?"

"Sir?"

"Take second squad and Estevez and take control of the medical facilities. Let their medicos retrieve and treat their personnel, too, but our man comes first. And if they fuck it up, kill them."

Leaving the diagram of the ship up, Esma pushed off to Richard's body, unbuckled him, and asked if Martin would take him to sick bay. Seeing he would, she took Richard's place, despite the blood she'd shed there. From there, she was able to pull up a much smaller image, one where she could see Marguerite and Khan, the wife, approaching the hangar. She followed their progress until they disappeared inside. In a few minutes, not more than ten, she saw the crew leaving but not going far.

Hangar Deck, UEPF *Spirit of Peace*

Khan, husband, met his wife and Marguerite on the hangar deck. Already, virtually the entire crew was assembled there, per the invaders' orders. They stood or sat on the deck, intermingled with the four cargo barges and the high admiral's barge.

Damn, thought Marguerite, looking at the cargo shuttles. *If I knew their codes by heart the way I know my own I might be better off taking one of those. They could, conceivably, make it to the transition point and then Earth on their own in greater safety and comfort.*

"We're ready to flee," Khan, husband, said, "but..." He swept his hand about the hangar deck, taking in the hundreds of demoralized crew present.

"I'm not going to open the hangar to space and kill my crew to make good my own escape," Wallenstein said. "I've done bad things, things I wish I hadn't, things I will go to my grave wishing I hadn't, but that's too much."

Turning to the crew, Khan, male, announced, "We have to get the high admiral someplace safe. You, they won't harm. My wife and I they might. Her, they *will*. So I need you all to assemble in the passageways outside, because we *are* going to open the hangar to space."

So that's what a human wave actually looks like, thought Khan, as he watched the crew bolt *en masse* from the hangar. More than once it locked up at the entrance in a flesh-filled traffic jam, until pressure from behind forced the jam through, usually to the sound of screaming.

At what cost in broken bones, I cannot imagine.

When the crowd had cleared away, leaving the hangar almost unoccupied, a couple of dozen—*no, thirty-two*, thought Khan, after a quick head count—still remained.

Raising one quizzical eyebrow, Khan fixed his gaze on a young woman—*well, yes, despite anti-agathics, this one really looks* young—who strode forth from the others.

"We talked it out among ourselves," the woman, an ensign, said. "None of us have any connection to down below. No families. No real friends. We're from Earth and we want to go back there. So we're going, too. Besides, you'll be making for one of the colonization ships and you'll need crew to run it."

Khan shot a questioning glance at Wallenstein, who drew herself up to full height and said, "It's going to be tight on my barge, but climb aboard and fit yourselves in as best you can."

Bridge, UEPF *Spirit of Peace* (under new management)

Esma kept her face very calm, watching the high admiral and a few dozen others board the barge. She even managed to keep calm when Robinson, possibly the new high admiral, demanded of Aguilar, "Well, where is that bitch Wallenstein? I demand she be found!"

"You're in no position," answered Aguilar, "to demand anything. You've done decent service and probably bought your own life and just possibly the life of that evil twat, the marchioness of Amnesty.

"I have no instructions to put you out of an airlock, High Admiral, but equally I have no instructions not to. We in the legions' officer and centurion corps are selected and trained for initiative. We are also trusted to use it. Don't make me use mine to decide that you would look good flopping around in vacuum like those two poor bastards who were blown out of the hole we made to get inside the ship.

"Do you understand?"

"Yes, sir," said Robinson. If a tone could have groveled, that tone would have been his face and belly down on the deck.

"That said," Aguilar continued, before asking of the bridge crew, "does anyone know where the high admiral, or the ex–high admiral, is?"

The rest of the crew said nothing, though the senior noncom, or warrant, who had pronounced that sick bay could give fine care, shot an inquisitive glance at Esma.

"I haven't seen her in some time," the girl said. "But I was the one who kept her schedule. She was supposed to be visiting three or four of the ships today, two inspections and two morale-building visits. Which of those she might be on . . . well, some things cannot be predicted or finely scheduled for."

"Ain't that the goddamned truth?" Aguilar said. "I suppose there's a fair chance that, if she's on one of the other ships, she's been torn limb from limb by the . . . hmmm . . . how many ships have mutinied, so far, and surrendered?"

"Let me check," Esma said . . . "Okay . . . *Harmony* . . . *Brotherhood* . . . *Annan* . . . it seems every ship of the line has. They're all sending shuttles down, too, to pick up their occupation force."

"Ensign . . . ?"

"Miranda," Esma offered.

"Thank you. Ensign Miranda, please put out to all ships that the former high admiral is wanted. Oh . . . and that failure to turn her over by whichever ship she's on will see that crew decimated. The old-fashioned way."

"The old-fashioned way?" she inquired, quite sure she wasn't going to like it.

"Yes. That means we'll break the crew into tens, those tens will draw lots, and the loser will be beaten to death by the remaining nine, who will be killed if they refuse."

Esma gulped. "We'll just pass that on, then, won't we? Communications?"

"Yes, Ensign."

"Pass that on to the other ships, would you?"

Hangar Deck, *Spirit of Peace* (under new management)

Marguerite was likely the best pilot present, even though between the Khans and her thirty-two, for lack of a better term, "loyalists," there were at least seven qualified pilots. Thus, she took the pilot's station on the left and had Khan, husband, seated to her right. Most of the passengers were sitting ass down on the deck, there not being enough seats for them. No one complained. Indeed, no one complained even knowing that there were not enough—not *nearly* enough—EVA suits for them in the event of an accident or taking fire from the ship they were escaping.

She wanted to minimize the time between launch and discovery. Thus, she ran through the steps in preflight she didn't really trust anyone to handle on her behalf. That was quick, though, *I'm not that rusty.*

When the barge was ready, she lifted it slightly off the deck and at the same time began sucking the atmosphere out of the hangar. There was an emergency procedure for blowing the shuttle doors, and she considered using it, but decided against because, *In the first place, it's very noticeable and I don't want to be noticed, but in the second, about every third time someone has tried that the shuttle ended up getting wrecked.*

The fleet had come a long way, maintenance-wise, since she'd taken over. Nonetheless, she still spared a glance at the balloon warning system some clever prole had come up with when it hadn't been possible to trust the installed pressure warning system.

"And that's it," she announced, "Khan, open the doors."

Khan had already taken control of them. At her word he clicked an icon on her screen. The hangar began to open into space.

Bridge, *Spirit of Peace* (under new management)

I wonder if I'd be so brave, Esma wondered, *if I wasn't pretty sure that I—or the way I look, anyway—matter enough to Patricio to keep me from being beaten to death by nine crewmen chosen at random.*

She risked a brief glance into the small screen on Richard's former command chair. The hangar was open to space with Marguerite's barge moving slowly outward. Once it was gone, she saw that they hadn't bothered to close the hangar off.

Close it myself, if I can figure out how? I'd better get it closed or they might figure out just who left and just who covered for her. I don't know that they will. I don't even know how they might. But they still might. But, then, if the crew that were on the deck report she was there, and they might, my cousins here might figure out I let her go.

No, wait. As is, Marguerite takes all the blame herself. They have no idea I've been covering for her and probably no idea of how. So let it ride. They'll see the crew gathered outside the hangar, but no time soon. By then . . . well, by then I may be on my way to Balboa.

Admiral's Barge, *Spirit of Peace* (under new management)

Marguerite's heart didn't begin to slow until she knew that the tail of her barge was past the hangar doors. Until then, *they could have overridden my command and slammed the things shut on me, with us only partway through. The lucky ones would be the ones crushed by the doors and, since I'm forward, I wouldn't be among them.*

The next problem . . .

The next problem, in fact, were the five antimeteor cannon, three mounted amidships, equilaterally, and two toward the bow. The two toward the bow really didn't concern her. *By the time they can bear we'll be out of range in a race between the barge and the pellets.*

One of the central cannon, on the other hand, would be able to bear once she was a few hundred meters from the stern. *And if I keep a course to delay that for the maximum time, it only means that* three *of them, rather than one, will be able to bear.*

The cannon were semiautomatically directed. They could read direction, speed, and mass, with UEPF shuttles normally being out of their engagement parameters. On the other hand, for certain things, not just inbound meteorites, meteors, and asteroids but also presumptively nuclear warheads launched from below or satellites that might have been in orbit but steerable, the cannon were set for: "Forgiveness is easier to obtain than permission; blast it."

For other things, they *needed* express permission.

"Thank all the gods," Khan said, "that the cannon need express permission to engage something with our profile. If they'd been set on complete automatic . . . oh . . . oh, shit."

"What?" Wallenstein asked.

"Set on automatic . . . oh, shit . . ."

"'Oh, shit?'" Wallenstein asked. "What's this 'oh, shit' about?"

Bridge, *Spirit of Peace* (under new management)

"High Admiral's barge leaving the hangar deck," the computer intoned all over the ship. "High Admiral's barge leaving the hangar deck."

"What?" demanded Robinson. "That bitch is getting away? I'll not stand for it!"

"What the fuck is going on?" Aguilar in turn demanded to know. He picked a member of the bridge crew at random, pointed his twenty gauge, and said, "Start talking fast or you're dead."

The crewman blanched, then said, "I don't know any of the hows, but the ship will notify the crew when the high admiral's barge or the captain's pinnace leave or arrive. It did that. So apparently she got to the hangar deck and bugged out. Or somebody did."

"She can control the hangar from her own barge," said another.

Aguilar shot an accusing glance at Esma.

"I don't know, Tribune," the girl lied. "She was *supposed* to be visiting other ships. Maybe she was delayed and didn't bother to let me know. Maybe she was having a little fling on the side. It happens."

Aguilar narrowed eyes and lips. He didn't believe her but couldn't prove it and didn't want to risk Carrera's or—worse—Fernandez's wrath by throttling their prime agent.

"Fine," he said, in a voice that left no doubt he didn't believe her. He turned his attention back to the sailor he'd threatened. "You people have cannon of sorts for defense from meteorites and such. How do I make them work?"

The terrified crewman's eyes went automatically to gunnery.

"I see," said Aguilar, shifting his shotgun. "Engage that boat," he said. "Now."

"It's not that easy," gunnery answered. "There are protocols that have to be followed."

"Then follow them and shoot that thing out of space."

"I can help there," Esma said, as if trying to redeem a mistake she'd made.

Admiral's Barge

"There's no help for it now," Marguerite said. "If I've

never said so, and I probably didn't, you and your wife have been among my most cherished subordinates. I hope we'll meet in the great beyo—"

"*Peace* is firing," Khan announced.

Bridge, *Spirit of Peace* (under new management)

"Gunnery," Esma commanded, "turn target acquisition over to me."

"Aye, Ensign."

Esma looked in her small screen. She could see what she presumed was a barge carrying Wallenstein, heading straight away to sternward. On a chance, she looked for whatever ship had brought the boarders. It wasn't still on the hull, she found, so she did an automated search until she found it. Looking closely, she saw nothing that would distinguish it from the current high admiral's barge, at least from this angle. After making a few adjustments, she then sent the image she'd found to the main screen, where it replaced the diagram of the ship. She increased the size, which seemed to have the effect of reducing the resolution.

"That's it," she ordered. "Gunnery, engage with everything that will bear."

"Aye . . . ma'am." Hesitantly, gunnery's finger pressed a firing button.

Instantly, four streams of incandescent slugs shot away from the *Spirit of Peace*. Two of the streams were close enough together that they could be mistaken for a single stream—at least they could be mistaken by someone who didn't know any better. A few seconds passed. The streams of slugs lost some of their incandescence, almost disappearing in space. And then the shuttle began to spark as pieces of it started to fly off at random. On the view screen, it rapidly disintegrated before blooming into a great burning flower.

The bridge crew gasped as one, except for one crewwoman who began softly to weep, her head on her arms over her console.

"Capture would have been better," Aguilar said, "but this will do."

"No, it won't," corrected Robinson. Even so, he smiled at the image on the screen and said, "Die, bitch!"

Admiral's Barge

"What the . . . ?"

"*Peace* fired at the shuttle, Robinson's old barge, I'd presume, that brought those pirates to the ship. I wonder if it was because it somehow fit the targeting parameters—though I can't imagine how—or the ship made a mistake as to which barge was which . . . or maybe it was a delayed fire command being acted on."

"Or maybe one of the crew sabotaged the boarders," Marguerite opined. "I doubt we'll ever know. Take the con. Keep this course for the nonce, at least until we're out of effective range of anyone's cannon, then set course for the *Juncker.*"

"Be about three weeks," he said. "I'd recommend either getting out the games or setting my wife loose to entertain our passengers . . . or both."

"Both?"

Khan nodded very affirmatively. "Three weeks is a long time. Both."

Bridge, *Spirit of Peace* (under new management)

At this point, Aguilar's feelings—and he'd never been among the least suspicious of people—where Esma was concerned, had gone from mild appreciation to *deep* suspicion. Therefore, when she asked permission to go and check on the people in sick bay, he'd said, "Sure, but first give me the gun and then . . . Corporal Morales?"

"Yes, Tribune?"

"Escort her. Take one other man."

"You know the ship better than I do, miss," Morales said. "Lead the way."

Rather than trying to take the inexperienced Balboans through the gravity-free spine, Esma led them to one of the elevators. Three, even four, normally would have been no problem, but when two of the three were in bulky Volgan space suits it was a very tight fit indeed.

Pressed enough, rather *com*pressed enough, that she could barely breathe, Esma commanded, "Section thirty-one."

The elevator said nothing in return, but began to move sternward at rather more than a walking pace, stopped and opened up to another corridor in something under a minute.

"It's that way," Esma said, pointing with her chin.

Without another word she moved off, using a grip on a hand rail where there wasn't yet enough gravity to give her feet purchase. The two Balboans followed, but rather less deftly.

Gravity built up quickly as they moved away from the spine, though, with the Coriolis force, it was an awkward kind of gravity.

Morales noticed the red crosses that dotted the passageway at about eye level, along with arrows pointing outward. *Makes sense*, he thought.

It wasn't very long before they reached sick bay. The hatch opened automatically, allowing Esma and the other two to enter.

Morales could have cared less about the Earthpig wounded, but he was very pleased to see Estevez not merely alive but conscious, though with some of the Earther medicos clustered about him like a flock of hens.

I suppose it didn't hurt matters any that they're pretty sure we'll slaughter the lot if our man doesn't make it.

Esma asked one of them, "The earl of Care?"

That medic pointed inward, toward the spine, and answered, "In there."

Informing Morales where she was going, Esma walked a bit unsteadily toward the ship's morgue. A hatch *whoosh*ed open for her. She entered and saw the still clothed and still bloody corpse upon a gurney.

She walked to it, her knees threatening to buckle under her. She steadied a bit once she could use the gurney for support. It suddenly became very real. She saw again Richard about to take out the Balboan's shuttle. She heard herself warning him not to. She saw the sad smile. *Did he know about me all along?*

She saw herself, as if through another's eyes, firing. She saw the bullets strike and the blood burst forth. She saw too much.

With deep regret and still deeper inner pain, Esma murmured, "Richard, I'm so sorry, so *terribly* sorry." Then she lay her head down on his bloody chest and began to cry for the mortal sin she had committed against one whom she knew had truly loved her.

CHAPTER TWENTY

Equō nē crēdite, Teucrī! Quidquid id est, timeō
    Danaōs et dōna ferentes.
(Put no faith in the horse, Trojans. Whatever it is,
    I fear the Greeks, even when bearing gifts.)
                    —Laocoön, in Virgil's *Aeneid*

Task Force Jesuit,
Cordoban-Santa Josefinan Border

The command post was almost empty, this time of the morning, darker than three feet up a well-digger's ass. Overhead, the Smilodon stalked the Leaping Maiden.

Coming in from off in the distance, one could hear the whistle and shriek of mortars and artillery. Sometimes one might hear a blast of three, too, though as often as not the enemy were using white phosphorus, which was a better marking round in many circumstances. It wasn't particularly impressive, really, just shells in ones and twos and threes, never hitting the same spot but playing around for a while then stopping.

It's the assholes preregistering on our positions, thought Claudio. *Seen it before. Hell,* done *it before. Every gun registering between three and six targets—who knows, maybe more—so that we can't really guess as to their main effort when they decide they're ready to break us.*

Claudio looked over at the map, tacked to a tent wall and covered with acetate. It was annotated with recent reconnaissance reports of the Santa Josefinan buildup around Task Force Jesuit's forward trace. Of late, those reports hadn't been so much about the who, what, when, and where of things, as they had been about, "The sonsabitches are as thick as fleas out there and we couldn't get through their counter-reconnaissance to find out anything."

More ominous, still, were the spots marked with, "Patrol X, disappeared and believed destroyed."

Time to turn ourselves over to the Cordobans for internment? Maybe. If not today or tomorrow, then soon. Why, oh, fucking why did I ever accept being recalled to duty? He sighed and then mentally answered his own question: *Because you love this shit and would rather lose doing this than win at anything else. Idiot.*

Marciano shook his head with a sad smile. "Well, at least their carrier's gone elsewhere. That's something."

Someone knocked on the upright pole by the normal entrance to the tent. Claudio looked over to see Stefano Collea standing next to a tall, very slender, and rather pale-looking sort. He looked slightly familiar but... *can't quite place him. Certainly doesn't look Cordoban.*

Collea said, "General Marciano? Sir... there's... there's someone here to see you."

Claudio suddenly attached a name to the face and a rank to the insignia. "Captain . . . Gold, isn't it?"

"Yes, sir. I'm surprised you remembered; we were only in the same room maybe twice, and were never introduced."

"You briefed your chief on one of those occasions. It was not a happy time. That's what made your name stick in my mind."

Gold sighed, ruefully. "Yeah . . . something about DFC12 pallets and shipping containers. Oh, well."

"Yes," Claudio chuckled, "that was it. How can I help you, Captain Gold? I'm afraid our hospitality is limited and you might get bombed . . ."

"I'm . . . well . . . actually, sir, I was sent to help you."

"Sent?"

"Yes, sir; by the *Duque* . . ."

"*Et dona ferentes.*"

"I wonder how he does that?" Gold did actually wonder aloud.

"Does what?" Marciano asked.

"Predicts things like that. He said you would say exactly that. Oh, and that I was to . . ." Gold reached into an inside pocket of his blue jacket, a move which immediately made him the focus of two suddenly hostile rifle and pistol muzzles.

"Easy, gentlemen," Gold said, "it's only a letter."

Carefully, Gold drew out the letter and passed it to Marciano.

With a shrug, the Tuscan general took the letter, walked a few steps to a makeshift desk, leaned his rear on the desk, and thumb-sliced the letter open. He took out the thin sheaf, took one look, and said, "It's hard to believe anyone descended from Adam and Eve could have such shitty handwriting."

"Yes, sir," agreed Gold. "He didn't say you would say that but he *did* say that there's a typed copy inside."

"Of *course* he did." Claudio thumbed through the thin sheaf, placed what had been the top half onto the desk, and began to read, silently.

"Old Comrade," the letter began. *"It's been too many years. I hope, when all of this is settled, you'll be my guest for a few weeks, or months. It would be a fine thing to get us all together, you, myself, Sada, Qabaash, the entire gang. That, however, has to await events.*

"Right now, from every report I've had, you've done a fine job of withdrawing to the Santa Josefina-Cordoba border. You've got secure flanks. You've probably mostly solved your supply problems by buying on the open market and the black market in Cordoba.

"But there you will sit until the money runs out. And, if you've been paying attention to events in the Tauran Union, the money's not only running out, but what you have left is probably close to worthless. There will not be any more coming; the Tauran Union is effectively dead. No, don't pretend to mourn; you're not going to miss those arrogant, corrupt bureaucratic bastards any more than I am.

"It may or may not have occurred to you, but if you've been paying for supplies from the Cordobans with Tauran currency they are not going to be happy with you, right about now. Maybe marching over the border and getting interned wouldn't be such a great idea after all."

"Hadn't really thought about that," Marciano muttered. "Stefano?"

"Sir?"

"What's the exchange rate now, Tauran to Federated States Drachma?"

"I was going to mention that at tonight's command and staff. Short version? We're nearly broke."

"*Hummph.* How *does* that bastard predict . . ."

Marciano went back to the letter. He read until he came to the line, "*Go ahead and check with your staff. See where you stand financially.*"

"God dammit!"

"*So your choices are almost all bad: stay and be destroyed, eventually cross the border and be interned, if you're lucky, or, maybe, take the way out I'm offering you. Now stop reading for a bit and ask Captain Gold what he has to offer you.*"

Marciano looked directly at Gold. "Do you know what's in this letter?"

"Probably, sir, at least in broad terms."

"He says to ask you what you have to offer."

Gold smiled. "Oh, that one's easy, sir. He wants me to park my ship off shore, load you all, and take you out to sea, where he's arranged for one large and two midsized airships to take you home. To that end, I've got a fair number of small boats, enough to take everybody out in . . . mmmm . . . let's say forty lifts. Maybe fifty. I have three-quarters of a million daily rations."

"Stefano?"

"Two months, sir. Maybe two and a half. If we could

take off the couple of weeks' worth we have left, maybe three months."

Marciano considered that. He asked, "Our heavy weapons? We don't have much left but . . ."

"I'm carrying two batteries of light artillery, our batteries, not yours; so twenty-four guns and about twenty thousand shells. Mortars are similar. Enough machine guns and such to at least make up your materiel losses. Actually, way more than enough."

Nodding, Claudio went back to the letter.

"You're not going to be able to get everything out, not in the one night you will have to get it out. And you probably can take none of your really heavy equipment, so I've added what I could spare, along with enough rifles and machine guns for a full corps."

"God dammit!"

He read on for a bit, then asked, "Vehicles?"

"A few light ones for coordination, a dozen medium trucks, and perhaps a third enough prime movers for the artillery."

"Hell, if we have to, we can round up horses and confiscate civilian cars. We've certainly had enough practice at *that* lately. Okay."

"As to where your target should be, I am torn between whether you should go for a port, or should try to liberate a capital and then go for a port. You could land in Castille, since they stayed out of the war, but they might intern you, so I can't recommend it. The Anglians are a paranoid and often resentful lot; I don't recommend there. Gaul? Maybe you should save Gaul for one of our colleagues who, yes, lives. You'll know who I mean."

"Janier is alive?" he asked Gold.

"I have no idea, sir."

"Must be Janier." Claudio chuckled, once again. "Frog bastard's too mean to die."

"*So if not Gaul, then where? I think you should at least think about going home and starting the liberation of Tuscany.*

"*Note, this is a freebie. No charge for the ship, the airships, the food, the arms, the ammunition or the other supplies. Or you can pay in now-worthless Tauros, if you like. Up to you. All I really demand is that you just put the arms and other equipment to good use. The only caveat to this is that, between you, me, and Gold—oh, and I suppose some of your immediate staff—we know what's going on, but the rest of the world needs to think you hired a random ship which you had given a laundry list to buy and load for you and the same for the airships. And, in fact, the ship is off my books, not part of the classis, not in the hidden reserve, not manned by Balboans, except for Gold, while the airships are genuine civilian hires with no connection to Balboa. Or not officially, anyway.*

"*It's important for a couple of reasons. One is that you and your men need to be the Taurans who never surrendered, who may have been worn out but were never actually beaten in the field. Since your force was Pan-Tauran, you are also the best force for this. You will be the exception that lets people keep their chins high, after so many disasters.*

"*The other thing is that, well, frankly, the history books are not going to be kind to you. You know it. I know it.*

And we both have a pretty good idea of how unfair that will be.

"*Rather, the* other *history books are not going to be kind to you. I guarantee you, however, that Balboan and Santa Josefinan history books will be* extremely *kind to you, since we understand that the courage of one's enemies does one honor.*

"*Now figure out how to get on that goddamned ship and do it!*

"*Good luck.*"

"*Carrera.*"

"What a son of a bitch," Marciano said. "Like it's going to be that easy. Hmmm . . . speaking of easy, Captain Gold, how many rubber boats did you say you have?"

"Two dozen, sir, with motors."

"It's going to be harder than you think; we have wounded I will not leave behind. Rall!"

"Sir?"

"Start working on an escape plan. Now, Captain Gold, when can your ship be here?"

"We could be here tomorrow night, sir. Actually, we could be here in four hours. But I recommend we wait until three nights from tonight. In the first place you will need time to plan and coordinate. In the second, it's going to be only one moon, and that at a thin sliver of illumination, three nights hence. Finally, I've got to have my crew get the boats ready, which is harder than it sounds."

"Got that, Rall?"

"Got it."

Claudio looked back at the letter.

"*PS: I'll restrain the Santa Josefinans and the*

reinforcements I sent them for three days from when Gold tells me you agree."

"God dammit!"

"PPS: While we didn't put an instructor aboard for political education—too many languages to deal with already—we do have a container full of copies of Historia y Filosofia Moral, *English translation. You may find it useful to distribute these."*

Sergente Maggiore Chiarello, short, olive, and formerly pudgy, stared down at the tripod-mounted machine gun before him with a distinct lack of enthusiasm. As an engineer, yes, building things was his job, but this was something more in line with a mechanical engineer's duties.

"Which I am not."

"Sergeant Major?" asked Chiarello's assistant for the project, a *Caporale* Borroni, taller, skinnier, and both more intelligent and more innocent looking.

"I am not—*we* are not—mechanical engineers, Borroni. But the general, via the colonel, via *Capitano* Ederle wants us to fix this fucking machine gun so it will fire a burst of eight or ten rounds every twenty to sixty minutes. And, I confess, I have no idea how to do that."

"No, I'm not one, either," Borroni admitted. "But how hard can it be?"

Chiarello fixed Borroni with a baleful glare.

"Oh, come on, *Sergente* Maggiore, we can do this. Let's just take it a step at a time. Now first, what have we got to work with for power, because we're going to need some kind of power?"

"I can tell you more easily what we don't have, *Caporale*, we don't have a generator, solar, or windup. We don't have a motor that can run off a battery, even though we could spare the batteries from the vehicles we're about to burn. What's left?"

Borroni thought for a moment, then answered, brightly, "We have gravity and water."

"Well, yes," Chiarello admitted, "I suppose we do. How far does that get us?"

"It gets us to a way to pull on a rope or cable to depress a trigger," Borroni answered.

"But we need to have it fire intermittently."

"So we fix whatever we use to catch the water to spill," said Borroni. "Let's go scrounge some wood, nails, and cord . . . and a jerry can. Oh, and some weights; rocks will do. I think I have a way to do this."

The key thing had been to have the men fire at random spots, irregularly, every night. This they'd done. It even seemed to deter the Santa Josefinan patrols that had become increasingly bold as the numbers of guerillas around Task Force Jesuit had grown.

Overlooking the main highway connecting the capitals of Santa Josefina and Cordoba, sat a machine gun on a tripod, the whole assembly seemingly bound in wood and wire. The aiming point for the machine gun wasn't the highway, but a copse of trees to the west of it. The fire did, naturally, pass over the highway. This had been preset sometime over the last three days and nights.

The machine gun, of course, had a trigger. Normally, this model could hardly be said to have had a hair trigger, what with ten to twelve pounds of pull required to fire it. A lever system and a cam, with the cam sitting in front of the trigger, effectively dropped that to about one pound. A small framework, likewise of wood, kept the lever and cam in place.

From the lever ran a length of wire, stout stuff, pulled from some damaged electronics. The level also extended down past the cam. This had a quarter-pound or so rock at the bottom end.

The wire at the top of the lever ran first to a fairly good-sized rock, maybe a pound or so, around which the wire was wrapped. From there it went to a bound-together wooden apparatus, two tripods with a crosspiece. The wire then went over the crosspiece and down to a roughly one-quart can, scrounged from the mess, with a make-do wire handle running connected on opposite sides, just a tad above the midway point. A piece of cord was further attached to the can, extending up from the bottom, and affixed to a higher stake. such that it would tip the can at some point in its descent.

The can was connected to the handle by the wire. Over that, a twenty-liter water can released water in a steady drip, drip, drip. Testing had shown that the can would be filled about every forty minutes.

As it filled, it pulled on the rock, lifting it from the ground. Eventually, the rock was pulled enough that between it and the water can, enough force was applied to the trigger, via the lever and the cam, to activate it.

Brpbrpbrpbrpbrpbrpbrpbrpbrp.

At that point the can ran out of slack to its bottom cord, which tipped it, spilling much if not all of the water. Then the rock fell back to earth, pulling the can up and leaving enough slack for the gun to stop firing and the trigger to reset. Then the can started filling with water again.

Chiarello and Borroni had been busy engineers. They'd also had help, once they'd figured out how to do it. Maybe five minutes later, a different machine gun threw a burst at a different copse of woods. And a few minutes after that, a rifle fired. Sometimes, a single mortar shell lanced out, to fall among the guerillas' positions with a thunderous blast. The mortars used a very different arrangement and could only fire once, each.

Somewhere down range, a young Santa Josefinan guerilla crossed himself and sent a silent prayer of thanks to the Almighty that it hadn't been him in that machine gun's sights. Or the sights of the other one. Or those of any of the riflemen. Or under the mortar's deadly, indirect gaze.

Of course, no one was in the machine guns' sights really. Neither was anyone in any of the other sights. Nor, except maybe by fluke, was anyone downrange of the rifles or in the burst radius of the mortars' shells.

Indeed, the machine gunner was currently at the beach, awaiting his turn to be picked up by either a rubber boat or a commandeered fishing boat; you never really knew until the transportation showed up and you were directed to this stop or that. Likewise standing by was the crew of the other gun, rather, all the other guns, plus a large number of riflemen, and more than a few mortar crews.

The engineers were going to be among the last out. This was because they were busy putting in a few mines in some obvious places and a much large number of warning signs that insisted a given area was mined.

It was actually harder than it sounded, because these fake minefields had to be by the numbers enough to convince people they were real. That meant stringing barbed wire on three sides of the field, leaving the front open toward the enemy, lifting and replacing clods of earth in a pattern that looked like a deliberate minefield, putting thin rods in places to look like tilt rod mines, and running what would appear to be trip wires from central points.

A lot of this, of course, had been done over the last three days. But there were certain things, laying actual mines and booby traps being the biggie, that had to be done at the last minute. And that meant a very, very dark last minute.

"Hurry up, dammit, Borroni," ordered Chiarello. "I do *not* want to be left behind and captured or have to run to Cordoba and be interned. Neither do you."

"Sergeant Major," answered the soldier addressed, "maybe it's been a while for you since you worked with mines, but these things are fucking *dangerous*. You *really* want me to rush them? You want me to rush them when I'm having to do everything by *feel*?"

"Just go as quickly as you can . . . while being safe."

The spot chosen for the evacuation was a cove, sheltered by sand dunes and cliffs, about halfway up the coast from the forward trace to the Cordoban border. There were two spots, close together, where a boat with some draft could get in to wading distance and depth from the shore. For most of the rest it was a gently sloped, sandy beach without much in the way of either cover or impediments.

There were colored lights on the beach, facing out toward the ship and well shielded from view from anywhere but to sea. Four of the colored lights, blue, green, yellow, and red, were for six, each, of the rubber boats moving to and from the *Alberto Helada*. A fifth, in orange, marked the pickup point for the four decent-sized fishing boats and dozen small craft the Taurans had managed to scrounge.

Gold was favorably impressed by the behavior of the men—*oh, and some women, too; mustn't forget the ladies*—of Task Force Jesuit on the beach.

Sure, he thought, *there's a little confusion. Bound to be when you've got fourteen or fifteen languages in the same small area and the* lingua franca, *English, is native to almost none of them.*

Yeah, a little confusion, but no panic. And this kind of thing is like a neon sign, inviting panic in.

He heard a burst of machine gun fire, a long burst, somewhere to the north. *Ours, I think, one of the semi-robotic ones the Taurans rigged up.*

A group of about twenty, led by an MP, trotted by, kicking up sand. They said nothing, so Gold couldn't make a guess at the nationality. *Big boys, though; I'm guessing Hordalander tankers.*

He thought back to earlier in the day, when he'd seen a crew of Hordalanders, big bastards, all, crying like babies as they applied thermite grenades to their tank's breach block, engine, final drive, and transmission. The radios and thermal imager had been taken off their mounts and put over the engine, so that the thermite would burn through them before melting its way through the engine block.

The driver had been particularly pathetic, bent over at the waist in front of his station, face buried in folded arms resting on the tank's glacis, shoulders shaking with the sobbing of pure grief.

I suppose it had been their home, or maybe a family member, Gold had thought. *Well, and don't I feel pretty much the same way about* Alberto? *Sure I do.*

The wounded had posed a particular problem, since many of them had to be lifted and carried. This included even some of the walking wounded, since many bore wounds that precluded climbing up the net the *Alberto Helada*'s crew had let down the side. The ship hadn't had a suitable lift, either, but the men rigged up something with the davits for the ship's boats, which had also been tossed into the fray, running between the ship and pickup point orange.

Even with the davits, his exec had reported to Gold that it was a goat fuck at the ship. This had led to a change in loading plans. Now, all the wounded lay or sat in lines by the colored pickup points. Every boat leaving shore now departed with two, usually one each walking and litter-borne, though those numbers could vary. And, instead of stopping first by the nets, the boats went to the davits, rigged their wounded to the falls there, saw them off, and only then went for the nets.

That was, the exec reported, a cluster fuck, too, but less of one than the other way they'd been trying, with boats nearly full of nothing but wounded, with a few medics, and the davits overtasked.

He wasn't keeping close track of the frequency the
boats came to shore, but Gold had the impression the
turn-around times had shortened. He also had the
impression that they hadn't shortened enough.

"Captain Gold? Captain Gold? Can you come here,
please?"

That was Marciano's voice. Gold followed it to find
both the general and his chief of staff, Ralls, in furious
discussion.

"Here, General," Gold announced himself.

"We should have given you a radio operator to follow
you around," Claudio said. "Silly of us, I suppose, but
we've never . . ."

"Never done anything like this before?" Gold offered.

"Never. And that means," Claudio said, "that we're not
going to make it, the most we're going to be able to get
off is perhaps six-tenths, and that would demand our
running the boats till shortly after sunrise. And *that*, as my
chief of staff points out, means the Santa Josefinans will
attack before seven thirty in the morning.'

"You can't wait that long," Gold replied. "I'll need to
get my ship at least moving over the horizon, and
preferably have it over the horizon, before the first hint
of light."

"We know," Ralls said. "The point of discussion is
whether or not we should send half the men back to man
our forward trace again, or just keep bugging out all day,
and do a fighting withdrawal to the beach."

"You want my advice?" Gold asked. At Marciano's nod,
he said, "Fine, I think we need to wait another day."

"Wish we hadn't torched the tanks," Rall said.

Marciano laughed, ruefully, and said, "Wish in one hand..."

It was in the aftermath of this discussion that Gold saw—no, not saw exactly, but *felt* the first signs of... *No, not panic, but the ones being sent back to the line are... sullen? Resentful? At least those. Can't say I blame them.*

Meanwhile, I'm not precisely orgasmic with glee at having to order my ship over the horizon while stuck here, myself.

CHAPTER TWENTY-ONE

Fixed Fortifications are monuments to the stupidity
of Man.   —George S. Patton, Jr.

Not quite so much as fixed ideas are.
                                        —Patricio Carrera

Mortal Danger is an effective antidote to fixed ideas.
                                        —Erwin Rommel

World League, First Landing,
Federated States of Columbia

Lourdes didn't know about the attack on the *Spirit of
Peace.* She had never been cleared to know about it. This
wasn't because Carrera didn't trust her, but that, with
something this important he didn't trust *anybody*
completely. Neither had the word yet broken in First
Landing, though it wouldn't be long delayed.

She was a lovely woman, Lourdes, even now as she
entered middle age. Tall and slender, willowy, really, with

enormous brown eyes and full, sensuous lips; if she was not the beauty Carrera's first wife, Linda, had been, still she turned heads and even stopped conversations when she entered a room. She wished she had been able to stop the conversation she was currently engaged in.

Or change it, anyway.

The ambassador to the World League from Valparaiso, Filipe Bazaar, looked slightly ashamed. Middling of height, with salt and pepper hair—all gray at the temples—dressed in formal diplomatic attire with a diagonal sash running over his shoulder and across his chest, the ambassador cut a rather dashing figure. A retired admiral, he was, too, a not uncommon background for highly placed public servants in Valparaiso.

"I'm sorry, Mrs. Carrera, truly sorry and from the bottom of my heart. But, no, my government has decided not to provide a squadron of fighters to, as it turns out, cover the attack on the Earther base."

Before she could comment, the Valparaisan held up a hand, palm toward her, and explained, "We could send a brigade of mountain troops to help defend your country because that was only against the Taurans and Zhong, neither of whom would have nuked us from space. But the UEPF just might, over this, and that is a risk my government will not—cannot—take."

Since it was her son's life at stake in this, Lourdes found it hard to keep her voice calm and her claws out of the ambassador's face. So it was not entirely calmly that she replied, "If you—your government—had told us this before, we might have been able to make alternate arrangements."

Bazaar winced slightly at her tone, but rebounded quickly. "You never told us what the fighters were for before," he explained, reasonably. "We thought it would be backup air cover, over your own country, and for that we'd have been there if and when called. We're not afraid to fight, you see, only to be exterminated like roaches. I'm sorry, as I said, but you have only yourselves to blame for this."

The problem is that it's all true, Lourdes thought. *We never did let them in on why we needed the fighters so we can't complain that they're not willing to do something we never asked them to be prepared to do. But we're still talking the life of my son; I see no need to be reasonable . . . except that, still, it's not their fault and especially not his.*

Grasping at straws, Lourdes asked, "Would you be willing to let us stage some fighters through you?"

"We would not," Bazaar replied. "And even if we would, my military attaché tells me that you have nothing suitable, nothing bellicose, anyway, in your entire aerial legion, that would range from Balboa to the nearest airfield in Valparaiso and nothing that would get from any airfield in Valparaiso to Atlantis Island. And none of your fighters have in-flight refueling capability, so, no, we can't do that, either, even if we wanted to. Which my president does not."

I hadn't known any of that, Lourdes thought. *I really don't know as much about our own military as I ought to. So ours won't range and . . . hmmm.*

"Airships could carry disassembled fighters and land them, but they'd never get there in time. Our aircraft carrier?" she asked.

"Too far away, I understand, to do you any good in anything like good time. Moreover, it carries not a single modern fighter," Bazaar replied. "You can chase down helicopters and slow-moving cargo planes, but you would be left behind trying to chase down even the slowest jet transport."

Lourdes' hands began to tremble slightly. She managed to keep her voice calm as she said, "Excuse me, Ambassador Bazaar; I need to call my country."

Sub camp C, *Ciudad* Balboa

Carrera had returned to Balboa tired, but not half as exhausted as the flight warrant, Montoya, who had been doing all the heavy lifting. He'd dismissed his pilot with the advice to, "Get some sleep. Or get laid and then get some sleep."

Then he, himself, had retired to his own quarters to follow the same advice. He'd just managed to close his eyes when Jamey Soult opened the door and announced, "It's your wife on the encrypted phone, sir. 'Urgent,' she says. 'The worst emergency of your life or hers,' she says."

Word traveled quickly in the concrete confines of the general staff bunkers. Both Kuralski and Fernandez were standing by, by the time a bleary-eyed Carrera reached the secure phone.

"Oh, shit," Carrera said, after Lourdes had given him the dread news. "Shit, shit, shit, shit, shit." His face had gone suddenly very pale. *What the fuck is wrong with me? I don't* make *this kind of mistake.*

"What's that, *Duque*?" Omar Fernandez asked.

"I think I made a very bad mistake, Omar, one that we cannot fix. Oh, crap . . . they're going to have to find a new phrase for 'fuck up,' now, because I have fucked up badly enough that the phrase is now worn out."

"And that mistake was . . . ?"

"Call it wishful thinking on steroids. Believing the Valparaisans would get caught up enough in enthusiasm for the war that they'd deploy the fighters they'd earmarked for our defense, if called upon, to cover the ALTA and the attack on Atlantis, when we asked for that instead."

"I wouldn't be too hard on yourself, *Duque*," Fernandez said. "We simply *couldn't* let the Valpos, or anyone else, in on the secret. And we have nothing . . ." Fernandez let the thought trail off; it had been a statement, anyway, not a question. "That's worse than you know."

"Oh?"

"Our ambassador in Wellington reported that ten Zhong heavy aircraft, two of them likely to be for in-flight refueling, landed a while ago and have been sitting there. Se-67s; they can carry about a maniple, plus, typically, a couple of pieces of light armor, what we call 'Ocelots,' or their version of them. The other two were probably Se-87s—refuelers—just based on how long they spent refueling. It's entirely possible that more are coming."

"Oh, joy." Carrera certainly didn't sound joyful. "So they're going where? And how heavy? What *will* they carry?"

"We don't know. If we'd never attacked Atlantis then

I'd have been sure they were heading for the lodgment the Zhong have, against expectations, managed to carve out to our east. Since we *have* attacked the base . . ."

"How long to get there from Wellington?"

"Probably nine or ten hours after they take off. It's impossible to calculate their fuel burn without knowing what they're carrying. Impossible to say when they're going to take off, too."

Carrera stormed to the door to his quarters and practically tore it off its hinges. "Get me in communication with my *son*!"

Atlantis Base

Ham felt the flush of victory, with the base's town firmly in his hands, the first threats passed to Wallenstein, and the terror being spread throughout the fleet. The actual base, which was more of a not so small town, was built around a fair-sized trapezoidal bay, the same bay in which the damaged ALTA now rocked at anchor. From the corniche along the shores of the bay, the town climbed up steep slopes that led to crests now occupied by seven maniples of Balboan cadets under fairly adult leadership.

Except for me, thought Hamilcar. *I'm in charge and I am* not *an adult.*

From his command post in the town, Ham mused on the situation.

I've got seven maniples here now, plus one back at Beach Red, one guarding very important prisoners, one around the helicopters' refuel and rearm point, and one in reserve, but collocated with the artillery battery, and not far from the helicopters.

That's probably about as good as it—

Ham's thoughts were interrupted by the same short, brown commo sergeant who had previously connected him with the old man. Once again, the sergeant handed Ham a radio handset, saying this time, "It's the *Duque* on the line and he says he needs to talk to you. It's a better connection than before—a different Federated States' communications satellite came up over the horizon—so you can speak at greater length this time."

Ham slithered backwards, then sat up and took the handset, nodding gratefully. "Ham here, Da—*what!?* . . . Oh . . . Oh, hell . . . And you don't know how much more might be coming?

"No, actually, Dad, it's not all that much consolation that you're taking the blame for this. Awfully big of you, of course, but me and my cadets are just left out here to twist slowly in the sun . . . no, no, I suppose that's not very charitable.

"Seven hours, huh? . . . And Fernandez says another dozen heavy lifters have arrived at Wellington to refuel? So I'm looking at what? A brigade? A big brigade? . . . Maybe a division? Yeah, okay, shit . . . No, I don't think we have the horses to handle that . . . We needed those fighters . . . someone's fighters, anyway.

"Okay, keep me posted. We'll do our best. Ham, out."

It was a paler Ham who handed the microphone back to the commo sergeant. He looked at his map, asking himself, *Where are those Zhong Paras going to make their jump? This isn't something I've ever studied. Maybe . . .*

"Get Tribune Cano here, ASAP," he told the sergeant.

"It was never my specialty, either, Ham," Cano said. "I've been a foot soldier and even a horse cavalryman; but do I *look* stupid enough to jump out of a perfectly good airplane or airship?"

"I was afraid of that. I wonder if Alena..."

"She's sedated and ashore," Cano said. "The doctors cleaned her out and sewed her up. But, you know...she's smarter doped up than any five geniuses on tea and coffee."

"Can she be moved?" asked Ham.

Cano shook his head. "I'd rather not, if it can be avoided at all."

"It can't be. We need her...*I* need her, here. Use whatever means you need but get her to me."

"Funniest damned thing," Cano said, an hour later, shortly after the helicopter brought his stretcher-bound wife to a plateau at the base of the ridge. A team of six husky cadets was already carrying her up the rocky slope to bring her to Ham. Cano had left them to their task, while he trotted upward to report to Ham. "She'd already refused her painkillers. Started refusing about the time you and I were talking. I filled her in, as best I could, but...well... she never really seems surprised, does she?"

Ham shrugged. "You're just her husband; I'm her son by a different mother. She's a witch; everyone knows this. She sees all and..." Ham let the sentenced drift off. unfinished. Instead, he shouldered his own pack, picked up his rifle, and trotted down the slope to meet her halfway.

At least she's not obviously bleeding, Ham thought, when he reached the stretcher. *Bad enough that I had to put her through this; I couldn't stand the thought of harming her more than that.*

The cadets lugging Alena stopped when Ham reached them. Gently, they lowered her to the ground, letting the built-in metal stirrups keep her a few inches above it.

Ham was about to apologize when Alena held up her hand. "No need, Iskandr; you needed me; I came. How may I help advance your holy work?"

"I don't know what's going on, Alena, but the old man tells me I've got at least a brigade of Zhong Paras inbound, half getting here in maybe six hours and half sometime after that. No, we don't know how long after."

"Zhong?" Alena the witch mused. She mused, but then she winced. Still, she was able to say, "I can see where they'd come, yes, given that the empress is the high admiral's lover. Yes, before you ask, of *course* I have the clearance to know about our...mmm...most *highly* placed spy. And the Zhong are also a lot closer than the Tauran Union, so maybe more able to get something there quicker.

"I'm a little surprised they had much to spare, given their commitment to their lodgment in Balboa."

"Imagine *my* surprise," Ham said, sardonically, "when the old man told me."

Alena shook an unsteady finger at him. "Don't be bitter, Iskandr. I don't know if anyone, ever, has had so much on his own shoulders alone for such a great war. Anyone can make a mistake. Except for you, of course.

"In any case, my lord, none of that matters. What

matters is defending yourself and your command from some very elite soldiers, while accomplishing your mission."

"Well, without fighter cover, our first line of defense are the air defense vehicles on the ship. It isn't much but..."

"They must come off the ship and be landed, Iskandr," Alena said, with both heat and force. She cast her eyes heavenward. "I do not know what kind of weapons the Earthpigs can launch from space, but that they have something I have no doubt of."

"Yes, yes," Ham agreed. He looked over at Cano.

"I'll see to it, Ham." Cano turned and beckoned over a young cadet bearing a radio on his back.

"They are," Alena continued, with another wince, "doing one or another thing. Either they intend to seize this for themselves or they intend to return it to the Earthers. I think the former very unlikely, Iskandr, because even if the Zhong empress were doing nothing but playing the whore with Admiral Wallenstein, for sheer advantage, the fact remains that they have her and can force her to relinquish any hold they might gain on this place. So they really do intend only to defend it from us. Oh, and I suppose to destroy us in the process. That might be a good revenge for what was done to the carrier we sank that was loaded with civilians as well as for what happened to them around the *Isla Real*, wouldn't it?

"So you are the soldier, Iskandr. You are young, yes, but have a raw talent to rival—possibly to exceed—your father's. They are coming to take the base and destroy you. How would *you* do that?"

***

Ham walked alone, pacing back and forth across a sort of natural corniche carved into the slope. *They're going to jump onto the island and try to grab a field somewhere. But then . . . on the flattest patch of ground big enough to take a long-range jet cargo plane . . . Flat ground? With a jet? Yeah . . . maybe. They're using older Volgan designs, pretty much like we do, and those tend to be rough field capable. Se-67s, the old man said they were, probably eight of them. So two battalions are coming, maybe with a regimental headquarters split up among them.*

It seems pretty easy, drop one battalion around the base, to hold us in, and one on the best or second best area suitable for a rough landing. The battalion that holds us inside the base probably gets joined by the second battalion, while the landing area builds up. When they've got a couple of regiments or even a division they come and destroy us. And we'll have failed. I don't want to even think *about what it would mean to the old man and the country to fail. And I* really *don't want to think about setting off a nuke.*

So can I divide my forces to either hold the base or possibly destroy the battalion that will secure the landing area? Yeah . . . no.

Second option, go after the one that will secure the landing area. Might be able to do that. I mean, I've seen drops before, even if I've never done one. And I've read about them. They're as bad as amphibious or worse. Total chaos, in other words, at least for a while.

No, that won't work. If they can't land outside the base, because I'm outside of it, follow-on echelons may just take their chances and land inside it. And there's a concrete

strip there, which has got to be better than a rough one.
And once they land, I cannot take the base back.

So can I use my limited armor, the helicopters, and
maybe the guns to seriously fuck up the landing outside?
But then, how to get them back inside? Okay, that's
obvious enough; I'll need to attack to create a temporary
gap in their perimeter to bring the armor back in.

Ham stood up straight and began to look around at the
slope on which he stood. He noticed one smoking tower,
one of the smashed ones from the initial barrage.

"Hmmmm," he muttered. *But maybe I can do*
something else, too.

Cano had been standing over his wife, far enough away
to give the boy room to think, close enough to be ready to
hand while still being able to hold his wife's hand.

Alena—as always, watching her god carefully—noticed
that Ham had stopped his perambulations and, where
he'd been bunched over with his hands clasped behind
his back before, he'd now straightened up.

Smiling with absolute confidence, even through her
pain, the green-eyed witch said, "Iskandr is ready,
husband. Go to him."

By the time David trotted up, Ham was bent over
again, this time on one knee, with his map unfolded
besides him and his hands busily forming the dirt into a
scale model of the bay, the base, and the slope.

Looking down, Cano could see larger pebbles dotting
the inner military crest of the slope. He was about to ask,
when Ham said, "We must attack, Tribune. We must

attack holding nothing back except a guard on the special prisoners, and a thin screen on the reverse slope of the ridge around the town . . ."

Ham proceeded to sketch out the scheme of maneuver to strike the more distant landing and then to create a gap to get that strike group back. "And when we're done," he finished, "we take up a defense around the perimeter.

"Make it happen."

Cano was a little shocked when he found himself answering, "Yes, sir."

"And I want you to have a chat with whoever was responsible for those mostly bogus laser towers. I don't see why we can't get some use out of the ones remaining."

Even as the staff worked to turn Ham's will into orders, one could still hear the sounds of skirmishing and building clearing toward the southern end of the base. Here, however, at the central park, those sounds were faint and becoming fainter. For the nonce, David Cano was free for other matters.

"Who here was in charge of or worked with the laser defensive turrets?" David Cano asked over the handheld megaphone. He spoke to the group, much the largest, composed of those who could not be linked to the crews of one of the ships. "Come forward; I'm not planning on hurting you. What, nobody? I see."

David left the speaker button keyed while saying to the same intel warrant that had overseen the segregation of the prisoners, "We don't have enough crosses set up yet. Go grab two hundred people at random, men, women, children, both sexes and all ages. Then nail them up to the walls..."

At about that time, someone inside the group of captives shouted a rough translation. The group, itself, then pushed forward half a dozen men, three of them uniformed.

Looking them over and raising one eyebrow, David asked, "May I assume that you six are responsible? Are there any others?"

The six identified prisoners turned around and called out names and gestured until there were between two and three times more of them, standing there, in front of the crowd.

"Come forward. As I said, you will not be harmed, at least as long as you cooperate." Slowly, hesitantly, the men and women came forward.

"Who is senior?" David asked.

The prisoners looked side to side, exchanging glances, until one stepped forth. "I suppose I am."

"Sir," David corrected.

"Sir. I suppose I am, sir."

"Good, come with me, please. The rest of you have a seat where you are. You'll be fed and watered here. Also let my warrant officer know if you have any injured among you. We're not especially well equipped in that department but we'll do what we can."

"Sir," asked one of them, "can we use our own hospital?"

"Yes of—your *own* hospital? Your own ... tell me, how good are your medical facilities?"

"Best on the planet, sir, by a lot."

"GET MY WIFE TO THE EARTHERS' HOSPITAL!"

Seeing a group of cadets racing to Alena's stretcher, Cano then turned back to this key group of prisoners. He led the senior prisoner toward where Castro-Nyere and the other two Class Ones still writhed on their crosses. "What's your name and rank?"

"Commander Juncker," the prisoner answered.

"Good, 'Juncker.' How many of the defense turrets still work or can be made to work?"

"I don't know."

"How would you find out?"

"I wouldn't."

"I see," David said, congenially. "Mr. Robles?"

"Sir?"

"We'll be needing another crosspiece and four more spikes."

"I'll get right on it, sir."

"I meant," said Juncker, with a gulp, "that I couldn't from here. There is a control building not far from here. I can find out there."

"Ah, good. Lead on, Commander Juncker." With a motion of his head, David indicated that two armed cadets were to follow.

CHAPTER TWENTY-TWO

He will meet no suave discussion, but the instant,
  white-hot, wild,
Wakened female of the species warring as for spouse
  and child.
  —Rudyard Kipling, *The Female of the Species*

First Landing, Federated States of Columbia

Not being on the public dime, Lourdes and her entourage were billeted on one half of one floor of one wing of a five-star hotel in this, the largest and second most expensive city in the Federated States. The carpets were deep. The furniture was all handcrafted, mostly antique, and criminally expensive. On the walls hung art from both Terra Nova's two-hundred-odd nations and thousands of cultures, as well as prized pieces auctioned off by the Peace Fleet (officially to bring culture to the benighted heathens of the new world, but really to fund the fleet).

That later had led to a team of Fernandez's best antibug men sweeping all the rooms with extraordinary care, and leaving the bugs in place in all but one of them, with signs posted to be "Careful what you say; the walls have ears."

It was in the one room where the bugs had been "accidentally" shorted out that Lourdes paced frantically, head down, stomach a-churn, contemplating the battalions of Zhong Paras heading to attack her only son. Her only company—two armed bodyguards with diplomatic immunity to cover their pistols better than their suit jackets could hope to, and Matthias Esterhazy— followed her with their eyes as she pounded to and fro.

What can I do? What can I do?

My boy is commanding mostly boys, themselves. They're not that well trained. They're not really that well equipped. Better trained and better equipped than Earthpig space-squids is a very low bar.

And that was all deliberate. Patricio said every addition to their arsenal, every extra day that might be spent on training them, was potentially an arrow pointing right at them and tipping off the UEPF that something was up. I understand that . . . well, almost, I do.

And I understand that this was important, that the war ultimately wasn't over and won until not only the Tauran Union was wrecked, but the UEPF as well. Okay, too, yes, it was worth it to the planet to risk my only son on that.

But it was hardly worth it to ME!

Will that fat pig of a Valparisan understand that we now have the entire UEPF? Was that really the only reason they refused to send the fighters? Maybe . . . maybe they were afraid of us. After all, they're just another corrupt oligarchy, like the rest of our Latin "allies." Maybe

they've come to realize the threat we represent to their
ruling class. I wonder...

She stopped her pacing and suddenly, inexplicably,
smiled. Turning to one of the bodyguards, she said,

"I need to talk to the *Duque*. Please set it up."

Forty-five minutes later she returned to the swept
area, looking somber but determined. "He said to give
it a try," she said to Esterhazy, without mentioning what
"it" was. "Get my driver to bring the limo around. We're
going to go pay a visit to the ambassador to the World
League from Valparaiso. Oh, and pick up our new vassal
on the way."

World League, First Landing,
Federated States of Columbia

Lourdes carried the firearms in a satchel through the
security checkpoint. As an ambassador her person was
effectively sanctified, beyond the insult of a search or even
a mandatory pass through a metal detector. This was long-
established practice at the World League, even for various
terrorists who were absolutely *known* to be carrying
weapons in.

With the small group walked someone whose slump
was the very image, the Platonic essence, of dejection and
despair, the former ambassador of the UEPF to the World
League,

She passed the satchel to Esterhazy, once past the
entrance. Then they all stopped off at her office for the
guards to reequip themselves.

"And now, gentlemen, let's go for that high-level diplomatic talk with Valparaiso . . ."

Felipe Bazaar, the ambassador to the World League from Valparaiso, would never have dreamt of having his own armed guards in his office. Thus, when Lourdes entered with Esterhazy and one of the guards, leaving the other to block the door, there was only a female secretary, thin like Lourdes but much smaller, to bar the way. Carrera's wife sent the girl sprawling on the floor, with the caution, "Sit there and shut up if you want to see tomorrow's sunrise." She directed the other guard to keep the secretary supine, quiet, and away from the phone.

Inside his office, the ambassador arose from his massive Silverwood desk in a good simulacrum of high dudgeon. "What's the meaning of this?" he demanded.

"Sit down, shut up, and listen you fat, overstuffed goose. I have wonderful news! Simply *wonderful!*"

The ambassador was sufficiently nonplussed that he sank slowly back into his chair, hands resting on the desk to ease his way down.

Esterhazy went to stand behind Bazaar and to one side. He was not a small man; the intimidating effect was profound.

With a finger, Lourdes directed the former UEPF's ambassatrix to a seat.

Bazaar noticed and was about to ask when Lourdes offered. "Why, *that* is my wonderful news. Ambassatrix, please tell Bazaar about the grand news."

Bazaar thought the Old Earther would fall into tears as she said, "The Peace Fleet has surrendered to the

Timocratic Republic of Balboa. All facilities, property, art, and personnel are likewise surrendered."

The Valparaisan hoped it didn't show on his face but, *Holy shit, now they own us.*

"That's right," Lourdes said. "Now we own you. I have only the one son, you know, Ambassador," Lourdes began. "Did you have any brothers or sisters?"

"A brother, two sisters," Bazaar answered. "Why?"

"Well, I was wondering if you ever noticed—sons often do not—how much better you—you and your brother—were treated than were your sisters, by your mother. Possibly even by your father, but it's mostly a mother thing? It's especially strong in we Hispanic types. Well, Hispanics and Arabs. I'm sure you already knew that, of course."

Bazaar shrugged as if to say, *Well, of course boys are better treated than girls. It's the way of the world.*

Lourdes nodded. *In this, at least, we understand each other.*

"Now Hamilcar is my only son," she continued. "And I am past the time I am likely to conceive another. I want you to imagine how much better, even than you were, you would have been treated had you been an only son, with no hope of more. Is there anything your mother would not have done for you?"

"Pro . . . bably not," Bazaar hesitantly agreed.

Lourdes face turned to flesh-toned ice. "So when I tell you that if Valparaiso doesn't get a squadron of fighters in the air to cover my son, I will personally push the button to nuke your half-dozen largest cities, you will understand that I mean it, yes?"

Bazaar's eyes grew wide. "What nonsense is this? Bullshit! Complete and utter—"

"Hajar, Ambassador Bazaar, Hajar.

"What? Did you really think nukes go off by themselves? Accidentally?" She began to laugh, softly and then with enthusiasm.

"Oh, no, *Mister* Ambassador. We nuked Hajar. My husband nuked Hajar. My husband who also has one son left, and trends pretty faithful, hence is not going to have another, destroyed Hajar. He killed at least three million people, most of them innocent, in revenge over the murder of his first family. We nuked them and we can nuke twenty more. And we have the means of delivering them to your cities that you cannot even detect, let alone resist. Do you think he now—He with the blood of millions on his hands? Him, a charming monster?—will hesitate to destroy you if you let his only boy be killed?"

She stood and walked partway around the ambassador's desk, stopping to pick up a red phone. She pushed the phone in front of his face.

"This *is* the secure phone, yes? Good. I want you to get on this secure phone to your government—right now, while I watch and listen—and let them know in no uncertain terms that, while the UEPF *might* have attacked you if you had gone to my boy's aid, we will *annihilate* you if you do not."

"But—but, we've given you help in this war. Shed our blood for you. How can you do this? How can you even threaten to do this?"

"What have you done for us lately?" she sniffed. "The *phone*, Mister Ambassador. The phone right *now*."

Bazaar didn't have to dial, a simple push of the button was sufficient to connect him with the home office. "Put me through to the president," he said, then waited for something under a minute for the connection to be made.

"Yes, Mr. President, Ambassador Bazaar . . . it's about the Balboans' request for fighter support for their attack on the UEPF's base . . . yes, Mr. President, I know we didn't agree to it in advance . . . yes, they know it, too, and don't care . . . yes, they're also aware we were afraid of UEPF retaliation . . . Mr. President, but that excuse is dead now; the UEPF is theirs. Their military commander's wife informs me that we either send those fighters or *they* will nuke us . . . Yes, as a matter of fact I *do* believe her."

Lourdes couldn't quite—neither did she really try to—make out the stream of curses and obscenities coming from the phone. Even so, Bazaar pressed it tighter to his ear to make sure she didn't. She could tell the flood had passed when he moved it slightly away from his ear and said, "We're willing to try a bluff. A dozen of our most capable jet fighters will depart with two refuelers within the half hour. But they will not be armed."

"If the bluff works, fine," she replied, "but, speaking for myself, I would consider that a very thin reed on which to hang your chances of not being destroyed by us."

Choukoutien, *Ming Zhong Guo*, Terra Nova

Meaningless, useless courtiers clustered about the throne room, each resplendent in brightly colored, embroidered robes, and not a one of them of any value to the emperor.

A new courtier approached through the main entrance. Begging permission to approach the throne, he skipped the usual self-abasement and simply hurried to the emperor's side.

"Your majesty," whispered Li An Ming, into the emperor's ear, "I have terrible news."

The Zhong emperor braced himself, thinking, *What can that evil bitch come up with that is worse than what she has already put me through?*

Mustering what little dignity the empress had left him, the emperor asked, "And this would be?"

"I am afraid that Her Imperial Majesty has been killed. I just received word. The killers—the Balboans, as it turns out—are asking what we'd like done with the body. They say they can deliver it, but it may take a few days."

"Done with the body? Done with the *body*?" All the useless, meaningless, and splendidly berobed present looked up in surprise at the emperor's suddenly raised voice.

For the first time since he'd been forced to marry her, the Zhong emperor began to truly and sincerely laugh. "Feed it to pigs! No . . . no, that's not good enough. Toss it into an open-pit shit house. No, no, wait, that's isn't quite enough either.

"Ask them to send the bitch's corpse to me. I'll find something appropriate.

"And now, where is my minister of foreign relations and my minister of war?"

"Oh, and one other thing, Your Imperial Majesty," Li An Ming continued. "It seems the enemy has captured the entire Peace Fleet."

The emperor paled, not so much for being a fan of the Earthpigs as that this interjected a dreadful level of uncertainty into his life. "I want my minister for foreign relations, finance, information, internal security, and my minister of war *now*!"

The throne room was cleared now, cleared except for the three ministers the emperor had demanded, plus Li An Ming, who was there because he understood the apparatus by which the late empress had ruled the empire.

"Peace," insisted the emperor, right arm pounding the armrest of his throne for emphasis. "I want peace with the Balboans and I want our fleet and army—what's left of them—back."

"What if they demand reparations, Your Majesty?" asked Finance. "What if they demand ransom even for the men they haven't captured?"

"Then we shall pay it," said the emperor. "Whatever the late imperial bitch's sins, and they were *many*, she had a good deal to do with holding the empire together. Without her, I will *need* that army. Badly."

"I can call the airborne and special forces group back from Wellington," said War. "For the ones on their island and ashore, we lack the strength to withdraw them without Balboan permission. Our fleet admiral, Wanyan Liang, lacks the strength to evacuate them in the face of the Balboan air force and"—here War shuddered at the memory of the roll of losses—"especially in the face of the coastal artillery of their fortress island."

"I will," said Foreign Affairs, "have our ambassador to

the World League approach theirs and see what can be agreed to. It may take a while—several days to several months—to work out arrangements."

"I don't think you quite understand," the emperor said. "The bitch sold the people on the war via the Propaganda Ministry. The lies flew thick and fast, each more incredible than the last—or, if credible, credible only because they were so consistent! With the war lost and her dead—I cannot even turn the cunt over to the people's justice now!—the odds of rebellion here are . . ." The emperor looked pointedly at Li An Ming. As right-hand man for the late empress, he knew better than most the state of the empire.

"Dangerously high, Your Majesty."

The emperor shifted gaze to Internal Security, who likewise agreed, "Not inevitable but, yes, Your Majesty, dangerously likely."

"So you see, I *need* that army. I must have it. Not in several months but at least the beginnings of it within the week."

Finance nodded, then bowed. "I will make it happen, Your Majesty. Please issue the authorization; much gold—much!—will certainly be required."

"I shall."

"And Information?"

"Yes, Your Majesty?"

"You have twenty-four hours to come up with a plan to pacify the people, as long as they can be pacified, and put all the blame on my late empress."

"Yes, Your Majesty."

"Now go!"

The ministers began to shuffle out of the throne room, until Finance turned around and asked, "Your Majesty, what if they want more gold than we have?"

"Where can we get more?"

"The Federated States; they have the largest reserves on the planet, more than four times ours."

The emperor drummed his fingers for a few minutes, thinking hard, then thundered, "Get me the Minister of Trade!"

Estado Mayor, Sub camp C, *Ciudad* Balboa, Balboa

Carrera didn't like the look on Fernandez's face. The latter sat framed in the light pouring through the doorway into Carrera's concrete office.

"Out with it, Omar."

With a grimace, Fernandez laid out the bad news. "We haven't been able to break back into the satellite network, neither the FSC's nor the Tauran Union's—and the Zhong's was always out of the question—but our embassy in Wellington informs us that the Zhong air transport fleet there built up to some fifty-seven heavies and eight or nine refuelers. They're flying out now. And I think we all know where they're going."

"Shit. Where are the Valparisan fighters?"

"Oh, they've landed on the airstrip at Atlantis Base. Moreover, they sent out three C-31s with ground crews, a mobile radar set, and sundry odds and ends. I had someone look at the ordnance they brought. Though they said they'd fly them unarmed, in fact they sent along a dozen air-to-air missiles, one per plane. Sadly for us, however, and worse for the cadets, a dozen, divided by two, for likelihood of a kill, and then further divided by fifty-seven plus eight or nine, means a division of Zhong Paras on the island. Sure, they take out two or three planes. Maybe even four. It's not enough even to deter the Zhong."

An office drone stuck his head in the door. "*Duque*, your wife is on the line from First Landing, in the Federated States. Shall I patch it through here?"

"Yes, thank you," Carrera said. "And please close the door and post yourself as a guard on it."

"Wilco, *Duque*."

It took maybe ten seconds for all that to happen. At the flashing light signal, Carrera picked up the secure phone on his desk. He'd barely gotten the formal, "Yes, love," out before Lourdes launched into a breathless narrative.

"Patricio, I am sitting here with the Zhong ambassador to the World League. He's asked for an armistice in place, without a formal surrender of his country's forces, and repatriation without payment. I've told him this is impossible, that his empire has damaged our infrastructure, destroyed our buildings, killed and wounded our citizens, and committed numerous war crimes against us, from torture to biological warfare. I have insisted upon unconditional surrender, reparations, payments for the return of prisoners, an admission of guilt and apology, and turning over to us any war criminals, such as we may identify, that will not be among the prisoners."

Carrera looked at Fernandez and mouthed, *Have someone notify the president.* Fernandez wheeled around, opened the door, and told the office drone to get him.

Biological warfare? thought Carrera. *Well, sure, we accused them of it. After all, the Zhong always claim biological warfare is being waged by their enemies. Nobody believes them, of course, except left-wing academics, but they still always claim it, though this time we got our accusations in first.*

We sort of had to. We knew beyond a shadow of a doubt that the cratering of the Isla Real was going to a create a huge breeding ground for mosquitoes, and that those would bear malaria, dengue, yellow fever, black vomit fever, LLU-5, break-back fever, thotovirus-bravo-terranoviensis, and God alone knows what else. Moreover, we were going to be relatively protected and they were going to be extremely vulnerable. So we had to accuse them first.

"Am I on the speaker, Ambassatrix?"

Catching the hint, Lourdes replied, "You are, *Duque.*"

"And the name of the Zhong ambassador is?"

A new voice piped in, speaking in surprisingly accentless English. "I am Ambassador Shen Song."

"Very good. I will ask your indulgence for a few minutes, while the president is summoned and this call transferred to his conference room."

Parilla, Carrera, and Fernandez all clustered at one end of a long conference table. The former, who was also president of the republic, was able to get around now on his own, following a severe heart attack brought on, in good part, by Carrera's insubordination. In the middle of that end of the table sat a wired-in speaker, currently shut off. Situation maps that mirrored those in the operations cell were affixed to the walls. "The Zhong are asking for peace?" Parilla asked. "I confess, I am surprised."

"And we need to make peace, Raul," Carrera said. "We *desperately* need to make peace."

"And that surprises me even more. What is this, our *Dux Bellorum*, the great Patricio Carrera, wants *peace?* What is the world coming to?"

"They're got about a division of Paras heading for Atlantis, Raul. My kid can't take those on, though he'll try."

"And the Valparisans your wife browbeat and threatened into sending aid?"

"They sent what they said they would. But, as it turns out, it's not enough."

"So . . . peace, then," Parilla mused. "It's not such a bad word, I suppose. Whatever will we do with the time saved?"

Carrera recognized that Parilla was being sardonic; the once brotherly-close relationship between them had frayed a bit under both the pressures of war and Carrera's penchant for heart attack–inducing insubordination.

Finally, Parilla said, "Fine, let's talk to this Shen Song."

Carrera tapped the speaker. "Ambassatrix, Ambassador; the President of the Republic is here now, and listening. I have already told him of my wife's demands, which are our demands. However, he assures me that everything is negotiable."

"In the first place, Mr. President," Shen Song began,

"the demand for payment for the return of our fighting men is simply too high, given that they are still undefeated in the field. We cannot and will not countenance paying more than a third of the cost to the Taurans . . ."

Carrera and Fernandez exchanged glances. *If they are willing to pay anything, then they want this to end as much as we do. But what of the aerial armada heading toward Atlantis?*

Atlantis Base

The armor and the gunships were out in position to strike any of the three most likely drop zones. Around the base, the cadets were as well dug in as time allowed, and with some depth in the defense gained by occupying and fortifying key buildings. A short cohort of cadets was also poised to attack to open up a route for the armor to escape after it savaged the descending Zhong Paras as best it could.

Meanwhile, Hamilcar Carrera stood on the military crest of the ridge, Tribune Cano beside him, and cursed, "Come on, damn you, come on. We can't wait forever!"

Yincheng, Zhong Empire

Sixty-five heavy-lift aircraft, hovering about from twenty to thirty-five thousand feet, all wanting to land, represented an unusually, and dangerously, high workload for the air traffic controllers of Yincheng Air Base, which was also the home base of the Paras.

A nervous flight lieutenant, Rong Yuyao, glanced at his fuel gauge. Tapping his radio to life, he called down to the control tower. "Look, you misbegotten sons of low-ranked, back passage whores, we cannot stay up in the sky forever!"

"Everybody's got problems, Lieutenant Rong," answered one of the controllers. "We'll bring you down in good time."

BdL *Dos Lindas*, *Mar Furioso*

Roderigo Fosa read the decoded message with mixed feelings. *It would have been glorious, after all, the biggest naval battle since the Great Global War.*

"What's it say, Skipper?" asked Sergeant Major Ramirez. "Good news? Bad?"

"It says, short version, 'Peace has been arranged with the Zhong Empire. Their fleet is to steam at flank speed for their main base in the Eastern *Furioso*. Do not interfere with them or harass them. Return to Balboa. Fight only in self-defense. Assume blockade around Zhong lodgment. Stop and board all ships heading for the Zhong lodgment. Only food and medical supplies come through until they're evacuated. Any of them that can fit on the ships can leave. Bravo Zulu. Carrera.'"

Ramirez nodded. "I'm not really sorry," he said. "I think we'd have won, but we'd have lost a lot of good men and boys in the winning."

"Yeah, Top, we would have. And we've got this consolation; you know why he had us interned?"

"I assumed it was part of the great master plan," Ramirez answered.

"Well, yes, it was, but the plan had two parts. One was just what we did, come out slugging at a time most convenient for us and least convenient for the Zhong. But the other part . . ."

"Yes, sir?"

"He wants the crews of the fleet intact to take over the ships of the former United Earth Peace Fleet. And I think he wants them for an eventual expedition to liberate Old Earth."

"Bastard does think ahead, doesn't he?"

"Oh, yeah."

CHAPTER TWENTY-THREE

Men want a battle to fight, an adventure to live, and a beauty to rescue. That is what is written in their hearts. That is what little boys play at. That is what men's movies are about. You just see it. It is undeniable.

—John Eldredge

Sachsen, enroute to Leinenfeld

Khalid's auto zipped past abandoned cars, abandoned towns, and the occasional pillar of fire and smoke rising from some of each.

"Your name is Moslem," Alix accused. "You've helped the Moslems here to rise up. But you say you are not Moslem."

"I'm a Druze," Khalid replied, still keeping his eyes on the road.

"And you two?" she asked of Tim and Fritz.

"I'm an atheist," Tim admitted. "Though I don't mind those who still believe."

"I'm a true infidel," Fritz said. "I went back to the

Roman Catholicism of my grandparents. I'm working on bringing Tim to Holy Mother Church, too."

"Why, then . . . ?"

"Why Balboa?" Khalid asked.

"Why so much *loyalty* to Balboa?"

"They're probably the most Catholic country left on the planet," Fritz explained. "You want to find the 'church militant'? Look there."

"They don't try to shove religion down your throat," Tim said, nodding his head in Fritz's direction and adding, "Except for this one, and he, at least, *means* well."

Khalid remained silent for a moment, then asked, "Do you know anything about the Druze?"

"Near enough to nothing."

"We're a heretical sect, if you ask some of *them*," Khalid said. "Though some of them, a few, consider us to be a sect of Islam. We're mostly ignorant of our own religion; a fairly small minority is educated in it and the rest of us simply abide by certain principles. Among these principles is patriotism. We are loyal to the country in which we live.

"In my case I was recruited in Sumer, after my family was murdered. I took revenge for that, oh, a hundred times over and down to the last generation. And in the course of that, I gradually ceased being a Sumeri and just as gradually became a Balboan. My friends were Balboan, good men, good soldiers, and a privilege to fight beside. I acquired a house in Balboa, though it's been rented out many more years than I've lived in it.

"Why I even . . ."

"What?" Alix prodded.

"I used to date a girl, the sister of a comrade. Thought a lot about marrying her but, in the end, realized that my job and marriage aren't compatible. Maybe when the war is finally, fully over. Maybe."

Tauran Union Defense Agency Headquarters, Lumiere, Gaul

Troopers Braiden and Proctor, manning the window farthest from the corner, busied themselves with a long-running, high-points contest of gin rummy. The window to the left of them was manned, but with a table pulled up to cover the central part of the window and with a number of peepholes shot through the table. The holes were covered with dark cloth, paper, or cardboard, so that anyone looking to snipe at it couldn't know when it was manned and being watched out from. Greene roved from position to position. Corporal Dawes sat close to Captain Turenge, who sat on a desk with the earpiece from a radio stuck in her ear.

Campbell, meanwhile, sitting on the floor in the corner, spent the time terrifying Houston with horrible tales of his likely fate if the building should fall. This couldn't be too far off; the Moslems had bent the flanks in such that the building was now isolated, food was getting short, and even the prodigious supply of ammunition from the sub-basement running low. Campbell was, in fact, pretty sure they were all fucked.

"Shut up, please." Turenge held up a hand to stop Campbell's harassment of the detested Houston. She cupped the other over the earpiece, and closed her eyes, concentrating hard on the weak signal. After a few minutes, she looked up and said, "The enemy have taken the Peace Fleet. It has surrendered in its entirety. They own space."

"Holy shit," said Campbell, while thinking, *Twenty-four space suits, new. That's sure as shit what they were for.*

"Amazing," said Braiden, "little country like that and now they own space."

"Just get back to the game, Jim," said Proctor. "Space can wait."

That news wasn't the least dark spot of the world situation. Supposedly, both Gaul and Anglia had managed to come up with their ransom to get their troops back. Sachsen had not and Tuscany was still trying, as were some of the lesser states that had contributed troops. The Balboans, however, were still playing hardball, diplomatically: "You, the members of the Tauran Union, claimed to be a single superstate and made war upon us, as such. We cannot release any prisoners until either the full sum is paid for all of them, or, in the alternative, a given state secedes from the Tauran Union."

This had led Anglia, Haarlem, and Hordaland to officially leave the Union, no deals, no caveats, just simple secession. Even so, none of the troops had yet been released.

Task Force Jesuit, Cordoban-Santa Josefinan Border

There could be no other night for this; everyone who was getting out had to get out now.

With Eris rising and Hecate hanging low in the western sky, Marciano's MPs began leading the first wave of escapees for this night out from the assembly areas in which they'd been waiting north and down to the beach.

"Quiet," was the MP watchword and command, "for God's sake be *quiet.*"

To help with that, and with some other things, the machine guns on water-drip delay began firing at about the time the first several hundred departed from just behind the forward trace. Rifles, several dozen, joined in that, while some mortars, not excess to needs but worth expending to get the men out, joined in with random shells at random times, one shell and time per mortar, period.

Gold wasn't sure why the sense of despair was gone that he'd felt after the last attempt had been called off halfway through, but he didn't sense it this evening.

I suppose it could be that the Santa Josefinans didn't attack today, as I am sure some of them expected to happen. But I think there's some fear, still. Maybe it's only fear of getting lost and left behind, but it's there.

Tonight, Gold had a radio operator assigned to him, a Hordalander tank driver who'd had to put his own tank down. The boy didn't have much to say; he carried and monitored the radio and was ready to transmit any suggestions to Marciano or Rall or to bring Peter to them for consultations. Meanwhile, Peter had contact with his own ship, the *Alberto Helada,* via a small but powerful radio, the shape and size of a brick. It was through this that the ship informed him that they'd reached their anchorage, that they'd dispatched the small rubber boats as well as the ones the Taurans had commandeered that had been sent out with the freighter to hide.

Gold began to feel some of the burden of fear—in his case, fear of failure—lift from him as the first boats began shuttling the Taurans out to the *Helada*.

Claudio appeared out of the seeming air. "The loading's going well," the general said.

"Yes, sir," Gold agreed. "With most of the wounded taken off yesterday, tonight should go faster."

"I hope so," Marciano agreed. "As a gesture of good will...well, sort of...at Rall's suggestion, I left all our booze and a good deal of food for the locals when they figure out what's going on. International good will, and all."

Command Post, Second Cohort, *Tercio la Negrita*, First Santa Josefinan Infantry Legion

Dinner, this evening, had consisted of a few ounces of stale bread, a canteen cup of watery soup, with perhaps two ounces of monkey in it, and half a candy bar from a stockpile that the Taurans had somehow missed.

God, I'm hungry, thought Ignacio Macera, for about the two hundredth time. *Artillery ammunition they've managed to bring up a lot better than they have food.*

The tent for Macera's command post was a commandeered civilian job, not especially large, that the troops had painted green and brown with some latex paint they'd looted from a store. The paint was already beginning to peel off.

There was enough room inside for Macera, his rather

small staff, and a few guests. Such meetings as he'd had to have since coming to this spot were generally done outside, in a narrow draw with some protection from direct and indirect fire, but absolutely none from rain and mosquitoes.

The wind, the same wind that was, for the nonce, keeping the mosquitoes off, carried on it the aroma of a dozen different styles of savory stew and at least one of baking bread.

God, I'm hungry, Macera thought. *So are my boys.*

There was reason for the hunger. The Taurans had, in their flight, stripped the country pretty much bare, shooting any food animals they couldn't take with them. Because of the damage to the roads and bridges, as well as the confiscation and sabotage of the dray animals and trucks the country normally could have provided, only a thin trickle of food was actually reaching the troops. Supposedly a small freighter was being filled with provisions back at *Puerto Bruselas* but, if so, it hadn't even been dispatched yet. Nothing, in any case, had come by sea.

Standing outside the tent, facing northeast in the direction of the Tauran defenses, and torturing himself with the smell of the food, Macera heard a long burst fired from a single machine gun. The tracers he could not see. Neither could he hear the repetitive *crack* of the bullets' passage.

Something about the sound of that Tauran machine guns and the other weapons he heard firing bugged Macera. He couldn't quite put his finger on the whys of it, either, and that also annoyed him to no end.

The intensity is about the same, he thought. *And nothing about it seems too high or too low . . . but still it bugs me.*

He cleared his mind, sat down on a makeshift camp stool, and just concentrated while listening. He waited a short time. A different machine gun fired. He knew it was different because with this one he *could* hear the passage of the bullets.

He waited still longer. Both machine guns to his front fired again, one after—though far from immediately after—the other.

It wasn't the gap between bursts of either of the machine guns that alerted him, oh, no. *It's that the gap between that first one firing and the second one firing were just about exactly the same. It's been three times now and the difference in time between them was exactly the same, give or take ten seconds. I call "bullshit."*

"Get me my reserve commander!" Macera shouted to one of the runners in the command post.

Do I let higher know what's up? No, I might be wrong and they'd just laugh over it. But I am allowed to do reconnaissance without asking permission and nobody told me it couldn't be a reconnaissance in force.

The reserve maniple was under the command of a junior tribune, a young black officer somewhat improbably named "Henry Morgan."

Morgan had started the war as a platoon leader, with charge of fewer than forty men. Now, with not much of a jump in rank, he commanded something north of six hundred. This was partly the result of casualties among the tercio's officer corps, but more because of the flood of new recruits, flocking to the winning side.

It stretched his group of leaders to the breaking point,

that human flood, with corporals leading what were really platoons, for example, and maybe a properly trained private or two to help them. Or maybe not.

"Henrique," Macera called him, after Morgan reported in, largely because he knew it annoyed the youngster, "I am beginning to suspect we're having the wool pulled over our eyes."

"Sir?"

"Have you been listening to the machine guns? I mean the other side's."

"Not really, sir, no."

"I have. Do you know that there's one that, after it fires, another will fire in five minutes and forty-five seconds, plus or minus ten? Now why would a machine gun crew do that? Why would it be firing with such—and I use this term in its full meaning—*clocklike precision*?"

Unseen in the darkness, and Morgan was dark enough to be truly unseen in the darkness, a light dawned. "Those motherfuckers! They're abandoning their position and marching into internment in Cordoba, aren't they!?"

"And, see, Henry"—the young man noticed that this time his boss used his proper name—"that's why I had you in the reserve, because you're far and away my smartest maniple commander. Now, I'm coming along, but here's what I want you to do . . ."

The formation was more or less V shaped, with the upstretched arms of the V pointing toward the Taurans and the reserve platoon down at the pointy base. Morgan took the point of one two-hundred-man "platoon," while Macera took the other. A centurion took the rear to kick

the asses of stragglers. The reserve was held in a closer
formation by the first centurion.

Neither side had any barbed wire up to impede
progress or channelize their enemies into the beaten
zones of machine guns. Even without the barbed wire,
though, progress was difficult, given the very limited
illumination provided by Erie, now well past apogee.

All the way from the rear to where he was on point,
Macera could hear the first centurion, saying, "SHUT
THE FUCK UP, YOU DICKHEADS!"

*Yeah, these rabble are making enough noise that one
man shouting is hardly going to alert the Taurans any
more than the rank and file already have.*

The first notice any of them had that they'd reached
the Tauran lines was a trip wire, over by Morgan's arm of
the V, that set off a shooting flame–powered shrieking
whistle. Half a minute after that, Morgan called Macera
over the radio; "Boss, I could see by the light from that
warning device. The fuckers have taken to their heels.
They're not here."

As if to refute that, a machine gun fired a long burst to
Macera's front. From where he stood he could now see the
tracers, one in five, skipping over the ground to strike
somewhere off to his rear. Macera stopped where he was,
consulted his watch, and waited . . . for five minutes and
thirty-eight seconds when the other machine gun let loose.

"No big surprise there, is there?" he asked, rhetorically.

Whipping out his compass, Macera noted the direction
toward each of those two Tauran machine guns. Physically
pointing the corporals concerned in the right direction,
he told off first one platoon, and then another, "Get rid of

that machine gun. I don't think there's anyone there but be careful, even so."

With the remainder of the maniple, about a hundred men, Macera continued on to the northeast. At one point in time, he almost fell into a trench, seeing—or, rather, *sensing*—it in the nick of time.

"Empty, too. Those dirty bastards."

Past the high ground the Taurans had chosen for the defensive positions, he could hear generators going and make out lights. One set of lights was upwind of him, not too far off. From it came the most tempting smells.

Morgan called again; voice breaking and full of the sound of tears of frustration. "It's the men, sir . . . they broke ranks and assaulted one of the . . . well . . . I guess they're field kitchens. They won't fucking listen to anything. They're just standing around, stuffing their faces with bread and soup. Should I shoot a couple of them?"

Before Macera could answer he heard the sound of about a hundred pairs of rushing feet, racing by him in the dark and heading toward the lights from which came those most tempting smells.

Fuck.

"No, Henry, there's nothing to be done. Well . . . try to get some local security set up with the ones who've already grabbed some food. But you won't get them moving again until they've eaten or the food's run out."

"Sir, they left us a *lot* of food. I don't think we'll run out anytime soon. Oh, shit; they left booze, too!"

From the sheltered cove from which the bulk of the troops were being evacuated Marciano could hear the occasional trip-wire device being set off. He looked at the sky, consulted his watch, and then asked Rall, "Are we going to make it? Before daybreak, I mean."

"Yes," Rall answered, with a good deal of satisfaction in his voice.

"Where did you learn the trick with the food, Rall?"

"My great-grandfather. He was a regimental commander in the Great Global War. When I was a boy he told me about breaking contact with some Volgans who were poised to overrun his regiment by having the cooks make soup and leaving it there. Only works when your enemy's starving, though."

"The Santa Josefinan politicians?"

"They're trussed up with a key to their chains on one of Chiarello's water clocks. They should be able to get themselves loose and cross into Cordoba on time. But, you know, sir, if not, fuck 'em; it's not like we owe them anything."

Marciano almost laughed, but contented himself with, "Very good."

"The Cordoban 'workers'?"

"Paid off and sent home."

"Those men worked hard for us. I hate to have paid them in worthless—"

"We didn't, sir," said Rall. "Instead, we sent them home with a rifle and about two hundred rounds, each. They seemed happy with that."

Suddenly Gold was there, standing to one side of the two Taurans, his Hordalander RTO in tow.

"That's it, sir," Gold said, "we're next."

Marciano looked east to see the first glimmering of

sunrise flickering on the clouds overhead. He, too, could smell the soup he'd denied himself and his men. "Seems like I haven't eaten in days. How's the food on your ship, Captain?"

Muelle 81, *Ciudad* Balboa, Balboa

The mess sections for the prisoners had put out a very impressive spread for the event, in about two dozen different cuisines.

Given that about ninety-eight percent of what they had to work with came from cans, thought Carrera, *I'm genuinely impressed.*

A huge tent, one which, on another planet at another time, might have been called an "Oktoberfest tent," had been raised over a section of the parking lot north of the pier. Some hastily nailed together but solid-looking stairs led from asphalt to the trailer. There were also a couple of microphones on stands, with wires leading off to various controls, amplifiers, and speakers.

On chairs and benches, alone or at tables, some six thousand senior officers and noncoms were gathered. Nearly all had disposable plates either in front of them or balanced on their legs or held in one hand. Guards, mostly pro forma, formed a ring around the tent. At one end, a stake and platform trailer did stand in service for a rostrum.

"IF YOU WOULD ALL SHUT THE FUCK UP NOW?" intoned RSM Ayres, standing atop the trailer. He didn't need the speaker system that had been set up to fill the tent with sound. The noise *immediately* died down to a whisper.

Still scorning the use of the microphone, Ayres announced, "Our gracious captor would like a word with us."

Carrera, himself, was as chipper as could be. *And why not? I went into that conference with the Zhong ambassador expecting to have to order my son to surrender—which order the little bastard might just have disobeyed—and let the Zhong go scot-free. Instead, I let Task Force Wu go scot-free, which I wanted to do, anyway, get paid fifty percent of the hostage cost of the Taurans, for people we haven't even captured yet, get a score or so of Zhong, and a few attached Tauran, intel types to hang on war crimes charges—oh, they're guilty as sin, but then, so am I—to mollify the people. And all I really had to trade over it was Wu's boys and dropping the demand for an admission of guilt. Better still, my boy's mission is a complete success.*

But they had us. I still don't fully understand— personal failing, to be sure—why they knuckled under at all. Maybe Lourdes will.

Carrera, who had been sitting next to the Mendozas, Jorge and Marqueli, stepped up, climbed the steps, walked to the microphone, and began, "I couldn't possibly think to outdo the RSM in sheer, unenhanced volume." That got a laugh, one somewhat lost on some of the attendees who either hadn't grown up with English as a first language or were terribly, terribly innocent. Ayres understood the double entendre perfectly well, of course, and unconsciously preened a bit.

"We have a problem," Carrera continued. "Many states have already agreed to the fee we're charging to send you guys back and have made arrangements to send it. That's been not as hard as expected, since so many of them keep their gold, or most of it, in a vault in First Landing in the Federated States. Had you guys known that? I hadn't, actually.

"But others have not. I sense that this isn't because they're unwilling to ransom you, as that the rebellions that broke out when you and your men were *so* unwisely sent here have simply overturned your societies; hence, that there's no one in a position to pay.

"And why do I insist on payment, since I'm sure you're wondering about that, especially given how well you've been treated and the excellent chance that, once you go back and set your countries to right, we will find ourselves bosom buddies, in a long and fruitful—hell, maybe perpetual—alliance.

"It's simple: our cities are in ruins from bombing or fighting or both. Our infrastructure, barring only the Transitway, is a mess. And the Transitway, too, took enough near misses that it needs work before we can use it again.

"Powerlines and waterlines are cut, bridges down, roads cratered, and with a burgeoning mosquito and other insect population that is very likely to bring all kinds of disease upon us.

"Moreover, I have to set things up to care for tens of thousands of wounded, *hundreds* of thousands of widows and orphans, or the dependents of the crippled, and rebuild everything. I bear you—hell, all of Balboa bears you; we know you were sent here by stinking Kosmos who despised you even more than they despised us—well, we bear you nothing but good will. I say it again: we bear you soldiers nothing but good will. But I've *got* to have that gold. No, cash won't do; the Tauro has become effectively worthless, and you're going to need the Federated States Drachmae you already have."

He paused for a bit, letting the need sink in.

"So, could I let you go on credit? I certainly would like to. Here's the problem: any of you who swear out a bond, payable to Balboa, to cover your release, will then no longer be fighting for your own countries. Oh, no; you would be, and—more importantly—would be *seen* to be, fighting for me. I wouldn't do that to you or to your cause.

"So why don't I let go those whose countries have paid? As long as you're part of the Tauran Union, you have to answer for all the Tauran Union.

"Why don't I let go those countries which have paid and which have seceded from the Tauran Union? I don't know that you're enough, on your own, to liberate your countries.

"RSM?"

"Sir?" Ayres replied.

"There are anywhere from a couple of hundred thousand to a half a million Moslems who've risen in rebellion in Anglia. And by that I mean only the men; there are probably two or three times as many women, girls, and boys, providing support. Can the Anglians here liberate, say, your capital, against those odds? Can they even besiege it?"

Ayres did a bit of military math in his head, divided the

result of that by stone and brick, and came up with, "NO FUCKING WAY, SIR."

"General Janier"—Bertrand Janier, still wheelchair bound as his bones continued to knit, was sitting with the mass—"your country had the largest single contingent here. Can you liberate Gaul on your own?"

Someone from the Psychological Operations Tercio hurried to Janier's side with a microphone. "Not a chance, Patricio. The Anglians' half million are about three times that size in Gaul."

"So, you see," Carrera continued, "I cannot, not in good conscience, let these individual national contingents go. It would be futile."

"IF *YOU* LED US, WE COULD DO IT," shouted Ayres. That got a considerable murmur of what certainly sounded like approval. Indeed, it was likely a strong majority of the Taurans who thought that a rather splendid idea.

"Can't do it. Same problem as mentioned: you would be fighting for me, the great enemy, rather than yourselves. Although . . ."

"YES, SIR?" asked Ayres, for the crowd.

"Personally, I think your best bet is General Janier. No, before you start, just shut up. RSM?"

"THE CROWD WILL, ONCE AGAIN, SHUT THE FUCK UP!"

"He did as good a job, given the hand he was dealt, as anyone could be expected to. He's used to commanding you, and you're used to him. He knows his business. Therefore, I nominate Bertrand Janier to command you. RSM?"

"ALL IN FAVOR?"

The "Ayes" were somewhat subdued . . .

"OPPOSED?"

. . . but the "Nays" were an obvious minority.

"I BELIEVE THE MOTION CARRIED, SIR."

Down on the floor, with tears in his eyes, Janier thought, *Thank you, Patricio, from the bottom of my heart, for this chance to redeem my reputation and honor. You are the best enemy a man could have.*

Janier, like Ayres, had been in on the choreography for this event for some days. They'd even rehearsed it. Even so, he blinked a few times, to clear his eyes, and swallowed hard, to clear his throat, then beckoned the PSYOP type with the microphone over. "A suggestion, Patricio?"

"Yes, Bertrand."

"What if we, here, declare a New Tauran . . . no, not Union . . . aha, a new Tauran Confederation. Just us soldiers; *we* do it. And then we sign it, on our own behalf. What if we created a confederational constitution, here, to which we append our signatures and pledge—how did that phrase go? Aha, I remember—'our lives, our fortunes, and our scared honor'."

"I suppose . . . the old Tauran Union being impliedly declared dead . . . that Balboa would recognize the new confederation. Mr. and Mrs. Mendoza, would you see fit to helping the Taurans draft a new constitution, one—I assume this is what they want—something like ours, but addressing the peculiarities of Tauran circumstances?"

As rehearsed, Jorge and Marqueli exchanged doubtful glances, then leaned in to whisper to each other. The whispering amounted to repetitive "rhubarb and garbage," but after a prearranged time, they separated and stood up. "We'd be proud to help, sir," said Jorge, "but we'd need a committee to direct our help toward."

"General Janier?"

"I will appoint a committee by nations, *Duque.*"

"Very good," Carrera answered. "but you look like you have a doubt, Bertrand."

"Well, Patricio, it's your rather harsh laws on treason?"

"I see. Well . . . this is different, you know. With us never having recognized the TU as a legitimate country—which it never was—it is impossible to commit treason against it. Those we charged and tried were committing treason, not against the TU, but against Anglia, Gaul, Tuscany, etcetera."

Janier nodded soberly, just as it had been rehearsed, then asked, "Would Balboa be willing to forgo payment from those states neither in secession nor yet being able to pay until we had liberated those states?"

"Do you object to my holding them until the ransoms are paid?"

"I do," Janier answered, "and yet I understand, I am sure we *all* understand your position. Just let us go, hold the ones you must, and we will put top efforts into liberating them as soon as practical. There will, after all, be much hard fighting ahead and we shall need replacements."

"All right," Carrera said, "we'll do it. We'll take a chance on you to set all things aright. Is there anything else?"

"We are going to need," said Janier, "a great deal of rope."

At that the assembly closed, amidst fierce cheering and multinational war cries.

CHAPTER TWENTY-FOUR

It was men who stopped slavery. It was men who ran up the stairs in the Twin Towers to rescue people. It was men who gave up their seats on the lifeboats of the *Titanic*. Men are made to take risks and live passionately on behalf of others.   —John Eldredge

Thirty-two miles northwest of Leinenfeld, Sachsen

The five naked, dark-skinned bodies swayed gently in the breeze from ropes encircling now very lengthened necks. On their own, these could not have been the giveaway. Like the bodies, the faces of these were blackened and showed swollen, blackened tongues protruding. They—a man, a woman, two boys, and a girl—weren't obviously Moslem, or Sachsen, or, indeed, obviously anything but corpses. Tim, who was possibly a little more in tune with some of life's shadier realities than most, looked from the halted car at the largest corpse and said, "Circumcised; they're Moslems."

***

They'd figured out early on that neither back roads nor *Autobahnen* really would do, on their own, entirely. The roads connected small towns, and it was precisely in those small towns that sundry *evilwickednaughtybadbadbad*, antiprogressive, *doubleplusungood*, and reactionary *burghers* had been ignoring both propaganda and law concerning firearms, religiously secreting and maintaining great-*grossvati's* stock of everything from rifles to machine guns to grenades to *panzerfaeuste*. A good deal, probably most, of the ammunition was unserviceable, but the arms, themselves, were fine.

Sadly, arms or not, there was no chain of command to get the towns together for any purpose higher than point self-defense. Still, under the direction of their local mayor, or fire or police chief, or perhaps a retired officer or *Hauptfeldwebel*, many of these towns had quickly transformed themselves into hedgehogs on steroids.

With some of these, Alix, *sans* makeup, had been able to talk them into unhindered passage and even get some help. Others, though, had taken to the "shoot first and ask questions later" approach.

And it was very damned hard to tell which was which before it was too late. That inability lay at the core of how they lost Tim.

"Okay, everybody, this is a non-Moslem town that looks ready for harsh measures," Khalid said. "Drop your Islamic gear, hide your travel passes, and look Sachsen. Alix, wipe your face of makeup and look as girly and Aryan as you possibly can."

Once that was done, Khalid started moving forward

again. The road twisted a bit, even as it went up and down over hill and dale. After a particularly sharp turn, he slammed on the brakes again. There was another group of hanging corpses, fresher and whiter than the previous set. It was also smaller, consisting of two men, hands tied, necks stretched, and feet just a few tempting inches off the ground.

Tim looked and began to say, "Those aren't . . ." when the first shots rang out.

Khalid was quick, very quick, but he wasn't quicker than a bullet. By the time he had the car in reverse, a bullet had hit the radiator, while another had come through the windshield, struck Tim just above the nose, and sent the top of his skull, along with a good bit of brains and blood, to strike the roof and fall back on Alix, sitting in the backseat.

Alix screamed loudly enough almost to burst eardrums. Fritz just sat, paralyzed with a mix of horror and fear, staring at the remains of Tim's head. Khalid paid attention to neither, his own head and body twisted one hundred and eighty degrees, as he drove backwards out of the ambush's kill zone.

He almost missed the turn, screeching his tires on the pavement as the car swerved and skidded, ever closer to a deep drainage ditch by the side of the road. Khalid muttered various curses in Arabic under his breath as he fought the car for control.

As the car sped backwards, it left a cloud of steam, almost like a smoke screen, between it and whoever had fired. This may have even helped a bit.

Once out of line of sight, Khalid executed a deft

three-point turn on a road so narrow it should have permitted no such thing. Then, after flipping the shifter back into forward, he sped away, cursing the steam that half blocked his vision every meter of the way.

While Fritz dug a shallow grave for Tim, and Alix stood guard, after having cleaned out the blood and brains in the car, Khalid shook his head doubtfully over his field-expedient radiator repair. They were hidden in a small but dense wood.

He'd taken some chewing gum, some fibers Alix pulled from one of the emergency tampons in her purse, and a screw of about the right size he'd removed from a nonessential part of the engine compartment, specifically one that helped hold on one of the headlights. The gum was for a watertight seal, the fibers to help hold the gum together, and the screw . . .

Well, something's got to keep the gum in place. If we're lucky, this might get us halfway to Leinenfeld. If.

Fritz had never officiated at a funeral before, of course, though he sometimes toyed with the idea of bucking for the priesthood. He'd never even attended a Catholic funeral or graveside service. Hence, naturally, his words were, however heartfelt, not necessarily theologically sound. On the other hand . . .

"God, I don't know what to say, so I can only say what's in my heart. Take to your heart the soul of our brother, Tim. He was a good man and a good agent, one who was driven from every version of Your religion by the attitudes and actions of others. Overlook his atheism, Lord, for he knew no better. Remember, please, that he gave his life doing Your work."

"Amen," offered Alix, followed by Fritz and then Khalid.

The dirt from the shallow grave was piled close to the narrow slit in the earth. While Fritz used his shovel to backfill the hole, Alix and Khalid used their feet to push the dirt back. It was the work of several hours for Fritz to have excavated it, but of only about fifteen minutes to fill it back in and pack it.

"Okay," said Khalid, once the hole containing Tim was filled. "Let's go. With luck we can reach Leinenfeld by morning . . . if the radiator holds up."

**MV *Alberto Helada, Mar Furioso,*
a hundred and five miles off the coast of Cordoba**

Airships could have four modes of lift. One was by displacement of air with lighter-than-air gas, or aerostatic lift. Another was aerodynamic lift, or lift obtained via the shape of the airship, itself, with a curved surface atop and a fairly flat surface below, like an airplane wing, to create lower pressure above it than below, when it moved forward. A third, usable by some forms, was to employ an angle of attack, with the nose of the airship held higher than the tail. Lastly, the airships could, some of them, use vectored thrust. This is to say that they could direct the fans that propelled them downwards, or upwards, or to the sides, to direct the airship vertically and steer it horizontally.

The airships hired by Carrera, on the sly, to extract the Taurans of Task Force Jesuit from the *Helada* could use all of these.

One such hovered over the *Helada,* with two more in echelon left, not especially far away. Marciano couldn't see the name of the other two, but the one overhead had *Pegasus* proudly emblazoned underneath.

The airship could possibly have landed or, at least, come down low enough to lower a ramp. Gold and the airship's captain, in consultation over the radio, had decided this just wasn't worth the risk. Instead, with the various fans keeping it in position, the airship had let down four of what amounted to troop ladders, two each fore and one aft, up which the hale members of Task Force Jesuit scrambled. Amidships, a pallet was let down, to take the heavier stores and the wounded. The pallet was lined up magnetically with the square hole from which it was let down.

Marciano's staff had spent three days working with a half dozen of the airships' officers to figure out the load plan.

"Did I ever mention, Rall, that I'm afraid of heights? Yep, absolutely scared shitless. I even hate to fly, though I can put on a good face about it."

The Sachsen looked at the Tuscan mountain infantryman with incredulity. "Then the mountains . . . ?"

"Were in good part about conquering fear," Marciano finished. "Conquer one; conquer others. 'We become brave by doing brave acts,' and all."

Rall nodded; he understood the principle of the thing. "Are you afraid about going home? About what we'll find when we get there?"

"'Shitless,'" Marciano quoted his own word.

"Do you really think Carrera set up the rebellion? It's pretty ruthless, even for him."

"No doubt in my mind. He hates the Kosmos, the Cosmopolitan Progressives, maybe even more than he hated the Salafi *Ikhwan*. I saw it occasionally in Pashtia, just how much he loathed them. So kill a few million civilians to destroy the Kosmos? Lives well spent, in his view."

Again, Rall nodded. "Where are we going, once we load?"

"He—Carrera—gave us all the leeway we might want. He only suggested my capital. I think...maybe...he doesn't really understand Taurus. Tuscany is on the periphery, and was never a great power, whatever our pretension. We need to go somewhere else. Maybe Anglia. Maybe Gaul."

"Not Sachsen?"

"No. Your national troops haven't been released yet, so we'd be liberating a kind of vacuum."

"Gaul, then," Rall said. "It's a good stepping-off point for Sachsen, too."

"There is that," Claudio agreed. "Okay, let's say Gaul. The Columbian newspapers say Lumiere, the capital, is under siege and beginning to starve. So do we go for it or a port?"

"Port helps the others, Janier's force. But I think we'll get a lot more gratitude from the Gauls if we save their capital from falling."

"Can we do both?" Marciano asked.

"Can we risk the chance that in doing the one it will be too late to do the other?"

Claudio clasped his hands behind his back, stared down at the deck, and proceeded to think very hard about that question. Finally, he decided, "Lumiere, then. Go start drawing up the plans."

"Loading will take more than a day, maybe closer to two. Then three and a half days to fly. We can be in Lumiere in five days, six at the outside."

"Plan on six, Rall. If nothing else, our experience of the last few days should let us know never to expect plans involving complex issues of transportation to ever work out on time."

Tauran Union Defense Agency Headquarters, Lumiere, Gaul

More than the fire, Jan had decided, *more than the demons and the torture, Hell is a place that stinks and where the stink never fully goes away.*

Oddly, she found herself thinking in accentless French.

The stench came from two very similar sources. One were the bodies of the Moslems who lay in the streets all around, and at the base of the building for the several dozen killed inside and unceremoniously dumped out the windows. So far, there hadn't even been so much as a suggestion from either side of a truce to bury the bodies.

The worse stench, though, was from the inside. There were some large refrigerators in the former cafeterias, and a few corpses had been stashed there. No, they weren't working, with the electricity down, but at least they were airtight.

There were too many bodies, though, for that. They'd taken to putting them in rooms in the basement. The cool down there had partially slowed down the decay, and the stench that went with it, but only that. And once those bodies started turning, it turned out that the system of vents let the reek reach every nook and cranny of the headquarters. Stuffing the outlets with whatever was to hand hadn't helped all that much, either. The aroma of decay still managed to get through, somehow.

Probably just as well there's been nothing to eat for three days, Jan thought. *I couldn't eat anything anyway.*

The outside situation, too, had gotten worse. To take her little section as a microcosm of the entire building, where she'd once been able to have herself, Turenge, Sergeant Greene, Corporal Dawes, and the other seven troopers watch just one corner, now, since the flanks had folded and the Moslems could come from any direction, she'd had to take over responsibility for the rear corner, as well. That was being watched by the sergeant and five troopers, while she had five—plus herself—Houston, Turenge, Dawes, Braiden, and Proctor, to watch over this one.

At least when Turenge and Dawes aren't off shagging, I do. I swear, I don't know where they find the energy. He's nothing but skin, bones, muscle, and blood, while she could have used to gain a few pounds even before the rebellion broke out. Good luck to them, anyway. I almost wish it were me.

A bullet pinged into the room from some outside, unknown source. After passing through some of the furniture piled up against the window, it buried itself in the wall, knocking out a small shower of plaster and some chips of paint.

Jan glanced around the room. "Where the fuck is Houston?" she asked.

"I never noticed him leaving," said Turenge. Braiden and Proctor just shrugged, adding, "Small loss if he took off."

"No," Jan corrected, "it's a big loss if the swine parleys intel about our situation for his own life. Man the fucking windows and see if he's trying to defect."

"I've got the son of a bitch," said Braiden, "out on the boulevard. He must have slipped out a low window. Who could imagine him getting that pudgy, out-of-shape body to the ground? He's got one hand up and is waving a small white flag with the other."

Jan bolted to Braiden's window and peered through a small gap in the furniture. "Ki . . . kill him."

The shot came almost in the same instant, leaving one fairly worthless major stretched out, lifeless, on the pavement that fronted the headquarters.

Sixteen Kilometers Northwest of Leinenfeld, Sachsen

Khalid pounded on the car's hood with a mix of anger and frustration. Not only had his repair blown, but the car had overheated to the point the engine seized up. There'd be no expedient fix for this problem.

"What now?" Alix asked. "I'm a girl, not a wimp; I can walk."

"Sure you can," Khalid agreed, "in decent boots or walking shoes. Have you noticed what you have on your feet lately?"

Alix didn't need to look down. She knew she had sensible pumps on, office wear. Indeed, she'd been coming from the local office when she'd been grabbed.

"I can *still* walk."

Khalid looked at Fritz, who shrugged and said, "Let her try."

"All right; let's get what we need from the car."

From where the car finally died, near the town of Lippe, to the outskirts of Leinenfeld, ran an irregular but dense forest. Trails wound through it, well-trod in happier times but, even so, still unmarked on Khalid's map. He cursed the place roundly until Alix pointed out, "There are trail guides for the tourists and hikers. We just need to find a dispenser."

This proved fairly easy. There were dispensers all around a peculiar monument to some long-ago victory of Sachsens over Tuscans.

Before looking at the map of the trails, Khalid pulled a small compass out of his pack. "Fortunately, I've had this course, too."

"You went to *Cazador* School?" Fritz asked, a trace of awe in his voice.

"Yes, fairly early on in my career," Khalid answered.

"What's this school about?" Alix asked.

"Just a combat leadership course," Khalid replied.

"It's really fucking hard," Fritz corrected.

Khalid spent a few moments orienting the map, looked

at it, looked left, looked, right, looked at the compass again, and then pointed to one particular trail, saying, "that way."

Muelle 81, *Ciudad* Balboa

The huge tent was largely empty now, the consortium of officers and senior noncoms returned to their billets aboard the holding ships. Only a small cadre hung out at one end with the Mendozas, trying to hammer out a constitution. Barring those couple of dozen, however, the rest all awaited the outcome of talks between their commander, their enemy's commander, and the commander of the combined Tauran fleets, Admiral Pellew.

The fleets that had mattered, of the Tauran Expeditionary Force that had set out to capture Balboa, had been Gallic and Anglian. Others had contributed, of course, but those were the leaders and it was to those that the lesser national fleets had attached themselves. Even there, since the Gauls had been given command of the ground forces, the Anglians had been accorded command of the combined fleets, under their own flag officer, Pellew.

It was true, too, that whatever accord the ground forces might reach among themselves, nobody was going anywhere by surface vessel in the face of opposition from the fleet. Whether or not there would be opposition . . .

"I confess," said Pellew, who was typically as tall and slender as any other Anglian Sea Dog, "I don't know what to do. Not only is the Union parliament scattered or destroyed, none of Her Majesty's ministers are available, either. There is no quorum for anything, no orders that mean anything. And I am beginning to run out of fuel that I cannot pay to replace, what with the complete collapse of Tauran currency and finances. Moreover, Cienfuegos, which was our naval logistic base, has devolved into revolution bordering on utter chaos. I don't know where to turn. I have no legitimate new orders and I have no way to get the orders I had overturned."

Janier sympathized. He thought well of the Anglian and had since very early on in the war. *Soldiers, after all, can march when in their natural element, but warships are holes in the water, surrounded by steel, into which we pour money.*

"You bombed the shit out of the tank farm on your side of the Transitway," Carrera said, glumly, "or I could float you the fuel until you get finances straightened out. Rather, I could have except that you also bombed the shit out of every dock at the Port of Cristobal, so there's no place for you to tie up, either, even if I had the fuel, which I don't.

"But," Carrera continued, "and this is extremely important, Admiral, is it fair to say that you will interpose no objection to the return of the men I hold?"

"What," asked Pellew, "do they plan on doing?"

"Just returning to liberate our homelands," Janier replied.

Pellew gave a skeptical look, pointing with his chin at the ad hoc constitutional convention at the opposite end of the tent. The arguments had, on occasion, gotten loud enough for him to catch the drift of their purpose.

Janier wagged a finger. "I didn't say, after all, nor limit, just *who* we intend to liberate our homelands from."

"Did you ever take an oath to the Tauran Union, Admiral?" Carrera asked.

"Well, no, my oath was to Her Majesty."

"As mine was to the *Republique de Gaul*," Janier added.

"If she were not incommunicado, what do you think the queen would want you to do? Do you really imagine she *wouldn't* want you and Bertrand to liberate her country?"

"Put that way, I suppose she would."

"So in what way does your duty lie anywhere but in escorting Bertrand's forces back to Taurus?"

"Okay, fine," Pellew agreed. "But I still don't have any fuel. And I am not going to go down in history as a man who surrendered his fleet to an army."

The Gaul said, "Hmmm . . ."

"Yes, Bertrand?" asked both of the others, simultaneously.

"Oh, surrender, of course, would be impossible. But I was just thinking; if you, Admiral Pellew, sold a warship or two to Balboa, and, if you, *Duque* Carrera, paid enough—oh, in gold, to be sure—for the fleet to fully refuel . . ."

Carrera looked contemplative for a moment, then said, "Well, I suppose Balboa *could* use a pair of destroyers and maybe another cruiser . . ."

"I lack the authority," Pellew said, simply.

Janier and Carrera both shrugged. "Just a thought," said the latter.

"But . . . ummm . . . General Janier, don't you outrank

the admiral of your fleet? I'm not a scholar of Gallic Naval Regulations and law, but ..."

Janier looked at Carrera. "I wonder if I could perhaps borrow a helicopter. I'd like to pay a visit to an old friend ... at sea."

Aircraft Carrier *Charlemagne*, Shimmering Sea

The admiral of the Gallic Navy had his own quarters aboard ship, with his own small staff, his own domestic staff, and his own mess. At the moment, the mess was cleared out, but for the admiral, Teste, and Janier, recently brought to the ship by a Balboan helicopter.

"What do I care about fuel?" asked Teste. "The carrier is nuclear powered and, frankly, we can move faster—a lot faster—than the Balboans' sneaky little plastic submarines can hope to catch us."

"Your escorts?" Janier asked. "They need fuel."

"But I don't need *them*!" Teste replied.

Janier smiled, slightly, asking, "So would you mind trading one of them, the *Jean Baptiste*, say, for something else you might need? Like fuel for the rest of the fleet?"

"But I don't *need*—"

"But I *do*! I need, especially, the amphibious assault ships and the helicopters they carry! I need the guns of the *Charles Martel*! I need the attack aircraft of this ship! I need a way to land our forces on a potentially hostile shore, near a port."

"You're really going to try to liberate home?" Teste asked. "You're going to be badly outnumbered."

"We'll have help," Janier said. "And even if we didn't, I'd still have to try. The country demands it."

Teste sat silently for a long minute. "You really think we still have a country, Bertrand? A country is just a people; and our people could hardly wait to sell their sovereignty, sell their nationhood, to the Tauran Union. And now it's under enemy occupation. Not that it wasn't, already, while the TU held sway."

Now it was Janier who sat silently for an even longer minute. When he spoke again, it was with a question. "Do you know what our national flaws really are?"

Teste sneered, though not at Janier, specifically. "Our people are fantasists. They act out their dreams. They refuse to face rea—"

"No, that's not it; none of that is quite it, though I can see why you think it. Our real flaw, and I think it must go back all the way to Old Earth, is that we give too much unearned and undeserved credit to the intellectual, and we have too great a taste—amounting, even, to an addiction—to having the appearance of elegance in everything.

"That, old friend, is how the TU sold itself to the people; it was the darling of the intellectuals and their running dogs, the intelligentsia, so the people—who wanted to be just like those—bought their lies. And because it was the intellectual class and the intelligentsia selling the package, they were good at the only thing they've ever been good at: making a bad idea sound elegant to those who are desperate for elegance, or the appearance of it, in all things."

Teste rocked his head from side to side. "So what's the

point of your going back, then? The same swine will still mislead the people as they always have. You'll be liberating them from backwards Moslems in favor of mere frauds, hypocrites, and hedonists. Frankly, the Moslems are better people, even if they're flawed. They, at least, are sincere."

"What if we're not going to do that?" Janier asked. "What if we're going to put them under . . . well . . ."—the general drew a sheaf of papers from the inside pocket of his jacket—"read this."

"What is it?"

"It's a draft of our new, confederate, constitution."

Muelle 81, *Ciudad* Balboa

Soult sat in the driver's seat, as usual. He, at least, was protected from the afternoon rain by the roof over the four-by-four. Carrera stood outside, leaning against the hood of the vehicle, with rain dripping off the wide-brimmed jungle hat he favored when he didn't need to wear a helmet. Carrera held out a glass in his left hand, which Soult duly refilled. The warrant then, after somber and sober reflection, poured himself a small one. Carrera sipped at the legionary rum carefully—the stuff was *strong*—arms folded, watching the sixteenth ship being pushed out by tugs to sail out of the harbor, and then onward to Taurus. Only a few contingents remained, though one of those, the Sachsens, were large enough to need several ships just for themselves.

Just as a precaution, he'd trebled the guard on the

Sachsen ships, and made sure their engines were partially disassembled.

Finally sick of the rain, and with the freighter fading to a dim outline, Carrera said, "Fuck it," and walked around the four-by-four, plopping himself down on the passenger's seat.

"The thing is, Jamey, what the fuck are we going to do with another cruiser?"

CHAPTER TWENTY-FIVE

> Then Saul said to his armor-bearer, "Draw your
> sword and run me through with it, or these
> uncircumcised men will come and run me through
> and torture me!"
> —1 Samuel, 31:4, Christian Standard Bible

Outside Leinenfeld, Sachsen

The woods had held through to within about a mile of
their target address, 2 Brunnenstrasse, the residence of
Ann-Marie Maybach, mistress to the Sachsen Minister of
Finance, Olaf Kubier-Schmidt.

"We could probably go further," Khalid said, "but I think
we'd be better off holding up near here until nightfall."

"Near here," in this context, and after a bit of
exploration, turned out to mean holed up inside an office
some ways down a deep tunnel. The tunnel itself had
been dug long before for the trains that weren't running
in Sachsen for the nonce. It had, once upon a Great
Global War, done service as an air raid shelter.

Of course, the door just *had* to be both very stout and locked.

"Not a problem," Khalid said to Alix, "we've *both* had that course."

"Standard part of the training package," Fritz explained. "Shall I?" he asked Khalid.

"Sure, probably better if you do. I need to crank the power for my computer, go outside to get a satellite link, and get a message to Fernandez that we're within a mile of the target and that we intend to take our target tomorrow. We need him to have the extraction helicopters ready to move with an instant's notice."

"We've never discussed that," Alix observed. "What do you mean by 'take'?"

"I mean we'll go into the apartment with as much violence as called for, then ask him to come with us, and, if he doesn't, I'll apply as much pain as needed to get cooperation."

"Oh. That works for me. What about his girlfriend?"

"That's a really good question to which I don't have a really good answer. Ideally, she's calm and collected and wants to come with us with a fervent desperation. If it's not ideal . . ."

"And ideal is never the way to bet it," interrupted Fritz.

" . . . then we may have to knock her out and tie her up, or beat her silly and carry her, or . . . harsh, I know . . . kill her."

"*Kill* her? My God, why? And could you kill a woman?"

Khalid's answering smile was quite sad. "Remember when I said I had revenge for my murdered family down to the last generation? Yes, I can kill a woman."

Changing the subject, he told Alix, "Take your shoes off and rest your feet. Clean them. If you know how to bandage and moleskin a blister, there's a first-aid kit in my pack. If you don't, wait for me and I'll see to your feet when I get back."

Tauran Union Defense Agency Headquarters, Lumiere, Gaul

Casualties had been getting bad enough that Jan Campbell's crew had had to take over the same sector of the ground flow as they'd held above it, allowing the four remaining of the previous defenders to take over their old area, upstairs.

The Anglians had lost two men, both to head shots, since they'd moved. Those bodies were also stuffed into one of the basement rooms. Moreover, the stench was, if anything, worse down here where there was less of a chance of a breeze to waft it away.

Sergeant Greene came from the back side area held by the other half of the section and, while standing in the door, gave her a head and eyes signal, inviting her to a *tête-à-tête* out in the central area. The door, by rights, should have been blocked off and a passageway been carved through the wall, covered by some furniture. It was on Jan's list to have done but, for now, *They're just too weak and hungry*.

Telling Turenge that she was in charge until Jan returned—"And being in charge means no shagging, Captain"—the major followed her senior noncom out.

"You know, ma'am," Greene said, "I've become the

senior noncom—well, the senior infantry noncom—in the headquarters. There's a Gallic tanker and a Sachsen admin guy who outrank me, but they sought me out and made it clear that they defer to my judgment. I walked around, right after they came to me, and did a little checking.

"Fully one-quarter of the people we have manning the defense here were civilians until we handed them rifles. Their first day of training was on the job. There are less than fifty grenades left in the whole building. The average machine gunner is down to under five hundred rounds and the average rifleman has a bit over sixty. We've still got a little night-vision capability, enough, say, for twenty men for about three hours. That's how few batteries we have left.

"There is literally no food left in stores, though some of the troops have a half a meal or so secreted about their person."

"And?"

"And so it's my judgment that it's time to try to cut our way out of here."

"We should have done that some time ago," Jan said. "We couldn't, because we were key to the defense and, while we were here, the flanks wouldn't fold. Or so we thought."

"Our holding here helped," Greene admitted. "But it was a miracle they hung on as long as they did. The fat and overaged veterans they pulled in to form a militia just weren't up to it, long run."

"If they'd been Balboans, they'd have been up to it."

"Maybe so," Greene conceded, "but we have a serious dearth of Balboans here and on our side."

"Point," it was Jan's turn to concede. "So how do we get

out of here? Who do we take? What about the wounded? We *can't* leave them to be captured. They'll be skinned alive. Literally."

Greene sighed with inexpressible weariness, and that not merely physical. "There's enough morphine to give the ones who can't walk out on their own power a pleasant enough send-off."

"Kill our own? How can we do that?""

"Oh, the usual way, I'd imagine," the sergeant said.

Jan felt a trace of heat rising. "That's *not* what I meant."

"I *know* what you meant, ma'am. Would it actually make you feel better if I told you that our senior medic, that Gallic senior sergeant, Pangracs, will do the injecting?"

Her head hung. "I suppose it wouldn't. Okay, let's say we're going to try; have we informed the senior officer commanding or are we just going to leave him in the lurch?"

"Oh, did I neglect to mention it? The last officer senior to you took a bullet through the spine. You're in charge, *Major.* And I took the liberty of calling a meeting of the remaining section chiefs for two hours from now."

"Why two hours?"

"Because you and I are going to need that much to come up with a plan. There's no more time for discussion; when they get here you need to give them an *order.*"

Airship *Pegasus*, enroute to Taurus

Marciano's force lacked even a tourist map of their own

countries. Fortunately, the *Pegasus* was able to print off the very best maps available to the public.

Unfortunately, the ship could only print off maps on standard, eight-by-eleven inch paper. This, while taped together to form several larger wholes, was less than optimal. Especially when paper or tape tore.

On a different sheaf of papers, Claudio had a copy of the new constitution approved by the main force under Janier. So far, he hadn't shared it with anyone but Rall and del Collea. It was time now, though, time before they voted—as he thought they had to vote—on their target.

There was no assembly hall on the ship big enough for everyone. There was no way to bring over even representatives from the other two, smaller airships. There *was*, however, a local video system that could patch into the other two ships and into every room and public spacing on all of them. With a camera focused on his face, seated at a table in the *Pegasus'* main dining room, and with about three hundred and fifty senior officers and noncoms as his audience, Marciano began.

"In a few minutes, or perhaps an hour, or perhaps even two, we're going to be voting on where we're going to try to land in our home continent. Before we get to that, we have to know why we're going to land and what we're going to try to do.

"I'll tell you right up front, that whatever we decide will make no difference on our own. The main force that was captured in Balboa, and which has been ransomed, has already voted. They accept the constitution I am about to discuss with you. Since they're about twenty or more times our size, we're already outvoted and outgunned in the matter."

Claudio paused to take a drink of water, then gave off a couple of small coughs to clear his throat.

"Point the first: the constitution we propose to vote on is not a parliamentary system. It's rather more like the Federated States', with two houses that are elected differently and of different composition, but equally strong. It has also an executive, called a 'Consul,' and a high court."

Claudio snorted with a grim humor. "Hell, in Taurus we change our constitutions at the drop of a hat. One could even make the straight-faced argument that we do not have, and never have had, a genuine constitution in our history. It's probably true that for most, maybe all, of us, our national governments at one time or another were set up about the same way.

"There are some differences, though. This constitution"—and here Claudio waved the thin sheaf of paper— "is only about eight thousand words. In Taurus, in trying to legislate all kinds of newly found, vote-buying, 'rights' into our constitutions, while legislating away as many others that might prove inconvenient to the state, our constitutions can run as many pages. Or, at least, they seem like they do.

"Each branch of government, as far as the constitution goes, has a slightly different focus. For example, the two houses of the legislature have enumerated powers, and not too many of those. The executive, on the other hand, has no listed powers, but only responsibilities the powers to meet which are said to be there. The high court, conversely, has a mix of both, along with some things that are forbidden to it and some things over which it can have no choice. There are, for example, some ten crimes which have mandatory death penalties for everyone, and a special mandatory death penalty for any member of the court who should vote in such a way as to increase the power of the court.

"There is also a list of misdemeanors which have only two penalties, flogging and jail, no fines allowed.

"But the big thing, the really huge thing, that makes this different from what we're used to is that no one votes or holds public office or the position of a decision-making bureaucrat without having first volunteered for, served in, and been honorably discharged from the armed forces of what is to be the 'Tauran Confederation.'"

Marciano stopped then, to wait for the cheering to die down.

Leinenfeld, Sachsen

They must have looked convincing enough; they hardly ever had to produce the imam-signed certificates of appreciation cum travel passes. Tonight was no exception to this rule.

The streets were mostly darkened but not empty. Gangs of newly minted slaves swept and picked up garbage. Others, those of the new ruling class, walked around, invariably armed. Tents, too, had been set up in public places for *majlis*, and the powers that be stopped at these from time to time to meet and greet.

Khalid, Alix, and Fritz carried their arms openly, slung

or nestled in the crook of an arm. Khalid and Alix walked up front, with Fritz taking up the rear to cover the natural sway of Alix's posterior.

Alix suddenly stopped, staring at a black and white wanted poster, pasted up against one wall. She'd seen the same sorts of signs before; it was only the angle of this one and the presence of a stray moonbeam that caught her attention.

"That's *him*," she whispered to Khalid. "That's Olaf, the finance minister."

Khalid who, unlike Alix, could read the script said, "Interesting. They're offering . . . mmmm . . . let me think . . . one hundred thousand gold dinar . . . four and a quarter grams of fine gold each . . . about twenty million Federated States Drachma. That's not small change."

"No," agreed Alix, "it isn't."

Khalid continued to read, giving summaries as he did. "He's wanted alive . . . he is believed to be in hiding here in Leinenfeld . . . death for anyone who knowingly hides him or helps him escape . . ."

"The bastards want him to release the gold in the Federated States to them," was Alix's no doubt spot-on judgment. Now that she was tipped to the poster's existence, she realized they'd already passed quite a number of the things.

"Let's keep walking," Khalid said. "This means a couple of things. One is that we can't bluff our way out with him, we're going to either have to take him out clandestinely, or as if we're carting him off to the new local authorities—no, I don't think much of that idea, either—or maybe change the rendezvous to the roof of the house he's in.

"But the other thing is we can't necessarily expect him to come with us peacefully. Tell me, did he strike you as being very brave?"

"No," she replied, "if he'd been any more of a pussy, I'd have been willing to eat him."

Khalid barely suppressed a laugh. "Anyone ever tell you that you have a wild sense of humor? I'm almost tempted to actually take you to a whorehouse, if we could find one, and buy you a girl."

"Maybe later," she answered, with twinkling, mischievous eyes. He'd noticed that her flights of anger and depression had lessened a good deal in both anger and intensity as they'd gotten closer to their objective.

I like this woman enormously, thought Khalid. *It's entirely hopeless, of course.*

"In any case, we still have a worse problem than we thought. I need to look at the roof of the place, and the nearby roofs, as well."

The Leinenfeld *Bahnhof*, or train station, lay on the left, its two seven-windowed wind breaks parallel to and dividing the town's main road. Of course, no trains ran yet.

"I just noticed," said Khalid, "there are no traditional lampposts suitable for lynchings anywhere we've seen yet."

"The bulk of our politicians have very keen survival instincts," Alix replied. "I'm sure they had them replaced at public expense ages ago. But, if you look just ahead"— she pointed with her chin—"you will see that a number of them were not quite instinctive enough."

Khalid then did notice three bodies hanging by the

neck between the four columns of the entrance to what looked to him like an old town hall, or *Rathaus*.

"Here's our turn," Khalid said, putting the lynched politicos out of his mind. Immediately to their right, as they made the turn, was a white ashlar building. Under the moonlight, they could just make out the hand-painted sign, "Islamischevereinsbank."

Past the bank were what appeared to be apartments, one of them labeled "2."

"I hope," said Khalid, "that there aren't too many apartments for that one entrance."

"This keeps getting harder, doesn't it?" she asked.

"Before I make a pronouncement on that, let's see if we can't get up on the roof of one of these buildings. I need to find a pickup zone where we're not too likely to be shot at while we load. Failing that, we need one where we can hold them off while we await the helicopter... potentially for several hours, if we don't time it right."

Tauran Union Defense Agency Headquarters, Lumiere, Gaul

The "hospital," for certain highly constrained values of "hospital," had actually been set up in one of the latrines in the basement. It stank, of course, but at least there was running water. It was also reasonably protected from the more or less continuous sniper fire, while the tile floor and walls lent themselves to easy and certain cleaning.

There was still a goodly supply of denatured alcohol. The chief medic in the building, Gallic Sergeant Pangracs, had made enough alcohol lamps out of old cans and whatnot that one could see well enough to navigate, well enough to treat, to the extent he could treat, and well enough for Jan to see what he was doing.

If I can tell him to do it, I can at least give him moral support while he does.

Jan knew the number remaining to her by heart. There had been some seven hundred and twenty-five people when the rebellion broke out. Three hundred and eleven of those had been civilian, about two-thirds male, and over eighty percent Gauls. All of the civilian women had been ordered out, before the flanks collapsed, leaving two hundred and seven males. One hundred and fifty-one of those males had elected to stay and fight, while fifty-six had taken their leave. Since there hadn't been, initially, enough rifles for all of them, they'd been let go willingly. Of the one hundred and fifty-one, sixty-three were now dead, and stuffed into rooms in the basement, thirty-one among the walking wounded, fourteen among the nonambulatory and, in the main, "expectant" wounded, and only forty-three still able to fight.

Of the four hundred and fourteen military, some fifty-nine had been drafted to help form up and take charge of the civilian militia being raised outside the headquarters. Of the remaining three hundred and fifty-five, ninety-seven were dead, with all but one of their bodies rotting in the basement. One hundred and twenty-six had been more or less badly wounded. Of those, seventy-four had been evacuated before the flanks collapsed and the building was surrounded. Fifty-two, pus the fourteen civilians, were in the makeshift hospital under Sergeant Pangracs' care.

About half of those still able to fight were wounded to some extent. Even three of Jan's own SAS troopers bore wounds to some degree or another, though only one was serious.

Two hundred and six, including a few of the tougher women in that figure, and including also all of the walking wounded, remained approximately able to fight.

Two hundred and six, thought Jan, *including in that number some limpers and some lame, are all I have to try to cut our way out with. Or maybe a few less; some will certainly lose their nerve and stay behind.*

Pangracs was a big boy. She remembered him from earlier months as being rather beefy. Short rations, stress, and despair had slimmed him down almost to the point of emaciation. Looking at him caused her to look down at her own sadly deflated chest.

When this is all over, and if I come through, I am going to hit every restaurant in this city and eat at least one of everything on the menu . . . except escargot, of course, since they look like dusty but runny snot.

Sergeant Pangracs was speaking. He began with a question, "Is there anyone here who feels they can—on their own power, because there's no one to help you— make it out of here on their own? Anyone? Well, if you change your mind, let me know."

He's a lot more calm than I would be.

"We can't hold on here anymore. Those who are able are going to try to cut their way out. Those who can't . . . you have three choices, and they all suck. You can, in the first place, trust your future to our attackers. Anybody here not know what they let us see that they did to those two prisoners? You know, skinned alive? Right. Still, it's your choice.

"Choice number two: I've been treating your pain with morphine sulfate. A good many of you will have built up some immunity by now. I might have enough left for everyone, but I might not, either. What I do have is Fentanyl, enough to put down every elephant in Uhura. Well . . . *maybe* every elephant. There's no doubt, though, that it's enough for you.

"Thirdly, for those who demand certainty and don't mind leaving a mess behind, nine millimeter.

"But that's pretty much it. So let me ask again, who wants to try to walk out under their own power? Get up and walk to the major, over by the doorway."

There was a stirring among some of the cots and pallets. Eleven of the wounded stood, some swaying and some reasonably well, and one by balancing on his one remaining leg. Three of the eleven promptly either sank back to their pallets or fell over or simply collapsed where they stood.

The eight who could and were willing to try ambled or hopped over to Jan, who directed them to an assembly area, of sorts, on the ground level. For the remainder, Pangracs started to make his final set of daily rounds. He had one more noncom with him, plus a private, carrying ampoules and syringes on trays. There were also two bottles of medicinal brandy and several packs of cigarettes on the private's tray.

It's not like they're going to affect anyone's health for the worse, Jan thought.

At the first pallet was a thin man, looking about forty

years older then he was, and leaning against a couple of thin pillows. Pangracs took a small paper cup from one tray and asked, "Drink, Jacques?"

The answer came back in the form of a whisper, "I won't say 'no' but . . ."

Pangracs understood; Jacques couldn't rise. Using one hand, his left, to raise Jacques' head, he held the cup to his lips and more or less poured it in. That set Jacques to coughing, but not as much as did the cigarette lit by the private and placed between Jacques' lips.

"The neck, yes?" Jacques asked. "Which side?"

"Show me the left side," Pangracs answered. The wounded man took another drag of his cigarette, then twisted his head to offer the jugular. Pangracs held out his right hand for the syringe. He picked up a nearby alcohol lamp and held it near the neck to examine for the jugular. He found the pulsations, measured off a distance by sight, and then pronounced, "This will do well."

The vein was basically there for the taking. Pangracs placed the fingers of his left hand on the neck, pushed the needle in with a steady pressure from his right hand, and then depressed the plunger.

"Easy as caaaa . . ." Jacques said, around the drooping cigarette. In less than a minute, he was gone. The private scooped up the cigarette, squashed it out, then replaced in it Jacques' hand.

"I'm not a ghoul, Sergeant," the private said, indignantly. "What, did you think that I'd keep it?"

One down; fifty-seven more to go, thought Pangracs. *If I can keep my nerve up.*

Some were to prove at least physically easier. These

were the ones who already had an IV going, into which the Fentanyl could be injected without further pain. But IV or not, they *all* took a little bite out of Pangracs' soul.

Three hours later, and with the sun outside beginning to set, there was no more moaning in the makeshift hospital, no more cries of pain, nor requests for medication or water or food.

Jan had come and gone several times in those few hours, mostly to see to her troops. When she came back this time, even under the limited glow from the alcohol lamps, she thought Pangracs' eyes seemed red and puffy. Still, his voice was calm as he said, "I can't leave them. Two of them asked me to stay with them, not to leave them alone. I said I would, without thinking. Now I must.

"Can I have a rifle, a few magazines, and a couple of grenades?"

"I'm sure we've enough," Jan replied, "but . . ."

"I gave my word. Maybe I'd have stayed anyway, though; you don't euthanize fifty-eight comrades and just walk away from it untouched, you know, Major?"

"I understand," she said, *even if I don't actually* know *what you're feeling. But that you're wounded in the soul I don't doubt.* "I'll have someone bring you a rifle and two grenades."

CHAPTER TWENTY-SIX

Before embarking on a journey of revenge, dig two
graves.   —Confucius

Leinenfeld, Sachsen

After a half hour's clandestine cranking to charge the
computer's batteries, Khalid had sent back to
headquarters, in Balboa: "Pickup, two hours and forty-five
minutes from now, flat rooftop opposite target's house.
Expect hot pickup zone."

"And," said Khalid, "it's showtime."

After a time-killing stop as a coffee shop, operating
with flame rather than electricity, the three walked briskly
to 2 Brunnenstrasse, opened the door, and walked in as
though they had official business. Khalid almost choked
when the mailbox cum buzzer system failed to show any
such name as Ann-Marie Maybach. Then he realized,
"The dumb shit put this in his own name."

"Well," suggested Alix, "he's probably the one paying
for the rent and utilities."

"Likely," Khalid agreed. "Fritz, pick the lock."

Dropping to one knee, Fritz examined the lock closely, then pulled out his tool kit and selected a tension wrench and a pick from those. "This one's not especially hard," he said.

"Not especially hard" turned out to take almost two minutes. *Still faster than I could have done it,* thought Khalid.

"Let's go."

Quietly enough, all three passed through the door and went to the apartment on the second floor that the mailbox asserted was the finance minister's.

Fritz asked, "Pick this one? They'll almost certainly hear me do it."

In answer, Khalid simply applied an authoritative rap to the door, announcing himself as he commanded, *"Oeffnen. Polizei."*

The door sprang open with alacrity. Behind it stood a rather well-built and at least moderately pretty Sachsen girl, redheaded, with blue eyes.

"Frauelein Maybach?" Khalid asked.

"Yes," she answered, then demanded to know, "What took you so long? I had to . . . well . . . never mind. But I had to do that *and* pour half a bottle of whiskey into him to set him up for your arrival. He has a gun."

Alix figured it out first. *She has called the Sharia police for the reward. Timing has just gotten shitty.*

"Where's my money?" Ann-Marie demanded to know.

"You'll be able to pick it up from the police station tomorrow," Khalid replied. "We don't have a couple of mules with us to carry half a ton of gold."

"Well, I'll want a receipt for him anyway, some proof that you captured him through my intervention."

"Get a piece of paper, then," Khalid ordered her.

"We've got problems," Alix whispered.

"I know," replied Khalid. "What I don't know is . . ."

There was another knock on the door. Just as had Khalid, these interlopers ordered, *"Oeffnen, Polizei."*

"Go take care of the girl," Khalid quietly ordered. "Fritz, go with her." Then he flicked the safety off his rifle and informed the genuine Islamic police that the door was open. "Come in, it's open," he said.

As soon as the door opened, and Khalid had a chance to see that there were only two of them, he opened fire. The two Islamic police went down in a tangle of arms, legs, holed clothing and flesh, and a good deal of blood.

Alix came out of the bedroom in back with a handful of red hair attached to a handful of girl. At the living room, she let go of the hair to drop Ann-Marie's head to the hardwood floor. *Wham.*

Fritz emerged behind Alix, staggering under a great naked mass of lard with arms and legs. "He's drunk as shit, blind staggering drunk. I'll have to carry him."

"Right," Khalid said. "Let's go."

"What about the treacherous *bint*?" Alix asked. "Shouldn't we at least gag and tie her?"

"I'd like to brain the bitch but . . . Fraulein Maybach, can you stay here and keep your mouth shut or should we just kill you now?"

Nursing a bump on the back of her head where Alix had dropped her to the floor, the Sachsen women replied, "But what about my money?"

"Yeah, gag and tie her."

"Be better," said Alix, "if we shot her."

Szczyt, Jagelonia

Of the two IM-71s from what was called "the Siegfried Group," under contract to Fernandez in Balboa, the lead bird was piloted by a former Volgan major named Kira Robertaevna Chuikova. She was a compact little set of flight controls, was the ex-major, and a highly talented pilot. She hoped, if this thing came off, that she'd get an offer from the Balboans. It might or might not pay better, but it was likely to be a lot more fun.

As soon as she'd gotten the word, Chuikova and the other chief pilot had immediately launched, heading almost due west. She'd been told to travel nap of the earth, and to avoid major cities. The latter had been easy enough to do; there being only one major city in this part of Sachsen, but the first two hundred miles, near enough, had been across land so flat there was no irregular earth to fly in the nap of.

Idiots can't read a map.

It was a two-hour flight, straight line, at max speed. At cruise speed, and dodging main cities, two and a half was more like it. This meant that Khalid had timed things . . .

Leinenfeld, Sachsen

". . . *just that little bit off. Dammit. 'Course, that stupid, greedy redheaded bitch hadn't helped.*"

While an overladen Fritz staggered up the stairs to the pickup zone rooftop, and Alex took point for him, Khalid followed behind, walking up steps mostly backwards, while making sure no one was following too closely.

Then he heard a recently familiar voice, shrieking at the top of her lungs about how the infidels were stealing someone wanted by the new government. *Wonder how the bitch got out. Note to self, ask Alix if she was ever a girl scout and if she ever learned to tie a knot.*

By the time Khalid reached the rooftop, there was a sizable crowd—a sizable and *armed* crowd—collecting on the street and in a parking lot just off it. *And, one supposes, there'll be one more on the other street in a few minutes, too.*

Someone bearded and scruffy looking, but armed, popped their head around and loosed a round in Khalid's direction. The Druze returned the favor, but neither hit the other.

"And here," Khalid muttered to himself as he scampered higher up the stairs, "is where I curse myself for not saving out a dozen or two of grenades from all that largesse I brought to the mosques."

He emerged onto the roof to see that Fritz had dumped Olaf's still inebriated body on the asphalt, and was laying out five alcohol lamps to create a cross. Fritz struggled with a small cigarette lighter, but finally got the things lit.

Khalid told Alix, "Get eyes on those two towers to the west," even as he took up a prone position to engage anyone coming out of the same horizontal hatch he had.

Siegfried Group Helicopters One and Two

Her copilot saw them, the alcohol lamps, before Chuikova did. She ordered the other IM-71, "Kill running lights here. Circle overhead and look for threats, I'm going in."

"Roger."

Leinenfeld, Sachsen

A head emerged from the horizontal hatch. Khalid blew the top of it clean off. *There, that ought to discourage them a little. And . . . and . . . yes, there it is; what my comrades Cruz and Montoya told me was the sweetest sound in creation: friendly helicopters come to get you out of a tight jam.*

There were no running lights Khalid could see, but he could follow the helicopters pretty well by sound. One was circling overhead—*hope they've got decent night vision*—while another drew closer. Then, suddenly, the one that had been closing was there, on the roof, and bouncing a bit. He felt more than heard one of the door-mounted machine guns rip a few yards of cloth in the general direction of that horizontal hatch. *And I'm damned glad of it.*

Khalid ran to Fritz and helped him get Olaf back on his own broad shoulders. As Fritz reached the helicopter door, the door gunner jumped out and led him to the rear clamshell, then helped him hoist the finance minister aboard and lay him atop the flat surface of one of the interior extra fuel tanks.

Alix isn't used to this. I told her but without the experience . . . I'd better go get her.

Khalid ran around the front of the IM-71, rather than face the invisible whirring human blender of a tail rotor. He reached Alix and took one knee. "We did it, love! We did it! That toad of a finance minister safely aboard! Now it's our turn."

He reached down to lift her to her feet. She threw her arms around him, not out of desire but out of the sheer exhilaration of "Mission accomplished."

Then two things happened, almost simultaneously. First, she shuddered and fell—rather, was pushed, against him. Second, the overhead helicopter fired a long burst into one of the two towers to the west.

Feeling her go limp and slump against his chest, Khalid grabbed one arm, bent at the waist while draping that arm over one shoulder, stood with her torso dropped across his back. As soon as he did he felt a warm trickle running down his back. He ran for the back clamshells and hopefully some medical aid.

There was light to see by, inside the helicopter, once they'd risen far enough off the ground. With Alix dropped atop the extra fuel tank, the one Olaf was not corporeally overflowing, Khalid began tearing at her clothing to get at what he was pretty sure was a bullet wound. One of the door gunners brought over a first-aid kit, but shrugged to indicate he had no real idea how to use it.

Neither seeing nor feeling a wound in front, he flipped her on her side to examine her back. He didn't see a need to take her bra off; the entrance wound in her back was well above it.

Sucking chest wound, maybe. Khalid tore into the aviation first-aid kit, not understanding a word written therein. Some things were obvious, though. When he found a cravat-style bandage in plastic packaging, he ripped open the plastic, carefully, and pressed it over the entrance wound. He held it in place by hand until he could get Fritz's attention and get him to hold his hand on it. Then he used the bandage to tie the plastic in place. Finally, he eased her back to lie on her own back, hoping the weight would help to seal the wound before her lungs collapsed. Lastly, he covered her with her own bloody shirt against the windchill inside the IM-71.

She drifted in and out of consciousness, which might have been a good sign except that she kept getting more and more pale.

She's bleeding inside and there's nothing I can do about it. I'm worried about shock.

Khalid indicated to the door gunner that he needed a blanket but could neither make himself understood nor find one by scrounging. Ultimately, he took off his own shirt and covered her with that.

"Doesn't help. Shit."

Alix woke up toward the end. It was only for a minute but in that minute she had some very lucid seconds. She reached out one hand to take Khalid's, then let go of his to reach up and pull him down toward her.

"Thank you," she said. "Thank you for saving my country's army and my country."

Khalid felt her face, where it was pressed against his

cheek, twist into a smile. "I only told you I greatly preferred women. I didn't say I was entirely exclusive and closed-minded on the matter. I wish you had asked . . ."

Her hand dropped again and he took it. He told her back, "So do I."

Sometime between then and landing at Szcsen, he felt her body shudder, one, twice, the third time hard, and the fourth weakest of all. Her grip on his hand relaxed, let go, then bent at the wrist, fingers to the floor.

He stroked her now very relaxed and extremely pale face and repeated, even though she could no longer hear, "So do I."

Tauran Union Defense Agency Headquarters, Lumiere, Gaul

Jan felt compelled to ask Pangracs one more time, "Are you sure you won't try to break out with us?"

"No," he replied. "I stay here with them."

I could, I suppose, order him out. But what was the old saying? Ah, yes; it was "never give an order you already know won't be obeyed."

"I thought you would still hold to that but I had to ask," she said. "Good luck, Sergeant Pangracs."

"Good luck to you, too, Major Campbell."

"Sergeant Greene?" Campbell asked, in the open central area on the ground floor that they were using as an assembly area.

"Here, Major," Greene replied. She walked to him,

then looked out the same window he did, facing the network of fences and alleys, overfilled—and stinking— garbage cans and overbloated—and stinking even worse—dead bodies.

They couldn't see any of that with the naked eye, of course, because for their little attempt at escape, Jan and Greene had settled on a time of zero illumination, with not even the smallest of Terra Nova's three moons overhead.

And that was fine, because her people still had some night-vision capability and, based on their nearly complete ineffectuality at night, the rebels did not.

Campbell and Greene both watched silently as the little bit or remaining light set with the moon, Hecate, leaving the area behind the headquarters in utter pitch blackness.

"Time, I think, Major."

"Time, Sergeant Greene," she agreed.

"SAS," Greene said, just loudly enough to be heard in the building, "come with me."

Of the nine SAS Jan had started with, three were wounded. Only one of these was serious, however, leaving eight more or less capable of what was needed.

I'll take one SAS trooper with his arm in a cast or sling over any two others healthy and hale.

The SAS moved as silently as ghosts; friendly, careful, and mute, all eight. This was a bit surprising insofar as they carried with them a good quarter of all the ammunition remaining and *all* of the grenades but for the two they'd left Sergeant Pangracs.

Aided by their light-enhancing monoculars, the

troopers moved around overstuffed and rotten garbage cans, and all the rest. They avoided the bloated, stinking bodies, one footstep away from a noisy and explosive release of inner gas.

A cat snarled, defensively. This was enough to get Greene, Dawes, and the rest to stop and hunker down for ten full minutes. But when no light came from the buildings behind, and no window took on the shadow of an alert watchman, they resumed their movement.

Dawes, on point, held up a single hand to halt the party. Greene couldn't see the reason, but inferred it when his corporal squatted and bent, then appeared to be fiddling with something.

Aha, a trip wire of some kind, thought Sergeant Greene, correctly.

Slow as their movement was, the buildings behind were not far. Soon enough the entire party was standing underneath a window they'd taken special pains over to ensure that no glass remained to it.

For this, Greene went first, boosted up by Proctor and Braiden. They held him up, as high as they could, while he picked a few remaining shards from the frame, placing them carefully in a breast pocket lest they make any noise. Then he was in, turned around, and helping the next man in. Soon enough, here, too, eight men were inside enemy territory, complete unsuspected.

Based on the windows of the back building, Greene and Campbell figured six rooms. One SAS trooper went to each, with the corporal and the sergeant forming themselves into a reserve. Greene consulted his watch.

★★★

"Time, Turenge," Campbell said. Then more loudly, she said to the assembled almost two hundred, "Fix bayonets! Fix bayonets!"

The indoor assembly area rang with the metallic sound of knives turning firearms into spears.

"An' nuw ye fockers! If ye ever want to see yer loved ones agin . . . CHARGE!"

They did. Screaming and cursing and promising all manner of vile retributions on their besiegers, the mix of Anglian and Gaul and Sachsen, of Hordalander and Tuscan and even Castillian, in English and French and German and Spanish . . . and in Lord alone knew what else, the mob surged into the space between the buildings, moving as fast as they could for the other side.

Greene barely refrained from laughter as the true mob of rebels surged from where they had been defending back to face the headquarters. Already fire was lancing out at the charging Taurans. Over that cacophony, he told Dawes, "I'll reinforce the room on the right; you go center."

And that's what they did, joined the one trooper in each of those rooms who hung behind, unseen, firing into the backs of the Moslem rebels without so much as being suspected. One by one, fire in those rear rooms faded away as the rebels crumpled into death or agony.

"Through the windows," called Jan, in French, the most common tongue her people shared. "Help each other through the windows! No one will be forgotten."

My ass. We will lose and forget some, no help for it. But we'll lose less if no one even suspects he might be left behind.

She recognized Dawes in the window overhead. "Give me a hand up," she said to two nearby soldiers. They did, until Dawes was able to draw her up and into the window.

Greene met her there shortly, for he'd seen her going up to the window.

"They're going wild in here, Major," the sergeant said. "The wog corpses are being hacked to bits."

"Do you blame them?" she asked.

"Not in the slightest, but thought you might want to know. Also, I've kicked a patrol out to the other side of the street, just two men. They tell me they're sure the wogs were there, but that they all seem to have run off."

"Wonder why?"

Banlieue Vincennes

In the darkness, Marciano's airships came down close together about twenty miles outside of Lumiere, on the other side of a lower-class *banlieue*, replete with Moslem rebels. They came down out of small-arms range.

As the troops debarked, they immediately took up tactical formations and began a movement to contact to the *banlieue*. He didn't have enough ammunition to screw around with his artillery. The two batteries of 85mm, auxiliary propelled guns Carrera had sent along with the *Helada*, he'd reorganized into three, smaller batteries, in a single battalion. These took up overwatch positions to smash any attempt at resistance from the inhabitants of the towering apartment buildings.

As a matter of fact, yes, the men of the former Task

Force SJ, or Task Force Jesuit, had very different rules of engagement than the ones they'd operated under in Santa Josefina.

Taking one of the few light vehicles they had as a command car, Marciano took up a position to the left of one of his batteries, along a long ridge that faced the *banlieue* of Vincennes. He couldn't hear it, let alone see it, but he could see the men of one of the Gallic battalions scrambling for cover even as the radios sprang to life with reports of incoming fire and requests for support. One of the 85mm guns fired a white phosphorus round as a marker into an obviously guilty building. Marciano assumed it was confirmed, because within seconds of the shell's bursting into a white, flaming flower, all eight guns opened up with a mix of high explosive and white phosphorus. It wasn't long before the entire building was engulfed in smoke and flame.

"Teach you ungrateful bastards a sharp fucking lesson," muttered Claudio.

EPILOGUE

UEPF *Juncker*

The crew had never surrendered the ship, since they had neither family down below nor a Balboan boarding party close to hand. Instead, they'd just kept quiet, communicating with the high admiral, if, indeed, that's what she remained, via tightbeam. Apparently everyone aboard the rest of the fleet and down at Atlantis Base had likewise kept their mouths shut.

"Bring her around to face the Rift Transition Point," ordered Marguerite. "Take up slack on the sail to tack."

That last wasn't actually what the ships and their lightsails did, but it was as close a term as existed, and so it had become part of the naval lexicon.

There was one other element of the United Earth Peace Fleet that hadn't surrendered. These were the light cannon in the asteroid belt. They had announced their surrender, to save their families. But until a force came to occupy their base—and they had no shuttle of their own to bring one—they would do no harm . . . or not directly.

"Ask the light cannon to give us a starting push now," Wallenstein intoned.

Shortly thereafter the huge lightsail grew brighter, albeit not bright enough to see unaided from Terra Nova, not at this range. With excruciating slowness, the ship began to move. It was, after all, not one of the relatively sleek ships of the line of the former Peace Fleet, but a huge colonization ship that had been converted into a ferry for supplies. The supplies were mostly still there, which added to the mass.

"Transition in two weeks, seven hours, forty-three minutes, fifteen seconds, High Admiral," Navigation announced.

"Very good," Wallenstein said, though she said it with little trace of the warmth her voice had once held. "Khan, husband," she said, rising, "you have the con."

BdL ALTA

They'd sent out a bomb disposal team from the mainland who had figured out how to disarm the unexploded warhead and then proceeded to do so. Now, unencumbered and unthreatened, the assault transport was heading home to Balboa. Ham had turned over Atlantis Base to the noncadet regiment that had relieved him and then command of the cadets and their adult adjuncts to the senior adult officer aboard, retired to a shipping container doing duty as quarters and the seven other cadets who occupied it.

Now he lay on the top bunk, staring—so it seemed—

through the several shipping containers over his, through the expended missile deck, through atmosphere, and off into space, and possibly into another universe.

We'll never be safe with them *out there,* thought Carrera's boy. *We have to get out there, get on their side of the transition point, and take out their filthy government. We have no choice in this.*

Casa Linda, Balboa

The house had been bombed but not, as it turned out, to destruction. Even now bricklayers were fixing some of the structural damage, even as glaziers repaired the smashed windows, and a small team of interior designers and furniture venders redecorated.

Moreover, Lourdes had shown considerable presence of mind and selflessness, both, in securing some of the art. At the moment, for example, Carrera's prized portrait of his lost Linda was carried across the lawn by two men, both tall and strong, to its customary spot over the fireplace.

As the painting passed, Lourdes was there. Esma was there, too. And, moreover, they were each watching the other warily.

Silly of both of them, thought Carrera. *I'm just too old for two women, even if Lourdes would go for it, and, frankly, I'm too old for the young replica of my Linda, who—I must never forget—is* not *my Linda.*

But, equally, as sure as I am that I am too old, I am equally sure that I haven't the foggiest notion of what to

*do with and about her. Can't keep her here, even if I am
not laying a finger on her. Cruel to send her away, maybe.
And I am no kind of a matchmaker even if I wanted to be,
which—in her case—I do not.*

What to do, what to do? Well, the Tercio Amazona *took
some serious losses. Maybe I could ease her into there.
Maybe.*

*Things have way of turning out strangely. I think it's
going to be a golden age here for them and for all the other
kids. Now that the Sachsens have paid up, we're probably
the most gold-rich country in human history, per capita.
'Course, the key word there is think, not* know.

*One thing, though, I do know: the war is over and I
can take a rest, enjoy my wife, my kids, maybe soon
enough my grandkids. I can hardly wait to see the
disobedient monsters that Pililak puts out.*

GLOSSARY

AdC Aide de Camp, an assistant to a senior officer.

Adourgnac A Gallic brandy, alleged to have considerable medicinal value, produced from ten different kinds of grapes, of which the four principal ones are Maurice Baco, Cubzadais, Canut, and Trebbiano. There is an illegal digestif produced from the brandy that includes a highly dilute extract from the fruit of the tranzitree, qv.

Ala Plural: *alae*. Latin: Wing, as in wing of cavalry. Air Wing in the legion. Similar to tercio, qv.

ALTA MV A ship, owned by the Legions. The title is an acronym for "Armada Legionario, Transporte de Assalto."

Amid Arabic: Brigadier General.

Antania Plural: *antaniae*, septic-mouthed winged reptilians, possibly genengineered by the Noahs, AKA Moonbats.

ARE-12P A Gallic Infantry Fighting Vehicle.

Artem-Mikhail-23-465 Aurochs An obsolescent jet fighter, though much updated.

Artem-Mikhail 82 Aka "Mosaic D," an obsolete jet fighter, product improved in Balboan hands to be merely obsolescent.

ASW Anti-Submarine Warfare.

BdL *Barco de la Legion*, Ship of the legion.

Bellona Moon of Terra Nova.

Bolshiberry A fruit-bearing vine, believed to have been genengineered by the Noahs. The fruit is intensely poisonous to intelligent life.

Caltrop A four-pointed jack with sharp, barbed ends. Thirty-eight per meter of front give defensive capability roughly equivalent to triple standard concertina.

Caltrop Projector A drum filled with caltrops, a linear shaped charge, and low explosive booster, to scatter caltrops over a wide area on command.

Cazador Spanish: Hunter. Similar to Chasseur, Jaeger and Ranger. Light Infantry, especially selected and trained. Also a combat leader selection course within the *Legion del Cid*.

Chorley A grain of Terra Nova, apparently not native to Old Earth.

Classis Latin: Fleet or Naval Squadron.

Cohort Battalion, though in the legion these are large battalions.

Conex Metal shipping container, generally 8' × 8' × 20' or 40'.

Consensus When capitalized, the governing council of Old Earth, formerly the United Nations Security Council.

Corona Civilis Latin: Civic Crown. One of approximately thirty-seven awards available in the legion for specific and noteworthy events. The Civic Crown is given for saving the life of a soldier on the battlefield at risk of one's own.

Cricket A very short takeoff and landing aircraft used by the legion, for some purposes, in place of more expensive helicopters.

Diana A small magnet or flat metal plate intended to hide partially metal antipersonnel land mines by making everything give back the signature of a metal antipersonnel land mine.

Dustoff Medical evacuation, typically by air.

Eris Moon of Terra Nova.

Escopeta Spanish: Shotgun.

Estado Mayor Spanish: General Staff and, by extension, the building that houses it.

F-26 The Legion's standard assault rifle, in 6.5mm.

FMB Five-Minute Bomb.

FMB-I Five-Minute Bomb-Incendiary.

FMTIB Five-Minute Thermobaric and Incendiary Bomb.

FSD Federated States Drachma. Unit of money equivalent in value to 4.2 grams of silver.

GPR Ground Penetrating Radar.

Hecate Moon of Terra Nova.

Hieros Shrine or temple.

Huánuco A plant of Terra Nova from which an alkaloid substance is refined.

I Roman number one. Chief Operations Officer, his office, and his staff section.

Ia Operations officer dealing mostly with fire and maneuver, his office and his section, S- or G-3.

Ib Logistics Officer, his office and his section, S- or G-4.

Ic Intelligence Officer, his office and his section, S- or G-2.

II Adjutant, Personnel Officer, his office and his section, S- or G-1.

IM-71 A medium-lift cargo- and troop-carrying helicopter.

Ikhwan Arabic: Brotherhood.

Jaguar Volgan-built tank in legionary service.

Jaguar II Improved Jaguar.

Jizyah Special tax levied against non-Moslems living in Moslem lands.

Karez Underground aqueduct system.

Keffiyah Folded cloth Arab headdress.

Klick Kilometer. Note: Democracy ends where the metric system begins.

Kosmo Cosmopolitan Progressive. Similar to Tranzi on Old Earth.

Liwa Arabic: Major General.

Lorica Lightweight silk and liquid metal torso armor used by the legion.

LOTS Logistics Over The Shore, which is to say without port facilities.

LZ Landing Zone, a place where helicopters drop off troops and equipment.

Maniple Company.

Majlis Assembly, or a combination of that and cocktail hour, sans cocktails.

Makkah al Jedidah Arabic: New Mecca.

Mañana sera major Spanish, Balboan politico-military song: Tomorrow will be better.

MB Money Bomb.

MRL Multiple-Rocket Launcher.

Mujahadin Arabic: Holy Warriors (singular: mujahad).

Mukhabarat Mullah Arabic: Secret Police. Holy man, sometimes holy, sometimes not.

Na'ib 'Dabit Arabic: Sergeant Major.

Naik Corporal.

Naquib Arabic: Captain.

NGO Nongovernmental Organization.

Noahs Aliens that seeded Terra Nova with life, some from Old Earth, some possibly from other planets, some possibly genetically engineered, in the dim mists of prehistory. No definitive trace has ever been found of them.

Ocelot Volgan-built light armored vehicle mounting a 100mm gun and capable of carrying a squad of infantry in the back.

Meg Coastal Defense Submarine employed by the legion, also the shark, Carcharodon Megalodon, from which the submarine class draws its name.

M-26 A heavy barreled version of the F-26, serving as the legion's standard light machine gun.

PMC Precious metal certificate. High denomination legionary investment vehicle.

Progressivine A fruit-bearing vine found on Terra Nova. Believed to have been genengineered by the Noahs. The fruit is intensely poisonous to intelligent life.

Puma A much-improved Balboan tank, built in Volga and modified in Zion and Balboa.

Push As in "tactical push." Radio frequency or frequency-hopping sequence, so called from the action of pushing the button that activates the transmitter.

PZ Pickup Zone. A place where helicopters pick up troops, equipment, and supplies to move them somewhere else.

RGL Rocket Grenade Launcher.

Roland A Gallic main battle tank, or MBT.

RTO Radio-Telephone Operator.

Satan Triumphant A hot pepper of Terra Nova, generally unfit for human consumption, though sometimes used in food preservation and refinable into a blister agent for chemical warfare.

Sayidi Arabic form of respectful address, "Sir."

SCIB Shaped Charge Incendiary Bomb.

Sergeyevich-83 or Serg-83 A Volgan-designed, Zhong-built naval fighter bomber, capable of vertical takeoff and landing, and of carrying an ordnance load of about two tons.

SHEBSA *Servicio Helicoptores Balboenses, S.A.* Balboan Helicopter Service, part of the hidden reserve.

Sochaux S4 A Gallic four-wheel-drive light truck.

SPATHA Self-Propelled Anti-Tank Heavy Armor. A legionary tank destroyer, under development.

SPLAD Self-Propelled Laser Air Defense. A developed legionary antiaircraft system.

Subadar In ordinary use, a major or tribune III equivalent.

Sura A chapter in the Koran, of which there are 114.

Tercio Spanish: Regiment.

Tranzitree A fruit-bearing tree, believed to have been genengineered by the Noahs. The fruit is intensely poisonous to intelligent life.

Trixie A species of archaeopteryx brought to Terra Nova by the Noahs.

TUSF-B Tauran Union Security Force-Balboa.

UEPF United Earth Peace Fleet, the military arm of the Consensus in space.

Volcano A very large thermobaric bomb, set off primarily by a seismic fuse.

Yakamov A type of helicopter produced in Volga. It has no tail rotor.

LEGIONARY RANK EQUIVALENTS

Dux, Duque: indefinite rank, depending on position it can indicate anything from a Major General to a Field Marshall. Duque usually indicates the senior commander on the field.

Legate III: Brigadier General or Major General. Per the contract between the *Legion del Cid* and the Federated States of Columbia, a Legate III, when his unit is in service to the Federated States, is entitled to the standing and courtesies of a Lieutenant General. Typically commands a deployed legion, when a separate legion is deployed, the air *ala* or the naval *classis*, or serves as an executive for a deployed corps.

Legate II: Colonel, typically commands a tercio in the rear or serves on staff if deployed.

Legate I: Lieutenant Colonel, typically commands a cohort or serves on staff.

Tribune III: Major, serves on staff or sometimes, if

permitted to continue in command, commands a maniple.

Tribune II: Captain, typically commands a maniple.

Tribune I: First Lieutenant, typically serves as second in command of a maniple, commands a specialty platoon within the cohort's combat support maniple, or serves on staff.

Signifer: Second Lieutenant or Ensign, leads a platoon. Signifer is a temporary rank, and signifers are not considered part of the officer corps of the legions except as a matter of courtesy.

Sergeant Major: Sergeant Major with no necessary indication of level.

First Centurion: Senior noncommissioned officer of a maniple.

Senior Centurion: Master Sergeant but almost always the senior man within a platoon.

Centurion, J.G.: Sergeant First Class, sometimes commands a platoon but is usually the second in command.

Optio: Staff Sergeant, typically the second in command of a platoon.

Sergeant: Sergeant, typically leads a squad.

Corporal: Corporal, typically leads a team or crew or serves as second in command of a squad.

Legionario, or **Legionary**, or **Legionnaire**: private through specialist.

★★★

Note that, in addition, under legion regulations adopted in the Anno Condita 471, a soldier may elect to take what is called "Triarius Status." This locks the soldier into whatever rank he may be, but allows pay raises for longevity to continue. It is one way the legion has used to flatten the rank pyramid in the interests of reducing careerism. Thus, one may sometimes hear or read of a "Triarius Tribune III," typically a major-equivalent who has decided, with legion accord, that his highest and best use is in a particular staff slot or commanding a particular maniple. Given that the legion—with fewer than three percent officers, including signifers—has the smallest officer corps of any significant military formation on Terra Nova, and a very flat promotion pyramid, the Triarius system seems, perhaps, overkill. Since adoption, regulations permit but do not require Triarius status legionaries to be promoted one rank upon retirement.

DRAMATIS PERSONAE

Aleman, **Guillermo,** Crewman on the Coastal Defense Submarine, *Megalodon.*

Alena the Witch, Governess and worshipper of Hamilcar, first to recognize him as the avatar of Iskandr. Selectrix, supervisor and trainer of Ham's dozen Pashtun wives. Wife of Tribune Cano, of the legions and of the Pashtun Scouts. Alena, herself, doesn't know if she's a witch or just very observant and very bright. She only knows that she sees and knows things others miss.

Antonio Auletti, Sonarman, Coastal Defense Submarine, *Megalodon.*

Arbeit, Lucretia, Ex-marchioness of Amnesty Interplanetary and former Inspector General, UEPF.

Ayres, Regimental sergeant major, 57th Anglian Regiment of Foot.

Battaglia, Captain, UEPF *Spirit of Brotherhood.*

Braiden, **Jim,** Trooper, attached to Major Jan Campbell at the Tauran Defense Agency Headquarters.

Campos, Tribune, officer aboard Bdl ALTA.

Cano, **David,** Tribune, assigned to BdL ALTA. Husband of Alena the Witch.

Carrasco, Condor pilot and Cazador. Also flamethrower operator.

Carrera, **Hamilcar,** AKA "Iskandr." Cadet, son of Patricio Carrera and his second wife, Lourdes. Believed to be the reincarnation of Alexander the Great by the people of Alena the Witch and a god in his own right.

Carrera, Lourdes Nuñez de, Carrera's second wife. Tall, slender, huge eyed, multilingual. An independent thinker and brave; she is a she-bear in defense of her family. She, personally, foiled a coup against her husband and Parilla, for which service, along with her diplomatic service, a bill is pending in the Senate to make her a citizen of the Republic.

Carrera, **Patricio,** *Dux Bellorum*, or *Duque*, or *Duce*. Born Patrick Hennessey. Former officer in the Federated States Army, retired, moved to his late wife's—Linda Carrera de Hennessey's—native country of Balboa, raised an army to avenge the death of her and their children at the hands of Salafi terrorists. Currently commander of the *Legion del Cid*, a former private military corporation, now the armed forces of the Timocratic Republic of Balboa.

Carvajal, **Cristóbal de,** Legate, commanding BdL *Tadeo Kurita.*

Castro-Nyere, **Claudia,** Former UEPF ambassador to Santa Josefina, now quietly ranching her *latifundia* on Atlantis Island.

Cherensa, Tribune, Cazador officer, older and very experienced.

Chu, Conrad, Warrant officer, captain of the Coastal Defense Submarine, *Megalodon.*

Cleric, David, Corporal, 57th Anglian Regiment of Foot.

Collea, Stefano del, Aide de camp to Marciano.

Cruz, Ricardo, Sergeant major, Second Cohort Second Tercio.

Dawes, Junior noncom, attached to Major Jan Campbell at the Tauran Defense Agency Headquarters.

Debayle, Cordoban customs inspector.

Emperor, No name given. Official ruler of *Xing Zhong Guo.*

Fernandez, Omar, Chief of intelligence for Balboa.

Fosa, Roderigo, Legate and admiral, commanding the *classis*, or fleet, of the legion, recently released from internment in Santa Josefina, by virtue of Santa Josefina rejecting its neutral status and becoming an open ally of Balboa and co-belligerent in the current war. Nobody apparently saw this coming.

Francisco, Stakhanovite slave at *Finca* Mixcoatl.

Fritz, No other name given. Balboan agent in Sachsen.

Greene, Senior noncom, attached to Major Jan Campbell at the Tauran Defense Agency Headquarters.

Haukelid, Hordalander medical officer attached to Task Force Jesuit.

Hendryksen, **Kris,** Sergeant major, Army of Cimbria, captured in the first Tauran invasion.

Huerta, **Jose,** Warrant officer, XO of the Coastal Defense Submarine, *Megalodon*.

Johnson, Terry, Legate commanding the expedition built around the ALTA.

Khalid, Fernandez's premier agent for direct action and, on occasion, more subtle missions.

Khan, the husband, Commander aboard the UEPF *Spirit of Peace*, fleet intelligence officer.

Khan, **Iris,** AKA Khan, the wife, commander, Sociology Officer for the UEPF.

Kubier-Schmidt, Olaf, Sachsen finance minister.

Leon, **Manuel,** Condor pilot and Cazador.

Li An Ming, Assistant and couturier to Xingzhen, the Zhong empress.

Liu, Captain, Zhong destroyer *Changsha*, and commander of the two-ship flotilla of which it is a part.

Ma Chu, Lieutenant colonel, Zhong Marine Corps, AdC to Admiral Wanyan Liang.

Macera, **Ignacio,** Commander, Second Cohort, *Tercio la Negrita*.

Marciano, Claudio, General, Tuscan, called out of retirement to command Task Force Santa Josefina, better known as Task Force Jesuit.

Maybach, Ann-Marie, Young mistress of Olaf Kubier-Schmidt.

Mendes, Cadet in Vicente's platoon.

Mendoza, **Jorge,** Warrant officer and instructor in history and moral philosophy. Mendoza, a former tanker, was rendered legless and for a long time blinded by the destruction of his tank in Sumer.

Mendoza, Marqueli, Wife of Warrant Officer Jorge Mendoza. Ph.D. Author and philosopher in her own right, and, with her husband, one of the two main intellectual architects of the Timocratic Republic. Seconded to the propaganda ministry for some educational work in support of the war effort. The essence of pure feminine charm in a very compact package.

Miranda, **Esmeralda,** Ensign, former peasant girl of TransIsthmia, on old Earth, later enslaved. Saved by, first, the substitution of her sister, who was sacrificed and cannibalized by the neo-Azteca Nanauatli and then by the intervention of High Admiral Wallenstein. She has risen from slave to cabin girl to commissioned officer. As the latter, she has become an informant and spy for Fernandez, via her handler, Cass Aragon. Very young and the spitting image of Carrera's murdered first wife.

Morgan, **Henry,** Junior tribune, Santa Josefinan, commands a maniple of Second Cohort, *Tercio la Negrita.*

Moya, Cazador.

Negrón, Cadet in Vicente's platoon.

Pablo, Stakhanovite slave at *Finca* Mixcoatl.

Parilla, Raul, President of the Timocratic Republic of Balboa.

Proctor, Nat, Trooper, attached to Major Jan Campbell at the Tauran Defense Agency Headquarters.

Qabaash, Achmed, Brigadier, Army of Sumer. Legate, *Pro Tem, Legion del Cid.* Qabaash commands a brigade in the Presidential Guard of the Republic of Sumer, which brigade, sent to help Sumer's ally, Balboa, is appointed Forty-third Tercio, *Legion del Cid.*

Rall, Friedrich, *Oberst,* or colonel, executive officer for Task Force Jesuit.

Ramirez, Senior noncom of the *classis* (fleet), brother to the tribune commanding the artillery battery.

Ramirez, Alfonso, Tribune, battery commander of a light, eighty-five-millimeter artillery battery.

Robin, Christopher, Petty officer aboard *Spirit of Peace,* dragooned into going down to defend Atlantis Base.

Robinson, Martin, High admiral, UEPF, previously captured.

Rodrigues, Jorge, Cadet platoon sergeant, old friend and comrade of Ham's.

Salas, Legate, commanding the *Tercio la Negrita,* in Santa Josefina.

Shazli, Esther, Latifundia owner, Atlantis Island.

Sitnikov, Cadet in Vicente's platoon.

Speidel, Alix, Member of Sachsen *Reichstag,* lesbian, patriot.

Soult, Jamey, Warrant officer, Carrera's driver, confidante, and friend.

Temujin, Arpad, Son of Irene Temujin, condemned slave, lover of Miriamne, *Finca* Mixcoatl.

Temujin, Irene, Indentured servant, Atlantis Base. Former high functionary in Amnesty Interplanetary.

Tim, No other name given. Balboan agent in Sachsen.

Velasquez, Manuel, Legate commanding Second Cohort, Second Tercio.

Vicente, Arturo, Centurion, Cadet Rodrigues' platoon leader.

Villalobos, Legate commanding the *Tercio la Virgen*, in Santa Josefina.

Wallace, Bethany, Junior enlisted aboard *Spirit of Peace*, dragooned into going down to defend Atlantis Base.

Wallenstein, Marguerite, High admiral of the United Earth Peace Fleet, a fleet of observation in orbit above the Planet of Terra Nova. She acquired her position largely through the actions and intervention of Patricio Carrera. The high admiral is of the Reformed Druidic Faith, repentant for her previous ("and they were many, oh, many") sins. Still, she has a duty to her home planet to keep the barbarians of Terra Nova from breaking into space and trashing her system of government, even though she detests that system. She has a plan for Terra Nova, too, though that has proven, to date, somewhat problematic of execution. Lover of Xingzhen, the empress of *Xing Zhong Guo*.

Xingzhen, Empress of *Xing Zhong Guo*, or New Middle Kingdom. Real ruler of the Kingdom. Of indeterminate age but painfully beautiful. Rather despises most men. Lover of Marguerite Wallenstein.

ACKNOWLEDGEMENTS

In no particular order:

Yoli and Toni who, in their different ways, put up with me, Steve Saintonge, TBR (the Kriegsmarine contingent of the bar), Ori Pomerantz, James Lane, Jack Withrow, Tom Wallis, Thomas Mandell, Krenn, Jasper Paulsen, Matt Pethybridge, Conrad Chu, John Becker, Patrick Horne, Sam Swindell, David Rowberry, Tom Brophy, ARRSE (even if they don't know it), Bill Crenshaw, Andy and Fehrenbach at old Cambrai-Fritsch Kaserne, Dan Neely, T2M, Henrik Kiertzner, Greg Dougherty, Keith Glass, Leonid Panfil, Ernest Paxton, Chris Bagnall, Jean-Louis Beaufils, Chadd Newman, Jeremy Levitt, Bruce Cook, Sheinkin, Jasper Paulson, Keith Wilds, Charles Krin, Mark Bjertnes, Alex Shishkin, Larry Fry, Robert Hofrichter, Jim Braiden, Nat Proctor, Ned Brickley, Joel Salomon, John Biltz, Seamus Curran, Tommie Williams, Emeye, DanielRH, Tom Lindell, Arun Prabhu, Owen Baker, Jacob Tito, Peter Gold, Nigel the Kiwi, Joseph Turner, Dan Kemp, Robespierre, Jon LaForce, John Prigent, Phillip "Doc" Wohlrab, Chris Nuttall, Brian Carbin, Joseph Capdepon II, Mike Watson, Michal Swierczek, Harry Russell, James Gemind, Mike May, Guy Wheelock, Paul Arnold, Andrew Stocker, Nomad the Turk, Paul 11, Geoff Withnell, Joe Bond, Rod Graves,

Mike Sayer, Jeff Wilkes, Bob Allaband, John Jordan, Wade Harlow, Michele Chini, Jason Hobbs, Jim Curtis, Bob Oberlender, Darwin Concon, Dave Cleric, John Hoare, Paul Ashton, Scott Joseph, KC Ezell, and Justin Watson.

And finally, Modean Moon, who has edited almost all of these books and is worth rather more than her weight in gold.

RING OF FIRE SERIES

(with Eric Flint)

1635: The Papal Stakes   PB: 978-1-4516-3920-9 • $7.99
Up to their necks in papal assassins, power politics, murder, and mayhem, the uptimers need help and they need it quickly.

1636: Commander Cantrell in the West Indies
PB: 978-1-4767-8060-3 • $8.99
Oil. The Americas have it. The United States of Europe needs it. Enter Lieutenant-Commander Eddie Cantrell.

1636: The Vatican Sanction   HC: 978-1-4814-8277-6 • $25.00
Pope Urban has fled the Vatican and the traitor Borja. But assassins have followed him to France—and not only assassins! The Pope and his allies have fled right into the clutches of the vile Pedro Dolor.

STARFIRE SERIES

(with Steve White)

Extremis   PB: 978-1-4516-3814-1 • $7.99
They have traveled for centuries, slower than light, and now they have arrived at the planet they intend to make their new home: Earth. The fact that humanity is already living there is only a minor inconvenience.

Imperative   PB: 978-1-4814-8243-1 • $7.99
A resurrected star navy hero attempts to keep a fragile interstellar alliance together while battling and implacable alien adversary.

Oblivion   PB: 978-1-4814-8325-4 • $16.00
It's time to take a stand! For Earth! For Humanity! For the Pan-Sentient Union!

GUN RUNNER
A NEW SCIENCE FICTION ADVENTURE FROM
LARRY CORREIA & JOHN BROWN

THE HEART OF A WARRIOR
Soldier-turned-smuggler Jackson Rook has been hired to steal a state-of-the-art exosuit mech for a man known only as the Warlord— but when the Warlord's actions begin to remind him of the foes he fought in his youth, will he still see the mission through?

"[A] no-holds-barred page-turner that is part science fiction, part horror, and an absolute blast to read."
—*Bookreporter.com* on *Monster Hunter International* by Larry Correia

"Servant delivers solid pacing, a great setting, and a smart story that breaks away from genre conventions."
—Brandon Sanderson on *Servant* by John Brown

GUN RUNNER
HC: 978-1-9821-2516-5 • $25.00 US/$34.00 CAN

Available in bookstores everywhere.
Order ebooks online at www.baen.com.